I0654356

SPACE MARINERS:
CHILDREN OF RRAL

For Tui and Jeff
My friends from
New Zealand

SPACE MARINERS: CHILDREN OF RRAL

Book Five of the Endurian Universe

Joe Bergeron

Endurian Press

Space Mariners: Children of Rral is a work of fiction. Names, places, and incidents either are products of the author's imagination or are used fictitiously.

Copyright © 2015 by Joe Bergeron

All rights reserved. No part of this publication may be reproduced or transmitted in any form or by any means, electronic or mechanical, including photocopy, recording, or any information storage and retrieval system, without permission in writing from the author.

Cover illustration by Joe Bergeron.

Published by The Endurian Press

www.joebergeron.com

Chapter 1
The Lesser Wisp

The path to Earth was obvious. Kern Harner's remote probes had analyzed the Bronze Portal's ever-shifting multi-dimensional shape well enough to determine that one of its many corners lay in an outlying region of the nearby galaxy they called the Lesser Wisp.

Another clue was offered by the remnants of a remarkably long, sinuous wormhole which led also in that direction, possibly another shortcut to Earth that had been accessed in the recent past by agencies unknown.

Valjhar Cor set a course for the Wisp, a large barred spiral galaxy comparable in size and mass to the spiral they called the Greater Wisp, and far larger than the little galaxy that contained their home world of Rral. From this distance that loose spiral was only faintly visible to their naked eyes, though it could be viewed in some detail with the telescope Kern had installed beneath a bubble on *Mote's* outer hull.

They left the world Colibdis, its double sun, and its sparse galaxy behind, grateful to have escaped before the Prohibitor could track them there. For a few weeks they watched the Lesser Wisp's softly-lit disk expand beyond the large transparent dome atop *Mote's* bridge.

Though Earth offered them a goal, it was not an urgent one, merely one of curiosity. They were in no hurry to reach it, and enjoyed the quiet time of their passage, a chance to relax after their trials among the humans of Colibdis, and to adjust to the changes in their circumstances brought about by that adventure.

The former Elf princeling known as Cal-Cotavion rarely sat among them on the bridge. Though he'd been brought back from the brink of death by their science and by the power of the mystic Stones he commanded, he still suffered from his wounds, both mental and physical. Mostly he remained in the cabin they had modified to accommodate his immensely tall form, where he tortured himself with the Lights of the Stones, and also, as far as they could tell, begged the universe to forgive him for being alive.

Nearly as uncomfortable a presence was Kroy dal Ren. His encounter with one of the weird disembodied beings of Colibdis had jolted him into a new awareness and a partial mastery of his physical body and environment. As a result he now shambled around, gaping at everything and everyone, and even speaking, though his utterances were usually brief, and cryptic at best.

Kroy also liked to touch things, even things he didn't understand, which included everything. Kern carefully instructed all the ship's vital controls to be unresponsive to Kroy's touch. He and the others did their best to civilize the misplaced star-being, instructing him in the maintenance of his body, so that he need not moan and cry from the discomforts of hunger or thirst or exhaustion, and also so that he would not soil himself.

The problem became particularly acute when Kroy became aware of his body's long-thwarted sexual functions. When he appeared among them sporting the physical manifestation of his body's cycle it was cause for embarrassment and stifled mirth among them all. Luckily, Kroy had not yet made the connection between his discomfort and the female members of their company. Still, he plaintively asked for an explanation for his suffering, and requested relief.

As Valjhar was both their leader and the person most directly responsible for the star-being's occupancy of Kroy's body, the others would consider nothing but that Valjhar himself should instruct Kroy in the manual expression of the reproductive body, or "dropping the fish" as they called it, followed by the disposal of the eagerly flopping thing. Pimsie, Kern, and Shaula were thereafter reluctant to let Valjhar forget that indignity.

For Valjhar, the situation aboard ship was somewhat uncomfortable, though he strove to conceal that. He was still accepted as their leader, though so far he had only led them from one dangerous situation into another. He suspected their casual acknowledgement of his leadership was more due to their individual lack of interest in supplanting him than to any great confidence in his ability. They each had their own concerns to occupy them.

Kern Harner, still blissfully in love with the unimaginable prize that was Pimsie Flam, was often busy assisting her in her tireless effort to make *Mote* seem more homey. Except for the bridge itself, which Valjhar had declared inviolate, most of the ship's habitable volume had felt Pimsie's decorating hand. Tapestries woven from colored metallic threads hung in the corridors, depicting everyday scenes from distant Enblenol and the surrounding countryside. Most decks were covered by rugs in bold but simple geometric patterns, their substance and colors derived from strange materials Kern whipped up from the most unlikely sources. Mobiles hung from the overheads, with plates and spirals and fonces formed from various crystals, stirring slowly in the recirculated air. Pimsie had even attempted to paint, but so far she had not produced anything she liked well enough to display for very long.

Cal-Cotavion had been a difficult, prickly character for as long as Valjhar had known him. He was considerably more humble now that he'd taken on a burden that appeared to be beyond his strength. He grew even more morose as he pondered his own unworthiness and mourned the loss of his beloved Seren.

On those rare occasions when he appeared among them, Valjhar immediately became less critical of Cal's weakness. The sight and proximity of the Stones of Rral, shaded as they usually were by Cal's grey cloak, forced him to reevaluate the stamina of a person able to endure their weight and radiance with his frail mortal body, even if he did so only with difficulty.

Still more enigmatic was Shaula Alshain. She was quiet, always present, but always in the background, very observant, but saying little unless called upon to speak.

Valjhar, now fully aware of her capacity for violence and manipulation, did not trust her. The others accepted her more readily, but Valjhar could not bring himself to put aside his suspicions. He could not look at that young woman, so lovely and capable, and not be reminded of how blindly he had once mooned over her, or how his trust in her had harmed them all.

And Pimsie? Pimsie treated him with an amused patience she might apply to a child. She was not above wagging her finger at him whenever he did anything she considered particularly foolish.

At length *Mote* entered the Wisp's northern face at a steep angle, leaving only a few thousand light-years between it and Earth. Even so, that distance contained several thousand star systems at least, at some of which they lingered.

Nearly every star possessed multiple planets. Nearly half the time these included at least one world whose conditions roughly resembled those of Rral, Colibdis, or Smerkesh. These worlds invariably bore forms of organic life, or at least the remnants of such. Most of these were small and simple, but some were more complex forms, multicellular, or in some cases giant single-celled organisms consisting of great numbers of specialized organelles drifting within blobs of various plasms, cooperating only casually as the opportunities of their circulation arose. Meeting as they crawled across the spongy organic crusts of their worlds, these blobs would consume each other, though it was impossible to tell which was consuming which, or if in fact the result was not a simple merger.

A few worlds bore signs of extinct cultures and technologies. These were relics of recognizable civilizations, but the Rralians agreed their absence on other worlds did not necessarily indicate the absence of past intelligence, which might not always leave such obvious traces.

Sometimes the only detectable remnants of these ancient cultures were residual molecules of synthetic substances, or strange isotopes in the soil. A few had perished recently enough to leave visible ruins, sometimes very grand and sad. Kern gleaned bits of technology from these places. These he carefully analyzed, and sometimes duplicated, to make up in some small part for their lost access to the Compendium, that fabulous record of the scientific arts of Old Rral, a loss that still rankled him.

As far as they could tell, these various cultures had met their ends for disparate reasons. Sometimes it was a result of the natural evolution of their star. Sometimes it was caused by some great impact, nearby supernova, or other cosmic calamity. In most cases the reasons were obscure, smothered in too great a depth of time to be easily deciphered. Sometimes the Rralians suspected the natives might have bred the intelligence right out of themselves, to judge by the half-aware gleams in the eyes of the animals who still prowled among the ruins.

Still more bleak were the considerable numbers of orphaned, sunless planets they encountered in the interstellar regions. Some of these frozen orbs had evidently been alone for eons, while others bore chemical traces of life indicating they had been ejected from stellar systems. Some of the larger rogue planets had enough inner heat and volcanic activity to sustain a few pockets of relative warmth.

On one of these, a great and terrible civilization had once arisen, far from the influence of any sun. It had fallen into a hideous darkness of mind before its extinction, and only the Light of Cal-Cotavion's Stones had shielded the Mariners from the evil that remained there. After that they avoided all such sunless worlds, which were dark traps for their sensitive minds.

Across this barren wilderness of stars they roamed, eager now for Earth, which was probably still populated by thinking beings, even if they were only cousins of the violent, primitive people of Colibdis.

After a few years they reached the end of their trail, and knew that Earth must lie within a hundred light-years of their position.

But how to find it? The legends of Colibdis told them the Earth orbited a single sun, a powerful white one larger and hotter than the gentle golden star Sharn that had lit their days on Rral. But dozens of such stars burned nearby. They might have to visit each in turn.

Valjhar never forgot the look on Kern's face on the day they first detected signs of the proximity of Earth. They were nowhere near any of the candidate stars at the time, but nevertheless Kern looked up from his instrument console with an expression of round-eyed wonder.

"It's radio emissions, Valjhar, and not random. Artificial radio signals, I'm sure of it. Whatever the humans are doing on Earth, they obviously have some kind of a technical culture."

"What does it mean?" asked Pimsie in astonishment.

"The signals? I don't know. It will take me a while to figure out how to rectify them, if I even can. But I'll soon know the direction to Earth, there's no doubt of that."

A sense of anticipation and joy filled the ship. Soon they would have somewhere to go, and a living, vital people to meet. If the humans of Earth were less primitive than those of Colibdis, their planet might even become a second home for them, perhaps even one capable of confounding the persecution of the Prohibitor.

Only an hour later Kern began to laugh. "This is so simple! The humans—I assume it's them, anyway—encode information into the transmission by varying its strength.

I'll try matching various signal amplitudes to sound frequencies..."

Kern had built tiny speakers into the ship's controls for the sole purpose of providing audible alerts and other feedback. Now they took on a new purpose—they played music. It was faint and tinny, sounding very much as if it had crossed an immense distance to reach them.

"Music!" said Pimsie. "The humans send music across space. Oh, how wonderful."

The rhythm was fast and rambunctious, the melody meandering and unpredictable. No two phrases were exactly the same, though as they listened certain themes became apparent. It seemed fiery and chaotic, and Valjhar wasn't sure he liked it. But...it was *music*, the product of minds and hands much like his own.

All around them burned the nameless stars of a foreign galaxy. The sound of music, any music, emerging from that unimaginable star desert brought tears to Valjhar's eyes. Looking around, he saw he wasn't alone in that.

Kern and Pimsie leaped up and began to dance. Their joy was infectious, a bit annoying, and enviable. Valjhar soon threw up his hands, bounded over to Shaula where she sat wrapped in her green cloak, lifted her up, and also hopped and bounced around the deck with a clumsy abandon.

Shaula did not object to this. It was only when Valjhar looked into her hooded eyes that he faltered. What did he see in those impassive emerald depths? Was it resentment, boredom, or caution? Was that the slightest shade of a smile on her lips? It might be anything, as far as the bewildered Valjhar could determine.

Their dance slowed and halted. Shaula disengaged herself without a word, retreated, and returned to her seat, where she gazed out at the stars in silence.

Earth's sun turned out to be about seventy five light-years away. Kern steered the ship into a grand curve and set a course in that direction.

That night (according to the ship's arbitrary timekeeping), Valjhar, finding sleep elusive, stood alone on the bridge, watching the stars crawl by as he sighed disconsolately.

After a time he became aware that he was no longer alone. Pimsie at least must be asleep, for seated cross-legged on the deck was Nali, the Dreamfarer, the second and more ethereal of their hitchhikers from Colibdis.

"Hello, Nali."

"Hello, sweet Valjhar," she replied in her tinkling voice.

Valjhar smiled. This was the reason he found it possible to accept the presence of this strange spirit who shared Pimsie's body. She was not obtrusive, and she was kind.

Nali looked as usual: a slight, delicate figure, all of blue, wearing a tall funny hat. Her most distinctive features were her eyes, solid orbs of translucent green, apparently sightless, though somehow Valjhar always knew when she was looking at him.

"You know, Nali, that we're approaching Earth? We'll be there in a few more days."

"Yes. Already I begin to know their dreams."

"What are they like?"

"They are like the dreams of the people of Colibdis, full of beauty, terror, and yearning, but suffering more from doubt and confusion. They are something like you in this, Valjhar."

Nali removed her hat and studied it for a moment. She tossed it aside, and it lapsed into nothingness.

She began to melt and shift before his eyes. She grew larger, and her shadowy color lightened to a pale pink. Her ears shriveled into the small, flattened convolutions typical of humans. Her indigo curls straightened and paled to a snowy whiteness. Even her clothing changed. Her loose, nondescript garments fell away, and in their place appeared films of silver, pale green, and icy blue, emphasizing the exaggerated curves of her altered body.

She stood up, or rather drifted to her feet, causing her new raiment to flow around her like the sweep of nebulosity through time. She towered over Valjhar now, half again his size. Only her jade-like eyes remained the same, and the delicate skin around them remained bruised.

Valjhar gaped at her in awe and astonishment.

"Yes," she whispered. "I feel their dreams, and their desires, and I respond to them."

Chapter 2
An Introduction to Earth

Intercepting radio signals became impossible as *Mote* hurtled toward Earth at an effective speed many times greater than that of light. When the ship drew within the orbits of the white sun's outermost planets they stopped to reconnoiter the situation.

The difference was profound. Kern's receivers were now swamped with transmissions of every wavelength and means of modulation. In a mere seventy five years the humans had gone from a few simple broadcasts to thousands or even millions, a radio din bound to proclaim the human presence to any listener among hundreds of star systems, whether they intended this or not.

Kern needed time to learn how to tease all these signals apart, and more time to turn them into information they could understand. In the meantime they accelerated toward the inner planets, using their secondary propulsion system instead of the primary microjump drive, to assist with radio reception.

Earth was easy to identify with its large single moon, which had also figured in the legends of Colibdis. Its basic characteristics were easily determined: larger than Colibdis, and about the same size as Rral, with more land area than Rral, and a slightly warmer climate overall.

As they drew nearer to the planet Kern suddenly cut power to the drive, ending the ship's illusion of normal gravity and sending them all floating unexpectedly. Pimsie yipped.

"Why did you do that, Kern?" asked Valjhar. It was annoying. All the mobiles would become tangled, and then must be sorted out by hand to please Pimsie.

Kern, who remained strapped into his seat, frowned at his instruments. "Earth is surrounded by a fleet of space vehicles. Small ones, mostly, but hundreds of them, orbiting at various altitudes and inclinations."

That was enough to arouse Shaula Alshain from her lassitude. Showing more free-fall agility than the others, she floated upward, bounced off the invisible bubble, and landed beside Kern's console, whose chair she grabbed to stabilize herself. She studied Kern's displays with a keen eye.

"Do you think it's a defense mechanism like the one surrounding Rral?" asked Valjhar.

"Hard to say," said Shaula, "but I doubt it. These objects are not really well organized, especially the ones in the lower orbits. And none of them show much power output."

"We'll be careful anyway. Kern, please bleed off our real velocity and put us all back on the deck. We'll keep our distance until we understand what's going on here."

Valjhar felt himself relax as Kern oriented the ship and configured the thrusters. He gratefully returned to his seat as acceleration returned. For once they would not fling themselves headlong into an unknown situation. For once he had ordered a sensible, temperate course of action that should keep them all safe.

Pimsie gave him a quizzical little smile, as if reading his mind.

It didn't take long to determine that the satellites were passive, and that none of them had taken notice of their presence. *Mote* maintained a station between the Earth and its sun, looking down on Earth's sunlit half from an altitude well above almost all of the satellites.

Feeling secure, Kern resumed his analysis of the signals. "This is good," he said at length. "The humans are so profligate with their broadcasts that we'll be able to learn a lot about them without moving one skad closer to Earth."

"Yes, good," said Pimsie. "I don't want anything to do with the place until I'm sure they're civilized."

For the next few hours Valjhar, Shaula and Pimsie haunted the bridge while Kern analyzed the signals. Valjhar eventually became impatient enough to ask, "Anything yet, Kern?"

Kern frowned distractedly. "Not much so far. I can tell you these Earth people speak hundreds of different languages. Put any two of them together and they probably wouldn't be able to understand each other. I'm not even sure which language I should work on deciphering first. It's crazy."

More hours passed. Pimsie chatted with Shaula for a while, and then fell asleep in a chair.

Valjhar observed Kern closely as he began to slump in his seat. Kern gradually grew pale, and his breathing grew faster and more ragged. He began to look ill.

"What's wrong, Kern?" asked Valjhar quietly.

Kern glanced at Pimsie and back at Valjhar. "Not in front of Pimsie," he mouthed.

With a sinking feeling Valjhar motioned for Kern and Shaula to follow him off the bridge, leaving Pimsie asleep in a state of contented bliss. They descended the spiral staircase leading to the second of Mote's five primary decks, and thence to their dining room, which was bright and warm with Pimsie's decorations.

They took seats around the table. Kern was shaking and distraught. Valjhar poured him a mug of hot "fruit" tea, a concoction of sugar, citric and ascorbic acids, and a few other compounds that was the closest thing to a true tea they could make. After all this time, they were still not very successful at synthesizing complex foods.

"Tell us what you found, Kern," said Shaula.

Kern took a few moments to master himself. In a choked voice he said, "I don't know where to begin. Remember how you both thought the people of Colibdis were

12

dangerous savages? Well, their cousins on Earth have refined savagery into something of a genteel art form. They
have a somewhat advanced technological culture, but they
are rotten at heart."

"All of them?" said Valjhar. "Surely not."

"I suppose not, but even the most virtuous of them is
complicit in more forms of evil than I can even articulate."

"Go on, Kern," said Shaula. She didn't appear particularly surprised, but she of course came from a barbarous
world herself.

"All right. To begin with, there are over six billion humans on that planet."

"Billions? You don't mean—" began Valjhar.

"Billions. I mean billions. So all right, they have a
crowded planet. But...of that number, hundreds of millions,
maybe more than a billion, are so deprived they don't have
enough food to eat. They are starving. Every day, thousands
of those people starve to death. Do you understand what
that means? They have so little food that they die."

"Is there—some terrible food shortage on their planet?"
asked Valjhar.

"No. Not yet anyway. It's just that vast numbers of humans have almost nothing. A much smaller number has—
an inconceivable degree of wealth, vastly more than is
needed to meet their needs, or even to satisfy their wildest
desires. All by themselves they have the ability to eliminate
hunger and want. The richer *nations* could easily do it too,
but—it is not considered important."

"What's a *nation*?" asked Valjhar.

"That's another matter. This world is divided into rig-
idly defined political units called nations. Each one has a
separate government, often a separate language, and sometimes even a distinct religion, that being a supernatural in-
terpretation of reality based usually on ancient myths and
tales."

Now Valjhar's head was spinning as he tried to absorb all this. "Well, Smerkesh and Colibdis had their religions also."

"Yes, but they at least were based on reality, to a certain extent. I see no evidence that any of the multiple gods worshipped below have any real existence."

"Tell us what these 'nations' do consider important, Kern, if not the starvation of their people," said Shaula in a dull tone of voice.

Kern swallowed. "Weapons. They devote massive wealth to the creation and purchase of weapons. They use them to threaten each other and sometimes destroy each other in acts of highly organized violence. Armies often stream across the national borders to kill their neighbors and destroy their goods. As we speak, about a dozen different wars are happening on that hellish planet, big and small. But the richest individuals rarely suffer from them. They hire, coerce, or trick the poor and ignorant into murdering others for someone else's ends. But there's more about the food..."

Now Kern looked more haunted than ever.

"Many of the crops the humans grow go to feeding other creatures."

"So they have more concern for other species than for their own?" asked Valjhar.

Kern laughed bitterly. "No, it's nothing so benign. They raise these animals to eat. Oh, we know the humans of Colibdis did this as well, but not on this scale, and not with this much brutality. The Earth people raise billions of animals every year, often in the foulest conditions you can imagine, so they can later slaughter them in huge death camps, cut them up, and eat them."

Valjhar felt a surge of nausea. He supposed he was beginning to look as grey as Kern did. He glanced at Shaula, who sat watching Kern gravely.

Kern continued. "Earth is an amazing planet. It has a richer diversity of life than any we've yet encountered. It has several kinds of beings who are similar to humans in the magnitude of their intelligence, but not in the nature of their intelligence. But this possibility is usually disregarded by humans, and they too are killed or pushed aside with little concern. Earth has any number of obviously sentient, self-aware beings, some of which the humans use for food. It has at least a hundred times more plant and animal species than Rral. The humans estimate there are thousands of species they haven't even found and named. And every day, hundreds of these marvelous life forms, whose ancestry can be traced back over hundreds of millions of years, are wiped out by human activity. Made extinct!"

"Why?"

"It's because of the great number of humans and their amazingly profligate and destructive habits. They act without any foresight. They rip what they want out of their planet with no thought for its health, or even for their own future. And oh, Valjhar, this is only the beginning. The corruption and evil built into the various human societies is beyond belief. Their systems of trade and currency...it's labyrinthine beyond measure, and it's all concocted by the rich few to extract as much wealth as possible from the labor and suffering of the poor. Do you remember the Harbormaster of Enblenol, Randa's father? He controlled maybe ten or fifteen times the tarits of you and your father, more than anyone else in the city, and he was reckoned rich. In some of the more corrupt places on Earth, a person who owns an economic enterprise collects hundreds of times more money than the people he hires to do the actual work. Such people make money by virtue of having money, simply by owning things, rather than by doing anything useful. They have so much money that the bulk of it is literally useless to them. And yet they are often considered heroes. Often the people who work for them are grateful for the pittance they are allotted, as though their masters would have anything at all if they could not exploit these underlings. It's monstrous."

Kern lowered his eyes and folded his hands. "This is the gist of what I have learned so far about the abominable people of Earth."

"Then what are we doing here?"

They all wheeled to take in Pimsie as she stood in the doorway, blinking, her face flushed and twisted. "Again we find an inhabited world, and this is the worst one of all! Valjhar Cor, I don't want to meet these people. I don't want to see one. I don't want to get one bit closer to them, not even by the width of a hair."

Pimsie marched into the room, collapsed into a chair beside Kern, and leaned into him, nuzzling his shoulder and stroking his hair.

Valjhar looked away. "Shaula. How does what we've heard compare to your own home world?"

"In some ways it seems even worse. Yes, my people on Boosh were mercilessly exploited by the rulers there. But, those rulers were of a different species than us *Stotzis*. It seems these humans have little regard for their own kind, let alone for other kinds. Otherwise, I heard nothing very unfamiliar."

Valjhar sat brooding. They had crossed a great distance to reach this destination. They had no better place to go. They could not go home. Return to Colibdis? No, they could not again expose themselves to the malignant powers that dwelt there. They could search this galaxy at random, visit empty world after empty world, searching for—what? What was the goal of their wanderings, after all, other than sheer curiosity, and to evade the Prohibitor?

Valjhar shook himself in disgust and dissatisfaction. Whatever their future might hold, he could not insist that it include a people so egregious that his friends couldn't endure even the most superficial knowledge of their vileness.

"All right," he said. "I agree we should not risk contact with these people. I propose we remain where we are, and learn as much as we can about them from this distance, until we are satisfied, or until we can't stand any more."

"Good! Now I'm hungry." Pimsie jumped to her feet and pattered into the nearby kitchen, where she rattled around in the cabinets. "Why is there never anything good to eat on this ship? Oh, I'm sorry, Kern dear, I know you do your best. Can I get you anything?"

"No thank you, Pimsie. The last thing I am right now is hungry."

Kern, having also lost his appetite for studying the humans of Earth, left the task to Valjhar and Shaula. First they had to make sense of one or two of the human languages, and that alone took days. Kern was smarter than he was, Valjhar realized with chagrin. Valjhar was more willful. That was the main reason people tended to defer to him.

Shaula was mainly concerned with determining how dangerous the humans were, but Valjhar was more interested in their general nature and culture. He learned some specifics of their biochemistry and verified that their bodies worked along the same general lines as their own.

He also learned many other interesting details. Even the most favored humans had brief life spans. By the time they attained their maximum intellectual development they were already well into physical decline.

He also learned enough to try to answer one of Pimsie's questions.

"Valjhar, why are the humans so terrible?"

"I don't really know, but it might have something to do with their intelligence."

"Are they all idiots then?"

"No. A race of idiots could never have developed the technology they have, or dreamed up systems of myth and religion so elaborate, for that matter. But they have a much wider range of intelligence than we Rralians have. Hold on a moment; let me show you something."

Valjhar returned to the bridge with a drawing slate and a stylus. On it he drew a simple two-axis graph. He also drew a line slanting slightly upward from left to right.

"I don't have exact information on this, Pimsie, but this graph represents the intelligence distribution of Rralians, when measured using the same standards the humans employ. The vertical line indicates the percentage of people, and the horizontal line shows increasing intelligence, so any line or curve plotted here represents that proportion of the populace possessing a particular level of intelligence. Are you following me?"

Pimsie grimaced at him as if to say, "Of course, idiot."

"Er, yes. So, the slanted line represents our range of intelligence. You see that the line starts high, at about one hundred sixty on the scale the humans use, and then increases smoothly to about two hundred, into regions the human's tests can't measure. The point is, all Rralians have roughly the same intellectual capacity. Roughly. These tests measure only various kinds of analytical thinking. They don't address art or poetry or dreams. My own intellect falls toward the left, or in the stupider regions, as you might expect based on some of my actions over the years. Kern is higher, much closer to the right. I don't presume to guess where you'd fall on this scale, Pimsie."

She frowned. "How did you find your own score?"

"I found some of their intelligence tests and took them. I may have been hampered by my unfamiliarity with their languages; I'm not sure."

"All right, so what about the humans?"

Valjhar drew another line, this one curved, starting very low on the scale, sweeping upward to a gentle summit, and then plunging back down again.

"They call this a 'bell curve,' and it represents the range and distribution of human intelligence. Look at this peak, and see how low it lies on the intelligence scale. This is the average of human intelligence, and it encompasses vast numbers of people. If we encountered a Rralian who functioned at this low level, we would be greatly concerned. We would suspect a serious brain injury that had not yet healed. This is the human average. To the left their condition becomes even more dire, descending to even greater depths of stupidity. But observe the right. In that direction we find decreasing numbers of increasingly intelligent people. At the far right we find small numbers functioning at Rralian levels.

"All human advancement depends on this small minority. Without their imagination and capability, the humans would still be living in huts with walls of mud brick and scratching in the soil with sticks. Without these few, the humans couldn't even maintain the level of development they have now, let alone improve upon it."

"All right, but if the humans have these superior people to lead them, why are they still so barbarous?"

"Because their political systems do not favor intelligence in their leaders. In many cases leaders select themselves because of ruthlessness and greed, or they are chosen by the stupid masses because they appeal to their own ignorance and aggression. Many such people still have the predatory instincts of their distant ancestors. You see, it's not only the humans. Almost every creature on that planet fears some other creature that wants to kill and eat it. It's a constant struggle of life and death. The humans are more vicious than any, and more successful, but they are not unique in their savagery."

Pimsie requested, received, and completed the human intelligence tests. She declined to reveal her results to anyone. Shaula also took the tests, and with a rueful laugh tried to comfort Valjhar with the fact that by this measure she was slightly more stupid than he was.

After that Pimsie was rarely to be seen on the bridge. Occasionally her tousled blonde head would pop out of the stairwell long enough to ask "Have we learned enough about the planet of death yet?" and then she'd disappear again.

Kroy dal Ren sometimes appeared as well, to flop down on the deck and gaze at the luminous blue-and white planet that floated directly overhead. At times he would say things like, "It is dirty, it has dirty air lying in basins, its air is clogged with bad atoms that serve no purpose and release no light." Valjhar found it best to nod and agree with him, as he had no idea what Kroy meant by this.

Kern, wearing his scarlet and black engineering suit, busied himself puttering around the ship as he so often did. Ignoring the Earth as much as possible, he went about the bridge installing strange boxes and cones at various points on the already somewhat haphazard control consoles.

"These are audio transducers," he explained.

"Ah, excellent," said Valjhar. "I've always said we need more audio transducers around here."

Kern looked hurt. "Sarcasm, Valjhar? Yes, we do need them. Remember that Earth music we heard? I thought we might give it another try, and these should reproduce it much more accurately than the old speakers. Do you think you can find more music?"

"As much as you could possibly want."

In truth the satellites and many points on the planet's surface broadcast so much music it was almost impossible to sort it all out. Valjhar had been ignoring it, intent as he was on obtaining more concrete information about the humans.

He sighed and scanned through the waveforms of the various music broadcasts, looking for one that promised not to be too cacophonous. He finally selected one with a wide tonal range and a lot of complexity, though rhythmically it appeared to be a little chaotic.

"What do I need to do?"

"You've chosen something? Okay, just a moment..."

Kern fiddled around at one of the boards, and suddenly a vast sound filled the bridge. It was so rich and deep that at first Valjhar thought it was the sound of a storm. It took several seconds for the structure of the music to resolve itself in his mind, because it was unlike anything he had ever heard before. It rolled and thundered, with a driving beat behind it, or rather more than one, interacting in ways that multiplied the complexity and power of the whole.

Suddenly Pimsie appeared beside him, goggle-eyed. "They can sing like that?"

Sing? Yes, surely that vast, triumphant sound must be human voices, tens of them, or even hundreds, synchronized and mingling, magnified into a force that could almost make him believe in the gods of Earth.

Cal-Cotavion's grey-hooded head appeared in the stairwell. With his wooden staff in hand he mounted to the deck, then stood facing away from them, looking toward the stars as he took in the music.

The pace of that great chorus increased, its ardor grew more frenzied, the instruments launched into a wild climb up a celestial ladder to heights unknown and previously unseen, and then it was over.

A human voice, with its characteristically deep pitch, announced they had just heard the Symphony Number Nine by Beethoven.

"That was just the last few minutes of it," said Valjhar quietly. "Maybe we should listen to the whole thing sometime."

He silenced the audio and sagged back in his chair. He felt dazed, as though his mind had been expanded in a direction he didn't know existed. He doubted it would ever entirely return to its previous shape.

He looked around at his fellow travelers. Pimsie crouched on the deck, her head bowed, her yellow hair concealing her face. Shaula looked elated, spinning in her chair with a happy grin.

Kroy dal Ren stood nearby, weaving on his feet. "That was the closest thing to the voice of my people I have heard since I left them."

And that, thought Valjhar, *was perhaps the most coherent sentence you have ever uttered.*

Cal-Cotavion abruptly turned to face them. He raised his head. His hood fell back from his narrow, pallid face, exposing the bitter blue star of the Stone of Truth that burned on his brow. Valjhar winced. He knew Cal was about to unleash that thing, right there in their midst.

And he was right. The Stone flared brightly, and a pillar of azure radiance stabbed up through the dome and out toward the Earth. Cal staggered beneath it, as though the beam had a physical weight. It flickered and died, and Cal mercifully replaced his hood.

"How much Truth can that thing possibly reveal about an entire world with one single blast?" asked Valjhar in annoyance.

"That depends on the wielder, and his intentions. I can tell you this, my friend. That world and its people are in crisis. In fifty years it will be a very different place. It will be unrecognizable."

Valjhar was distracted by the sound of Kern's sobs, who sat hunched at his console, hiding his face in his arms as he wept.

"What's wrong, Kern?"

Kern looked up, and Valjhar had never seen him look more desolate.

"Valjhar...for days now I've wanted nothing more than to flee from this world and its people. They're violent, unreasoning monsters, as we all know. But Valjhar, look at what else they can do. If they can create and perform this music we just heard, what else can they do? Can we just abandon them when they possess such genius? I want to know more. I want to know what kind of artists they really are. I'm selfish; I want to learn all this, from and about them, even if it's dangerous to stay here."

"I can already tell you one other thing they have that might interest us, no matter where we go from here," said Valjhar. "They grow a lot of very promising fruits and vegetables."

Pimsie lifted her head and studied him with a gleam in her eye.

Chapter 3
In the Sun Room

The hospital's staff would not allow Rouse Farewell to lay in bed all day as she wished. She was not physically infirm, they told her. If she lingered in bed her body would deteriorate, and so would her mental condition, dragging her spirits down still further. She laughed at this, wondering how much lower they could go than a suicide attempt.

"You must get up and move around," they said. "We want you back. We want you to get better."

So with many profound sighs Rouse dragged herself out of her tiny room. Dressed in pyjamas and a dingy robe, she shuffled out toward the sun room, where she would sit for a while and observe some of the other nuts, lunatics, and idiots populating the institution.

She squinted as she entered the room. Today it was living up to its name, with powerful beams of sunlight entering the large windows.

The jigsaw puzzles and board games were ignored as usual. A dozen or so men and women sat around, mostly absorbed in the noise of their own minds. Some mumbled to themselves, some rocked back and forth, some sat quietly and stared.

Rouse detested them all. She did not belong here among these people. In some cases she knew what had happened to obliterate their personalities; in others she didn't. She knew her own actions had had actual causes, external causes whose validity anyone must acknowledge, if they were willing to look past the haze of happy-happy optimism that clouded their thoughts.

One of those great shafts of sunlight landed squarely on the chair occupied by a new patient. The light caught in his hospital-issue pyjamas, lending them a white fire that was hard to look at. Rouse squinted. A side effect of one of her medications was dilated pupils. That must be the problem.

This new joker, the one they called Cal, was a bit of an oddity. Though he was no more active than the others, he didn't appear to be as ruined or munted. He sat sprawled in his arm chair, his long legs all knees and angles, with his head back and the slightest smile resting on his lips. Rouse knew little about him, only that he'd been picked up on a farm somewhere in the Waikato and deemed incompetent.

He was certainly an odd-looking man, thin beneath his jammies. He had long, bony fingers. His face was narrow, somewhat irregular, yet still handsome in an undefinably exotic sort of way. His hair was an untended colorless mop. He was very pale. Rouse had never seen anyone quite like him.

His serene smile and posture of complete relaxation irritated her. She decided to go over and mess with him.

"So, mate, what kind of drugs do they have you on, to keep that daft smile on your face?" she asked as she stood over him with her arms crossed.

Cal opened his eyes and turned toward her. Their color was a startling pale grey.

"No drugs. I need no drugs to smile. I need only to be free."

Rouse smirked down at him. "Free? In case you haven't noticed, you're locked up in a looney bin."

"I am free in a way you can never understand."

His thick accent was also strange, clearly European, but she could not identify it. She could tell that he had to consider the choice and pronunciation of every word he spoke. He was certainly no Kiwi.

"Where are you from?" Not that she really expected an answer...

"I am from...other...I do not know your word." Cal held out one hand balled into a fist. He set a fingertip of his other hand to whirling around it.

Rouse stared at this. "Another planet?"

"Yes, I think so."

"Which one, Mars?"

"You will not know it. It is very far away."

"Very interesting."

"You are not surprised that I am from another planet?"

"No, why should I be? This is a nuthouse, after all."

"Yes. A nut house."

"Where's your spaceship?"

"I am not sure, but I think waiting somewhere toward your sun."

"Hmm. So you're an alien, and you find yourself confined to a mental hospital in New Zealand for some reason. You seem remarkably all right with that."

"Yes. This place, it reminds me of home. Not this poor house with all its quiet people, but the world itself. The sun and the sky are like those of my home. I am more heavy here, but I am also more light. My burden was taken from me."

"What burden was that?"

"My...magic gems."

"Of course, your magic gems. Who took them?"

"The men who stopped me and brought me here. They took my gems and my thing for talking, and left me only my clothes. They do not know what they have, for the gems are in their box, and they cannot open it. That is good, for they are very hard to look at. Without them I feel more at peace. Their Lights cannot burn me. I do not always think about my sins and faults. Here I can rest."

Cal rubbed his forehead. Rouse noticed there a little purplish spot, like a healing bruise, or a bit of frostbite.

"Did you tell them all this when you were taken, Cal?"

"Oh yes, that and more. But I do not think they believed me." Cal frowned. "No...I did not tell them about the gems."

26

"Well, that's good. They might have found that part especially hard to believe."

"I am not courteous." Cal rose to his feet with an unexpected grace. Rouse blinked in surprise. She was taller than most men, but this one was taller still by several inches. "I am Cal-Cotavion." He bowed to her.

"Cotavion? What sort of name is that, Armenian? My name is Rouse Farewell. Yeah, it's a dumb name, I know."

"It does not seem so to me."

"Well, it is. It's not even spelled as you pronounce it. The way it's spelled, you'd think it would be "Rowz". But it's not. It's not even "Rose". It's "Roos". Damn nuisance to have clever parents."

"Why are you in the nut house?"

Rouse flinched. Using this term in reference to Cal had seemed cheeky and funny, but hearing it directed back at herself felt otherwise. "Well...I tried to kill myself."

"Why?"

"That's what they've been trying to get at here for the past few weeks. It's not an easy story to tell."

Cal descended into his chair with a thoughtful expression. Rouse chose a seat beside him.

"If I had my gems, I could tell you why you did it."

"Really."

"Yes, really. Even without the gems, it is hard for me to not tell the truth. Their influence lingers."

Rouse detected a touch of vexation in Cal's reply, but it faded as his serene expression returned.

"Why do you hate yourself so much that you would kill yourself?"

"I don't hate myself!" snapped Rouse. "Why should I? There's not much wrong with me, except that my eyes are too wide open. I hate everyone else, or nearly all."

With so little provocation Rouse launched into a rant about her despair over the evils of the world. As usual, the deeper into her argument she got, the more foolish it all sounded to her, the more shallow, the more self-indulgent. But she could not deny that these were her real feelings about the human race.

"Maybe as a man from space you haven't noticed it yet, but we humans are a right mess. We're stupid and cruel and savage and destructive. We kill each other, and we kill everything else that lives on the slightest pretext, or for none at all. We torture and murder other creatures to put a sammie on our plate. We prey on each other without even having the decency to admit we're doing it. We lie and cheat and steal and we believe every kind of nonsense that some liar offers us. We're all idiots and fools. We're all so ridiculous in one way or another, even me. Certainly you. And I need a drink of water from talking so bloody much."

"So you hate others enough to kill yourself to escape them. Why not try to change them instead?"

Rouse laughed. "What could I do? The world has millions of people who are just as outraged as I am, and just as powerless. Whole groups of us...oppressed and beaten down, all over the world...the Palestinians, women all over Islam, the red indians in America, so many more...and look at me, a *pakeha* white girl in New Zealand, one of the calmest and most privileged places on Earth, and I still can't stand it. What if I lived in Africa? What if I had to work in an Asian sweatshop? What if I was Tibetan? But I'm none of those, and I still wind up in the looney bin under five kinds of medication that make it hard for me to add two and two, and with scars on my wrists."

Rouse held out her arms and regarded the bandages that still wrapped her self-inflicted wounds.

"The evil that people do, the madness, the cruelty, I feel it all around me, pressing in on me. It's breaking me. So many bloody idiots in the world, you know? I'm only twenty three years old. If I can't stand this world already, what can I expect when I'm older?"

Rouse abruptly stopped speaking. She was shaking. She felt an anxiety attack coming on, and she didn't want to collapse into a quivering heap in front of Cal.

"What you say about humans is what my friends also say," mused Cal.

"Your space friends have a keen eye then. Too bad they've abandoned you to the charity of the Ministry of Social Development."

Cal gave a calm little half shrug. "They will come for me. I am not alone. The dream spirit talks to me."

Nurse Piripi, a huge young Maori man, arrived to conduct Rouse to a therapy session. Rouse found it amusing that the hospital rarely entrusted her, a tall, athletic woman, to the care of the female nurses. Perhaps it was related to the fuss she'd made when the police arrived to prevent her suicide. She left the enigmatic Cal Cotavion glowing serenely in the sunlight.

Over the next few days Rouse made an effort to spend more time with Cal, helping him with his English. His stories grew more and more ridiculous. It turned out he was not only from another planet, he was also an Elf, or he had been, since apparently one could only be an Elf on his distant native world. Not only that, he had been a prince among Elves. Not only that, he had also been the rightful heir to the entire kingdom of Faerie. Finally, he was also a wizard, or had been, since magic only functioned on his native world. His lost magic gems, on the other hand, were not strictly magical after all, and were good anywhere in the universe, if only one could open their box.

Rouse found it difficult to hold back laughter when listening to Cal's solemn tones as he recited this nonsense. It very neatly explained his helplessness among the men of Earth despite his great magical pedigree. It was all a bit sloppy though, an awkward mixture of cliches from various strains of fantasy and science fiction. She was surprised he wasn't also a vampire.

Cal spoke longingly of his lost love Seren, the Faerie Queen. If Rouse understood him correctly, upon dumping him she had immediately turned to ultimate evil. She was also his cousin. That detail was a little creepy, but Rouse took it no more seriously than the rest of it.

Cal's alien companions were apparently space-faring hobbits of a sort, or perhaps gnomes, though he claimed never to have read Tolkien, or even to have heard of him. He might make a pretty good Elf if those movies she'd heard about ever went into production and they started hiring extras, Rouse thought.

One day, while describing her frustrations she blurted, "Cal, if they're so smart, why don't your little space friends come down and do something to help us pathetic ape men?"

"I don't think they will ever do that. They fear you too much."

Chapter 4
A Troubled Leader

Valjhar Cor paced the deck, now and then casting a fretful glance up at the glowing blue world that taunted him from above. He kept trying to tell himself that this latest disaster was not his fault. Yes, it was he who had suggested they obtain plants and seeds from Earth, but the others had all enthusiastically agreed. As the only human among them, Cal had offered to go alone, venturing down in a small space boat operated by remote control.

They had chosen their target with great care: New Zealand, a remote place far from the planet's main centers of military power, and free of any warfare. It had no dangerous animals. Sparsely populated, it was cultivated with a variety of fruits and vegetables. It was a place as peaceful as any that could be found on Earth, save for those frozen regions where nothing grew.

Cal had insisted on going with the Stones locked into a special box made by Kern, shielded by various metals to reduce their impact on anyone in their vicinity. It would make him less conspicuous, he'd said. But not inconspicuous enough, apparently.

They didn't yet know how exactly the humans had detected Cal. The space boat should have absorbed their radar. It gave off very little light and no other form of exhaust. All they knew was that men had arrived, and Cal's radio had been cut off. Kern had withdrawn the space boat before it could be seen. It had come back laden with various fruits, vines, roots, saplings and bushes. Why Cal had not jumped aboard the moment he became aware of the approaching humans was not known. Why he had not opened that box, exposing the Stones of Rral, and overawing the men with their irresistible power was also not known.

The plants and produce were in storage while the Rralians considered what to do about the missing Cal-Cotavion.

"Have you considered that maybe Cal meant to stay there all along?" said Shaula.

"He's not like them!" said Pimsie. "He's kind and gentle and humble."

"He is now," agreed Shaula, "but he was less so when we met him, as you'll recall. Like them or not, these are his people. He may have no future on Colibdis, but why not here?"

"I think he would have told us if leaving was his intention," said Valjhar. "We would hardly refuse him, as he would surely know. And he would have told us goodbye."

"Then we must get him back, wherever he is," said Shaula. "With a few precautions, the humans could do nothing to stop us."

"That would be very disruptive," said Valjhar. "As far as these people know, they're alone in the universe. They speculate about life outside their world, but they have no evidence of it. I'm not sure I'm willing to confront them with that knowledge."

"You are too cautious."

"Why should we care about disrupting them? This isn't *Star Trek*," said Kern.

"What's *Star Trek*?"

"One of their nearly infinite number of recorded entertainments. It's a fantasy about a near future time when humans freely explore their galaxy in huge ships of space. They encounter many species who are essentially just like themselves. I was pretty confused by it at first. You should watch it sometime. It's given me ideas about how to arrange our ship. If course it's pure fantasy. The humans are hundreds of years from understanding the physics that would make all that possible. At the rate they're consuming their planet, they don't have hundreds of years. They could turn that around, but far more of them are devoted to making the problem worse than to making it better."

"What has it got to do with our current situation?"

"The characters operate under a rule that forbids them from interfering with the natural development of other cultures by revealing themselves."

"I see. Do they ever violate this?"

"From what I've seen, yes, almost every time it's mentioned."

"I'm not ready to violate their rule yet, fictitious or otherwise."

"That's silly," said Pimsie. "We've freely announced ourselves on every other world we've visited."

"That's true," said Valjhar. "But on those worlds our presence created only local effects. This is a planet with a global network of instant communications, and a paranoid population always quivering on the brink of madness and overreaction. There's no telling what consequences it would have if we went charging in."

"You really should watch a little *Star Trek* though," said Kern. "It's really rather magnificent, this vision they have for their future. You can see that many of them truly aspire to explore the stars, as we do. Of course, it's very unlikely to ever come to pass for them."

Pimsie stamped her foot impatiently. "But what about Cal?"

"We don't know where they've taken him. There's been no mention of him among their broadcasts, or at least none that we've found. There are so many…we may need to find help from among the humans, if it's possible to do that discreetly."

"We can't just abandon Cal among those barbarians!"

Valjhar began to assure Pimsie that they wouldn't, but his words trailed off as he watched her. She gripped the arms of her chair and sat stiffly as her head slowly tilted back. Her eyes went blank, and her lips moved as though she were whispering to someone.

Her huge aqua eyes swiveled to Valjhar's with a disconcerting intensity. "I'm going to sleep now," she said. With that she sagged back in her chair, instantly asleep.

Kern bolted up and went to her, kneeling beside her and holding her limp hand.

Valjhar frowned and looked around the bridge, finding, as he'd expected, Nali in her new humanoid guise, her startling green gaze locked onto his. The films and veils that half-concealed her lush body wafted about as though underwater.

"Nali. I do not appreciate your forcing Pimsie asleep like this. It goes against your promise not to usurp her body, and it insults our hospitality toward you."

"But Valjhar, dear," Nali whispered, " I couldn't wait. I have important news for you. I know where Cal is."

Valjhar wasn't sure he should dismiss his complaint against the Dreamfarer so quickly, but he decided Cal took priority for the moment. "Where?"

"He has been taken to a place where people are confined, people whose dreams are unusually sad, or chaotic, or troubled."

"Has he been harmed?"

"No. His dreams are peaceful. He is not afraid."

"Do you know exactly where he is?" asked Shaula.

"I can lead you to him."

"All right then—"

"But there is more."

Nali turned back to Valjhar. "You say you need help from among the people of this world. I have found one who may be able to help, but he also needs help. He is lost, he needs guidance, he needs to be raised up. Once his mind is filled with the knowledge you can give him, he can be a strong ally to all of you."

Valjhar looked at Nali as he considered these unexpected words. "Very well. We will seek out this extraordinary human."

"He is the ultimate man of the sea. But he is not exactly human."

Chapter 5
Escalation

Rouse grew to like Cal more and more. Despite his absurd delusions, he was among the most lucid of her fellow patients, the calmest, and the most accepting. He was always ready to listen to her own complaints and tales of woe, his grave attention never wavering for as long as she cared to speak. The staff encouraged their friendship, hoping Cal would eventually reveal the truth about himself, and glad to see Rouse opening herself more freely to him than she did to her doctors and therapists. It was a start.

She asked Cal what he'd done to be apprehended and locked up.

"We have only poor food aboard our space ship. My friends sent me down to obtain plants and seeds that we might use to grow better food."

"So you were arrested for nicking crops from a farm?"

"Nicking? Oh no. I had a payment to leave. I was given a cube of gold about as big as my fist. We know how gold is valued here. I hope it was given to the farmer."

Somewhere, someone knew if a golden cube really figured into the story of Cal's capture.

Rouse blinked, surprised at herself for taking that possibility seriously, even for a moment.

Doctor Narby, one of the most sympathetic members of the hospital staff, told Rouse privately that Cal might soon be released. His crime was a minor one, after all, and he appeared to be harmless. The main obstacle to his freedom was uncertainty about his citizenship or immigration status, and of course the whole mystery of his identity.

Rouse wasn't the only one who benefitted from Cal's company. Many of the other patients also gravitated toward him, including some who had been otherwise mute and passive for months or years.

One day she walked into the sun room to find Old Man Seltzer—that wizened, toothless husk of a man whom she'd never known to do anything but sit in his yellowed robe and stare out the window—crouched on the floor before Cal and wheezing out his regrets about the way he'd treated his family and wasted his life.

Rouse halted and stared at this spectacle in amazement. The sight of that man's tear-streaked face, a man who had been no more animated than a Halloween figure on a front porch, was as disorienting as seeing the dead come back to life.

Doctor Narby further confided in her. It seemed the military—not the police, but the military—were pressuring the hospital to turn Cal over to them. So far the administration was resisting, on the basis that Cal was legally their patient and the military had not demonstrated any authority to supersede that. But if they were persistent it was only a matter of time before Cal would have to be surrendered.

This news came as another blow to Rouse's perception of reality. What possible interest could the military have in a befuddled mental patient caught foraging for food on a farm?

"Doctor Narby...do you have any of Cal's things? I mean the things he was carrying when he was picked up. His clothes, or...his box."

"His box? I don't know anything about a box. He has his clothes in his room, of course, but he only has the one outfit, and he doesn't seem too inclined to wear it. We may have to do something to encourage him to dress properly."

Doctor Narby eyed Rouse's own shabby ensemble with disapproval. "Dressing well and looking after one's appearance are important steps toward recovery and normalcy. Oh, I think we also have his walking stick. We didn't let him keep it, as it's quite large and could be dangerous. I think we stashed it in a closet someplace."

"May I see it?"

Doctor Narby looked at her uncertainly. "Well Rouse, I don't know. You know I've shared all this with you because of your interest in Cal, and because you're—or you were—studying to become a nurse."

Behind closed lips Rouse gritted her teeth in embarrassment. She hated to be reminded of this miserable irony.

"But letting you examine the personal effects of a patient? That really goes against patient confidentiality."

"Yes, of course you're right. But—"

"What do you hope to learn from it?"

"Clues about whether he's really a space elf," she wanted to say.

"Maybe a hint as to where he came from," was what she said.

"Hmm. I'll think about it, but I'm sure the police examined his things when he was arrested."

This response did not satisfy Rouse. She fretted about it for the rest of that day, and fumed sleeplessly in her narrow bed for most of that night. Yes, rules, rules, to hell with rules! Surely the risk of facing a few disapproving words was worth the possibility of learning something about that lanky, pale oddball in their midst.

The hospital was more utilitarian than grandiose, a collection of eighty low wood-framed structures built with all the charm and grace of a chain motel. Rumors abounded that it was due to be closed down, and already some of its wards had been emptied, its patients released or sent to mental wards attached to normal hospitals. It sat on five thousand acres of ancestral Iwi land, land the Iwi would probably like to have back someday.

So far Rouse had rarely left her ward to see the rest of the compound. It might be necessary for her to expand her range.

With the inklings of a scheme in her mind, Rouse was finally able to get to sleep. In the morning she had vague recollections of dreams involving a mysterious yet friendly female figure, but those memories soon dissipated.

She arose from her bed and studied herself in the mirror over her basin. Her long chestnut hair was tangled and in poor condition. Her green eyes appeared dull. Her habitual tan had faded, leaving behind a slightly blotchy paleness. She had always been notably curvaceous, but with her recent lassitude she had gained weight and now looked sloppy.

She frowned and got to work on herself. Just sorting out her hair took half an hour in the shower followed by an hour with a comb and brush. She had no makeup, not that she had ever favored it anyway, but she gave her face a good scrubbing. Finally, she opened her drawer and drew out clothing she hadn't bothered to wear in weeks. She chose a pair of khaki slacks and a russet tank top that still fit reasonably well.

Making a conscious effort to improve her posture and walk more confidently, Rouse left her room, strode down those bland corridors with their walls of pale institutional green, and out the door, the first time she'd voluntarily left the ward in weeks.

The feeling of sunlight on her face had grown so unfamiliar it was startling. It was a lovely day. The hospital grounds were far more appealing than the buildings themselves. The shades of green glowing in the foliage were also much to be preferred. The big ginkgo tree waved and rustled in the breeze.

Rouse wandered the grounds, studying its layout, and visiting the farm and gardens. Some of the more functional patients worked the various plots and fields, their faces shaded by wide-brimmed hats. It reminded Rouse of a van Gogh painting, and it also reminded her of how her depression, and her angry acceptance of it, had limited her life for so long now.

She felt an urge to find a secluded copse, strip off her clothes, and enjoy the sunlight and the balmy air, but that would not advance her plan to appear more normal. Instead she made it a point to spend an hour weeding a bed of tomato plants, making sure she was seen doing it. When she returned indoors she received approving glances from the nurses.

The next day she did much the same, also taking the time to talk with some of the other patients, generally making herself appear as engaged, and as normal, as she could, and also acting out the part of a nurse, to the extent that she could do so without seeming presumptuous.

On the third day she approached Cal Cotavion in his traditional posture of repose in a chair in the sun room. He opened his startling grey eyes to peer at her with mild interest. Had they been drugging him after all?

"Cal, why don't you come outside with me and walk the grounds? It's a perfect day, and you could use a bit of exercise."

"But I'm so comfortable here."

Rouse frowned. "No, that's no good, Cal. Come along. We grow food here, you know. Maybe you can grab something for your space friends."

Cal gave her a bleary frown in return. "Oh, very well. It all seems rather tiresome, though..." He unfolded himself from his chair and lumbered toward the door.

"No no, not dressed like that. Those jammies aren't for walking about outdoors, and anyway, they could stand to be washed. I thought you were a prince, not a hobo. Go put on your normal clothes."

Cal sighed. "As you say."

Rouse watched as Cal wandered off toward the men's residence area. She was apprehensive about whether he'd return or simply collapse into his bed to avoid her annoying company and unreasonable demands. After twenty minutes she was sure he'd made his escape, but then he reappeared from the shadowy corridor.

His clothes were disappointingly conventional: jeans, a grey button-down shirt, and sneakers. They looked new, but not in any way remarkable. Certainly they were not a space suit or an Elf costume.

Rouse escorted him out into the sunlight, now feeling a little impatient. Cal's too-ordinary clothing made her recent efforts seem like a waste of time. It seemed he was just some nutter after all, but she still liked him, so she walked him along, showing him this and that. Cal followed politely, occasionally comparing the flowers he saw with those he remembered from the magical forests of Faerie. Also, it seemed his world sometimes had one sun, and sometimes two. It must have been a pretty confusing place.

They came to a row of kiwifruit bushes whose fruits were just beginning to ripen. Cal cautiously picked one, sniffed it, and bit into it, skin, fuzz, and all. The green juices ran down his long chin.

Rouse laughed, startling herself. She couldn't remember how long it had been since she'd laughed at anything. She laughed again, since it was now possible to do so, and led Cal away by the arm after he'd picked a few more fruits. They found a bench beneath an apple tree and sat down in the shade. Lacking any implements, Rouse took a kiwifruit and ate it as Cal had. It wasn't as bad as she'd expected.

They sat there for a while trading stories, his fanciful and hers far more mundane. Cal treated her with a certain distant courtesy, never acknowledging her sex or making the slightest attempt to flirt. But how, thought Rouse, could she hope to compete with the memory of the Queen of Faerie?

As they chatted, Rouse's gaze wandered over Cal and his clothing, still idly searching for any anomaly that might feed her hopeful fantasies. But, the denim looked like denim, the shirt looked like cotton with plastic buttons, the stitching on the pockets and belt loops looked normal—

But wait.

A strange cold thrill ran up Rouse's spine. Cal's voice grew muffled, and time seemed to slow to a crawl.

The belt loops themselves—they didn't appear to be sewn onto the pants. Cal wasn't wearing a belt, but that wasn't unusual. The loops—Rouse extended a finger and put it through one of them, tugging at it. Cal halted in the middle of a sentence and looked at her askance, as though he were about to question her, but he did not.

The loop appeared to be fused into the waist, not stitched. That detail was not easy to see, and would scarcely be noticed except by someone who was looking for anything odd. Even so, it might simply indicate some method of manufacturing garments that she didn't know about.

"Cal, where did you get these clothes?"

"My friends made them for me, so I'd fit in if anyone saw me. I suppose they're adequate. Don't you like them?"

"They're fine." Rouse was breathless, and could say nothing more. In a daze she listened to Cal speak on until she blurted out, "Cal—would you like to get your magic gems back?"

That question took Cal aback, and he struggled for words until he finally replied.

"That is difficult. The longer I am without them, the more I begin to feel like my old self. But my old self—is not someone who should be encouraged. The gems are my responsibility, and their power should not go to waste. I must say yes—I would like to have them back. I am a poor person without them."

That night Rouse again tossed and turned, alternating between the most ludicrous fantasies and berating herself for basing so much nonsense on a set of peculiar belt loops. She lay awake until four in the morning, then abruptly sat up, her mind seething, with sleep as impossible as flying out the window would be, if she could get past the bars.

Somehow she must learn the truth. Short of subjecting Cal's clothes to chemical analysis, or possibly Cal himself, what more could she learn?

The next day she was scheduled for a therapy session with Doctor Narby. Rouse appeared early at the office suite, hoping that Narby would be absent or busy, giving Rouse a chance to look around. But, as it happened, the doctor was present and able to receive her at once.

"Rouse, you appear to have improved so much in just the past few days."

"Yes, doctor, I feel as if I have."

"You look better, you act better, and you're showing a more active interest in your surroundings. Even your color is coming back. You might want to use some sunscreen."

Rouse nodded, sensing a certain ambivalence in the doctor's manner.

"But, I am a little concerned that this improvement might be coming more from your interest in Cal than from within yourself."

Rouse smiled and shook her head. "Oh, no. I admit I find his case intriguing, and I'd like to help him, but there's no more to it than that."

Narby looked unconvinced. "It won't do for you to grow too attached to him, you know. He may not be with us much longer. You know this."

Rouse nodded thoughtfully. "Yes—I suppose that's why I'm trying so hard to get through to him, not knowing how much time I have left."

"Your interest in Cal—it's not romantic, is it?"

Rouse shook her head again. "No, no. That would be quite hopeless. You've heard his stories, haven't you? I'd have to be someone quite a bit more exotic to hold his attention."

"Yes, we've heard his stories, and we're interested in getting through to him too. We're considering stepping up our efforts to find out who he really is and where he's really from. We are running out of time." Doctor Narby appeared unsettled as she said this, which unsettled Rouse in turn.

The door opened and a nurse stuck her head in. "Excuse me, Doctor, sorry for interrupting your session. There's a disturbance in Ward G. Brendan Sykes is acting up, we think he may be reacting badly to a new medication. He punched Doctor Webb in the face, and Webb refuses to go near him again."

Doctor Narby rose from behind her desk and started out. "Okay, round up as many nurses and aides as you can. Sykes can be a mean one on his best days. Rouse, please wait here, I shouldn't be long."

Rouse was left alone in the office. She sat in her chair, looking around indecisively, and then lurched up and over to Narby's closet. When she opened the door it emitted a groan like a kind of warning.

Hanging within were a few garments—a jersey, a jacket, a raincoat. Leaning against the shadowy wall behind them was a tall, narrow object wrapped in what looked like plastic trash bags.

Stashed away in some closet, indeed. Stashed in your very *own* closet more likely, Doctor Narby.

Rouse reached in and lifted the staff, drew it out. It was surprisingly heavy and felt very hard in her hand.

She dared not examine it too closely, not knowing how much longer she would remain undisturbed, Neither could she bear to simply replace it and probably never have another chance to get her hands on it.

Shaking with nerves, Rouse opened the office door and peered out. She waited until a few nurses walked out of sight before she left the office. The narrower door of a broom closet was nearby. Rouse opened it, grabbed a mop, yanked off its head and discarded it, then quickly returned to Narby's office with the handle. There she transferred the plastic wrappings from the staff to the mop handle and placed the latter into the closet.

This left the naked staff in her hand. It was a length of pale, natural wood, stripped of any bark, knobby and irregular, quite unprepossessing in appearance. Its head looked like a root cluster than had been cut off at an angle. Rouse didn't recognize the grain, but she was hardly an expert on wood varieties, so that meant very little.

Rouse heard noises coming from the waiting area. She hastily opened the office window and looked out. Immediately below the window was a row of flowering shrubs. With a quick look around, Rouse stuck the staff through the window and dropped it behind the shrubs. She barely had time to close the window before the door opened and Doctor Narby entered.

"Well, that was a delight. Mr. Sykes was a demon—Rouse, dear? Are you all right? You look a little flustered."

"No, I'm fine. I was just worried about you. May I leave now? Our session is over, I think."

"Yes, of course, sorry for the interruption. We'll make up for it next time."

Rouse waited for twilight before she ventured outside and wandered as casually as she could over to Narby's office window. She saw the gleam of white wood behind the bushes and was relieved that the staff was still there. But, she could hardly just walk back to her room with it without attracting attention. Perhaps it would be better if it looked like she was seeking attention. She noticed a vine of white morning glories growing over a nearby trellis. The flowers were curled closed at this time of day, but they would have to do. Rouse freed a few feet of the vine and severed the stem. Retrieving the staff, she wrapped the flowers around it as though it were some sort of portable maypole. She then walked boldly forth, with her head held proudly high. When a few patients saw her she gave what she hoped was a regal nod and a smile of pride at her own eccentric behavior.

Crossing half the grounds, Rouse managed to make it to her own window without drawing any attention from the hospital staff. After a careful look around she thrust the staff through the bars of her open window and let it clatter to the floor. Only then did she feel the tension leave her body.

Rouse forced herself to sit through a normal meal in the refectory and then retreated to her room. She turned to the staff where it lay on the floor, and gasped.

The morning glories, far from withering, had opened to their full luminous extent. If anything, they appeared to give back more light than what fell on them.

Rouse sat in her chair, lifted the staff, and brought it to rest across her knees. She ran her hand over the wood. Its surface was cool, utterly smooth but not slick or slippery. It did not feel like wood. Rouse pushed her thumbnail into it as hard as she could. It left no dent or impression in whatever substance coated it.

Rouse felt herself slipping into a daze. "Calm down, Rouse," she muttered to herself. "Sometimes a staff is just a staff."

But not this staff. A strange silence descended over her room and over her mind. Moving without thinking, she hid the staff in her closet, got undressed, turned out the light, and got into bed.

The room was quiet but somehow alive. A little light leaked in through the blinds, but it was not enough to explain the soft glow that seemed to suffuse the walls. Rouse lay wide awake, staring at everything around her as though she'd never seen anything before. The fabric covering her chair, the cobweb hanging from a corner of the ceiling, every shadow, they all seemed changed somehow, no longer things to ignore or take for granted, but part of the great mystery surrounding her. For within her now a suspicion had grown to certainty, a certainty still based on very little, but nevertheless firm. The world was not as it had always seemed. Indeed, it contained things she had never known or considered, and nothing, no matter how common or mundane, was separate from this wider reality.

This revelation was not entirely a comfort to Rouse. She had always had a dim view of the world and especially of the people in it, but at least she'd thought she understood it, in all its hopelessness and indignity. Now she concluded that what little she understood was only a tiny part of an unknown whole. What might lay beyond that?

Rouse began to shake. She drew up her knees and clutched herself as she rocked back and forth, whimpering through an anxiety attack. The howling terror of a black and unknown universe clawed at her mind. Everything she'd ever done, everything she might ever do, frightened her and seemed no more meaningful or purposeful than an infant spattering mud on a wall.

She thought back to the bold words she had offered Cal. *I don't hate myself; why should I? I'm great; it's everyone else who is terrible.* But this was not true. Seeing herself now, she despised herself, a weakling, a mote blown helplessly by the winds of the universe, her destination unknown.

And yet—

In her closet was a wooden staff that caused flowers to flourish when they should only wither and die.

She clung to this thought, hugging herself until the storm of fear passed from her mind and permitted her to rest.

Chapter 6
The Man of the Sea

The Space Mariners sat together on the bridge of their starship *Mote*. Valjhar Cor looked around at his four friends and companions, who looked back at him with faces intent and apprehensive.

"My friends, before we begin our descent, let's remind ourselves of what we're about to undertake. We must rescue Cal-Cotavion. To do that, the Dreamfarer believes we should recruit the help of the so-called 'man of the sea'. And so we prepare to meet him. We will try to avoid contact with the humans, but that may not be possible. So let's not fool ourselves. We will enter their domain. We know they are savages, barbarians, living in societies that are deeply sick and destructive in almost every way. We are powerful, but few. They are many, and they have powers of their own, which they are all too eager to employ. It will be dangerous, but we will be together. Are we ready?"

An uncomfortable silence ensued.

Her face pale, Pimsie said, "You're sure we won't crash again?"

Kern laughed. "Pimsie my love, I think we'll be all right. *Mote* has evolved since those early landing mishaps, and so have our procedures."

"Anyway, you're supposed to be asleep when it comes time to actually land," said Shaula. "With any luck we'll be away by the time you wake up, and with a new friend on board, or so we hope."

"Will he be as huge as Cal?"

"We don't know for sure," said Valjhar.

A great shape loomed into view beyond the bubble. They had separated the main hull of *Mote* from the structure containing the primary power and drive units, and this was moving into view, its great wingspan and sweeping curves a reminder of Kern's fanciful approach to ship design. It would remain on station here at this sunward point while the rest of the ship ventured to the planet some eighty thousand miles away. The main hull's maneuvering lamps were more than capable of carrying it across such a short distance.

Valjhar sent the ship into an orbit that would slowly decrease the distance to Earth and also carry it around to the planet's night side. They could make the trip much faster under power, but they wished to avoid excessive speeds that would draw too much attention to themselves. The disadvantage was that they must make the trip in free fall, meaning there would be no semblance of gravity aboard the ship, a condition they always strove to avoid or minimize. It could be amusing for an hour or so, but tiresome after a day, and debilitating if prolonged for much longer.

Luckily their fall would not take much longer than a day. They spent many of the ensuing hours on the bridge, watching as that lovely yet menacing planet slowly expanded overhead.

Kern kept busy trying to identify the source of an excess of free hydrogen in the ship's air. Kroy dal Ren drifted about silently, the least inconvenienced of any of them by the lack of gravity, his mind occupied by whatever strange thoughts resided there.

Kern had made a few audio earpieces, inspired by what he'd seen on human media. Valjhar used one of these to listen to human voice transmissions, limiting them to his own skull to avoid unnerving Pimsie unnecessarily. He sought any sign that their approaching ship had been noticed. He found none, but learned much else of the day's events.

A man had set himself on fire to protest the slaughter of sentient beings to be used as food. In another place, men murdered and beheaded another man because he did not share their religious beliefs. In yet another, a few rich and powerful men manipulated the fantastic, labyrinthine financial structure they'd invented to oppress and impoverish the great majority of the population. Indeed, the baroque complexity of that whole imaginary edifice was among the greatest, yet most pernicious, products of the human mind, its functions so obscure that most of its victims had no understanding of their true status in the system.

Valjhar had to consciously hold his ears at a normal angle to prevent them from flattening and revealing the dismay and disgust he felt. They could not leave this planet soon enough to suit him.

As they slid around the world, its terminator and its night side came into view. It was easy to see the greatest concentrations of human population.

"Are their lands on fire?" asked Pimsie.

"No," said Shaula. "That's artificial lighting in their cities."

"Those are all cities? So many?" Pimsie stared up at the clots and fissures of molten light that webbed and outlined every continent. "It's hideous. It looks like wounds on their planet, like it's bleeding out into space."

"It is extremely wasteful, at the very least," said Shaula. "From what I've learned, I'd say these people are burning their way through a terminal fever that will soon leave them exhausted."

The world loomed ever closer, expanding until it filled the entire view offered by their bubble. As they approached the uppermost regions of its atmosphere Valjhar rolled *Mote* to present its bottom to the planet. The constellations of this corner of the so-called "Milky Way" galaxy came into view.

Valjhar warned his friends to strap themselves into their chairs and applied power to the maneuvering lamps to slow their descent. This instantly brought back a semblance of gravity.

They entered the atmosphere over Earth's largest ocean, a few thousand kiloskads northeast of New Zealand, the land where Cal had been captured and where, they believed, he still remained.

Valjhar swiveled in his chair to face Pimsie, who looked back at him from the shadowy dimness of the bridge.

"Pimsie, I hate to ask you to submit to this, but it's time for you to sleep."

"I don't mind. It's for an important reason. Good night." With so little fanfare her eyes closed, her head sagged back, and the Dreamfarer appeared beside her, smiling down at her fondly.

"Nali. Do you know the man of the sea's location?"

The Dreamfarer turned to regard him with her opaque eyes.

"Yes, he sleeps. I shall guide you."

Mote descended gently through thickening layers of air. The stars grew less distinct. A hiss became audible, swelling gradually into a mellow roar of wind. The ship sank through a layer of thin, icy clouds. Shaula kept a careful watch on their sensors while Kern monitored the ship's systems and Valjhar piloted it.

"Here. Descend here," said Nali.

"Valjhar, do you see those aircraft?" asked Shaula.

Valjhar eyed his own display. "Yes, I see them. They're not showing any awareness of us."

"There's one of them now!" cried Shaula, pointing.

Far off was a slowly moving cluster of tiny lights, some blinking in various colors. Valjhar shuddered, half drawn to its mystery, but regarding it as he would the passage of a dangerous animal. What deranged thoughts were passing through the minds of its passengers?

"I don't think they can detect us visually," said Kern. "And I'm pretty sure I've got their radar baffled."

Valjhar was relieved when they passed below the altitude of most of the thousands of aircraft plying Earth's skies at any given moment. The black ocean horizon appeared around them. Valjhar slowed to a near hover, losing height very gradually.

"The air outside is thick," said Shaula. "Warm. Humid."

"What about ships? On the water?"

"None nearby."

Valjhar stopped their descent only a hundred skads above the surface of the sea. For a few moments they simply looked out at their new environment. Valjhar imagined the great sailing ships of Rral plying these placid waters, traveling from one gentle, welcoming port to another.

Shaula directed her instruments downward. "These waters are shallow. They are full of life. I'm detecting creatures in sizes ranging from big enough to occupy this whole dome down to smaller than I can resolve. Most of them have streamlined shapes, but I'm imaging other body plans as well. Look at this."

A projected image appeared in the air. It showed what looked like a cluster of slender, sinuous vortexes attached to an amorphous central body. These tentacles flicked and swirled in an alluring manner, then suddenly came together to propel the creature rapidly forward.

"That individual is about three skads long."

"And our aquatic friend lives among them?" said Kern in surprise.

"And among these."

Another glowing form appeared, this one sleek, finned, and purposeful in its motions.

"Look at the density display," said Shaula. A simple skeleton glowed through the flesh, but more apparent were rows of sharp triangular teeth in the jaws. "This monster is about seven skads long. I doubt it uses those teeth to pluck seaweed. We're approaching a submerged reef."

"Here. He is here, below us" said Nali. "I have awakened him. He senses your ship, but he does not know what it is. You should not need me anymore. Goodbye for now, my friends."

And so she was gone. Pimsie started, sat up, and blinked sleepily. "Is it over?"

"No, sweetie," said Kern. "Nali turned you back over to yourself sooner than we expected."

"I'll try to attract his attention," said Valjhar. "I'll turn on the landing floodlight."

A brilliant pillar erupted beneath the ship. Its light flickered from the small waves marching nearby.

Shaula gasped. "I'm picking up a large shape, emerging from a cave. It's humanoid, look."

A third image appeared, a manlike form, kicking its legs, making wide sweeps of its arms. It was very powerfully built.

"For some reason I didn't really believe we'd find a human-like creature living in the sea, but there it is. It makes no sense. It's...he's...almost four skads long."

"That's huge!" said Pimsie.

Indeed it was, thought Valjhar. Pimsie was about one and a half skads tall. He himself was little more than two. He had sudden grave doubts about this mission. What use could this enormous alien creature be in their search for Cal?

"Well, here we are, we may as well go through with it," he said, as though he were answering a question posed by someone else.

A thousand skads to dockside lay a small island that appeared to be uninhabited.

"I'll try to lure him to that island. Hang on while I yaw the ship around."

Valjhar advanced the ship very slowly, and according to Shaula, their quarry followed. *Mote* approached the wide beach, climbed it to the tree line, and came to rest on the sand.

Valjhar stood up and sighed. "Well then. All ashore that's going ashore."

"Why do you always have to say that?" said Pimsie.

They made their way down through the decks to the excursion bay, all of them, even Kroy. Kern wore his engineering suit. Valjhar wore his dimension belt. Shaula carried her entropic weapon. Valjhar deemed them ready and lowered the ramp.

Warm, heavy, fragrant air rolled in from this new world.

Pimsie sniffed. "Well, I must say I like this air. It smells like flowers."

Walking side by side they descended the ramp and left the ship. They halted, waiting. The ship's lights illuminated the scene well enough, out to the gentle incoming waves and beyond.

Something bobbed out there among them, stationary relative to the passing waves, a dark ovoid revealing little.

"I think I see him," whispered Shaula.

"Everyone stand up straight," said Valjhar. "Whatever he is, we'll meet him proudly, not quaking like children." This was a moment when Valjhar fervently wished for Cal-Cotavion, his fearsome staff, and his Stone of Adamance.

That great head emerged from the water, followed by wide, sleek shoulders and a massive torso. The gigantic figure advanced on them at a slow pace, his long legs swinging two skads at a time.

Valjhar's eyes widened involuntarily as the great creature halted not far off, looming over them.

"Valjhar," muttered Pimsie nervously. "He's twice our height and must weigh ten times as much as any of us. He's a monster. What are we supposed to do with him?"

That was a question Valjhar was presently unable to answer. His gaze roved up and down their visitor's massive form. He had a sleek, glossy hide of a deep tan color wrapped around enormous muscles that moved and bulged when he shifted his weight. Each of his hands was big enough to envelop Valjhar's head. His wrists were about as thick as Valjhar's thighs. His head—all humans had ridiculous protruding noses, but this one was like a sharp-edged mountain peak with twin caves in the bottom. He had the usual convoluted human ears, long blond hair still wet from the sea, and his eyes—

One glance at his eyes changed Valjhar's perception of him at once. They were strange, his least human, and perhaps least Rralian feature...a deep, solid blue, with huge black pupils.

But the really striking thing about those eyes was the sharp intelligence that shone from them. The Man of the Sea studied them with such a wary but intense curiosity that Valjhar had no doubt he was confronting an equal. One by one he looked into those little faces, and one by one Valjhar saw their reactions change. Kern smiled. Pimsie had trouble meeting his gaze. Shaula looked back with a steady appraisal. Kroy—Kroy blinked and said, "Greetings, fellow monster."

Of course their guest had no idea what this meant. They would have to learn how to communicate with him, what he called himself, and what he was, if possible. Valjhar studied him again. He appeared to be breathing normally. Evidently he was not limited to an aquatic existence.

Valjhar caught the giant with what he hoped was an engaging, welcoming expression. He began to back toward the ship's ramp, beckoning their visitor to follow. The giant hesitated, then haltingly advanced. The others followed with varying degrees of enthusiasm.

"You are very trusting, Valjhar," said Pimsie. "In some cases, anyway."

"Do you think he'll betray us, Pimsie?" said Shaula.

"I don't think that's the right word. He can't betray us, because he hasn't made any commitment to us. If he makes one later, then we'll see."

"Your alter ego sees into his mind, and she seems to trust him."

"Nali? She's not my alter ego. I'm still my own person, with my own mind."

"I think he'll turn out to be a good person," said Kern cheerily.

"You're even more trusting than Valjhar."

They climbed into the excursion bay. The giant followed. The ramp closed. A few minutes later *Mote* lifted off into space.

Chapter 7
Disillusioned

Rouse's altered perceptions did not fade with the sunrise. When she felt steady enough to leave her room she made her way to the sun room, intending to find Cal and quietly inform him that she had his staff.

She was arrested by the sight of the human beings occupying that room. Yesterday she would have seen them as a collection of grey, shuffling losers and outcasts, most of them barely worthy of her attention. Today...today she didn't know what to make of them. They struck her as very strange, very unlikely, incredibly intricate beings inhabiting a world that otherwise knew no greater complexity than the simple physics of a star or the crystal structure of some mineral. And it wasn't just humans, it was all life, an elaborate organization of matter unlike any other. And it wasn't just biology, either. It was also the infinite worlds residing within each one of those skulls, inside every one of those squishy brains, even the most barren and desolate.

Somehow they did not seem natural.

She found Cal in his usual chair, but she halted at the sight of him, for he had changed.

Whereas before he had rested lazily in the chair, now he slumped in it, his hands limp and motionless. He stared into the distance with his mouth opened stupidly.

Rouse approached him, took a seat beside him, and reached out to touch his arm. "Cal!"

He turned to her with blank and tired eyes. "Rouse?"

"Yes, of course it's me. How are you? Are you all right?"

"Yes, I think so. They took me away. They put me in a room. I—don't remember anything else." He looked away, mumbling in a language Rouse did not recognize or under-stand.

The first flickering of anger began to burn within her.

"Cal," she whispered, "I have your staff."

Cal frowned in mild puzzlement. "My — staff?"

"Yes! You know, your staff. The one you told me you carried across space with your alien friends."

"Ah...yes."

Cal appeared to have nothing more to say.

Rouse stood up suddenly. "Cal, you stay here and rest. I'll be back to see you later." She marched out of the ward and directly to the office suite, where without announcing herself or asking permission she barged into Doctor Narby's office, startling her. Narby's face showed fear, and Rouse realized she'd better tamp down her rising wrath or risk being confined, or transferred to a more violent ward. Already Narby's hand was hovering near the panic button beneath her desk.

"Rouse? What are you doing here?"

"Doctor Narby," said Rouse with a forced calm. "What did you do to Cal?"

"You know I shouldn't discuss patient treatment with you."

"You shocked him, didn't you? You subjected him to ECT?"

Narby looked uncomfortable and dropped her gaze. "Well, yes we did. But it was a last resort, a last chance to break through his delusion and find out who he really is."

"Why would you try to do that with a therapy you know damages memory?"

"Because nothing else worked!" Now Narby's own anxiety and anger became apparent. "You don't understand. It was our last chance. The courts have ruled against us. We're to turn Cal over to the army tomorrow."

That announcement shocked and chilled Rouse's anger into retreat. "Tomorrow?" she repeated.

"Yes, and if they decide Cal is some sort of a threat, who's to say they won't use methods worse than ECT on that poor man?"

Rouse absorbed this information and then nodded.

"I see, Doctor. Sorry for my outburst. You know I'm concerned about Cal too."

"Yes, of course, dear. I wish there was more we could do for him."

Rouse returned to Cal in the sun room with her face a carefully controlled mask of neutrality. She found him in the same position and in the same dismal condition. He looked older, worn and tired, as if he'd been an inmate—she could no longer think of him as a patient—here for years, rather than days.

She knelt beside him and whispered, "Cal. Cal, look at me."

He turned his bleary gaze upon her.

"Get up. We're going for a walk."

With tentative movements Cal stood and trudged after her as she led him outdoors.

Feeling the light of the sun on her face calmed Rouse a little, but somehow it looked ghastly on Cal, accentuating his paleness, its harsh shadows making him look even more haggard.

"Come, Cal. I want you to show me where you live. Show me your window."

Cal obediently led the way along the walkways, past various wards, common areas, and utility buildings, until they stopped alongside a low, pale green structure similar to the one Rouse lived in. He pointed at a young cabbage tree, with its long, sharp leaves, growing beside the wall.

"My window lies behind that tree."

Rouse nodded. "Good, that makes it easier. Now listen carefully, Cal. After dinner tonight I want you to go straight to your room. Wait for me there. Wear your shoes and your street clothes. Do you understand?"

"All right, Rouse, but why? These people will not permit you to visit me in my room."

"That's why I'm coming in though the window. We're leaving this place, Cal. I'm taking you away."

"Away? But my friends—"

"Your friends haven't shown their little pixie faces in the week or two that you've been here. They'll just have to find you later, wherever we end up, if they're ever going to. You can't stay here. You're in danger."

"From who?"

Rouse looked down in shame. "From our military. Our government. From whoever decides that anything different must be suspicious, must be something to be feared."

"I see. Whatever you think is best, Rouse. I trust you. My own thoughts are not very clear at the moment."

"Eat well tonight, Cal. I'm not sure where our next meal will come from."

Rouse found it difficult to follow her own advice that evening as she sat in the women's refectory. She was too nervous to do more than nibble at her plate of nondescript institutional food. When she returned to her room she stared at her closet door for a few minutes, aware that she was about to introduce a large and unpredictable change into her life, a change that could not be undone or taken back.

Taking a deep breath, she opened the door and brought forth the staff. The morning glories that entwined it were still as fresh and luminous as they had been the last time she'd seen them.

Rouse opened her window and rested the head of the staff on the sill. She returned to the closet and brought out her shoulder bag, which she packed with a jacket and as many other items of clothing as would fit. She set the bag on the windowsill as well. It would just fit between the bars, she judged.

She sat on her bed, tried to collect herself, and waited for the late-setting January sun to decline and the twilight to begin. When a soft purple light suffused the world outside, she rose on unsteady feet, opened her door, and peeked out into the corridor. No one was about. The only sound was the buzzing of fluorescent lamps. She strolled out of the building as nonchalantly as she could.

Once out in that gentle dusk she made her way to her window. First she pulled out her bag, which was fat enough to make its passage through the bars a challenging exercise requiring energetic tugging and curses under her breath. Then out came the staff.

In the twilight, the pale staff and the flowers that adorned it seemed to take on an added luminosity. It did not emit any actual light, but it accepted whatever light fell upon it and somehow exalted it.

Rouse marched off, again brandishing the staff as though daring anyone to dispute her right to carry it. The grounds were quiet. The exterior lights were flickering on, but the twilight was still bright enough so that they were not glaring or obtrusive.

Tokanui Hospital was not far from being closed forever; everyone knew this. Its staff was much reduced in numbers. Only about two hundred patients remained. Many of the buildings were already shuttered and abandoned. Already it felt like a ghostly place.

Rouse made it to Cal's building without attracting any unwanted attention. There was his cabbage tree. She slipped behind it, grateful for its concealment. But Cal's window…Rouse's heart sank. This building had a taller foundation than hers, and as a result its windows were higher, almost out of reach. Not only that, but its bars looked thicker and stronger than those on her own window, and their frame was bolted to the wall more strongly. Finally, the window wasn't even opened. Was Cal there, and waiting for her?

She looked out from the shadows of the cabbage tree, uncertain of what to do. Maybe this wasn't meant to be. Maybe she should go back to her room, keep herself out of trouble, and leave Cal to whatever fate awaited him. For all she knew, the army had some valid reason to question him, or study him, or whatever they intended to do to him.

She reached up and grabbed the bars, shaking them, pulling as hard as she could, to the point of lifting herself off the ground until she could see inside. She spied Cal collapsed on his bed, asleep or unconscious, unaware of her presence. Rouse dropped down, gave the bars a few more futile tugs, and lowered her hands.

Maybe she should just slip away and drown herself somewhere. That would simplify things so much. It would relieve her of so much responsibility and uncertainty.

Or...

She lifted the staff and shoved its head between the bars, shattering the window. She lodged it firmly behind the window frame and pulled for all she was worth. She didn't care if she broke the staff. It was only a stick of wood. But the staff did not bend or break. Nor did the bars. That infuriated her—those wretched bars with their flaking paint, those thieves of freedom, they had no business defying her. With a mad determination she pulled, grunting with effort, and then she actually walked up the wall, pushing with her legs while hanging from the staff.

With a sudden ripping sound the bars pulled free on three sides, remaining barely attached on the fourth. Rouse fell to the ground, landing on her back, stunned and breathless.

When her head cleared she looked up to see Cal's puzzled face at the broken window, looking down at her.

"Oh, hello Rouse. I'm sorry, I forgot you were coming."

Rouse sat up. "Cal Cotavion. You open that window, climb out, and come down here right now."

"As you wish."

As Cal awkwardly clambered out, Rouse got to her feet and picked up the staff. The flowers were torn and shredded by the use she'd put them to. With some regret she cleared the remains away. When Cal stood beside her she handed him the staff. His hand closed around it naturally, but he still looked somehow incomplete.

"Come on, Cal."

She led him away, in the direction of the fading twilight. Cal walked a little unsteadily but with his head held high. Rouse made sure she didn't skulk either. They entered a grove of fruit trees, where Rouse paused to stuff her bag and pockets with as many apples and pears as they would hold.

Continuing on, they left the hospital's grounds behind without being challenged. It almost seemed anticlimactic.

"Where are we going, Rouse?"

Rouse pointed to an irregular mass looming on the western horizon. "That mountain's Pirongia. It's covered with bush and there's a big forested park around it too. I'm hoping we can hide out there, if we can reach it. Luckily there's not much between us except farmland."

They walked on into the deepening night.

Chapter 8
The Invasion of Earth

The Stingray moved among his tiny new acquaintances cautiously and gently. *Motes's* corridors and compartments were barely tall enough to allow Cal-Cotavion to walk upright, but Stingray was obliged to hunch over as he toured the ship. He accepted the ship, and indeed everything he saw, more easily than Valjhar had expected. Perhaps he saw little difference between their ship and the seagoing vessels he had encountered in the ocean.

Teaching him the basics of the Rralian language proved easy enough, thanks to his intelligence and his intense desire to communicate with them. Training him to produce the appropriate sounds was a greater challenge. He had no native speech, or at least no humanoid speech. The sounds he naturally produced were used for echolocation, very high-pitched and often painfully loud. He also had a vocal apparatus similar to theirs, but it had been of little use to him underwater, and he had to learn how to control it.

He learned English even more readily, because his brain was more human in its configuration, or so Valjhar supposed.

They derived his name from his account of his early years. Remarkably, he had once possessed a larval form completely unlike his present humanoid one. This had been similar to some of the large flattened fishes of Earth's oceans, called rays. A closer examination of his anatomy suggested the name Stingray. While he had dim memories of this stage of his life, he could not account for his origin.

Once they'd established an adequate basis of communication, Valjhar led Stingray to the parlor in the aft end of the ship, a space he selected because the overhead there was unusually high. Earth was not visible through the compartment's large ports. In the dim lighting they had a fine view of a star field and the curdled band of the galactic equator.

Stingray studied this for a while and then turned to Valjhar.

"What are you?"

"We come from the distant planet Rral. We are not native to Earth. We are wanderers among the stars." Valjhar could not resist feeling a swell of pride as he awaited Stingray's awed reaction to this pronouncement.

"Where are you going?"

Valjhar was immediately deflated. "Er...we don't know. We have no final destination in mind. As I said, we're wanderers."

"Why are you here?"

"We encountered people of human kind on another world, and there we learned that Earth is the source of that species. We have found very few intelligent species in our travels, so we were drawn here."

"Does that mean your little band is lonely? Do you enjoy your life as wanderers?"

"Well...some of us would prefer to settle down, ideally back on Rral, I admit."

"Why don't you?"

Now Valjhar was embarrassed. "We—uh—we can't. You see, our possession of this space ship violates the laws of Rral, and we are pursued by a very dangerous—machine man—for that crime. It has already nearly caught us more than once. It is called the Prohibitor. We don't dare stay in any one place for too long."

"So you're not so much wanderers, as—what's a good word—fugitives?"

"Yes. I must admit that is the case."

"What do you want from me?"

"We sent one of our group down to search for food. He is human, not Rralian like the rest of us. He was detected and taken captive by the Earth people."

"Go on."

"Another of us—the dream-spirit Nali...I'm not sure if you've seen her yet...told us that you might help us to recover him."

"And how might I do that?"

"We're not sure." *Perhaps by using the physical violence we are loath to employ,* thought Valjhar with a sense of shame. "Perhaps by means of your knowledge of humans—"

Stingray interrupted him with an alarming laugh that was neither human nor Rralian. "What knowledge? I've barely encountered them. I know nothing of their ways, except that they send ships through the sea, flying craft through the sky, and they drag huge destructive nets through the waters, killing everything in their path. Other than that, I know more about you than I do about them."

Valjhar was nonplussed. "Still, Nali thinks you might be of use to us..."

"Valjhar, stop. You and your people interest me, and I like you. I certainly enjoy being able to communicate with beings who are something like me, people who know much more about the universe than I do. I've spent a lot of time drifting on the surface of the ocean, looking up at the stars, and wondering what's up there. Thanks to you, I now have some idea. I would like to help you, but I'm not here to be of 'use' to you, or to anyone else."

"Of course. My apology for my poor choice of words. And my compliments on your rapid acquisition of language that allowed you to discern it."

"Language isn't a foreign concept to me. The speech of dolphins and whales has its own kind of subtlety."

While they worked to educate Stingray, the Rralians also tried to keep track of Cal through Nali.

"He has been injured," she reported sadly. "They've done something to dull his mind. But he is still unafraid."

Valjhar closed his eyes at this news, struggling to contain his grief.

"Also, he has left the place where they were keeping him."

"Left, or been removed?"

"Left of his own accord, I think."

"That's interesting. Can you follow him?"

"He is not asleep, but as he travels he often enters a half-aware state of musing and contemplation, in which he considers things beyond the range of his senses."

"He daydreams, then. And that is enough?"

"Enough for me to be aware of him."

Kern was Stingray's most enthusiastic tutor. He seemed to be amused by the huge creature, and was not intimidated. He had merged adjacent cabins to contain Stingray's bulk, and had offered to construct a water tank for the giant to dwell in. This Stingray had refused, stating that he was actually quite slow and clumsy in the water, at least compared to the creatures who were designed to live there. Also, transitioning from air to water breathing and back was neither a quick nor a pleasant process for him.

Valjhar continued to watch the situation as closely as possible, looking for the best moment to swoop in and recover Cal, wondering how a huge amphibious humanoid was supposed to assist in this, and watching for any sign that Cal was in imminent danger. When events came no closer to resolution over the next several hours he was about to trust to luck and begin the rescue when something unexpected happened.

Sitting at a console on the bridge, Kern's face lit up with surprise and joy. "Valjhar! It's a radio call from Cal!"

Valjhar sagged with relief. "It's about time. Let's hear what he has to say."

But the voice that emerged from the speakers was not Cal's. It spoke in English, Earth's most commonly used language, the language of New Zealand, and one the Rralians had taken care to study.

"All right, I don't know if this thing is even really a voice transmitter at all, but if it is, can anyone hear me?"

Kern turned an expression of dismay toward Valjhar. "It's an Earth human! He has Cal's radio."

"So it seems. Would you have expected them to understand its purpose?"

"Well, it's not really a radio as they would understand it, but it's also not a quantum device, which we don't use for fear of revealing ourselves to the Prohibitor. But if they can guess how to activate it, and they can detect its emissions at all, they might also guess what it's for. It's not too unlike some of the devices they've imagined in their entertainment shows."

"Hello? Hello? We know you've already recovered the man you left behind, and also apparently kidnapped one of our citizens. We need to talk to you."

"What is he raving about?" asked Shaula. "We haven't done any of that."

"I'm confused too," said Valjhar. "They must think we were behind Cal's escape, if escape he did. I'm not sure we should correct them on that. But I suppose we ought to respond somehow." He leaned toward the microphone on his console.

"Wait, Valjhar, don't!" cried Kern.

"Why not?"

"Well—compared to the humans, our voices are very high pitched. I'm afraid that if we speak to them sounding like children, they won't, er, take us seriously. It's something else I saw on *Star Trek*."

Valjhar almost laughed. Instead he said, "Pimsie? Would you mind fetching the Stingray up here, please? I think I have a job for him."

"Me? Why me? Oh, all right."

Pimsie slouched off down the stairs. Valjhar had noticed her tendency to avoid their giant guest, but he had no time to deal with that at the moment.

Soon that great blond head appeared in the stairwell, and those blue-black eyes swiveled to take in everything. Kern had not yet constructed a huge chair for him, so he sat cross-legged on the deck to avoid looming over them too much. He wore black clothing designed to reduce his apparent size.

"How may I help you, Valjhar?"

Valjhar explained the situation. "You have a deep voice, and you sound more human than we do. Would you respond to these people? Try to be non-committal. Don't give anything away."

"Very well."

Valjhar was about to further explain what Stingray should say, but he took the initiative by leaning toward a console and keying open a microphone. Truly, he had gone from a solitary life beneath the sea to a basic understanding of their technology with remarkable speed.

"Who is this that speaks?" he rumbled.

There, thought Valjhar. *That ought to give the humans something to think about.*

"This is the Security Intelligence Service of New Zealand. Who am I speaking to?"

"We choose not to identify ourselves. What do you want?"

"It will be difficult to conduct any negotiations if you refuse to identity yourselves."

"We are not aware of any need for negotiations."

"Not to get your man back, I suppose, but there is the matter of Miss Farewell, who we would like to have back, and you might like to have your items returned as well."

Stingray looked at Valjhar for guidance, but he could offer no information other than a puzzled expression.

"What items are those?" resumed Stingray.

"This intriguing communicator, and your mysterious block of metal, of course. Both of which are sources of immense interest to us, I must say."

At a gesture from Valjhar, Stingray said, "One moment," and cut his microphone.

"Metal block?" said Valjhar.

Kern looked troubled. "I'm afraid he must mean the box I made for the Stones. The way I made it, it appears featureless, and its biometric sensor won't open for any human but Cal. It's so heavy they'd think it was a solid object."

"So you're sure they can't open it? I'd hate to think of the result if those primitives were exposed to the Stones, especially without someone like Cal around to control them."

"The substance is harder than any of their tools. In between the layers of silver, lead, and other metals are carbon structures unlike anything they've yet discovered, perfectly deposited, atom by atom. I doubt they can concentrate enough energy to burn their way into it. Maybe one of their nuclear weapons would do it, but that would also scatter the Stones to who knows where. Maybe they could melt it in some great furnace."

"Let's hope they're not ready to resort to that. Could they damage or destroy the Stones themselves?"

"Who knows? I haven't been able to bring myself to try to analyze them. Who would want to study them that closely? But we've never seen them damaged. I'm not sure they're really even physical objects at all, in the sense that we understand that concept. Although they are subject to gravitation…I'm not sure what to think."

"I think we can assume that Cal has freed himself from his captivity and has taken an Earth woman, this 'Miss Farewell', with him for some reason."

"That's a poor assumption," said Shaula. "The humans are divided into any number of factions, many working against each other or at cross purposes. Cal and this woman could have been taken by any of them. It might even be the case that Farewell is the instigator."

"True," said Valjhar. "Let's try to get more information from Nali the next time we see her. In the meantime… Kern, can you locate the source of their transmission?"

"I already have, but it's moving quite fast, probably in an aircraft. That's not useful to us unless we want to stoop down and intercept them…which we could do."

"Hello, are you people still there?"

"I suppose we shouldn't keep our friend waiting," said Valjhar.

Stingray keyed the mike. "Yes, we are here."

"Look, let me level with you blokes. I'm making this call in an, er, unofficial capacity. I'm not supposed to be using this phone of yours at all. Some dangerous folks would be quite cross with me if they knew what I was do-ing."

"What folks?"

"The Americans."

Valjhar frowned. He recognized this as a reference to one of the most powerful, dangerous, and warlike nations on Earth.

"What do these 'Americans' have to do with any of this?" resumed Stingray.

"Well, they know you're out there. They detected your spacecraft when it swooped down to a place not far from Samoa a few days ago, and they've tracked it to its current sunward position."

Kern's wide eyes prompted Stingray to ask a question. "How?"

"Who knows? They don't share all their secrets with small fry like us. Do you know how many people work at our SIS? About three hundred and fifty in all. That's probably less than the Americans have working at the food service of one of their big intelligence campuses."

"Why are you telling us this?"

"We Kiwis don't want things to get out of hand. I mean, what harm have you aliens done? Sent down one confused gentleman to purchase a few fruits and veggies? You paid a very good price for them, too. But the Americans have a poor sense of humor when it comes to things they can't control. They've already got naval warships on their way here. We're not sure why."

"I'm no alien."

Even Valjhar could hear the surprise in the reply. "Not an alien? Well, mate, you've got one hell of a spaceship for a human being. No one down here has anything that could hover way out there like you're doing, that's for sure."

"I didn't say I was human, either."

More bafflement. "Not human or alien?"

"Yes. Why do you think those are the only two choices? There's a lot more to Earth than you seem to know."

"So it would appear. We would appreciate the return of our Miss Farewell, or at least we and her family would ask for some word from her, in case she has decided on her own to go off with you, to wherever you're going."

Stingray looked at Valjhar for guidance.

"I suppose we'll tell him," whispered Valjhar.

"We know nothing of any Miss Farewell."

"Indeed. May we infer then that you have not actually recovered your Mr. Cotavion?"

"I think that would be reasonable."

"I see. Well, if there are any loose ends you need to clean up around our islands before you depart, I advise you to do it quickly, before the Americans arrive in force."

"Loose ends?"

"Sorry, it means leftover tasks you haven't yet completed, or something like that."

"Thank you. There is one other matter. We cannot permit you to keep either our communicator, or our...block of metal."

The speakers were silent for several moments. When their mysterious communicant resumed his voice was hushed and hurried.

"I'm sorry, but those matters are out of my control. Both artifacts, along with myself, are already aboard an airplane on our way to the States. We wouldn't have wanted it that way, but once the Americans got wind of what we had, they pretty much insisted. They can be pretty persuasive. And I must sign off right now, good luck."

Valjhar and his friends sat looking at each other for a minute or so, absorbing this information and forming their conclusions.

"Well, he didn't sound *too* terrible..." said Pimsie grudgingly.

"No, he didn't," said Valjhar. "We learned on Colibdis that not all humans are mendacious. We can hope that even here, in this world's pervasive atmosphere of corruption and evil, some people may still possess their integrity."

"You mean like when he hinted we could bargain with them to get our things back, and then he said we couldn't? I didn't say he sounded good. Just not too terrible."

"We can't let them keep the Stones," said Shaula. "Whether they could ever understand and profit from our radio is debatable, but the Stones are another matter altogether."

"Yes. Kern, can you continue to track that aircraft?"

"Sure, now that it's pinpointed it won't escape my beady little eyes."

"Your eyes aren't beady!" objected Pimsie.

Kern grinned. "Anyway, they're about twelve hours away from that America place."

"Then we have that long to stop them," said Shaula. "We mustn't let them reach their destination. It's the center of military power on this world. If they make it there, it's hard to see how we could avoid a big, very visible fight that we might not even win."

"I suppose now we can't avoid some kind of a fight," said Valjhar with a sinking heart.

Suddenly the bridge was illuminated by a dazzling green light from above. Pimsie screeched. Shading his eyes with his hands, Valjhar squinted up through the bubble. A brilliant point of verdant fire blazed from one of the Earth's northern landmasses.

"Calm down, everyone," said Kern. "It's only a laser."

"Looks like they want us to know we're in their sights," said Shaula. "Is it coming from America?"

"It is."

"I find their behavior annoying. Kern, can we return their favor?" asked Valjhar.

"You know we can," grinned Kern. "We can illuminate half their continent, if we want to."

"Cycle our beam through all visible wavelengths. Let's show them how colorful we are."

"No!" cried Pimsie. "Don't let them drag you down to their level. Don't make this a game of tit for tat. Let's be ourselves here, please."

Shaken, Valjhar said, "You're right, Pimsie. I'm afraid their aggressive nature is infecting my thoughts."

"Wait, you're afraid of offending them by shining a light on them?" said Stingray. "I suppose your pacifism is admirable, but Shaula is right. You can't avoid a fight now if you want to recover your magic gems."

Shaula gave Stingray a look of speculative appreciation.

Valjhar brooded down at the strange lens on his belt: a minor artifact of Old Rral it was, but also a power beyond anything the humans understood.

"We could draw their aircraft into space, beyond the reach of any help. But that would kill everyone on board, if I'm not mistaken."

"You're not thinking big enough, Valjhar," said Kern. "I think we can handle it more elegantly than that. I have some ideas. Have a seat and buckle in, everybody, and tell Kroy to do the same. I'm taking us to the far side of that big moon of theirs. Let's see anyone spy on us there."

"If we enter their aircraft, they're bound to know we're aliens," said Shaula.

"Send me," said Stingray with a predatory grin. "Let them think the aliens are big and imposing."

"What about poor Cal while we're doing all this?" asked Pimsie.

Valjhar was startled; he had almost forgotten about Cal. "He'll have to wait. He seems to be doing all right on his own so far, and we'll just have to hope he can keep it up for a few hours more. He and, I suppose, this Miss Farewell."

Chapter 9
Tramping Through New Zealand

The part of the Waikato region surrounding the hospital was farmland, a green country networked by many small roads, dotted by houses and farm buildings, and providing little cover. This made it impossible for Rouse and Cal to move during daytime without being seen. On their first night's trek they managed to traverse about eight miles to the northern flank of the extinct Kakepuku volcano, whose heights were clothed in a tawa forest that permitted them to hide and rest during the following day.

The sky clouded over and a gentle, steady rain descended as they huddled beneath the trees. Somewhere nearby a North Island robin peeped out its call. A tui chuckled and chatted with itself somewhere else.

Cal slept lightly, spending most of the day calmly studying his surroundings, never straying far from Rouse. His condition improved as the effects of his shock treatment wore off.

Rouse was not so fortunate. She shivered in the rain, her light jacket and other clothing soaked through. She found it difficult to sleep. Cut off from her medications, her state of mind deteriorated further, until she began to harbor fearful thoughts of return and surrender, or even suicide. She lay with her head and shoulders propped against a tree. She began to whimper as she felt the onset of an anxiety attack.

Hearing this, Cal came over, leaned his staff against the trunk, sat beside her, and took her hand. He had very long fingers, and a pallid skin through which could be seen blue veins. His hand was cool.

"Cal," she said shakily, desperate for some kind of distraction, "tell me more about your fairy kingdom." By now it didn't even matter if she believed his stories or not.

"Oh yes, Faerie. It's been so long since I was there, and I've changed so much since then, that when I think back to that place it's like I'm imagining the life of someone who looks like me, but is not me. Faerie is in many ways an artificial land. The glamour of a false sky and sun are cast over it to make it seem more like Earth, because the first Elves came from this world and preferred that look to the thin violet sky and double sun of the rest of the Colibdis. The whole country glows with the Blue Magic that creates this illusion and enhances the abilities of the Elves and all the other creatures of Faerie. This same magic makes the land dangerous to mortals.

"As a bit of a magician myself, I always wondered about that spell, so stable, so permanent, yet apparently lacking anyone to maintain it. Having much time on my hands, I decided to investigate. Traveling throughout the land, I made a careful map, a process neither easy nor precise, as the landmarks of Faerie are somewhat changeable and fugitive. My map revealed nothing suspicious, but as I studied it my eye was always drawn to one specific place. In the west-central part of Faerie is a great wooded valley called Belmarden, considered the heart of Faerie due to its beauty, a country of great trees suffused with the blue twilight, and alive with the voices of spirits and sprites of every kind.

"Near the center of this valley is a large lake called the Fadelmere, known to have been created by the first inhabitants of Faerie, long ago. From the center of this lake juts a small, rocky island, and atop it stands an abandoned wizard's tower, little regarded, and with little lore that I could discover. For some reason I was drawn to this tower. Wishing to show off my powers, I used my clumsy spells to create a frozen pathway over the water so I could walk to it.

"I found that the tower was not abandoned after all. Hidden there behind veils of illusion was none other than old Avion himself, the founder of my House, the founder of Faerie itself, one of the first men ever to become fey, and the source of the Blue Magic. My grandfather—or was he my great grandfather? My memory is fading. In any event, a person long thought dead.

"Avion did not object to my presence. He seemed quite mad, though happily so, the most ebullient and joyful Elf I had ever known. Nor did he stint with his knowledge. He went so far as to teach me the spell of the Blue Magic. In theory I could have gone to any part of the world and created there my own version of Faerie. I had no desire to do so, as I would not remove myself from Seren.

"In my pride, I shared nothing of what I had learned, clutching those secrets to myself while gloating about my superior wisdom and knowledge. Even when I stood with Seren on the shores of the Fadelmere, with the island and tower faintly visible in the mist, I didn't say a word. I wonder if Avion ever shared that spell with anyone else. But enough of my foolishness. Have you no stories of yourself, and this exotic world of yours?"

Rouse blinked, emerging slowly from the spell cast by Cal's words.

"Me? You know enough of my story, don't you? I'm a tall, awkward, unattractive girl from the north shore of Auckland. My father is an engineer whose devotion to his home life is erratic at best. My mother is a florist and a neurotic creature whose fingertips often bleed from her relentless gnawing. My two brothers are essentially big dumb brutes of no appreciable erudition or taste, caring for nothing but rugby and the All Blacks. My grandfather lives with us and is a vegetable. Except for him, they're all ashamed and disappointed by their suicidal relative."

Cal turned his head slowly to regard her. His eyes focused on her with a care and attention she had not seen there before. He studied her for quite a while before he spoke.

"You say you are unattractive? The standards of beauty on this world must differ greatly from mine. You are no Elf, but any mortal should delight in your appearance."

Rouse laughed. "You're mad, but then we knew that already."

"Why do you say so?"

"Well, look at me. I'm dirty, my hair is dirty, soaking wet, plastered to my face..."

Cal gave her a wry look and shook his head. "Those who appreciate true beauty know to look beyond such superficial things."

Somehow the approaching storm of her anxiety attack had passed. The day was warming, and the rain relented, though the clouds remained.

"I think I can sleep now, if you can do without my delightful company for a while," she said.

"I will try to sleep as well. Nali may have something to tell me, and I must make myself available to her."

Rouse rolled her eyes at his fancies but was happy to let her head sag against his shoulder as she fell asleep.

Rouse awoke hours later while the sun slanted down through broken clouds in the west. She sat up with gummy eyes and took stock of herself. She was mostly dry, but her hair and clothes were stiff with dirt and sweat. She and Cal ate a couple of apples each, a meal appreciated but not fully adequate or satisfying, at least for Rouse.

She was not yet safe from the storms of her emotions. She could feel them roiling and simmering somewhere deep within her.

They lurked at the edge of the forest, high enough on the slope of the mountain to give them a commanding view of the countryside. The multiple peaks of Pirongia stood about twenty miles to the northwest. The tree-lined course of the Waipa River could be faintly seen closer to hand. In the foreground was the green patchwork of paddocks and fields that occupied almost all of this part of the Waikato. As twilight thickened the lights of numerous farms winked on, so many that threading a stealthy path between them would be a challenge.

They left their hiding place before full darkness to take full advantage of the short summer night, picking their way down the age-softened flank of the ancient volcano while the sound of night insects rose around them. The light of the waxing crescent moon assisted them for a while.

Soon they walked again among fields, ditches, and many fences. Dairy cows rested in many of the paddocks, motionless until they turned their heads to watch them pass by. Rouse, a city girl, had little experience with cattle, and could only hope that was all they'd do. What if they started mooing? What if they encountered a bull?

Often they heard dogs barking in the distance. Sometimes dogs ran wild in packs, Rouse had heard. As safe and gentle as this rolling country appeared during the day, to fugitives skulking through it at night it had a more sinister aspect.

Or it did to Rouse, anyway. Cal strode along calmly, his head held high, his staff matching the easy rhythm of his long legs. He looked as though he expected that staff to protect them from any possible threat.

The landscape grew darker as the moon set. Obstacles became harder to see, and they were forced to slow down. As she climbed through yet another fence, Rouse became aware that her intense focus on her surroundings forced her more turbulent thoughts from her mind. She would not fall apart tonight.

Sometime around midnight they heard the bass flutter of a helicopter and saw its lights probing the countryside off to the east. At the same time a police car with its lights flashing whirred by on a road a mile or so to the west, in their path.

Rouse's heart froze. So far they had seen no sign of any pursuit, but she was not so foolish as to hope these events were unrelated to them. Surely their escape, especially Cal's, would not be ignored.

"Cal, we have to be extra careful," Rouse whispered, though that served no real purpose. "Those vehicles are looking for us. The helicopter is especially dangerous. It could be on us in a moment, and there's not much cover out here."

"Looking for us? Why should they? Rouse, why was it so important to get me away from the hospital?"

Rouse inferred from the baffled tone of Cal's questions that he was still throwing off the effects of his shock therapy.

"Cal, I know you were enjoying your restful stay there, or at least you were until the moment they fried your brain. But it wasn't going to last. My government—they were eager to get their hands on you, and they were about to take you away."

"For what?"

"To find out who and what you really are."

"But I've explained that to anyone who has asked."

"Yes. But maybe they don't believe your story. Or maybe they do. I'm not sure which would be worse for you."

"Do you believe me, Rouse?"

"Yes," she said without thinking, startling herself. She laughed. "Yes, I believe you're an Elf prince from another planet, why not? And I don't even care if it's true or not. I believe it anyway. I want to live in the kind of world that has space Elves! If I'd believed in space Elves a few months ago I might never have—" She cut herself off. She did not want to talk about that.

The police car continued down the road, but then, a considerable distance away, it pulled over and killed its lights. Rouse didn't like the look of that. Then, even more ominously, the helicopter shut down its spotlight, but drifted in their direction, as they could see by its running lights.

"They won't be able to see us," said Cal.

"Won't they?" Rouse was no expert on police and military technology, but even she'd heard of things like night vision goggles and body heat sensors. Why else would that helicopter be flying without lights, if not to try those? "Cal, quick, look for cows. Are there cows nearby?"

"Cows? I think I see some resting in the next field ahead."

"Quick, get there, run!"

Cal loped on ahead, his staff trailing behind like a ghostly white tail. Rouse followed, keeping her eyes on him, hoping his night vision was better than hers. He gave a little hop but she didn't see why, finding out a moment later when she fell into a muddy ditch. She fell hard, landing on her face. She started to get up, but then decided it was easier to lay back down and pass out.

The next thing she was aware of was the loud thumping of the helicopter rotor in her ear. The next was the fragrant warmth of a large bovine body close beside her. Cal was there too, with his hand on her shoulder. Her face was wet and achy, and her teeth felt loose.

The cattle lifted their heads and bawled. Some heaved themselves to their feet and headed off toward the barn.

"Cal, we have to follow them," said Rouse in a croak.

"Why?"

"If the men in that helicopter detect two creatures not acting like cattle, they'll be on us in a second. Stay low and try to move like a cow!" Of course if the helicopter crew grew suspicious and snapped on their searchlight it was all over for them anyway.

At that moment a powerful light did come on...from the direction of the farmhouse and barn. It played over the helicopter, revealing it to be a military aircraft.

An angry voice reached them faintly. "Hey, you pirates, get away from my cattle! You're frightening them!"

A much louder voice boomed out from the helicopter's speakers. "Extinguish your light! This is a military search mission. Drop your light and remain where you are." The helicopter swung off toward the hapless farmer.

"Quick, Cal, forget the cattle. Run away!"

"Please make up your mind."

"Look, there's a line of trees ahead. If we can just get to them..."

They reached the trees, which were merely a narrow stand dividing one pasture from another. Among them they crouched as they breathlessly waited to see what the helicopter crew would do once they finished harassing the farmer.

Rouse became aware of a peculiar emotion as she watched. It was not an easy feeling to analyze, but finally she concluded it was excitement, possibly even triumph. They had eluded and defeated, at least temporarily, the overarmed and overzealous minions of oppression who sought to capture them. Or perhaps her feelings were related to the fact that her nose felt a bit smashed and blood was running from it. Her hair was full of mud.

Whatever it was...it was nice to be feeling something. Something real and genuine.

Having perhaps established that an indignant farmer with a spotlight was not an enemy combatant, the helicopter lifted off. It flew about in a desultory manner and then left the area, to Rouse's huge relief.

"Well, that's enough of that for one night," said Rouse. "Let's try to be far from here by sunrise."

"Are you all right? You took quite a fall. You were limp as a rag when I carried you over that fence."

"You carried me...? Well, of course you did. How else could I have gotten there? I'm all right, a bit shaken up, no worse. Come on then."

They scrambled off into the darkness. When they neared the road they went very cautiously indeed, knowing that the police car could be lurking anywhere nearby with its lights out. They waited until two other cars had passed, then darted across.

Once away from the road, they halted and looked around carefully. With no moon and a partly cloudy sky, Rouse could see very little. She saw a distant glow that she thought might be Hamilton, but she couldn't even be sure of that. It could be Te Awamutu or some other town instead. She realized to her dismay that she had become disoriented and no longer knew which direction to take. She frowned up at the stars, knowing too little about them to navigate by their light.

"Cal, I don't know which way to go," she murmured. "I'm lost."

"We still wish to go to that mountain you showed me, correct? Pirongia, was it?"

"Yes."

"Well, what's the problem? It's right over there." Cal pointed a long arm into the darkness.

"You—you can see it?"

"Yes, I can see it. I know my nose is rather long, but that doesn't mean I can smell it."

"Are you...somehow becoming Elfier as we sneak along?"

"I hardly think so. I think it's more a case of my having better night vision than you do at the moment. One of us has to."

"Right. Lead on then, Owl Eyes."

On they trudged until they reached another small stand of trees, where Rouse collapsed onto a fallen log. "I need to rest. That helicopter episode—took more out of me than I thought."

"Then let us rest."

"I'm so hungry. I think we're out of apples."

"There are cows nearby."

"I can hardly tear one open with my teeth and start gnawing on it."

"I believe they are milk cows."

"So?"

"Could you not milk one? Isn't that what mortals do?"

"Milk a cow?" Rouse had never considered that. And yet, why not? Farmers milked their cows every day; why shouldn't she as well? "But we have no container."

"You make many objections. Milk the cow directly into your mouth. Or simply suck from its teat."

"That—that's grotesque."

"Yes, it is, isn't it? Like so many things people do."

"I don't think I'm quite that desperate yet. Maybe we'll find something else." She got up and continued on before Cal could suggest she look for a nice fat weta to munch on.

Luckily they soon happened upon a garden plot, fenced against pests, but with an unlocked gate. The farmyard was not far off, lit by a ghastly security light, but the house itself was dark, which was fitting for this hour of the morning.

Rouse and Cal snuck into the garden as quietly as possible, fearing to alert the almost inevitable farm dog. The garden offered tomatoes, strawberries, and beans, not all perfectly ripe, but close enough for a hungry fugitive. That she could see well enough to find and pick them was due to the fact that the sky was already growing lighter.

Rouse filled her bag and her mouth as quickly as she could. Cal also sampled the produce, though not quite as voraciously.

Mumbling around a mouthful of strawberries, Rouse said, "Oh, I have some money, but if I leave it they'll know someone was here."

Cal shrugged.

"I'll tuck it here under this fertilizer can and hope they discover it later."

"The farmers will appreciate your honesty, I'm sure."

"Right. Let's go!"

With dawn not far off they were now obliged to seek a hiding place for the day. Lacking a convenient nearby volcano, their options were limited. Then quite suddenly they found themselves on the steep bank of the Waipa river, or rather a place where two substantial tributaries entered it. A few clumps of trees were visible on the far side.

"We shall have to swim or wade," said Rouse.

"Obviously."

"Unless you can walk across the water?" she snapped, irritated by Cal's increasingly haughty attitude.

"Not unless I can freeze it first, as I told you. But I cannot. My spells do not speak to or influence this world."

Rouse grimaced at the turbid flow. "This river is not very clean. Try not to drink any."

Then from behind them arose a sound Rouse had been dreading: the baying of dogs. "Oh no!"

"Hmm," said Cal. "It sounds as though our presence in the garden may have been discovered. Shall we plunge into the river?"

"What, and ruin my nice berries and tomatoes?" Rouse tried to make it into a joke, but in fact she was terrified. She felt so much worse a moment later when the sound of a helicopter assaulted them, seemingly from out of nowhere.

The helicopter loomed up suddenly with its side door opened and its searchlight swinging about. There would be no hiding from it this time. The light caught them seconds later.

"Well, I suppose they've got us this time!" shouted Rouse over the rotor noise.

"That glare is a poor substitute for a true Light."

Rouse had no idea what Cal was talking about, but her despair was too great to allow her to care.

The helicopter drew closer and a voice boomed out if it. "Stay where you are! Do not move or we will be forced to fire on you!"

"Fire? What does he mean?" said Cal. "Will they set fire to us?"

"No, they'll shoot us with their guns! They'll kill us!"

"Oh, I see."

Cal made what looked like a casual gesture and his staff disappeared. A harsh bang and whine sounded from the helicopter as one of its rotor blades spun off into the twilight. The copter lurched onto its side and crashed heavily into the grass, its remaining blades churning up mud and clumps of sod before disintegrating. Its engine roared and died.

The staff fell out of the darkness and stabbed into the earth like a spear, just a few feet away. Cal wrested it free. It was unharmed.

Rouse stared aghast at the ruins. "Cal, those soldiers...they may be dead. They are surely injured."

Cal's tone carried a chill as he replied. "No one, neither man nor Elf, should ever threaten another without risk of retaliation. To expect otherwise is cowardice."

"They only did as they were told."

Cal sniffed in contempt. "I might accept that excuse from a dog."

Rouse wondered if she were seeing a hint of the haughty Elf prince of old. She stared at him in a state halfway between awe and terror. "I—I didn't think you could do things like that anymore."

"All I did was toss my staff."

"No, that was more than a toss. That staff shot up like a missile."

"Did it? Hmm. Perhaps I'm not as familiar with the limitations of the human body as you are."

Something about that suggestion caused Rouse's jaw to drop and her thoughts to haze over as she considered it. She contemplated Cal's words in a daze until he interrupted her.

"Hadn't we better go?"

"Oh, yes. Cal, it's so much worse for us now that we've done this. Before they were only searching for us. Now they'll be hunting us. We can't afford to stop and rest. If we don't lose ourselves in the forests of Pirongia, there will be no hope for us."

Chapter 10
From the Moon to the Earth

For Valjhar, one advantage of lurking on the far side of Earth's huge moon was that all transmissions from Earth were cut off. That kept Valjhar from his obsessive, depressing, and frequently nauseating study of all the crimes and self-inflicted disasters befalling that world, the follies of a race in the terminal stage of its technological and social development.

There seemed to be no end to them, a reign of evil and stupidity in every continent, every "nation" of that teeming globe. He was left wondering if anything good ever happened on that world, or if perhaps the humans had no taste for anything that wasn't sickening or abhorrent. Even their entertainment usually focused on evil or destruction of one kind or another.

The view from the bridge was peaceful but sterile. This moon presented a tumbled, gritty grey landscape of boulders, dust, and craters, its shadows stark and definite in the unfiltered sunlight.

Kern had been very busy in the hours since they'd landed *Mote* here, wings and all. The largest result of his work was also the largest artificial structure on the moon, larger than *Mote* in volume, if not in width or mass. It stood out there in the vacuum, looking very much out of place, a bulbous ovoid contraption made from titanium sifted from the lunar soil.

Pimsie was also on the bridge, enjoying the weak lunar gravity. She would leap up almost high enough to bump her head on the bubble, then perform graceful dance moves and twirls on her way down, slowed noticeably by her billowing skirts. It was good to see her out and enjoying herself again. She had spent about five minutes studying Earth's various cultures before retreating to her cabin with the firm statement that she wanted nothing whatsoever to do with the humans of Earth, or Azure as she preferred to call it, noting its color and the preponderance of its waters.

A huge figure came into view outside the ship. It was Stingray wearing the menacing black pressure armor Kern had fashioned for him. The giant bounded away toward the metallic artifact while kicking up puffs of dust with every footfall.

Kern's voice popped out of the bridge speakers. "Valjhar, the *Fly Trap* is almost ready to go. Better get ready to raise the ship."

"*Fly Trap?*"

"I named it after one of the local plants. Well, not exactly local, I guess. An Earth plant. You know what I mean."

Outside, Stingray cycled through a hatch in the side of the *Fly Trap* and vanished.

Pimsie ceased her gyrations and settled into a chair, looking uneasy. Kern, Shaula, and Kroy bounced up the stairwell and onto the bridge. Kern went to a console and studied the displays, whose graphics had already been influenced by things he'd learned about Earth computers.

"Everything ready, Kern?" asked Valjhar.

"Yes, but I'm still picking up that hydrogen excess in the ship's air. It's not enough to hurt anything, but it's annoying not to know where it's coming from. Shall we be off?"

Valjhar spoke into his microphone. "Stingray? Are you ready to have an adventure?"

"Ready."

With no further ado Valjhar used *Mote's* maneuvering lamps to gently lift off and then hover a short distance off the surface.

"Remote Spaceship Commander Kern Harner now causing *Fly Trap* to tag along with us." The ovoid rose into view.

Valjhar brought them out from behind the moon, orienting *Mote* to place Earth directly overhead from their perspective.

"All right, everyone. There's no point in using the microjump drive to transit to Earth, because *Fly Trap* doesn't have one and couldn't keep up. We're running low on time, so we'll be making the trip at constant acceleration. Stay in your seats for a bit until you get used to the return of full gravity."

"Go, go, go," said Pimsie. "The sooner we get this over with, the sooner we can save Cal and get away from here."

Valjhar activated the main lamps, pushing them more firmly into their chairs and beginning their four hour translunar voyage. Kern reported that *Fly Trap* was matching them a short distance behind.

"Stingray, are you all right back there?" asked Valjhar.

"I'm a little cramped, but fine," came the terse reply. "But Kern, quick…where's the toilet in here?"

Kern looked panicky. "I didn't—I never—"

Kern's sputtering was interrupted by Stingray's unsettling laughter. "Just a joke, Commander."

Kern fought back a smile, but did not entirely succeed. "That's some real Earth humor, you ogre."

Pimsie, Valjhar could not help but notice, did not appear pleased by this display of camaraderie.

They used the time to rehearse and coordinate their plan of action upon reaching Earth. It would have to be executed smartly to succeed in the time remaining. Halfway across they were obliged to swing the ship about and start slowing down, lest they blow a substantial crater in the sea floor and end their travels as a cloud of vapor. When they'd removed their velocity relative to Earth, Valjhar led them down through the ship to the landing control bay, whose wide ports offered a view of the nearby planet below. The misty expanse of its so-called Pacific Ocean sparkled in the sunlight.

Shaula carefully studied her instruments. "There are a lot of airplanes down there...give me a moment to pick out the one we want...ah, there it is, on course and on schedule. But other planes have joined it. They are smaller, and I'm sure they are armed."

Kern shrugged. "I don't see how they can make any difference. Maybe to give those other pilots some stories to tell."

Valjhar parked *Mote* a thousand miles off the west coast of the North American continent, at an altitude just above the majority of the human's satellites. *Fly Trap* came into view and parked nearby, balancing on its propulsion lamps.

Valjhar stood up. "Well, friends, are we ready to retrieve one of the greatest treasures in the universe from these most unworthy beings? No offense, Stingray."

"Don't worry, I don't identify with them," said Stingray through the speakers. "I think this should be interesting."

The others also proclaimed their readiness, except for Kroy, who merely looked around with his usual birdlike incomprehension, and Pimsie, who sat with her arms crossed, looking impatient.

"Open the *Fly Trap*."

Like a treasure box that might be found on a woman's vanity, the ovoid hinged open, throwing off brilliant sun reflections as it did so, revealing within it a cavernous space.

"Shaula, please illuminate the target aircraft."

"Activating laser."

A pulsing red star appeared over the ocean far below, its motion barely apparent.

Now it was up to Valjhar. He activated the dimension modulator on his belt and opened its control interface, which appeared in his visual field as an array of numbers and graphics. The device's targeting beam would not be visible at this distance and through the vacuum, so he'd have to rely solely on those internal displays to perform this delicate long-range task.

"The plane is zigzagging, trying to avoid our laser," said Shaula. "Don't worry, I have them pinned down."

"Here goes," said Valjhar. The modulator gave out its strange influence, causing the space beneath the distant plane to expand rapidly, pushing the plane away from the planet.

"Valjhar, you've caught two of the escort planes in the warp effect...they're falling out of it, but they're already too high to function...their air-breathing engines have failed...they'll have trouble recovering," said Shaula.

Valjhar grimly shoved this information aside. He could not afford to be distracted from his task.

The airplane came into view very rapidly, close enough so that the laser was no longer needed to make it visible. Valjhar fought to keep it balanced, so that it wouldn't tumble out of control.

"It's losing air quickly," said Shaula. "It's not a spacecraft."

"Kern," said Valjhar.

"Right!" *Fly Trap* moved into position, engulfed the airplane, and closed. "I'm pressurizing the interior! They should be all right now. You can relax, Valjhar."

Valjhar did so gratefully. Now it was Stingray's turn.

Valjhar's monitor showed the view from the camera mounted on Stingray's helmet. The giant opened the interior door of the chamber he'd occupied and stepped out into the brightly lit main compartment of this makeshift flying hangar. The American plane rested on its belly on the deck. To their credit, the men on board had comprehended their situation well enough to open its doors and deploy ramps that permitted at least some of them to leave the plane with weapons in hand, looking around incredulously. Their attention was then riveted by Stingray, who was a most intimidating figure in his black armor and helmet with its bulbous optics.

Stingray spoke through the speakers placed around the chamber. His English carried a Rralian accent.

"I'm one of those weird aliens you people have been worrying about. We want our things back, the box and the communicator, and then we'll put you back down very gently and be on our way. You might as well hand them over to me now. You can't do anything about it."

One of the men spoke up. "I'm the commander of this aircraft. We don't know what you're talking about."

"No? Well, I'll just rip your plane to shreds looking for myself."

"We are armed and will resist you."

"Yes, yes, very impressive. Feel free to blast away. You won't hurt me, but you might manage to shoot holes in this pressure vessel you're in, killing yourselves for no reason."

"You don't talk much like an alien."

"What did you expect? Colloquial English is obviously not that hard to learn. Even you can do it. Quit wasting my time and hand over the items."

"I'm afraid I'm not authorized to do that."

"Oh? Well, I'm authorized by a superior authority to disregard your lack of authorization." With that Stingray strode forward, his every slow footfall creating an ominous metallic clang that echoed through the hangar.

"Open fire," said the commander in a tired voice, as though he recognized the futility of the action. Instantly Stingray was assaulted by a spray of projectiles from the soldier's rifles. The camera view jerked around a bit as a result, but Stingray was not deterred. Then his attackers began to fall as they were struck by ricochets.

"Idiots, you're only harming yourselves."

Apparently the human commander agreed. "Cease fire! Let's try to pull him down by hand."

"Are you serious?" cried one of the soldiers. "He's a giant bulletproof alien. Who knows what he can do to us?"

"Follow your orders!"

"I don't think so, Colonel. At the moment we're in space aboard a flying saucer, and as far as I'm concerned that breaks the chain of command. I'll sit this one out and see if I can help these other poor guys who shot themselves."

"Your military career is over, soldier."

"Yeah, well, maybe this way I'll eventually make it back to my wife and kid." He bowed to Stingray, dropped his weapon, and said, "Nice alien. Me no attack you, you no attack me, savvy?"

The man's defiance seemed to put new life into the colonel. "Coward! Let's go, men."

The other soldiers advanced, or at least the eight of them who were still in the fight. Stingray easily swept the first two aside, but then the other six leaped upon him at once and managed to topple and pin him beneath their weight.

"I suppose we should do something," said Valjhar.

"No, give him a second, they can't hurt him," said Kern. "Just watch."

Valjhar's view included only the arm of one of the men piled atop Stingray, but then that arm stiffened and jerked, and he heard many cries of distress. A moment later Stingray surged to his feet, throwing off his attackers like raindrops.

"What just happened?" asked Valjhar.

"Stingray shocked them."

"Shocked them? Is that a function you built into his armor?"

"No, he can do that with his body. Didn't you know?"

"No!"

Stingray resumed his march toward the plane. A couple of men made a half-hearted attempt to restrain him, but he shrugged them off with ease.

"Just how strong is he, anyway?" said Shaula.

"I don't know," said Kern. "He weighs at least twice as much as any of them, but he's more than twice as strong, that's for sure."

The inexorable giant reached the plane and half ran-half leaped his way up the ramp. The plane's interior was a jumble of chairs, consoles, cables, and hoses. It looked to Valjhar as if their unexpected boost into space hadn't been as smooth as he'd intended. Stingray made his way aft, looking left and right. Two more men burst out from a rear compartment and fired their hand weapons. Noting their absolute lack of any effect, they stood by passively as Stingray passed them by.

Entering the aft compartment, Stingray confronted a man wearing civilian clothing who looked up at him with wide eyes.

"My god, you are a right big bloke, aren't you?" This man spoke with what they recognized as a New Zealand accent.

"I'm still growing, too. Do you have something of ours?"

"No!" he shouted. "I'll never give them up, you alien monster!" To Valjhar's confusion, at the same time the man offered the jewel box and the radio to Stingray.

Stingray seemed to catch on faster than Valjhar. "Yes you will, Earth human, you must!" He accepted the proffered items, stowed them in a compartment in his armor, then took a few moments to stomp around and throw things about while his companion cried out in fear that may not have been entirely feigned.

Shaula laughed. "I'm beginning to like our frightening friend. He's much smarter than he looks."

"I'm not!" said Pimsie. "He's a brute."

Valjhar, who had a stony feeling in his stomach from watching this display of violence, was inclined to agree with Pimsie, but Kern said, "He's not. He's been quite gentle with them so far."

Stingray turned and reversed his course through the plane. He jumped down onto the hangar deck and faced the shaken, wounded group of soldiers who had accosted him.

"So, you're still growing, eh?" said their commander.

"That's right. I was sent in here because I'm the only one small enough to fit. I have what I came for now. I hope you haven't found your first contact with alien life too disappointing, assuming this was your first. If you hadn't been thieves, we would not have had to deal with you so harshly. We will now return you safely to the Earth. You won't be permitted to keep this vehicle either, so don't try."

Stingray turned toward the airlock chamber.

"I don't believe you're really an alien at all."

Stingray paused and looked back. "Oh?"

"I think you're just some kind of a freak."

"Think what you like."

"Why don't you prove me wrong? Take off your helmet and show me your face."

Stingray paused again.

"No, I couldn't do that to you. The sight of my face would blast your senses."

"What kind of a laboratory did you come out of?"

Aboard *Mote*, Pimsie gasped. "What a rude question!"

Still Stingray did not move.

"I don't know. Why don't you tell me?"

"I'm guessing a Russian or Chinese one. My country would never pull a trick like you."

"That's good to know."

"The spaceships and your magnetic ray, or whatever it is…that's impressive though. That's worrisome."

"Valjhar," said Shaula, "Rockets have been launched from North America. They are large and powerful, and headed this way."

Valjhar frowned. "Visitors?"

"Judging from where they came from, I'm pretty sure they're weapons. Very powerful weapons. We'd better not be here when they arrive."

"But their own warriors are still here among us."

"Maybe they think it's more important to destroy us than to preserve their people."

Valjhar winced and spoke to Stingray. "Stingray, the Americans have launched some kind of weapons against us. You have to get out of there now, unless you want to ride back down with them."

"Goodbye, Colonel. Have fun constructing your little theories about what has happened to you today, and why."

Chapter 11
A Farewell to Earth

They ran across the fields, their clothing soaked from the river crossing, not daring to stop or rest. Once they passed a farmer at work in a field of maize. He stared at them and yelled "You're those escaped nutters! I'll have the police on you!"

"Please don't report us," gasped Rouse, but she wasn't sure he even heard her.

Their only chance was to reach the Pirongia forest before a serious search for them could be mounted. It was only a few kilometers away now, but now that they'd crossed Highway 39 the land was becoming more irregular and more difficult to traverse. They found a dirt road that wound its way up a steep hillside, and beside it was a sizable patch of woods. This they entered, exhausted, needing to rest before the final dash into the main forest.

Both were sweating and dehydrated from the summer heat. Cal had for a long time seemed to defy the mortal weakness of his body, but it was showing at last, while Rouse was a drained, filthy mess. They collapsed among the trees and devoured the last of the fruit and beans they'd gathered at such expense, unconcerned about the muddy farm water that had soaked Rouse's bag.

Cal's face was twisted with misery and dissatisfaction. "If I hadn't deliberately deprived myself of the Stones, none of this would have happened."

"Why did you do that, Cal?"

Cal's pale eyes bored into hers from the green shadows of the forest. "You have no idea what it's like to wear them. You are always naked before them. You cannot conceive a thought or carry a sin that is contrary to any of the powers they represent without suffering their merciless wrath. No one with an imperfect heart can carry them and use them without pain. They confer great strength, but they demand so much in return.

"When I landed here I put the Stones aside to make myself less conspicuous for the task at hand. But when I was caught and arrested, the weakest part of me saw a chance to escape the weight of the Stones. I needed only to let those men take them from me, and I would be free of them. I could even tell myself that it wasn't my fault, that their loss was beyond my control. For the first time in years I could lie, if only to myself.

"What a relief it was, and what a terrible mistake. The more the Lights fade from my mind, the more my old self emerges. Their influence can never entirely vanish, but it can wane. You have seen the result. You have seen some of the old, vain, petty Cal-Cotavion, a person who should have been left behind on the other side of space. I'm sure my friends will try to recover the Stones, and that will put them in danger. If they fail, the presence of the Stones on this ignoble, misguided world will challenge and quite possibly destroy anyone who attempts to use them. And you are in the worst danger of all. No, I had the responsibility to bear the Stones, and I abandoned it. It's terrible to think how a person can be strong and steadfast for years, and then, in a single moment of weakness, throw it all away."

"Well...it's not as if you've done anything too awful...except for acting like a bit of a prat. Unless you mean what you did to that chopper."

"Chopper? Oh, no. That was self-defense, completely justified."

Clouds settled in again, bringing a likelihood of rain. Rouse welcomed them, for it made them more difficult to see from above. If it rained they might encounter some puddle or rivulet from which to slake her intense thirst.

Hearing nothing and detecting no immediate pursuit, they left their hiding place for the final dash to the great forested mountain, whose top vanished into the clouds a few kilometers ahead. The dirt road stuck to the ridge line, promised little if any traffic, and sped them along. These were the lowest slopes of Pirongia, still cultivated, but growing steadily higher and steeper, with more sheep in the paddocks and fewer cattle.

As they climbed, Cal and Rouse gained a better view of the area they'd left behind. They paused to catch their breath and looked back over that far green expanse. They saw nothing there to comfort them. They discerned the twinkling lights of at least half a dozen official vehicles prowling the roads, and some of them were heading in their direction. Rouse was sure there would soon be more, and worse to come.

It happened sooner than she'd supposed. Five deadly-looking planes dropped out of the clouds and whipped low over the landscape at a blinding speed. It wasn't until they'd passed that the terrible shrieking roar of their engines nearly blasted them off their feet.

"Well, that surely wasn't the New Zealand Air Force!" yelled Rouse over the receding rumble. "It must be the Americans. They must have sent one of their aircraft carriers. This is getting worse all the time. They must really believe...that aliens..."

She faltered and turned to look at Cal, who stood there watching her patiently as she raved about things he probably didn't fully understand.

Suddenly it was perfectly obvious to her that everything he'd told her, all of it, was nothing less than the truth, and that she was standing here with quite possibly the most remarkable person on Earth. Her previous skepticism now seemed idiotic, or worse, arrogant.

"Cal, why haven't your space friends come to rescue you?'

"I don't know. I'm sure they will as soon as they can."

"It's been weeks. You really think they're still around someplace? That they haven't abandoned you?"

Cal shook his head at this strange question. "Their hearts are more pure than human hearts. They are brilliant, but they have little understanding of the deceit, cunning, malice, and subtlety upon which so many humans base our lives. In many ways, the best ways, they are still children, for all that they have seen and done among the stars. They took me up to travel in their company. They will not forsake me."

"I hope I'll get to meet them. Let's give them all the time we can. Let's get ourselves into that bush!"

They set the best pace their aching bodies would allow for a kilometer or two before finally entering the blessed, welcoming shelter of the Pirongia forest. Even better, they quickly encountered a small stream. With a glad cry Rouse knelt beside it and plunged her head into it, then drank deeply. Cal also drank, though not as wildly or as desperately. He smiled at Rouse's antics.

Rouse peeled off her sweat-soaked, filthy shirt and then her bra, discarding both. She immersed her hair and as much of her torso as she could get into the stream's small pools, then stood up and wrung out her long chestnut mane as well as she could.

Noting Cal's calm regard, she said wryly, "You could do with a bit of a bath too, you know."

"Are you planning to go on dressed like that?"

"Why not? If anyone catches us, maybe they'll be so startled that they'll let us go."

"You might find yourself—needlessly scratched by these trees."

"Oh, I suppose you're right." She snatched up the shirt, rinsed it out, squished out the excess water, and drew it on, shivering. "Not very comfortable." She looked at the bra, then retrieved it and stuffed it into her bag. "I don't want to litter the park. My family used to come here on holiday when I was little."

"Considering the quality of your physique, that garment is unnecessary anyway."

Rouse laughed. "Thanks for putting it so nicely. Are you trying to flirt with me?"

"Flirt? No. As imposing as your body is, and as admirable as you are, you are not the Queen of Faerie."

"No, of course not. I'm only an escaped Kiwi mental patient." Despite the levity she had attempted to inject into this exchange, Rouse felt oddly crestfallen.

But Cal-Cotavion was having none of it. He approached her and placed his pale hands on her shoulders, the first time he had touched her that she could recall. His gaze had a peculiar intensity when seen from this distance.

"You, Rouse Farewell, are someone who has not allowed your thoughts and perceptions to be defined and limited by what is considered normal by the people around you. You have suffered for it, and you have despaired, but you have not faltered or given in to conformity. You are a strong argument for the worthiness of our race."

Rouse felt a strange thrill course through her at these words. "That's the nicest thing anyone ever said to me, I think."

A shrill scream erupted from somewhere above them. Rouse looked up just in time to see a bird, a falcon, plummet through a gap in the trees and snatch some hapless songbird out of the air. It brought its prey to the ground, dispatched it with a bite to the neck, glared at the two humans who were fortunate enough to witness its prowess, and flew off with its meal.

Rouse drew back, shuddered, and shook herself to throw off excess water from her clothes and hair.

"Well Cal, if you're not going to take full advantage of this lovely stream, let's be off. If we bear northwest I think we can pick up the Mahaukura Track toward the summit, assuming we can bushwhack our way through the intervening country, which might not be easy. It's pretty rugged up here."

The stream seemed to come from the right direction, so they followed it for some time as it climbed and diminished until it was nothing but a trickle. By then they were high enough so that the cloud deck seemed to flow by only a few feet above the damp treetops. By this time Rouse had lost all sense of direction beneath that sunless sky, and elected to just keep climbing until they came upon a track or something else she recognized.

After an hour or so of tramping through the wet, muddy bush the vegetation began to change. Tree ferns gave way to horopito shrubs and kamahi trees. The forest opened up, which would have exposed them to observation except that now they entered the cloud deck obscuring the summit of the mountain.

They stopped suddenly and spun at the sound of movement to their left, but it was only a few wild goats, briefly visible in the fog before they noticed the two humans and fled.

Rouse's heart pounded from fright and exhaustion. "I'm so hungry I'd like to leap on one of those beasts and tear its throat open with my teeth. Is that horrible of me?"

"I'm sure those animals would think so."

"What do Elves like to eat?"

"In Faerie we subsisted mainly on certain fruits, which we ate more for pleasure than from any real need. Since leaving Faerie I've found it necessary to become less particular, though eating anything which I must first kill and dissect is still repulsive to me."

"I'm too famished for such niceties. Anything is starting to look tasty to me—present company excluded, of course."

Cal looked around speculatively. "I must say—I feel more at home on this mountainside than I have at any time since I left my world. There is a hint of Faerie here."

"Oh, it must be the Patupaiarehe."

"The who?"

"A legendary tribe of mysterious fairies. The Maori say they are pale with light hair, and live in forests and on mountains. They are said to—"

Rouse was interrupted by the reedy sound of a flute tweedling somewhere off in the mists.

"—play flutes."

Cal looked toward the sound with interest but no apparent fear. "Let us investigate."

Rouse followed Cal with some trepidation, convinced she was truly about to leave behind all the fields she knew. She was correct. Seated on a rock a short distance away was a being unlike any she had ever seen. She resembled a human woman, but was tiny, with mobile rabbity ears set high on her head, sticking out from a mop of silvery hair. She wore a simple blue smock and little pointed shoes. Her eyes were closed as she played her wooden flute, but she opened them at the sound of their approach. Rouse gasped. Her eyes looked like big spheres of polished jade.

"Hello, Nali," said Cal. "It's good to see you are able to manifest yourself in this place."

"You know her?" said Rouse.

"Yes, she is a friend, though I have never seen her look exactly like this. She looks nearly human. But she is very changeable."

Nali's voice was a musical high-pitched whisper. "Hello, Cal-Cotavion. They are coming. They are nearly here."

Cal turned to Rouse with an elated expression. "There, you see? I told you they would not abandon me."

Nali's delicate little face crumpled into sadness. "But Cal, your enemies are nearer still. Beware."

And then she was gone.

"I—I take it—that was not one of the Patupaiarehe?"

Cal shrugged. "Who knows? Maybe in part. Nali's nature is not easy to define. But her warning is urgent. I fear we have run out of time."

It was true. The air throbbed with a distant vibration.

"Rouse—more helicopters?"

That question was enough to distract Rouse from her dazed contemplation of Nali. "Yes, and they will be worse. The American helicopters will be far more dangerous than our local ones. I wonder what lies they told to our government to permit them to operate here. At least they can't see us, but I have no idea what the American military can really do. They're terrible warmongers."

Those vibrations did not remain distant for long. Soon it became apparent that they were fairly surrounded by a ring of helicopters hovering unseen in the clouds. Cal gave Rouse a long, grave look.

"Rouse, you must leave me."

"What?"

"These warriors want me, not you. While they are occupied with me, you might escape. Go. Seek your own people and tell them how I coerced you to follow me."

"Coerced my backside! I'll not give you credit for this escape. I've come this far—"

"Rouse, I will always be grateful for what you've done for me, but I will not see you destroyed for it. You must be free to help guide this world and its people. Please go."

Desperate tears began to flow. "But I'm afraid I'll never see you again. How can I go back to my old boring life of no space elves?"

Cal smiled, the fullest and most human smile she had yet seen from him. It looked like it was a strain to achieve it. "I believe you will someday see me again. And even if you don't...space Elves will always exist, somewhere, among the many other wonders which await you."

With tear-blurred vision Rouse turned away and started back down the slope. She felt betrayed, she felt betraying, she felt rejected, she felt afraid, she felt grief, she felt guilty. It was a lot to deal with while weeping her way down a steep mountainside as she also struggled with exhaustion and drug withdrawals.

She heard faint thuds and scuffling noises all around her, with a hint of voices. Now she was afraid enough to taste her fear on her tongue. She decided not to descend any farther for fear of losing the concealment of the fog. Looking around, she spied an unusually tall kamahi tree whose top was almost lost in the mist. Choosing the stoutest of its multiple trunks, she shimmied up into its branches, where she perched on one as she tried to bring her breathing under control.

She was just in time. She was soon obliged to hold her breath as a group of three Yank soldiers emerged from the fog and headed in her direction. They were wary and purposeful in their movements, but they did not look up. They took up positions immediately beneath her tree and stood looking up the slope. One of them spoke into a radio.

"Bughunt Command, this is Unit Seven, over.

"Unit Seven, this is Command, go ahead, over."

"We are in position, no contacts to report, over."

"Understood, stand by to move in on my mark, out."

Bughunt? That's what they were calling this operation? That term of casual arrogance and macho stupidity set Rouse's teeth on edge.

"I wonder what that fucking alien looks like?"

"Didn't you listen at the briefing? He looks human. These fucking Kiwi idiots even had him in a mental hospital, for Christ's sake."

"Stupid bastards."

"Yeah, he even told them he was from another planet, is what I heard."

"Oh, so if some nut tells you he's an alien, you just gonna believe him? Idiot."

"Don't tell me you can't tell an alien by looking at him. Why would they even look human? That makes no sense."

"Remember, he's got some human woman with him too."

"Yeah, some cunt named Rose Farewell or something. I wonder what she's getting out of the deal?"

"Some nice alien dick, I guess."

Rouse seethed at their salacious laughter.

"I wonder if he speaks English? He might say 'Take me to your pussy, bitch.'"

He speaks better English than you, you bloody...

"I heard these aliens been shooting down our planes left and right."

"Well, I hope this one we got here makes a break for it in our direction. I'd love to be the first motherfucker on Earth to plug an alien."

That was enough for Rouse. All the fear and anxiety she carried within her crystallized into something new: a wild, reckless anger. She kept telling herself she didn't care if she lived or died. Why not die well, by wiping some of the scum off the face of the Earth?

She pushed herself off the branch. Her scream of fury did not begin until she was already falling. She dropped twenty feet or more, landing full on two of the soldiers, snapping bones and bearing them to the ground. Finding herself still on her feet and functional, she turned on the third man, who was raising his weapon toward her, but he was too close. She grabbed the rifle's barrel and swept it up just as he fired two rounds. Rouse yanked the weapon away from him. Before he could react she swung the weapon around and rammed the butt into his face as hard as she could. He staggered back but remained standing, so she did it again. He fell backwards. His hand moved toward his sidearm, but she leaped on him, stomping his wrist into the mud, and then again, until his hand went limp. She bent down, snatched out the pistol, and flung it away. She turned to look at the other two, but they appeared to be in no condition to trouble her for now.

Rouse studied the rifle in her hands, considered using it, then tossed the filthy thing into the bush.

The man whom she had battered spoke to her through a bloody mouth. "Miss Farewell? We aren't here to harm you."

"Yes, well, this Kiwi cunt heard the way you spoke about her. You just lie there and shut up."

A voice emerged from somewhere in the mud. "Unit Seven, this is Bughunt Command, report your status, over."

Rouse spied the radio and snatched it up, still in a fury. Finding the press-to-talk button, she snarled, "This is Rouse Farewell, a citizen of New Zealand, and I'll thank you bloody pack of thugs to get off our mountain."

"Farewell? Not gonna happen. Stay where you are. Out."

Then events again moved beyond what was possible in the world of guns and soldiers and human beings. A shadow moved smoothly overhead, a darkness in the clouds, huge and silent. It disappeared from view somewhere up the slope. A moment later came a great concussion from that direction, strong enough to bend trees and send leaves swirling even at this distance. Rouse was staggered. Gunfire erupted in the near distance.

A boom like thunder rolled down the mountainside. And Light erupted. Not the dull grey light of day that filtered through the clouds, but Light, a sublime radiance compounded of green, violet, blue, and white, a Light outside of nature and beyond all reason.

Rouse stared at that distant glow, entranced, and stumbled toward it. Her hips and knees gave her considerable pain from her fall, but that meant nothing to her. The virtue of that Light superseded all other cares. It overcame even her despair, for suddenly she desired to live, to plumb the mystery of what these Lights represented. For a wondrous, shining moment, her mind was clear, and all things were possible. Cal-Cotavion had come into his own again.

She heard a rapid rhythmic thudding from the foggy forest ahead, and from it ran a juggernaut. It was a huge figure clad in sleek black armor, or perhaps it was a robot, faceless, its head or helmet featureless except for two bulbous lenses.

"Rouse Farewell!" boomed out its voice.

Rouse began to raise her hand, but then she was shot, and then she was shot again, and she fell.

Aboard *Mote*, Valjhar grimly piloted its detached main hull over a murky New Zealand mountain. They had no more time for planning, and no more hope of slipping in and retrieving Cal without any fuss. If they didn't move now, Valjhar might well have Cal's death on his conscience. He might already have hesitated too long.

He stood with his friends in the ventral landing control room, searching the concealing mists through its great windows.

Kern studied instruments able to ignore the fog. "Their aircraft are approaching. The ones with those bizarre rotary wings. Oops, they're firing rockets at us."

"Can they hurt us?" asked Shaula.

"Not unless their rockets travel at relativistic speeds or can explode with similar energy. Here they come. Quite the flurry of them."

They heard a quick salvo of faint detonations and the ship vibrated slightly.

"Oh, while I'm thinking about it, let me jam their communications. There, that should be all the harm they can manage, unless they decide to blow up the entire mountain and wipe out everyone around it."

"I wouldn't put it past them," said Valjhar. "Really, how mad are these people? This is the first alien visitation they've ever experienced, as far as we know. They have no real idea of who we are or what we represent. And their first impulse is to destroy us?"

Shaula gave him a look that indicated her continued disbelief at his naivety. "Welcome to the world of non-Rralian humanoids. But consider this. If an alien ship were to approach Rral, how would its automated defense system react?"

"That's a good point, but that system is a remnant of Old Rral, like the Prohibitor. I'd like to think the present-day Rralians would not be so bloodthirsty."

They were as ready for a fight as they knew how to be, except for Pimsie, whom they'd agreed would stay in the ship, out of danger. Stingray sat on the deck in the menacing armor Kern had made for him.

At Pimsie's insistence, and to Valjhar's relief, Kern had added a helmet to his engineering suit, which they knew to be extremely durable on its own. His helmet wasn't as forbidding as Stingray's, with a transparent visor through which his eager face could be seen. Shaula's entropic weapon was at the ready, though she looked heartbreakingly vulnerable in her simple costume of green, white, and gold. Valjhar was no more protected. He wore his dimension belt over the indigo tunic he often affected, and that was the extent of his armament. Even Kroy was present, though Valjhar hoped only to keep him out of trouble rather than receive any aid from him.

"Valjhar, I think I see Cal on the synthetic imager!" said Kern. "Yes, that must be him. I even see his staff. He's surrounded!"

Valjhar glanced at the imager's display. "We can't land near there. Too many trees."

"I'll take care of that! Come on, landing party, let's get to the excursion bay. Our moment of glory has come!"

Into the fray, Children of Rral!
Rise up now, in defense of Cal!
A wizard he was, a prince, an Elf,
But now he can't defend himself!

It had been some time since Kern had last been moved to blurt out some improvised verse. Valjhar would have smiled if the moment hadn't been so tense.

"Yes, get back there, everyone, and prepare to disembark. Stingray, your job is to find Cal and put the Stones into his hands as fast as you can."

"I remember. I really hadn't planned on stopping to pick flowers."

The others moved aft to the excursion bay, leaving Valjhar alone with his unhappy thoughts. Why must they find themselves in conflict with every intelligent species they encountered? Maybe it would be best if in the future they avoided any they discovered, since they were apparently incapable of getting along with anyone.

But he didn't have much time to brood. A booming blast rocked the ship—Kern's proton beam, by the sound of it. Once again the Rralian engineering suit had been put to a novel and unintended use. The imager's 3-D display showed that a large elliptical area of the forest had been flattened. Valjhar would find time to feel guilty about that later, he was sure. For now he moved the ship toward the clearing and landed a little harder than he'd intended to. He ran aft to join the others, activating the dimension belt as he did so.

The ramp in the excursion bay was down, revealing a grey scene of cloudy chaos. He didn't immediately see Stingray or Cal, but was relieved to see that Kern, Shaula, and Kroy had had sense enough to stay together, not far from the ship. Kern was posing dramatically, doing things with the engineering suit that were undoubtedly highly disconcerting to whoever they were directed against. Shaula was firing her entropic weapon with calm precision, her targets being weapons and vehicles rather than people, or so Valjhar hoped. Kroy stood there blinking in confusion.

Valjhar took a deep breath and ran from the shelter of the ship to join them. Human weapons popped all around them, but few if any of them seemed to be directed at them.

"Where's Cal?" asked Valjhar.

Kern pointed. "Stingray ran off in that direction. I assume the big oaf knows what he's doing."

Kroy's confusion seemed to be rubbing off on Valjhar, and it was getting worse. "I'm dizzy. Is there something wrong with our air adaptation?"

"Huh?" said Kern. "Wait a second. Our voices are higher pitched too! Let me check...it's the air! It's full of hydrogen!"

"That makes no sense," said Shaula. "Earth's air has almost no free hydrogen, and even if it did..."

"It would drift up and escape."

"So much dirty air here," said Kroy. "I am trying to clean it."

The other three turned to look at Kroy. "What are you talking about? asked Valjhar.

"Look." Kroy bent down and filled his cupped hand with water from a puddle. "The air here is so fouled that it lies on the ground after falling from the sky."

"Air? Water? Oxygen? No!" said Kern. "Ahhhh! Hydrogen! Kroy is a star being! His natural environment is a sea of hydrogen. To him, hydrogen that's chemically bonded to oxygen is polluted and inert."

Shaula said, "Kroy? Are you somehow breaking down the water to release hydrogen?"

"Yes he is," said Kern. "Look, this puddle is bubbling."

"Kroy, however you're doing this, you must stop!" said Valjhar. "If you build up too much hydrogen, it could explode and kill everyone!"

Kroy's expression changed. Valjhar could not define the emotion registered there. Any correlation between the mind of the star being who inhabited that skull and the emotions of a Rralian was slight at best.

A group of large helmeted figures loomed out from the mist. "Watch out, they're coming back," said Shaula.

The sound of several detonations reached their ears. Canisters billowing vapor thumped down among them. Valjhar felt an instant pain in his eyes, his mouth, and his lungs.

"It's some kind of noxious gas!" cried Kern. "Quick, everyone back in the ship!" They staggered and stumbled back up the ramp, into the bay. "All of you, get back behind the space boats, and cover your ears! It's time for a little chemistry experiment."

The ensuing blast turned out to be less than Valjhar had expected, more of a subdued *whomp* than an explosion. Kern looked a bit disappointed as they rejoined him outside the ship. The soldiers who had launched the gas canisters could no longer be seen.

Kern shrugged. "Oh well, at least the hydrogen blast burned off the gas, as I'd hoped."

Valjhar said, "Kroy, please do not release any more hydrogen."

"I am tired of being here among you in this thin, cold place and in this poor body."

Valjhar studied Kroy's inscrutable face in disbelief and growing anger. "Is that so? Perhaps you should have considered that before you so whimsically decided to invade the poor boy whose body and brain you usurped? I for one would be happy to put you back where you came from, but we don't know how. Now kindly stop making more trouble for us while we try to rescue our friend and comrade."

"A friend who is in great danger while we stand here bickering," said Shaula. "Let's go!"

114

Kern commanded *Mote's* egress ramp to close. "Let them waste their little projectiles trying to shoot holes in that ship. Maybe it will keep them amused while we go save Cal."

They ran down the slope in the direction Stingray had taken. Kroy accompanied them with a sullen reluctance. They followed Stingray's trail, partly through muddy footprints and mashed foliage, and partly through a line of injured, broken soldiers they found along the way. Valjhar's thoughts tried to veer away from them, to avoid confronting the reality of Stingray's violence. It seemed certain he was still wreaking such havoc not far ahead, for the sounds of gunfire and men's cries were concentrated in that direction.

Soon the warring figures resolved out of the mist. Stingray was striding forward, ignoring the massed fire of the squads of soldiers who were arrayed in an arc ahead of him. Luckily there were no ricochets. Kern had learned that lesson and coated Stingray's armor with an energy-absorbing substance.

And there, huddled just beyond the soldiers...was that Cal-Cotavion? Was that his proud figure, hunched over in the mud? With soldiers standing over him, aiming their weapons at his head?

Suddenly Valjhar was less concerned about ricochets and the well-being of the men who were attacking them. He keyed his radio and said, "Stingray, we're close behind you. Do you see that prisoner up ahead?"

"Yes. That's Cal?"

"Yes. Be alert for strange events." Valjhar turned to Shaula and Kern. "Shaula, please disarm those men who are threatening Cal. I'll handle the others. Kern, please prevent any of them from escaping. I want them all to see what's about to happen next. It will do them good."

The merest touch of Shaula's entropic weapon was enough to render the weapons of her enemies inoperable. Valjhar dealt with the soldiers firing at Stingray in a way still more subtle. He greatly expanded an area of space in front of them, with the effect of increasing the distance their bullets had to travel, causing them to fall to the ground after what looked like only a few feet.

Valjhar undid the effect just before Stingray reached that area. He leaped on the soldiers, who cast their empty weapons aside and tried to flee. They found themselves unable to move, as the mud and rock at their feet had reached up and gripped their ankles, thanks to Kern and his ability to manipulate matter. They cowered aside as Stingray passed among them.

But the two who were guarding Cal—though their guns were useless, one of them drew a huge knife as he scowled down at the defeated Cal.

Shaula calmly raised her entropic weapon and fired. The knife dissolved, and the soldier's hand shriveled into something sickening to behold.

"Oops," said Shaula.

Valjhar fought down his nausea and horror. "Stingray. Stingray, the Stones."

Stingray produced the box from its compartment. He knelt beside Cal, put his hand on his shoulder, and spoke softly to him.

Valjhar turned to Shaula. "That man's hand..."

"Don't you start, Valjhar Cor. He was about to kill Cal. The weapon's effect is sometimes imprecise. It had to be done."

One of the trapped soldiers chose that moment to speak up. "Speak English, you little freaks."

Shaula whirled on him and did him the courtesy of replying in that language. "What?"

"I said speak English. I like to know what's going on when I'm facing the things that are about to murder me."

That ignited Shaula's anger into a white-hot flame such as Valjhar had never seen before. "Murder? But you can't be murdered, can you soldier? Can soldiers be murdered?

Isn't this war? Didn't your leaders decide this is a war? Doesn't calling this a war turn killing into something other than murder? Isn't that what they tell you when you put on that uniform and take up those weapons? If I killed you, wouldn't you only be a casualty? A chance victim of war? Isn't that how you people think?" By this point she was screaming, and the man quailed back, despite outweighing her by a factor of at least three.

Shaula turned away. "So much like my home planet, so stupid…"

Valjhar found himself taking her in his arms, not fully understanding her, but wishing to comfort her. He couldn't remember the last time he'd touched her.

What he saw over her shoulder caused him to say, "Shaula. Look there."

Cal and Stingray were rising together, slowly, with Cal leaning on his staff. Stingray offered him that fateful box, and Cal accepted it.

"Valjhar, many more humans are coming," said Kern. Valjhar could hear them trampling the foliage.

Cal-Cotavion slid open the box. At once the Lights began to flow from it. Without hesitation he drew out the Stones and put them on, tossing their empty container aside as though he expected never to need it again.

Cal was transformed. He seemed to grow larger, straighter, while at the same time his posture showed the weight of the Stones. The very earth trembled beneath him and the touch of his staff. He raised his head, revealing the merciless blue star of the Stone of Truth. Valjhar flinched away. He was better able to endure the presence of the Stones than he'd once been, but he would never be comfortable in their Lights.

Stingray had fallen down, overwhelmed. He sat in the mud beside Cal, who turned to speak to him. "You. My friend Rouse is somewhere down the mountain, and she is alone. You must find her. Send word the moment you do."

Without a word Stingray staggered to his feet and ran off into the fog.

And then Cal unleashed the power of the Stones, all at once, creating a cold blaze that drew forth cries of anguish and wonder from everyone present: humans, Rralians, and Booshites alike. Valjhar turned his face away. He could only look sidelong at the mingled Lights. They made plain too many personal faults that he preferred to remain unexamined.

Cal turned to the soldier with the ruined hand and took his wrist. He held it up to the glare of the Ring of Life and focused its yellowish-green Light into a ray that gleamed and sparkled over that melted flesh. The man screeched and tried to pull away, but Cal-Cotavion's grip could not be broken.

Cal released the soldier, who stared at his hand with wide eyes.

"Your hand will not die. You may even regain its use, but it will never be the same again. I can do no more for you."

"Thank—thank you."

"I am sorry your hunt for me led you to this disfigurement."

"So am I. I see now that I was wrong. We were all wrong. What we are doing here is wrong. You came here looking only for food, and we turned that into—this. Who are you?"

"I am Cal-Cotavion of Faerie." The four Stones again pulsed with radiance, bathing a hundred men and a few small aliens with powers that had previously never been more than ideas to them, or ideals. Some men fainted. Some wept. Others stumbled away, cursing themselves.

"I think this battle is over," said Valjhar.

Their radios spoke. "Stingray here. Cal-Cotavion, I've found your friend. Come at once. She is dying."

Cal whirled. To Valjhar he seemed to move in slow motion, to more plainly show the mixture of dread and panic on his pale face. He vanished down the slope, and it was not clear if he was running, flying, or using a means of locomotion somewhere in between.

Valjhar and his friends followed as best they could, trusting that their attackers had been made harmless by Cal's display of power. They had not very far to go. They found Stingray standing guard over a woman's body. He had removed his helmet, and his face showed grief and fascination as he looked upon her. Cal-Cotavion knelt beside her. The others approached. Rouse Farewell had been shot twice, once in the hip and once in the head, a terrible wound that had removed part of the left side of her skull and exposed her brain. It was a sight so dreadful that Valjhar was obliged to look away, lest he collapse. Kern fell to his knees and hid his face.

"She will not die," said Cal. He brought the Ring of Life to bear with an intensity that Valjhar had never seen before. He blasted her with it, straining to such an extent that it seemed as though some of his own life was flowing into her. The reflected glare alone was enough to make Valjhar tingle and shiver with renewed vitality. "She will not die."

Nor were the other Stones inert. "Rouse has a great potential to exemplify the forces embodied in these Stones." As Cal bent over her, the Stone of Inner Light, dangling from its chain, brushed along her breast. "She sees too clearly and cares too deeply. These are her only faults. May she find her own path to Light in this world, and beyond."

Cal turned to look at Valjhar, who was moved by the pain and regret so clear on his face. "We must not leave her here. Because of her assistance to me, she is now an outlaw, a criminal, in her own land."

"Should we take her with us? To the stars, I mean?"

"No, she is too much a creature of this world. But we mustn't leave her here on these islands. We must find a safe, peaceful place for her, a place where she might rest."

"Yes, let's get her to the ship. Stingray, if you'd..."

Cal interrupted. "I will carry her. She shall not die, as long as I am near her."

"We can help to heal her," said Kern. "We already have some experience in repairing broken humans. Though her poor head..."

Cal lifted and cradled her in one arm as if she were a sleeping child. He hurried toward the ship while the others surrounded him like watchful guardians. They reached the ship without incident, but found many soldiers standing around it, gaping up at it with their weapons lowered. Waiting within, Pimsie lowered the ramp. Cal, Kern, Pimsie and Kroy disappeared into the ship.

Valjhar's attention was diverted by a soldier whose uniform was more elaborate than the others.

"Whatever you creatures are, don't come back. It's not worth it, for either side."

Valjhar paused on the threshold of his ship, of freedom, of safety. "You're half right. You can't imagine what we could offer to your people. Right now you are just barely advanced enough to understand and benefit from our knowledge, but that will be a very short-lived pinnacle. Your civilization will soon collapse, but its fall won't be our doing. We will not return. We have seen enough of you. Now please leave, all of you. We don't want you to be injured when we raise our ship."

Actually the soldiers were in no danger from that, but the implied threat still had the desired effect of getting them to leave.

Stingray moved to climb the ramp, but Valjhar stopped him. "Stingray. Nali told us you would be a strong ally for us in our time of need, and so you have been. Thank you.

Where would you like us to take you now? We can see you off in any part of the world, wet or dry."

Stingray appeared confused and taken aback. After a few moments he mastered himself and said, "Oh. If that's how it's going to be, I'll just make my own way to the coast from here. It's not far. Here, take back your armor."

Shaula, who had been waiting nearby, stepped up calmly. "Valjhar, I'd like a private word with you, please. Stingray, kindly do not budge from this spot."

Puzzled, Valjhar followed Shaula around the ship until they were out of sight and earshot of Stingray. Valjhar faced her expectantly.

Shaula slapped him hard across the face. Valjhar reeled back in shock and confusion. "What...?"

"Valjhar Cor, you are at times still a very stupid boy. You are going to abandon Stingray here? He's done our dirty work for us, so now you'll just drop him off somewhere with a nice pat on the back?"

"This is his world—"

"Idiot! You saw how the humans dealt with him. You heard what they said about him. He is not one of them. He's a freak to them, remember? What does Earth hold for him? Can he walk among humans in peace and safety? No. The best he can do here is to live in the sea like an animal, trying to avoid their fishing nets."

"What makes you think he wants to go with us?"

"The expression that appeared on his face when you turned him out should be enough, you nitwit. Of course he wants to go with us. We've educated him and shown him the path to the stars. We're his only friends!"

"But he's so—so—"

"So what? So big? We occupy only a third of the volume of the ship as it is. Kern could easily modify some of it to accommodate him. You know how he likes to tinker with things like that."

"I was going to say so violent."

121

Shaula stamped her feet as she tried to contain her anger and exasperation. "Violent? His violence was very useful to you when we needed to do uncomfortable things, wasn't it? Violent? Do you think he's more violent than I am? I think he's been quite restrained, considering he could rip the limbs off anyone on this planet without trying. Violent? Do you think he's more dangerous than Kroy? But Kroy looks like you, doesn't he? So do I. Does that make it all right? Just how narrow minded are you Rralians, anyway? Do you really have anything to offer the humans, other than better machines? I wish Cal were here right now with his Stone of Truth. I'd really like to see how you'd answer me, with that thing shining on you."

Valjhar was mortified. "You are right."

"I'm right? That was a very fast change of view."

Valjhar tried to smile. "It must be the latent scientist in all us Rralians. When we are confronted with an equation whose terms agree, we cannot argue with it, even when the terms are emotional and the equation is a moral argument."

"All right, maybe there's still some hope for you. Honestly, what Pimsie sees in you...come on."

They returned to Stingray, who awaited them with awkward apprehension. Valjhar approached him and took his hand, three times the size of his own.

"Stingray...I am sorry. I did not fully understand your desires. If you would like to join us on our journey among the stars, we would be honored to have you."

Stingray looked down at him with those disconcerting blue-black eyes.

"All right, Valjhar, thank you. If you truly think I have a place among you, I will be happy to join you."

Shaula took Stingray's other hand and led him into the ship. "Come on, let's go see if we can do anything for Rouse Farewell."

Valjhar remained outside for a moment, looking around at the alien landscape he was about to vacate. He entered the ship and closed the ramp. *Mote's* internal air blew into the bay, replacing the air of Earth with all its scents and odors, forever, or so Valjhar hoped.

Chapter 12
Rouse at Rest

Rouse awoke in a large, plaster-walled room with a rough wooden floor. She lay on a bed that was nothing more than a platform with a thin pad atop it. Two multi-paned windows were open, admitting a sharp breeze and affording a glimpse of a deep blue sky. Other than a few wooden benches and some shelves along the walls, the room was empty and unadorned, and very quiet.

Rouse had no idea where she was, nor did she feel like investigating. Her hip throbbed with pain, and the left side of her face and head burned and ached. She was soon annoyed at herself for waking up and wished she could pass out again.

Moving slowly she brought up a hand to examine her head. Her slightest touch brought new pain, but more, she discovered her hair was gone! Well, not quite gone. Her scalp was covered with stubble. She suspected she'd been unconscious for quite some time.

As she lay there trying to assemble her thoughts an unusual man entered the room. He was small and dark with close-cropped hair and a kind smile. His age was anywhere between thirty and seventy, she guessed. His only garments were some bright red robes that left his arms and one shoulder bare.

"Ah yes, Miss Farewell, you have awakened, good. Please, don't try to get up. I welcome you. My name is Sonam Pena, and I am the abbot here. Oh, you are in a *dzong*. A monastery. In Bhutan, the Dragon Land. I hope you like dragons."

"Hello." Rouse's voice sounded small and weak to her own ears. "Bhutan? How did I get here?"

"Well, it was a very strange business, very strange. A man appeared out of nowhere, carrying you, and this is something odd, because our *dzong* is not easy to reach. He was a very strange man, very strange. I hate to keep using that word, but there you are. He appeared to be Western, what we could see of him, and he was even more Western than most, more Western than you, if you know what I mean. Lighter. He spoke—strangely; there is that word again. He said his name was—"

"Cal."

"Yes, Cal! You know him? Good, good. He told us we must care for you, and hide you, until you are well. A strange request, but oh, he was very convincing. We couldn't see much of him because he was wrapped in a grey hooded cloak. But somehow he glowed. He glowed with power. All our monks came out to see him. We knew we were in the presence of a most holy man. I agreed to do as he wished, and that was before he made his offering, which was quite a large cube of gold, more than enough to improve our diets considerably over the winter. And so here you are."

"What happened to me?"

"You don't know? We were told you were shot. You don't remember?"

"No. I remember being…in a hospital. I remember Cal. We escaped together. But it's all hazy. I'm not sure what I remember about him. Did you shave my head?"

"Eh? No, you arrived with your head shaved quite smooth, I assume because of your surgery."

"My surgery?"

"Yes, yes. But ask me no more for now, please. I have brought in someone to look after you, a friend of the *dzongs*, someone who knows more about the wider world than do we poor simple monks. I will send him in to you. It is a pleasure to meet you and to see you awake."

Sonam Pena turned and left. A few moments later another man entered, also Asian, but this one quite different. He was taller, younger, and dressed in what she saw as a more normal fashion. The most striking thing about his appearance was his incongruous blue eyes. He smiled as he saw her.

"Are you…a doctor?" asked Rouse.

"A doctor? No. I do have a graduate degree in mineralogy, but I'm not a medical doctor. When I'm helping the monasteries I go by the name of Sapphire." He pointed two fingers at his eyes. "You can see why. Unusual, I know. I suppose I'm a mutant, but not the kind who gains super powers. Just blue eyes. How are you feeling?"

"I'm sore. My head hurts. So does my hip. Can you tell me what happened to me?"

"Why don't you see for yourself? Don't worry, it isn't as bad as it probably feels." Sapphire pulled a small mirror from his jacket and handed it to Rouse.

Rouse examined herself. The immediate shock was the sight of her nearly bald head, but after studying it for a few moments she thought she could live with it. After that came the startling realization that much of the left side of her cranium had apparently been opened up. A large oblong patch of skin had been removed and reattached…or replaced. The seam…it was too neat for her to think of it as an incision…was barely raised and slightly reddened.

"My scalp was injured?"

"Actually we think it was more than that, but we don't know exactly how much more."

Rouse frowned. "Has no one asked the doctors?"

"Rouse, we don't know who performed your surgery. The monks were told you were shot. That's about all we know. Your story is quite a sensation in New Zealand, but the details are vague."

"I don't remember being shot. I don't even remember being attacked." Rouse noticed her hand that was holding the mirror. She'd lost the bandage covering her wrist long ago, but the wound there...it was gone. There was barely even a scar, just a nearly imperceptible line of whiteness.

"What do you remember?"

Rouse lowered the mirror and forced her thoughts back in time. "I remember being in the hospital. I remember meeting Cal. He told me a lot of outlandish stories about Elves and fairies. I remember thinking that someone was after him, and that I needed to get him away. I remember being outside, and darkness, and the bush...that's about all. Anything else is just vague impressions. Do you think I have...brain damage?"

Sapphire came closer and held her hand. "I don't know, maybe. The monks have been careful to keep your presence here a secret. They haven't brought in a doctor. The man who brought you here assured them you were out of danger. Do you know who that man was?"

"Not for certain. I'm told it was Cal. I feel it was him. I wonder how in the world he brought me here to this distant place, and where he's gone to. I hope he's safe, wherever he is."

Rouse thought to examine her hip. Sapphire discreetly turned away as she lifted the sheet that covered her. She found a smaller wound, also neatly closed and already healing. She pushed at her pelvis, which produced an ache, but at least it seemed to be in one piece. She wiggled her legs and experienced only minor pain.

"Are you cold?" asked Sapphire. "These monasteries are unheated, I'm afraid."

"No, I'm all right," said Rouse absently. "I'm in a bit of a daze, though. To wake up in Bhutan, of all places, without even knowing how I got here, having had mysterious surgery...it's all pretty strange."

"Yes, of course it is. Are you afraid?"

"No. No, I'm not. That's also new. What I am though is tired. I'd like to go back to sleep. If you don't mind, I'd like to talk to you later."

"Certainly. Would you like me to close the windows?"

"No, I'm fine. I like the air here."

When Rouse awoke, the room was dark except for a wick flickering in a little bowl of oil. Already she felt better and stronger...and hungrier. This was exacerbated by an aroma filtering in through the door from some other part of the monastery. Rouse was wondering if she dared to get up to investigate when the door opened, admitting Sapphire, who carried a tray. With a smile for her he placed it on one of the wooden benches and beckoned to her.

"Rouse, do you feel like having a bit of dinner? I think you can trust yourself to get out of bed for a little while."

"I would love something to eat. I'm starving. I literally can't remember the last time I had a decent meal, or any meal, really. But there is the little matter of my wardrobe.

"Oh, of course. I'm afraid your clothes were declared a lost cause, but you'll find some authentic local replacements here on the shelf. I'm afraid you'll not find them very stylish. I'll just step out while you dress..."

Rouse laughed. "Don't bother, unless you'd be offended. I've never been all that modest, and I see no reason to change now." She began to roll off the bed, but soon found it wise to move in a more gingerly manner.

"Er...I'll just turn my back then," said Sapphire.

"As you like." Walking cautiously, Rouse went to examine the small pile of clothing. She found a red blouse and a little black jacket, both of which she drew on. Beneath them was folded a large square of striped cloth. "What's this for?"

Sapphire looked over his shoulder. "That's intended to wrap around your waist as a skirt."

"A skirt? I haven't worn a skirt or dress since I was nine years old. It's too long. I'll fold it in half."

"That might raise a few eyebrows. The dress code here is very conservative."

"Hmm. All right, out of respect for my hosts I'll wear it as it's intended. For now."

"Thank you. Shall we eat?"

Rouse and Sapphire sat on opposite ends of the bench. Between them Sapphire laid out two bowls of soup, a pot of tea, and two cups. Rouse spooned up some of the soup. It consisted of rice, lentils, and vegetables, and it was quite spicy. She began to slurp it down.

Sapphire laughed. "In the future, if you are offered food by a native Bhutanese, the polite form is to refuse once or twice before finally accepting."

"I'll keep that in mind."

"Would you like some butter? I find it goes well in the soup."

Rouse frowned in mild puzzlement. "No, thank you. I think I've gone off dairy foods for some reason. Sapphire, where are you from?"

"The closest thing I have to a home base is in London, but my work keeps me on the move."

"What work is that? Looking after mysterious Kiwi refugees?"

"Occasionally! By day I'm a gemologist. That's a fancy way of saying I hunt for, study, and deal in various gemstones from all around the world. It's sort of an obsession of mine."

"Gemstones. Yes, I can see how that could be very interesting. And by night?"

"Well, that's when I go by Sapphire, which seems backwards, I admit. You see, I'm also an ardent Buddhist, a phrase that also seems a bit difficult to parse. Sometimes the Buddhists and their various monasteries and temples have troubles that go beyond the scope of their traditional competencies, so to speak, and then I try to help. In addition to having a good eye for gems, I have certain other skills which are sometimes of use. I'm a bit more worldly than the usual monk or lama."

"My, how mysterious. And here you are, eating soup with a nobody like me."

"You appear to be a somebody. At least, the governments of New Zealand and the United States of America seem to think so."

"The Yanks? What do they want with me?"

Sapphire watched her carefully. "I gather they believe you've been consorting with aliens from outer space."

Rouse dropped her spoon and laughed loudly. "What? Me? Aliens?" She laughed about that for quite some time.

Chapter 13
Mariners on Trial

They'd left Earth and its stellar neighborhood far behind, to everyone's relief. *Mote* proceeded toward the center of the Milky Way. They had never yet explored a galactic core, and this one seemed as good an example as any.

Mote's small crew occupied themselves in various ways as usual. Stingray had essentially become Kern's apprentice. They were usually together, sometimes to Pimsie's evident annoyance. Stingray was determined to master their technology and make himself as useful as possible. He studied incessantly and was especially interested in ship design. Already his knowledge of *Mote* and its functions and principles was nearly equal to Valjhar's own.

Kern was delighted to have a companion who took as much interest in these technical matters as he did himself. Together they rearranged much of the ship's interior to increase efficiency and accommodate Stingray's giant frame, leaving a frustrated Pimsie to follow behind them and redo all her decorations in their wake.

"Valjhar, your monster is messing up all my work," complained Pimsie.

Valjhar was growing tired of Pimsie's apparently unwarranted distrust of Stingray. "Which monster?"

"You know who I mean! My mobiles alone are a shambles! What are you going to do about it?"

"Nothing, besides offer to help you replace your ornaments and tapestries when they're through. I do miss seeing them. The mobiles can be hung higher, I suppose."

"Hmph, you're useless."

But Valjhar had the impression she was secretly somewhat pleased by his offer. He was barely wise enough to give her the last word.

Pimsie was further placated when Kern and Stingray proposed building a large garden compartment for growing their new food crops. She eagerly assisted in its design.

Valjhar did his best not to dwell on Earth and their misadventure there, but he was not always successful. In particular, in unguarded moments he often flashed back to Rouse Farewell, who had suffered so terribly for her devotion to Cal.

They had taken her to the ship's medikum, placing her in a tank where she lay perfectly suspended on a floating mesh. Cal had bathed her with a gentle, steady ray from his green ring.

Pimsie had fussed about Rouse with a look of pity and horror on her face, washing her, applying pads of fluffed membrane to her hip wound to stop the bleeding. That terrible head wound would require far more attention.

Doing more was the province of Kern. Though he did not relish the role, only he had the deep understanding of their technology and of biology needed to make him somewhat effective as a physician. His normally ruddy face was purple with terror from the responsibility he faced.

Valjhar felt guilty. How many months and years had he idled away, moping and mooning when he might have been studying to share this burden?

Kern spoke in a shaky voice. "Pimsie...do we still have any of that serum we derived from...from..."

"From my poor lost pony, I know what you're trying to say. Yes, I think we still have some in your cryofreezer thingie or whatever it is. I'll get it."

"If you need any other tissues or substances, take them from me," said Stingray.

"No. Better from me," said Cal. "I am as human as she is."

"I need to patch this poor girl's skull at least. And I see...I see her brain has some kind of membrane that has ruptured...human anatomy..." Kern's nerve broke. He withdrew and began to shake and cry. Pimsie hurried to comfort him.

"Kern Harner, my friend, we have no time for this," said Cal. The Stone he'd pinned to his shirt collar, the Stone of Adamance, was normally the least conspicuous of the four, but now it came into its own. Its violet Light was deep and insistent, filling Kern and the rest of them with the resolve they needed to face this gruesome task. It was so much worse, Valjhar thought, to confront such injuries in a person who lacked the ability to heal. It was heartbreaking.

In the end Kern did take blood and various tissues from Cal, modified them slightly, encouraged them to grow, and used them to make crude repairs to Rouse's skin and dura. He fashioned a plate to repair her skull from an amorphous ceramic material much stronger than human bone. He repaired her broken hip by building filaments of helical carbon within the bone. Then he'd gone off and wept himself to sleep.

Cal continued to lavish his Lights on his friend's unconscious body. Cal wanted to make sure of their continued influence over her, he'd said, even if she retained no conscious memory of them.

Valjhar missed Cal-Cotavion; they all did. It had come as a shock to them all when he'd stated his intention to remain behind on Earth. Though he and his Stones had never been the most comfortable shipmates, Valjhar had the utmost respect for anyone who could wear and wield them for so long, even if he had recently faltered. They'd shared so many adventures together that the ship didn't feel the same without him. Their entire venture felt more precarious without the ever-present influence of the Stones.

A distraught Pimsie had urged that they equip Cal with a communications device, but she had of necessity been refused.

"If we gave him a quantum signaler that powerful it would be like a beacon to the Prohibitor," said Kern with regret. "It would be attracted either to Cal or to us, and either would be unpleasant."

"I'm not surprised that he chose to remain," Shaula had said. "At least there he's among his own kind, more or less."

"He'll be more alone on Azure than he is among us," said Pimsie. "No one there will understand him. What will he do? Stay with Rouse Farewell?"

"No," said Valjhar. "He told me he thought she should make her own path, rather than follow his. I believe he will seclude himself and try to remain inconspicuous while he struggles to master the Stones. And himself. Even if he should be discovered...he's so powerful, it's hard to see how anyone could really trouble him."

"He could return to Colibdis," said Shaula.

"What?"

"Have you forgotten? Somewhere back on that planet is a gateway that leads straight to his home world."

"I had almost forgotten that. Well, if he chooses to do that I hope he'll do it mindfully, with full awareness of the difficulties he would face with Seren. But still—he would have to find that gateway first."

Cal had left Valjhar with a private warning. "The being you call Kroy dal Ren is unable to perceive you, the others, or the world, as representing anything truly real. It is all simply too foreign to his true nature. Beware of him. I will not be there to intervene, should he awaken to his true power."

"I'm sure you know all this through your Stone of Truth," said Valjhar. "Can't you also use it to make Kroy see the truth about us and his situation?"

"The Stone reveals Truth, yes. But it does not provide understanding of the truth, if the ability to understand it is not already present."

Valjhar thereafter made it a point to keep a close eye on the hydrogen content of the ship's air. He rarely saw Kroy, who increasingly kept to himself, but he was aware of him as a troublesome, possibly dangerous presence who would eventually have to be dealt with.

Eventually turned out to be sooner than the confrontation-averse Valjhar had hoped. The hydrogen reading began to creep up in the vicinity of Kroy's cabin, while water vapor began to decline.

Valjhar sighed. There was no help for it; they would have to do something. To that end he called a meeting on the bridge, including a sullen, fretful Kroy.

They sat in a circle looking uncomfortable. Kroy hung his head, not meeting their eyes.

Valjhar began, "Kroy, why are you releasing more hydrogen into the ship? It can't escape and it builds up. You endanger us all."

"Why do you call me by that name? It is the name of this body. It is not my name."

"It's the name of the person who occupied that body before you evicted him," said Valjhar. "If you don't like it, what should we call you?"

"We have no names. We are together and we are one."

"Then you'll just have to settle for Kroy dal Ren. I repeat my question. Why are you still making hydrogen?"

"Better yet, how are you making it?" asked Kern. "Splitting water molecules takes energy, and usually some kind of apparatus. You seem to do it by being in the same room with it."

"I don't think I can explain it to you. To you, hydrogen is but one of many forms of cold matter. To us it is life, it is everything, it is our world. It surrounds us. It extends forever. We can feel it. We know it. We can touch it. It has taken me a long time to begin to do that again from the confines of this frigid body, with its many solid and liquid substances. But I begin to learn how to free it. It is only a first step."

"A step towards what?" said Valjhar.

"Toward making a new home for myself."

Valjhar felt a chill at these seemingly innocuous words.

"Nuclear fusion." said Kern. "Like inside a star."

"But that's absurd," said Shaula. "Even I know it's impossible to fuse hydrogen with your mind!"

"It's also impossible to split water with your mind," said Kern. "Yet Kroy can do it. We already know there are low-energy ways to coax small quantities of hydrogen to fuse. Kroy says he has some kind of special bond with the element. Who know what kind of a mind really dwells in that Rralian skull? Surely not exactly the same mind that lived as a magnetically organized plasma inside a star, if only because our squishy brains are so very different."

"Surely it was his magnetic-plasma form that enabled him to fuse hydrogen, and not his mind. And why would he and his people even need to? Don't stars naturally produce fusion on their own?"

"That's a good question," said Valjhar. "Kroy?"

"I am not sure how to answer, because our world cannot be described with the words you use to describe this world of locations and separateness. Usually our wold is full of light, and all is good. Sometimes the light fails, and a dreadful cold and silence descends upon us. When that happens we take hold of the world and urge it to grant us light again."

"Hmm. What do you make of that, Kern?"

Kern appeared mesmerized by Kern's cryptic account. "Just a guess...I'd say Kroy and his friends normally reside in their star's fusion zone, where they exchange peace and love and whatever else they do there. But maybe sometimes one or more of them rises too high, or is churned up by convection, and there's no more fusion, not enough energy for them to hold themselves together. That's when they use their magnetic fields to constrict some local hydrogen to warm themselves up until they fall back to where they belong."

"Kroy. Do you realize that even if you did manage to fuse hydrogen, you'd instantly vaporize yourself and everything around you?"

"Then send me back to where I came from."

"Send you back? Your star is nearly three million light years away. We could go back there, but it would be a terrible nuisance. Then we'd have to build another huge quantum bridge device. We'd probably have to do that on the dreadful planet Smerkesh, a place we never wish to see again. Then we'd have to try to transmit you back into the star, and you'd have to hope you'd be able to reconstruct your old form instead of just dissipating there. Meanwhile we'd be left with Kroy's empty body, lifeless, an even worse reminder of the friend we lost than you are now. Is there anything else we can do to satisfy you?"

"Yes. I wish to mate with one of the females."

Stingray laughed loudly until a glare from Pimsie silenced him.

"What?" said Valjhar in disbelief.

"I realize now that this is what this body craves."

"I thought I showed you how to—"

"It is not enough. The relief gained is not sufficient."

Well, I'm pretty much obliged to find it sufficient myself, you obnoxious... Instead of saying this aloud, Valjhar said, "All right then. Females? Do we have any volunteers?"

"No!" cried Pimsie. "Kern is my mate, and I'll have no other!"

"The dark-haired one, then," said Kroy.

"Don't look at me, Kroy," said Shaula quietly. "I have no intention of bearing your child. Your little fish can continue to flop around in your bed."

"Shaula?" said Pimsie in surprise. "Do you mean you have no ability to control your own fertility?"

"No, Pimsie. That's yet another Rralian gift we poor Booshites lack."

"That would be awful!"

"You heard them, Kroy," said Valjhar.

"If they reject me, I shall continue to..."

"Wait," interrupted Kern. "I just thought of something. Shaula, as a Booshite you probably can't interbreed with a Rralian anyway, despite our superficial similarities. You should be safe to mate with Kroy."

Shaula gave Kern a long, inscrutable look. Kern, it seemed to Valjhar, would have done better to keep this helpful thought to himself.

But Shaula surprised him. She stood up from her chair and sauntered over to Kroy with a smile that struck Valjhar as somehow dangerous. "Well then, Kroy, if you're sure that's all it would take to get you to relax..." She reached out and caressed his cheek.

Kroy looked up at her and did indeed relax, to the extent that he closed his eyes and slid out of his chair to collapse into a limp heap on the deck.

Shaula looked down at him in satisfaction.

"What did you do to him?" asked Pimsie, aghast.

Shaula displayed her palm, where a small device was concealed. "Sedative. I had a feeling things might go awry if we confronted him like this."

Stingray smiled at her appreciatively.

"But why? Not just because he wanted to...er..."

"Have sex with me? No, because he's extremely dangerous, and we can't permit him to remain conscious any longer."

Valjhar sputtered. "Surely that's an overreaction. We can monitor the hydrogen—"

Shaula raised her hand to interrupt him. "Valjhar, so far Kroy has confined himself to liberating the hydrogen in water in the air. If he becomes disgruntled enough, what's to stop him from splitting the water in our bodies? Or freeing the hydrogen in any of the other compounds in our bodies? That would be instant death for us. I'm surprised I have to explain this to you science geniuses."

The three Rralians looked at each other.

"I don't think Kroy would ever—" began Kern, but he couldn't finish.

Stingray spoke up. "Kern, even I can see that he doesn't regard the rest of you as true life forms. I think he sees himself as living through a bad dream, to put it in humanoid terms."

"Cal told me something similar to this as well," admitted Valjhar.

They all looked at each other uncomfortably.

"Then what shall we do with him?" asked Valjhar.

"If we're not willing to undo the mistake we made in bringing him here in the first place," said Shaula, looking at Valjhar very pointedly, "I say we keep him deeply unconscious until we think of something better."

Valjhar felt as if he'd been struck a blow. "That—that seems like a—"

"Betrayal? Yes, it does. But it will be a reversible betrayal, which is more than you can say about the betrayal he seems likely to pull on us eventually. It's a hard, bitter, nasty, pragmatic decision. If you refuse to do it, I won't blame you or object. I know it's an insult to your thinking and your way of doing things. I'll take my chances with him, if you and the others prefer."

"We could freeze him," said Kern.

"Is that safe?" said Stingray.

"Yes, we Rralians actually freeze quite well. We should be able to revive him whenever we wish. It would also be the least messy way of handling this."

"But only until...we think of a better answer for poor Kroy, right?" said Pimsie.

"Yes. Of course," said Valjhar.

Somehow it seemed as though the decision had already been made, by mutual if reluctant consent. Valjhar resolved to carry it out at once, while their unanimity still held. They carried Kroy's limp body to a compartment with an empty freezer they usually used for food storage. They folded Kroy's body to fit within it and sealed the door.

As they worked they uniformly grew more and more miserable. Soon Kroy's heart would stop beating and his blood would solidify. Valjhar felt like they were not only betraying the helpless creature, but killing him as well. From the crumpling faces around him Valjhar knew he was not alone in feeling this way.

Pimsie reeled away from them and cried "No! I can't go through with this. Take him out of there! This is monstrous. What are we turning into, a pack of humans? Keep him unconscious, but don't freeze him. I'll look after him until we find a way to let him be happy."

Valjhar was so relieved to hear this that he nearly wept with gratitude to Pimsie. He threw open the freezer door and hauled out Kroy's already chilled body.

Cal-Cotavion would have chastised them with the merciless glare of the Stone of Inner Light, to their betterment. As it was, their own consciences must suffice.

Chapter 14
The Falcon's Eyrie

Rouse rapidly regained her strength. Two days after her awakening she asked to be shown the rest of the monastery. Sapphire obliged her, assisting her as she roamed about on still unsteady legs.

The monks took this opportunity to present themselves, a hundred or so of them, males of all ages, all dressed in red robes, all smiling and friendly. Most of them seemed to revere Sapphire above any interest they had in Rouse, which was fine with her. She had no desire to become a center of attention.

Sapphire led Rouse onto a terrace where they could take in the monastery's precarious situation and the spectacular view it afforded. The structure was perched high on a very steep mountainside, looking out over a deep valley whose dark green trees were dusted with snow. Grey clouds blew past on a brisk wind, sometimes enveloping them and obscuring the view.

"I think I've heard of this place!" said Rouse. "Isn't it the Tiger...the Tiger's..."

Sapphire chuckled. "The Tiger's Nest? No. That place is too well known, and too thick with tourists, to be an effective hiding place for you. Bhutan has many *dzongs*. This one is known as the Falcon's Eyrie, and it is better named. There are actually a few nesting pairs of peregrine falcons around here, but there are no tigers at Paro Valley. In fact I think I hear a falcon now."

Over the sound of the wind Rouse heard a series of quick, harsh cries. She never saw the bird, but its hunting call was thrilling nevertheless.

Over the next days Sapphire proved willing to introduce her to the precepts of his form of Buddhism, which he explained was an idiosyncratic mixture of the Tibetan, Sōtō and Za Zen traditions. For the pure Tibetan form he wryly advised her to consult the abbot or one of the other monks, as he did not wish to confuse her with his own peculiar views.

"One of the basic tools we use to approach awakening is the cultivation of mindfulness, or awareness, but I don't think I have to explain that to you. I've rarely met someone with such a clear eye as yours."

"It's not so difficult in a place like this. So quiet and peaceful. So few distractions. It helps too that the few people around me are also busy cultivating awareness and simplicity. Have you ever felt that being surrounded by people who are full of turmoil and confusion is like—being immersed in a terrible noise that you can never tune out?"

"Yes indeed. Learning to tune out that noise, or at least to be aware of it dispassionately, is one of the skills we seek to learn. Tell me, Rouse, have you always been this way?"

"What way, mindful? No. For most of my life my mind and thoughts have been as clogged up and congested as anyone else's, or even more so. That made it difficult for me to perceive the world without seeing it through the dark and muddled filter of my own misery. Something changed me, something when I was in that mental hospital, I suppose. I'd like to credit the wonderful therapy I received there, but I'm not so sure. When I think about it deeply I see—morning glories. As though that makes any sense. I wonder if I'll ever remember more."

Rouse reached up and rapped her knuckles on her skull injury. The sound was distinctly different than the dull thud of knuckles on normal bone. She gave Sapphire a wry grimace. "I'm not exactly sure what's in this knob of mine anymore. Have you noticed my hair?"

"Yes...the patch over your wound is growing in differently. It's silvery rather than your normal dark reddish color."

"Yes, but I don't think it will stay that way. The color is coming back around the edges of the wound." She shrugged and smiled. "Who knows what's going on with me?"

"That uncertainty doesn't seem to concern you very much."

"It doesn't. I have obviously survived something very damaging and dangerous. I survived only because someone, somewhere, thought I was worth the effort. It's as if I now have a second life. Why was I granted this? I don't know. I'm sure it will all play out—appropriately. But I'm thinking I should avoid self-absorption, too, and not overthink myself too much."

More days passed. To assist Rouse in regaining her full mobility, Sapphire taught her some basic yoga techniques. She also had other willing coaches in the form of some of the other monks. In fact she rarely lacked for company whenever she was outside of her chamber, including some of the youngest monks, boys really, who liked to hover around her, giggling and talking among themselves in their native tongue. Rouse had the feeling their whispers were not entirely chaste.

Fortunately, the boys were learning English. Therefore they were able to understand her when she suggested they not allow her to distract them from their studies. They ruefully took the hint and mostly left her in peace after that.

Rouse learned something about those other skills Sapphire had hinted at possessing...he admitted to being an expert at several schools of martial arts. Rouse raised a skeptical eyebrow as he mentioned this.

"Yes, I know, Rouse, this is rather a cliché. Asian man knows martial arts, oh, how tiresome, I know."

"Actually, I was thinking that learning how to fight seems incompatible with the study of Buddhism."

"Ah, well, there is that. I prefer to think of it as a means of training and disciplining my body and mind."

"So you don't get into fights?"

"I do whatever I can to avoid them."

Rouse laughed. "That's not a very definitive answer."

Sapphire smiled and shrugged. "In an age of ubiquitous firearms, knowing how to fight with my hands and feet doesn't make me quite as invincible as I might like. I prefer to remain alive, even though I'm not supposed to be overly attached to life. Thus I try not to fight. I'm really quite a retiring individual."

Rouse sighed. "I wonder what's going on in the outside world? I suppose everyone has forgotten about me by now, or at least I hope so."

"Sorry to disappoint you, but they haven't. Your story is pretty big in New Zealand. You should see the stories in Woman's Weekly. And it has had surprising prominence and longevity in the wider world as well."

"Why should anyone be so interested in some girl who ran away from a mental hospital? And then got shot by un-known parties? And then was saved by other, even more mysterious unknown parties? And then vanished? But no, they can't know all those details...can they?"

"No, the story being circulated is that you were kid-napped by the mystery man Cal Cotavion, and that your government is eager to return you to your family. You should also see the videos of your parents pleading with your kidnappers to release you."

Rouse laughed again. "My parents, who visited me ex-actly once while I was in the hospital, and then probably went home and told their neighbors I'd emigrated to Aus-tralia. But still, I suppose they must care about me at least a little. I wonder when I'll be able to see them again."

"I would advise you not to try to contact them any time soon. The fact that this story is being kept alive tells me that someone powerful is very much interested in finding either you or this Cotavion person."

"Poor Cal! I wish I could remember more about him. He must still be around somewhere. Maybe I'll see him again someday."

"If you do, would you mind introducing me to him? I have a few questions I'd like to pose to him as well."

"Really? Why, do you think there's something—peculiar about him?"

"I think there's something peculiar about the whole incident, and I'm certain you do too. Things are quieter now. Yet somehow—"

"Somehow this was only the beginning...not only for me, but for the whole world. Yes, I feel that too. There's something on the horizon. It's like the lookouts on the *Titanic* spying that iceberg for the first time. The ship tries to veer away, it tries to stop, but it's too late. The ship is too recklessly fast. It has too much momentum and it can't be turned in time. It needs...it needs..."

"A bigger rudder."

"Yes. A bigger rudder."

Chapter 15
A Planet for Mariners

A voyage of five thousand light years brought *Mote* to an extensive region of dust and gas, including star-forming nebulae brightly lit by clusters of young blue stars. The effect was of a dark, foggy night in the countryside with a few scattered villages casting their lights into the mist.

As they traveled, the Rralians kept a close watch on their instruments for any signs of intelligence. Shortly after leaving Earth they had detected peculiarities in the spectrum of a planet in a yellow binary system, but it was off their course, and they didn't feel like investigating after their too-recent harrowing experiences on Earth.

Other than that they'd detected nothing until they approached this dim and cloudy region of space. Then their readings were ambiguous. They found a regular array of widely spaced radiation sources whose energy output was clearly unnatural, with a weak gamma emission, a strong infrared signal, and several ever-changing spikes in optical wavelengths. Their telescope showed the closest of these as a star shining in one pure color after another, gradually shifting to each color in turn with no obvious timing or order. The object was a dozen light-years away and showed no more detail, yet it must be massive to emit that much energy.

It was impossible to determine the purpose of these devices, or stations, or whatever they were, which made them seem all the more ominous. Though the Mariners had no evidence they were in any way hostile, their experiences had left them less trusting than they once had been.

"If someone uses those colored lights to communicate, their conversations must be very slow, considering how far apart they are," said Kern. "Some of them are so buried in dust clouds that I can't detect their visible light at all, only their infrared."

"Maybe they're using some kind of transcendental signaling," said Valjhar.

"If they're that advanced, we'd better be extra careful. They could conceivably detect us even at this distance."

"They're just floating out there, shining colored lights," said Pimsie. "We have no reason to think they're dangerous. Speaking of colored lights, I wish we could just ask Cal about them. I'm not sure twelve light-years would mean much to his Stone of Truth."

Her suggestion made Valjhar uncomfortable. "I'm not sure about the rest of you, but I prefer to learn about things through logic, observation, and my own intelligence rather than through magic gems."

"That seems silly. After all, the Stones were made with Rralian logic and intelligence, weren't they?"

"If I may speak for my exalted ancestor, Starn Harner... I'm not sure he'd say it was logic that produced the Stones," said Kern.

Pimsie frowned at him. "Oh well, the Stones and Cal are thousands of light-years away anyway."

"Have you considered arming your ship?" asked Stingray.

Shaula perked up at this question. Pimsie looked away.

"We've considered it," said Valjhar carefully. "But so far there has been no need."

"That's good to know, but what do you plan to do? Wait until there is a need, and then build your weapons?"

Shaula smirked in a way that annoyed Valjhar. "That argument sounds familiar," she said.

"We have our personal weapons," said Valjhar, stiffly.

"That's fine, but what if you're away from the ship? What if Pimsie is the only one aboard? What if—"

"All right, you've made your point. Kern?"

Kern shrugged. "It wouldn't be difficult to build some simple weapons. All we need are raw materials. It would take more than what we have on hand."

"I'll be happy to locate a suitable star system near our course," said Shaula.

"I still say you're being paranoid," said Pimsie. "It's not like there are any humans around here to endanger us."

Finding a useful star system turned out to be easy enough. They veered slightly to enter the domain of a small, Sharn-like star with many planets. Among them was a smallish gas giant with several moons, a pale aqua globe similar to Neptune in Earth's star system, though much closer to its sun. Its moons were mostly rocky and metallic, leading them to choose the largest of them as their new shipyard.

Kern prepared the way by venturing out in a space suit and constructing a cradle to hold the ship well off the ground. When it was ready, Valjhar guided *Mote* into its new berth, where it hung suspended forty skads above the surface of slag and craters. Those great, pointless wings sagged slightly in the moon's light gravity.

"Moon, I name thee...er, Drydockia," said Kern. He looked up at the huge misty orb hanging overhead. "And you, planet...I call you Flamaria, because your color reminds me of the eyes of the most beautiful girl in four galaxies."

Valjhar caught Pimsie about to roll those eyes, but she recovered and instead offered a pretty giggle.

Working together, Kern and Stingray soon devised a design for weapons. They would be simple tunable lasers, like those already mounted on the ship but much more powerful, until something more subtle or powerful turned out to be necessary. There would be two, each with its own power supply, each attached to the lower part of the wing structure by a black fin that would double as a heat radiator.

Even more exciting (to Kern at least), they would be detachable, and able to maneuver and operate independently.

While this work progressed, Valjhar and Shaula kept a careful watch on the alien array, but they observed no changes and no sign of detection. Otherwise Valjhar mostly brooded on the bridge and felt useless and disgruntled.

Like most brooders, he kept it to himself until somebody took the trouble to ask what was troubling him. That person was Shaula.

"I'm still safe to talk to, aren't I?" she said, reacting to Valjhar's seeming reluctance to respond to her question.

"Yes, of course," he said. He could hardly give any other answer as long as he shared the same ship with her.

"Then what's bothering you?"

"I don't like the idea of turning *Mote* into some kind of—warship. I know you've always been in favor of it, but it makes me uncomfortable."

"Do you know what I'm really in favor of?"

"What?"

"I'm in favor of none of us being killed by some threat we can neither foresee nor imagine."

"That sounds reasonable, but so far we've encountered nothing that a couple of laser cannons were needed to defend us from."

"If that keeps up, we'll never need to fire them, and your conscience will be clear."

Valjhar brushed this aside. "Even when we needed to blast Loki's moon, Kern's engineering suit was better suited to the task."

"Kern can't be everywhere. He's not always wearing the suit. Sometimes he's asleep. The lasers will make us safer."

"Not against threats we can't imagine."

"I suppose not. Valjhar, these are minimal weapons. They will not turn us into a roving mob of marauding space vikings. But let me remind you once again...I will do whatever is necessary to protect everyone on this ship."

Valjhar turned in his chair and gave her a considered look.

"Are you still hoping to someday join the Select, or the Cosmic Patrol, or whatever you call it?"

"No, I accept my failure to be worthy of that. I accept that I am now the most that I will ever be. But I have not lost my determination to protect the innocent."

"Are we really so innocent?"

"You are innocence itself. All of you, except for Cal, but he knows it, and suffers for it."

"Really? What if someday we encounter someone who needs to be protected from us?"

Shaula was taken aback, but only briefly. "Then that is what I will do. Let's be careful to make sure that need never arises."

Valjhar turned away and threw his hands in the air. "Why are we even out here, putting ourselves in these situations? We have no goal, no aim. We move on so the Prohibitor doesn't find us again. I try to tell myself we're out here to learn and grow, but are we?"

"We both know very well why we're out here," said Shaula quietly. "It's because if I had remained on Rral, your Prohibitor would have taken me or destroyed me, and you and the others would not allow that to happen, even though the cost to all of you has been so great. I can never forget that. Never. The others have managed to forgive me for manipulating you, but you haven't, and that means I can't forgive myself, either."

"You're right, I haven't," blurted Valjhar.

That silenced them both, leaving them to share a weirdly companionable form of misery.

For years they had lived in the proximity of a small blue crystal that embodied the very concept of Truth. It had made it impossible for any of them to lie to each other, not that the Rralians had ever been much inclined to do so anyway. Shaula's words, and her remorse, could not be doubted.

What would it take to allow Valjhar to take her words into his heart? Perhaps, he thought, the Stone of Adamance was having its influence on him as well, and not in a positive way.

Valjhar soon learned that Kern was thinking about more than weapons, possibly abetted by his faithful sidekick Stingray. Kern approached Valjhar with a mysterious smile on his face and pointed up through the bridge bubble at the blue-green planet floating in its tidally-locked position.

"Valjhar, I've been studying that planet up there in my spare moments."

"And?"

"It's mostly water. It has a planet-wide liquid ocean maybe ten thousand kiloskads deep."

"Hmm?"

"And a thick gaseous atmosphere too, of course. But not too bad. Surface pressure is about twice Rralian standard. Unbreathable, I'm sure, but warm enough."

"Very interesting. What about it?"

"Well..." It looked as though Kern scarcely dared to say this next part, "I thought it might be an interesting place to go sailing."

"Sailing?"

"Yes, Flamaria has everything we need! Water, wind..."

"You want to build a ship?"

Kern grinned. "We have a ship. It's *Mote*."

"*Mote* is not a sailing ship," said Valjhar, feeling as though he were informing Kern that Pimsie was not a picture frame.

"Oh, but it could be. Stingray and I have studied it closely. We detach the main hull, of course. We add a system of automated masts and sails which can be rigged and controlled from the bridge. We add a few more simple external structures and hey, we have a sailing ship. Maybe not the sleekest one ever, but perfectly functional. What do you think?"

Valjhar wasn't sure what to think. He stared up through the dome at that huge, mysterious ball of water and tried to imagine what it would be like to sail across such an alien, unbounded sea.

Finally he shrugged, and a tentative smile of his own appeared on his face. "Why not? It's not as if we have anything better or more urgent to do."

Kern nodded enthusiastically and dashed off below.

He and Stingray asked Valjhar to take charge of the design of the rigging and other modifications, deferring to his superior nautical knowledge. Valjhar immersed himself in this task with delight. What a pleasure, to do at last something he knew he could do well! He settled on a folding two-masted fore-and-aft rigging arrangement, with simple square sails, and rigging simpler than he would have liked, to minimize the risk of trouble with the powered lines and spars. Probably no one would wish to climb the mast to free a tangle of fouled lines.

Kern and Stingray spent a few days outside the ship engaged in the construction. The engineering suit gathered, processed, and shaped raw elements from the surface of Drydockia into a variety of components. Stingray was strong enough to manhandle most of the parts into place. Kern could have used the magnetic and electrostatic powers of the suit to do the same thing, but he was pleased to allow Stingray more involvement.

Whenever she wasn't gardening, or caring for Kroy, Pimsie often sat on the bridge watching morosely as her mate occupied his days with activities that had very little to do with her. Now and then she cast Valjhar a reproachful look, as though she blamed him for her neglect.

They added a deep and heavy keel to the underside of the ship, with a rudder just aft of the excursion ramp. The

folding masts, rigging, and sails were by far the most complicated parts and took the most time. They also added a
railed, open platform, a weather deck, just before the
bridge, in case conditions proved mild enough to permit
them to step outside now and then, though this seemed unlikely.

The most frivolous thing Kern added was in the bridge
itself. The rudder would be controlled by a traditional
ship's wheel, made of actual wood, or at least the closest
approximation Kern could make by compressing leftover
stalks and stems from their garden plants.

He presented this proudly as a finishing touch to his
project. "*Mote* is ready to set sail, Captain! We can leave at
your discretion."

"Kern, this thing we're about to do...is it safe?"

"Safe? Well, it's unlike anything we've done before,
descending into a planet like this. We can't be sure what
we'll encounter. I can't guarantee it will be completely
safe, any more than anything else we do is safe. Does this
mean you don't want to do it anymore?"

The look on Kern's face made it plain that he was about
to have his heart broken if Valjhar backed away now.
Standing beyond him, Pimsie gave Valjhar a pleading look.
Unable to guess what she was pleading for, Valjhar decided
to literally cast caution to the winds.

Valjhar pointed upward. "Release all moorings, Mister
Harner. There's a fair breeze blowing up above."

A laughing Kern ran below to prepare for their depar-
ture. That left Valjhar alone on the bridge with Pimsie, who
fixed him with a bright but inscrutable gaze.

"Well, Pimsie, are you pleased with my decision, or
not?"

"Valjhar, which am I closer to, my brain or my heart?"

Valjhar felt he was on dangerous ground here, but he
must answer honestly. "Your heart."

"That's right. It's always my heart, no matter what my brain has to say about anything. My heart is my center. You may infer my answer from that."

Valjhar nodded speechlessly, impressed.

"Kern did all this for you, to give you something to work on and look forward to, so you wouldn't be so sad and gloomy all the time. No, don't object, you've done a poor job of hiding it. I'm going along with this plan, for the sake of Kern and his generous heart. I would have preferred a beautiful, sunny world to sail on, but I'll take this. I'm not very afraid."

Valjhar could only nod in reply, half hypnotized.

Pimsie gave him a shy smile. "Always ask me what's best to do, Valjhar. I won't lead you astray."

"Maybe I shall."

"But always ask me in secret. We don't want everyone thinking I'm in charge, in case something goes wrong."

When Kern declared everything ready, Valjhar called everyone to the bridge, except for the unconscious Kroy, of course, who was secured to his bed in the Medikum.

"Strap in, friends. You know we've had some problems with landings in the past, and this one will be especially unusual. Possibly even a bit turbulent. Kern, am I free to lift off?"

"Yes, but be careful to take us straight up. You don't want to hit any of the wing attachment fittings with the keel or rudder."

Valjhar lit the maneuvering lamps and guided *Mote* up and away from its cradle, leaving the wings and main propulsion systems berthed below. Quite soon they crossed from the gravitational domain of Drydockia into the dominance of Flamaria. Valjhar rolled the ship to put the immense planet beneath them and allowed it to pull them towards it. Slowly the misty horizon around them expanded, and flattened, until it looked like they were descending toward a flat, infinite plane of cloud, not a curved planet, a reminder of just how huge this world really was.

Valjhar applied power to slow their descent, pressing them into their chairs. "We should enter the first cloud deck at any moment," he said, and indeed it was true. In an instant their view of the stars, the dust clouds, and the bright glowing nebulae was blotted out by a smooth blankness. Although totally expected, it nevertheless felt ominous. The ride grew a bit bumpy, but as yet it was nothing serious.

After several kiloskads of this they broke out into a deep zone of clear air that presented a dim but formidable vista. They looked into a limitless depth of air bounded above and below by vastnesses of cloud. The clouds toward which they descended were furrowed by great chasms running east and west, obviously shaped by winds on a colossal scale. Even at this distance they could see how fragments of scud were being whirled along and obliterated.

"Er, Valjhar, I'm showing wind speeds approaching the speed of sound down there," said Kern. "I'm not sure we should dive right in."

"All right, I'll match speed with one of those flows and then enter it. It could still be a little rough, everyone."

They didn't have to wait that long for things to become a little rough.

"Something funny on the speed-shift radar just below us—oops!" Kern's exclamation came as the ship shook and bucked around them, throwing them around in their seats. Valjhar fought to keep the ship more or less level.

"I think that funny thing would be called turbulence, Kern," said Shaula wryly.

"I'm going to take us down a little more aggressively," said Valjhar. "I want to get through this."

They all rose up in their restraints as Valjhar powered their way down while also gaining speed relative to the wind currents below. They broke free of the layer of turbulence and their ride smoothed out, except for an occasional jolt.

Valjhar decided to descend into one of the cloud canyons, where the winds were strongest but not as turbulent as in the adjacent clouds, at least according to their speed-shift radar. By now they could hear the roar of wind outside the ship, but a strange silence took hold as they entered that great river of wind at the same speed as the wind itself. Down they drifted, while walls of cloud rose on either side. The bottom drew near. It did not look inviting. It did not look soft and safe, like fluffy clouds. Rather it looked like they were about to land on a hard surface at a very high speed.

Just as they were about to make the transition, Kern said, "Uh, Valjhar...", but it was too late. This new cloud layer was also moving at a high speed, but in the opposite direction. The extreme wind shear grabbed *Mote* and forced it to pitch over violently, pointing the ship's bow straight down. Suddenly they were all hanging in their restraints. After they were finished crying out and shouting they could still hear crashes and bangs coming from the lower decks as objects that were inadequately secured flew about. The ship fell. The thrust lanterns mounted in its bow were not strong enough to support it in this gravity.

Valjhar fought with the controls as the ship continued to be buffeted by chaotic winds. By now he'd lost all sense of orientation and had to concentrate on his floating horizon display to understand the ship's true attitude. He struggled to pull up the bow and get the stronger ventral lanterns back beneath them.

As they descended, the view outside grew dimmer and dimmer until finally it was black. Kern or Stingray or someone thought to turn on the external lights, but all that did was produce a diffuse glow in the fog.

"So far this isn't as much fun as I'd hoped it would be," said Kern unhappily.

The ship gradually began to come right. The winds of this inhospitable world roared around them. A heavy rain drummed down onto the dome. They'd traversed galaxies with nothing but that bubble field separating them from the vacuum and radiation of deep space, but here it seemed a thin and insubstantial protection.

And then, a blessing. They broke free of those roiling clouds into a clear area of lighter winds and unknown depth. They passed out of the rain, at least for now. Their lights vanished into the blackness without a trace.

"Um, Valjhar..." began Kern tentatively.

Still shaken, Valjhar disliked what he heard in Kern's tone. "What is it now?"

"There's something strange on the synthetic imager, still far below us. It looks...like a huge mountain ridge, over a hundred kiloskads high. Or maybe it's a sand dune. It seems pretty smooth and regular."

"Wait, mountains? Sand dunes? Isn't there supposed to be an ocean down there?"

"Whatever it is, there's more than one," said Shaula. "There's a whole system of them, parallel to each other, as far as I can detect."

"They're moving from west to east," said Stingray, eying his own display. "They're waves."

"Waves?!" Valjhar thought furiously. "Of course they're waves. This is a planet with a world-wide ocean of nearly unlimited depth. No land masses to get in the way. Strong, steady winds. There's nothing to stop waves from building higher and higher, traveling around the world over and over. I wouldn't be surprised if each one was a nearly permanent feature of the planet. Why didn't we foresee this?"

"Waves a hundred kiloskads high?" sputtered Pimsie. "Valjhar, why are we still going down?"

"Pimsie's right," said Stingray. "Valjhar, are you sure you still want to do this?"

In fact Valjhar was very unsure he still wanted to do this, though something about the way Stingray stuck up for Pimsie irritated him. Nevertheless, he said, "You're both right, this is foolish. Hang on tight, everyone, I'm about to blast us out of this violent soup as fast as we can go."

By great good fortune this plan was interrupted by the last sound any of them wanted to hear. It was an alarm, a mournful wail that announced the detection of the unique energy signature that accompanied the materialization of the Prohibitor.

It was a sound Stingray had never heard. "What's that?"

Valjhar ignored him in his panic. "No! How is this possible? It's never caught up with us this fast before. Not nearly."

"Where is it? Where is it?" cried Pimsie, looking around as though the sinister golden figure might appear on the bridge with them.

"The signal is coming from Drydockia," frowned Kern. "Let's check the cameras on the ship's wing section."

These showed a peaceful scene of the shadowy wing, still supported by the scaffolding they'd built, with a nebulous sky beckoning all around.

But then a golden spark arced into view, swiftly resolving into the hated form of the Prohibitor, with its strange, sinuous movements and the blank, impassive mask of its red-eyed face. Or rather its three-eyed face, with the third usually lidded and located above and between the other two.

Now that lid was sliding open. A terrible light was rising behind it. Despite the distance between them, the Mariners could not help crying out in fear.

"I'm going to fire the laser cannons at it!" cried Kern.

"No, don't!" replied Valjhar. "The control signal will lead it right to us. Whatever it's going to do, we can't stop it now."

What it did was methodically destroy the wings, engines, lasers, and support structure with a blazing thread of energy they had never been able to analyze or understand. The final sight their cameras transmitted was that beam transforming into an even more incomprehensible form, a ghostly influence that dissolved Kern's lovingly-made structure into nothingness and drew its very essence directly into itself.

The image went dark. The Mariners looked at each other with haunted eyes.

"My ship! My poor ship!" said Kern.

"*This* is your ship, Kern," said Stingray. "It's keeping us alive right now. That other part can be replaced."

"Well, for now we can't flee or escape," said Shaula.

"That's it then," said Valjhar. "I'm taking us down."

"Down?" quavered Pimsie.

"Yes, I'm putting us right into the water, giant seas or no giant seas. Then we're going to power the ship down as much as possible, to make us inconspicuous. We'll hide in this ball of murk until we figure out what to do."

Valjhar congratulated himself on his confident, decisive tone even as he fought down the fear and uncertainty that filled him.

A brilliant flash of light illuminated their frightened faces.

Seconds later a peal of thunder rolled in.

"Lightning," said Shaula. "It's only lightning."

"Yes, and did anyone else get a glimpse of those waves during the flash?" asked a subdued Stingray. "I did. They're...extremely impressive. And I've seen some waves in my time."

"We'll all know how impressive they are in about five minutes," said Valjhar. "I'm going to set us down on the peak of one. Might as well know the worst right away."

He watched the slow crawl of the mountainous waves on his synthetic imaging display. "Mountainous" wasn't really the word for them...they were far taller than any mountains he'd ever seen or heard of, unless an asteroid could be considered a flying mountain. He matched course and speed with the nearest of them and descended toward it as quickly as was safe. *Mote's* lights gleamed off its immense, glassy surface for a moment or two, and then with a huge, jarring splash they were down.

The wave crest was broad, and for the moment *Mote* remained level. Valjhar released his harness and sprang to the ship's wheel, taking control of the rudder.

"Everyone stay in your seats. Kern, deploy the masts and rig the sails. We'll need to maintain some headway or we won't be able to control the ship. If we wind up sideways on the flank of one of these monsters we could capsize. Stingray, shut down all ship's systems except what's needed to keep us alive and in control of the ship."

As Valjhar watched the masts raise themselves through the mist and spray he felt an unexpected thrill. Against all odds, in the strangest way he could imagine, he was finally about to become the captain of a sailing ship. His father Vinjhar's wish for him would be fulfilled, though in a manner he could never have predicted or imagined.

Mote began to tilt down toward the stern as the wave crest passed. The booms rotated out from the masts, the canisters protecting the sails retracted, and an ingenious system of cables and motorized pulleys unreeled the glistening fabric. They filled with wind, and all at once *Mote* stopped wallowing and became a living sailing vessel.

The bow pitched up more and more steeply, ten degrees, twenty, thirty. Valjhar, standing behind the wheel, was obliged to hang on tightly to avoid sliding down the deck. Down and down they plunged, kiloskad after kiloskad. Valjhar grew tired from clinging to the wheel. He listened to the wind in the rigging (a sound transmitted through the hull, as the bubble field would never deign to respond to anything as feeble as sound) and watched the rain wash down over that bubble.

At last the ship began to level out. The enormous swells had a wavelength of at least a hundred and fifty kiloskads, so the troughs between them were broad, affording them several minutes of rest.

Valjhar turned his head to look back at his wide-eyed crew. They all looked shaken and apprehensive, except for Stingray, who gave Valjhar a look of level appraisal until he was distracted by Kern's attempt at levity.

"Well, Stingray, wouldn't you like to go swimming?"

Stingray snorted. "I wasn't exactly crazy about spending my life in the sea even back on Earth. It's usually cold, it's always damp, it's dark, and it's full of large animals who sometimes tried to eat me. Swim in this alien murk? No thanks, I'll stay warm and dry in here, thanks."

"What are we going to do about the Prohibitor?" asked Pimsie.

Valjhar had almost forgotten the reason they were riding this gargantuan sea in the first place. "We'll have to assume it's looking for us. It knows we can't get far without the main drive."

"But it won't necessarily look for us here, on this planet," said Shaula.

"I expect she's right," said Stingray. "After all, you'd have to be a little crazy to come down here. This system has several other planets that aren't quite so challenging."

"For all it knows, we landed on Drydockia to install a new, more compact power source and star drive," said Kern. "I doubt it would think we might be installing sails. Or wheels, or any other ridiculous thing."

"All right, we'll assume we're fairly safe where we are, at least from the Prohibitor. Maybe we can wait it out until it leaves and goes elsewhere."

"Valjhar, why are you all so afraid of this thing?" asked Stingray.

"It's very powerful."

"You're also very powerful."

"It's also relentless and implacable."

"And yet I note you're all still alive and well."

Valjhar sputtered, briefly at a loss for words. "We've had several narrow escapes."

"Poor Randa didn't escape," said Pimsie.

"Randa?"

Valjhar replied. "A friend we…left behind on Rral."

"She was killed?"

"He. We're not sure, but he was badly injured at least."

"I'm still not sure why you're so intent on hiding from this Prohibitor. You're no longer the helpless children you were back on your planet, trying to escape some monstrous power that nevertheless somehow never managed to kill you, or even stop you. I'd be amazed if its power is greater than that of all of you combined."

Valjhar could not long consider Stingray's startling words before he was distracted by the ship's increasing tilt toward the bow as the next wave caught up with them. Rather than hanging from the wheel, Valjhar now leaned against it as he skillfully guided *Mote* to keep its stern to the rising swell. Luckily the sail controls were easily at hand, mounted on stalks coming off the wheel column, so he could adjust them as needed as well.

Up and up they surged, kiloskad after kiloskad. The ship creaked and popped as the unfamiliar pressure of the thick local atmosphere eased off, and the interior grew cooler as they left those murky depths behind.

"I think I'm happy it's too dark down here to let us see the actual size of this wave we're mounting," said Kern. "I think that would be a little scary."

Their ascent took even longer than expected because the ship slid down the surface of the wave like a surfboard. Valjhar reefed the sails to minimize this effect, concerned that they might never reach the top and be forever pushed along in a constant thirty degree downward pitch.

The wisdom of reducing their sail area became even more apparent as they finally crested the wave and encountered screaming wind velocities that tore the wave top into a sheet of mist and foam.

"I hope we come up with a plan to leave pretty soon," said Pimsie, "because I think we'll all get tired of this ride quite fast."

"Would anyone other than me like to know the composition of this ocean we're riding?" asked Kern.

"How do you expect to get a sample?" said Valjhar.

"The atmospheric pressure up here is acceptable, and it's cold out but not too bad. Nothing we can breathe, of course. I suppose we could pop out onto the weather deck long enough to grab some water as it goes sheeting by. Who's with me?"

"Not me, Kern Harner, and not you either, not if you know what's good for you," said Pimsie angrily. "I don't care if we're floating on an ocean of sugarwort punch, you're not going out there for so little reason."

"I withdraw my question," said a sheepish Kern.

"I'll go," said Valjhar, not wishing to be buffaloed by Pimsie.

"I'll go too," said Shaula, though she sounded none too happy about it.

"You're both idiots," said Pimsie.

"Come on Shaula, we'd better hurry if we're going to make it out and in before we start down again. Kern, can you handle the ship for a few minutes?"

"Er...I guess so."

Valjhar and Shaula hurried down the staircase and into the next deck down. Just forward was the dorsal hatch and airlock that led up to the weather deck. Already they could feel the ship beginning to tilt again. They had little time. They grabbed breather masks off a rack on the bulkhead, ignoring the full spacesuits hanging beside them. Valjhar took an extra mask, intending to use it as an improvised collection vessel.

They entered the airlock, gave each other a look of mutual apprehension, and donned the masks.

"Ready?" asked Valjhar. Shaula nodded. Valjhar opened a valve. The ship's air, temporarily at a slightly higher pressure than the outside air, hissed out. The raw air of Flamaria was cold. Valjhar climbed a short ladder and unlatched the overhead hatch, which was instantly torn from his grip by the shrieking wind and slammed back on its hinge. The wind that entered the hatch was enough to buffet Valjhar and Shaula nearly off their feet. Water from rain and spray began to pour into the airlock.

"Valjhar, I don't think we should go out there," said Shaula.

Valjhar bit his lip. "I think you're right, but we have to at least close the hatch. I'll climb up and you hold onto my ankles, all right?"

"Yes, but hurry."

Valjhar dropped the spare mask and began to mount the ladder. It was more than little Valjhar Cor could manage. As soon as he poked his head through the hatch the wind took it and slammed it into the hatch, stunning him. He reached up but still could not grasp the hatch handle, not that he could have closed it against that wind anyway. And then, to show just how puny he was against the forces he had so foolishly chosen to challenge, the frigid blast grabbed him bodily, breaking Shaula's desperate grip, pulled him out and whirled him aloft.

The mask was ripped from his face. As if in a dream Valjhar had a glimpse of his friends on the bridge, staring at him in horror as he sailed off beyond the bow, narrowly missing the masts and rigging. He was flung into the water with enough force to stun him again. He sank at once. The water was warm and stung his eyes. His skin began to burn.

He could see nothing. He wouldn't be able to hold his breath for long.

As he prepared to drown, Valjhar hoped Pimsie would not blame Kern for his own rash foolishness.

At least it was quiet here. Maybe he wouldn't even notice the transition to death.

Perhaps it had happened already. Otherwise, what were those strange lights? Two parallel rows of soft blue lights, curved and undulating, sliding by somewhere below him, or above, as he could not tell the difference. Their motion, and the regularity of their spacing, were hypnotic. Valjhar was pleased that his last view of anything in life was something so mysterious and intriguing.

Soon his consciousness would fade and he would die. No Rralian possessed the reflex that would force him to try to breathe if he knew it was futile, so the dwindling oxygen in his lungs and blood would be his demise. Already the strange lights were growing less distinct. He became aware of a pulsing series of high-pitched sounds, and then something huge and powerful took hold of him and pushed him roughly through the water. He broke the surface and something was pushed onto his face...a mask?

Valjhar breathed in and his mind cleared instantly. He saw the lights of *Mote* not far ahead, or below, as it was already tilting down the surface of the wave. In that faint glow he saw the face of Stingray, maskless, his face strained, his eyes bulging, as he churned through the stinging water toward the ship. He leaped clear of it, carrying Valjhar as he would an infant, landing halfway up the curved, slippery hull, barely managing to scramble up the ladder leading to the weather deck, and thence down into the airlock.

Valjhar collapsed onto the deck, gasping into his mask as Stingray began to force the hatch closed with phenomenal strength.

Valjhar looked around the little chamber. Something was missing.

"Shaula! Where's Shaula?"

Stingray looked at him in horror but could make no reply without breathing in those useless, acrid gasses.

Without thinking, Valjhar secured his mask and climbed the ladder, squirming through Stingray's arms as he did so. The wind was less now, and he flung himself back into the sea, able at least now to breathe. The water immediately around the ship was lit by its lights, but Valjhar saw nothing in that murky haze, certainly not Shaula. It was all he could do to not sink beneath the limited influence of those lights. It was as if he were made of lead. Somewhere in these limitless alien depths was Shaula Alshain. If he must sink to the solid core of the planet, unknown megaskads below, to find her, then sink he would.

Again Valjhar heard those peculiar high-pitched sounds. Again the massive form of Stingray, churning through that wet dimness, his eyes closed against those painful waters. Unerringly Stingray approached Valjhar and clutched him with irresistible strength. And then, below, out of range of the ship's lights...those twin undulating rows of luminous orbs. Stingray paused on his way to the surface, facing them. Then, inexplicably, he resumed his powerful swim, straight down, toward the lights, into darkness, despite Valjhar's protests and struggles. The alien lights loomed huge, far larger than Valjhar had supposed, and then they were among them. They collided with something that felt rubbery and smooth. After a moment Stingray turned away, rising toward the surface, his speed faltering. Only when they neared the ship could Valjhar see Shaula's limp form clasped in Stingray's other arm. He could also see the strained desperation on Stingray's face as he fought toward the surface.

They broke the surface near the ship, which by now was well on its way down the slope of the current gigantic wave, its heaving surface extending vastly beyond the range of the ship's lights. Without the use of his arms, it was all Stingray could do to even remain near the ship, and he looked up at its wet, slick curving side with despair.

Valjhar took a deep breath, removed his mask and held it over Stingray's mouth and nose. That was as much of his great head as the mask was able to cover, and its shape was wrong to create a proper seal. Nevertheless Stingray released his breath with enough force to almost dislodge the mask, and then he sucked in great lungfuls, though his pained expression made it clear that he was also drawing in some of the ammonia-tainted air of this world.

Valjhar found himself wishing that *Mote* were not quite so sleek as the weakened Stingray looked for a possible route up. A few external handholds would not be amiss.

"Hold on, Valjhar," rasped Stingray as he clumsily transferred Shaula to the same arm that held Valjhar, squeezing them together painfully. Valjhar clutched Shaula's cold, limp form. What had Stingray decided to do?

The answer came a moment later when Stingray surged out of the water with a frantic thrust of his legs. They slammed against the ship's hull and somehow clung there. Stingray's free hand was clinging to one of the attachment points for the sail rigging!

"Valjhar, hold onto Pimsie, I mean Shaula, as tightly as you can. I'm going to toss you onto a higher part of the ship. Put on your mask."

It was painful to hear Stingray trying to talk over the rush and roar of this world. Valjhar took the mask, drew from it a single, shuddering breath, and then put it on Shaula. Her eyes fluttered open, but they did not look at him, and appeared sightless.

Valjhar wrapped his arms and legs around Shaula and nodded at Stingray to show he was ready. A moment later he found himself tumbling through the air. It was a perfect toss, though Shaula almost knocked that precious lungful of air out of him as she landed atop him. Valjhar stood up, lifting her sodden, sagging body. They were right beside the bridge and the bezel that generated its bubble field, but the dorsal hatch was still some distance off, beneath the scaffolding that supported the weather deck, uphill because of the pitch of the ship on the wave.

Valjhar was preparing to try to dash up to it when he was distracted by movement. There was Kern, wearing the engineering suit and a mask, waving at him frantically from the bridge and beckoning. He had abandoned the helm. The ship was beginning to yaw and was in danger of broaching. Surely he didn't mean to...

But he did. The bubble field vanished, and the atmosphere of Flamaria rushed in to fill it. Valjhar tumbled over the bezel and onto the deck. He tucked Shaula beneath a console while Kern slapped another mask over his face. Valjhar rose and fought his way to the wheel, turning the rudder hard over to bring their stern back into the wind. The still-fierce wind threatened to tear him away again, but he held on.

"Stingray! Stingray's still out there!" he shouted, his voice unnaturally deep in the thickening air.

"I'll get him!"

But Stingray did not need to be gotten. Through some prodigy of strength and endurance he came crawling over the bezel and flopped down onto the deck.

Over the roar of the wind and waves Kern yelled, "I've built up some air pressure in the top deck! I'm going to release it into the bridge and displace this bad air!"

That was all the explanation they received. The release of pressurized air from below was like an explosion. After an instant of this Kern restored the bubble field, and a measure of peace and quiet was restored to the bridge.

Stingray lay on the deck coughing, gasping, and retching. Valjhar cautiously removed his mask. Their normal air was not perfectly restored, and still bore the stench of rot and ammonia that marked the air and water of the unflatteringly-named Flamaria.

Shaula still lay unmoving. Valjhar ripped off her mask and was horrified to find it filled with stinking water that must have come from her lungs. Her eyes were open and blank, and Valjhar could feel no pulse.

The world went black before Valjhar's eyes and mind. He had gotten Shaula killed. She had sacrificed her life to try to save his.

"I will do whatever is necessary to protect everyone on this ship," she had said. And she had given the attempt her all, without thought, without a word.

Too broken to weep, too blind to see, he was barely aware of it when Stingray loomed up and snatched Shaula up from the deck. He held her by the ankles, draining the remaining fluid from her lungs, and even swung her back and forth.

Pimsie burst up from below, coughing in the foul air. "Shaula! She's dead! What are you doing?"

"He's trying to save her," said Kern.

"This tough little pixie will not die if I can help it," said Stingray. He lay her back down on the deck, knelt beside her, and tore away her outer garments. He placed his huge hands on her chest, completely covering it.

"Hey!" objected Pimsie.

"Pimsie, quiet," said Valjhar, a desperate hope expanding in his heart.

Shaula's body jerked, then lay still. Stingray frowned, which could never be a welcome sight even if he was on your side, and she jerked again, more violently.

And she breathed. She blinked rapidly, and drew in ragged breaths. She turned her head to the side and vomited out a puddle of vile water.

White light exploded in Valjhar's mind. He too had returned to life.

Long before anyone thought she ought to try, Shaula sat up and struggled to speak. "Something—there's something down there."

"Yes. Something huge," said Stingray.

Valjhar regarded him with a kind of hero worship. "I saw it too, or them, or whatever it was. What was it? Some kind of creature?"

"I don't know."

Chapter 16
Rouse on the Loose

Four months after her arrival at the Falcon's Eyrie, the abbot Sonam Pena took Rouse aside and spoke to her with his head lowered in embarrassment.

"Miss Farewell, you have recovered very well, better than anyone could have expected, and we are all so happy to see you looking well."

Rouse gave the man a little smile of forgiveness for whatever he was about to say next.

"But now, well, now I'm afraid I must ask you to leave our monastery."

"Oh? I hope I have not given any offense."

"Oh no, not at all. Your behavior has been most proper and respectable, within the limits of your Western upbringing. But...increasingly we find that your presence here becomes a source of...disruption."

"How so?"

The abbot shrugged and looked uncomfortable. "You see...as you have recovered, and your hair has grown out, you have become more and more...noticeable. This is especially an issue among our younger monks. We have enough trouble as it is, guiding them away from thoughts and activities which are not especially...monkish. But you...well, any male would find you distracting, whether he was dressed in red robes or no." He darted a glance into her eyes. "I hope you understand. I see you are amused by these signs of our spiritual imperfection."

Rouse tried not to laugh. "Well, perhaps I'd say I'm flattered. Of course I'll do as you ask. I am very grateful to you and your whole community for sheltering me over these past months. I'll never forget it, and I don't want to cause you any more trouble. May I have another day or two to prepare to leave, and to say goodbye to everyone?"

She was gladly granted this leniency. Mainly she wanted to confer with Sapphire, who had rarely been far from her side throughout this lengthy period. For the past few weeks, with her strength waxing, he had even taken to instructing her in the rudiments of some of the martial and contemplative disciplines he practiced.

Once during a sparring match she attempted a spinning kick, though she had only seen him perform one once and had no instruction. When she landed she observed that Sapphire had backed away and was regarding her with great surprise.

"Was it really that bad?" she laughed.

"Rouse, while you were in the air you performed three full revolutions."

"Oh? Is that so unusual?"

"Unusual? I'd never seen it done. I couldn't do it. I don't know how you stayed in the air so long."

Rouse laughed again. "Well, maybe I'm not as familiar with the limitations of the human body as you are."

For some reason that comment stopped them both. Rouse felt as though time had frozen, her thoughts hazed over by deja vu.

When she again became aware of her surroundings she found Sapphire giving her a very searching look.

"Rouse Farewell, I expect to hear great things about you someday."

"Oh, I hope not, because that will probably mean I've gotten into a lot of trouble."

"Where are you planning to go?"

"I don't really know. I suppose I'll just drift around here in Asia for a while."

"Does that idea frighten you?"

"No," she said, surprising herself a little. "No, I'm not likely to encounter anyone more frightening than a human being, and I'm one of those myself, so we should be on even terms."

Sapphire smiled and presented her with a canvas satchel he'd laid upon a table. "You'll need this." Rouse rifled through it. Among a few other items it contained a New Zealand passport stamped with visas for several neighboring countries.

Rouse was delighted. "What? Where did you get this?"

Sapphire shrugged modestly. "I have many resourceful and creative friends."

"So my name is Susan Allen now?"

"Yes. A name designed to attract little attention."

"And this photo...oh yes, you were so persistent with your camera last week. Well, thanks for this new lease on life."

Sapphire bowed to her. "Since I have the honor of knowing your real name, I will reveal mine as well. It is Rinchen Norbu Raintree. I'm a member of a most interesting and diverse family."

A few days later Rouse found herself wandering the streets of Kathmandu, having made her way there from Bhutan via various rickety buses and much walking. From there she slipped across the border into northern India, heading northwest, into Kashmir and thence into Pakistan. From there her vague plan was to travel into China via the Karakoram Highway.

While wandering through a market in Islamabad, Rouse observed a pair of Western tourists trying to conclude a transaction with a merchant whose language they did not speak. In exchange for a small brass pitcher the man hesitantly laid a fairly large bill onto the palm of the merchant, a weathered man who smiled and nodded at them but made no move to return any change.

Rouse shook her head and approached the trio. She surprised the merchant by placing her hand on his arm and smiling down at him. He looked back at her with increasing doubt and finally fumbled through a little metal box for a fair wad of cash which he gave to the tourists. Rouse released him. He gave a rueful shrug and she laughed, thanking him, using one of the very few phrases of Urdu she knew.

Rouse began to walk away, but the couple stopped her to offer thanks. From their accents they were obviously from North America.

"Thank you so much," said the woman, who was in her thirties and had dark hair confined by a scarf. "I wish we had your savvy for negotiating with the locals here!"

Rouse brushed this aside. "Not so much savvy. I could see in his eyes that he was happy to cheat you, that's all." She turned to walk away again.

"Wait!"

Rouse wasn't eager to involve herself with these people, but out of politeness she halted and turned back.

"Are you alone here?"

"Yes," said Rouse.

"Isn't that a bit risky? I mean, a white woman here in this country, all on her own?"

"Oh, I don't know. I don't feel terribly threatened. Do you?"

"Well, we do feel pretty much out of our element, or I do, anyway. You see, this is our adventure tourism trip, and I have to admit we're a little out of our comfort zone here."

"I'm sure you'll be fine. Good—"

The man spoke up cautiously. "You seem to be at ease here. If you're not too busy, could we hire you to guide us?"

Rouse laughed. "Why, do I look like such a ragamuffin that I need to find work?" She shook her head. "I've only just arrived here myself. I don't speak the language and I don't know my way around. No, I'm sure you can find a more qualified guide than me."

They both looked disappointed. Rouse found herself feeling a little sorry for them. "Where are you off to from here?"

"Well, we had planned to take the bus up the Karakoram Highway to Kashgar, but we've heard so many scary stories about it that I'm not sure if we dare," said the woman.

Rouse looked down and considered for a few moments, then gave a mental shrug and said, "As it happens, I'm planning to do exactly the same thing. If you like, we can ride the same bus together and keep each other company." She didn't actually feel any need for company, but she felt these people could use someone to keep an eye on them.

They lit up at once. "Yes, that would be wonderful, thank you!" said the woman. "Please, let us buy you dinner at our hotel, and we can get acquainted."

Rouse gamely tagged along, sharing an American-style meal in an American-style restaurant in an American-style hotel...not very adventurous. As it turned out, they were from Minneapolis, Minnesota. She was Amy Krause, a nurse practitioner, traveling with her husband Kevin, who was a landscaper. They said they wanted to get out and see some exotic corners of the world while they still considered themselves young enough to endure the required hardships. Rouse thought there might be more behind their trip than they were letting on. Kevin was reserved and a little tense, watching his wife with covert care. Amy was very talkative, rambling even, with a kind of taut, feverish volubility that reminded Rouse of the glossy skin of an overinflated balloon.

Rouse had trouble finding something she cared to eat from a menu that mostly offered dead animals. Finally she settled on a creole dish, with the provision that the shrimp be omitted. She doubted that shrimp were sentient enough to warrant her consideration, but decided it was best to give them the benefit of the doubt.

Amy Krause tried to insist on paying Rouse's bus fare, but Rouse assured her she could afford it, as was perfectly true. Not all the gold left by her mysterious benefactor had gone to enrich the monastery. Some if it had become a fair stack of cash concealed in her inner jacket pocket. Amy even offered to get Rouse a room at their hotel, but Rouse was content with a more humble but also less generic estab-lishment not too far away. She walked there after dinner, lost in thought. She was not oblivious to the many eyes that regarded her from the shadows of the darkened streets, but they did not concern her, either.

In the morning Rouse rounded up her charges and to-gether they boarded the bus. They were the only Westerners aboard, a fact which made the Krauses uneasy. The other passengers were a cross-section of every ethnic group to be found in southern and central Asia: Pakistanis, Afghans, Chinese, Sikhs, Uyghurs, Tajiks, and more. The bus itself was surprisingly bland and modern, but its interior featured more local color...rows of little brass bells attached to the ceiling, and panels with colorful, elaborate designs where advertising placards would be on a similar Western bus.

They had arrived so early that they were able to secure seats at the front of the bus. Kevin and Amy sat together, across the aisle from Rouse. Eventually someone claimed the window seat beside her...a small, shy-looking balding man with a glossy brown scalp. He mumbled some greeting at Rouse and Rouse nodded back.

The three Westerners settled in. Rouse observed that their fellow passengers appeared to anticipate the journey with little excitement. Most of them looked sleepy, surly, and in some cases apprehensive. Their regard for the misfit trio in the front of the bus was not very friendly.

"I don't think they like us," whispered Amy.

"Pakistan is an American ally," said Kevin with wooden conviction.

"Their government may be. I'm not so sure about the people."

"I wouldn't worry about them too much," said Rouse with a yawn. "They all have business of their own, and their own reasons for making this journey. I doubt that picking on a pair of American tourists will be a high priority for them."

"Susan, how can you be so blasé about this trip?" asked Amy. "Have you done it before?"

"Oh no, never. But I'm not really blasé. I'm deeply interested in everything around me. I just prefer to be interested calmly."

The bus departed in due time, or perhaps a little later. Rouse was happy to see the sprawling city of Islamabad thin out and recede behind them. It was a city carefully planned, with broad streets and shining white buildings, but to Rouse it seemed sterile and unwelcoming.

At first the highway was straight and bland as it slowly climbed toward the tangled knot of mountains visible on the misty horizon. Rouse soon tuned out the jangly music pouring from the speakers overhead. Tuning out Amy took a little longer. She was very ill at ease, constantly fidgeting, casting what she thought were surreptitious looks back at her fellow passengers, biting her lip, and appearing generally anxious. Finally Kevin leaned over and whispered in her ear. She fumbled out a bottle of water and used it to swallow a pill. After a few minutes she seemed to calm down, or perhaps become unaware of her surroundings. Eventually she fell asleep. Only when she went limp and began to snore lightly did Kevin gingerly lean across her to whisper to Rouse, looking reluctant and uncomfortable as he did so.

It took him a few moments to collect his thoughts, then he spoke in a rapid whisper.

"Susan—Amy has some problems, and I think you can see that. She was burned out by her work, and she had a breakdown. She's always been sensitive and fragile. She's worked hard to recover, and she insisted on taking this trip to test herself. She thought some kind of Eastern mysticism she'd find here might help her. But she's stressed by this new environment and having trouble keeping herself together. I just thought I should explain. Thanks for coming along with us. I know we weren't exactly in your plans."

Rouse only nodded in reply. She did not mention her own background in psychiatric nursing, let alone as a former mental patient, out of concern that it might make her identity as the still-notorious Rouse Farewell too obvious. Kevin's confession did dispose her to take Amy's flightiness more seriously. She felt chastened. She must not allow herself to become so impressed with her own newfound equanimity that she grew dismissive of the pain of others who had not enjoyed her peculiar advantages. Amy was brave to be here at all...braver than Rouse herself would have been just a few short months ago.

Kevin settled back into his seat and closed his eyes in an obvious attempt to keep himself calm. Rouse studied Amy more closely than she had before. Though asleep, she did not appear to be very relaxed. Her expression remained somewhat taut and anxious. She appeared to be in her mid thirties, but her complexion was drawn and haggard despite her attempts to hide this with makeup. This woman was tired beyond the capacity of a drug-induced nap to cure.

Rouse sighed and looked away. To take in the view through her window she was forced to look past her seat mate. He ventured a single glance into her eyes and then withdrew into himself, carefully avoiding her gaze. Rouse was aware of a degree of discomfort on his part, but doubted she could communicate with him, and so let him be.

The landscape became more and more empty as they rolled along. Scrubby plains rose gradually into greener hills. The road grew increasingly tortuous as it wound among these fertile hills, many of them terraced for agriculture. It passed many towns and villages until, hours later, it plunged down a steep slope into the broader valley of the Indus River, a mighty flow green with glacial sediments from high above. Past the town of Thakot the highway entered the wild country that lay between their bus and China. The road was no longer paved, but had dwindled to a narrow dirt track, barely wide enough for two vehicles to pass each other. Thus it would remain for most of the way to China. At 1,300 kilometers in length, the KKH could be traversed in two leisurely days of driving...if it weren't the KKH. Their trip would take considerably longer.

Somewhere ahead rose a tangled mass of mountains...the confluence of the Karakorum, Himalaya, Kunlun, and a few other mountain ranges of legendary stature and reputation. For now they bumped along the Indus Valley as it gradually narrowed, with tall brown ridges limiting their view to either side. The pale green river was huge and turbulent. The month was June, and the vast snowpack of the higher mountains was beginning to make its way down toward the sea.

The bumpiness woke Amy, who looked around blearily. Rouse wished she had not slept through so much of the day. Not only had it deprived her of some of the experience she had come here for, but it might make it difficult for her to sleep well tonight. Rouse did not think it likely that Amy Krause was suited to sleepless nights in strange places.

At least she had missed some of their driver's terrible driving. The valley had by now narrowed into a gorge, and the road was carved out high on its western wall, far above the river, and getting higher all the time. In Pakistan they drove on the left, just as they did in New Zealand, at least in theory. The road was very narrow, and often their bus roared along the middle of it, lurching to the left only when a truck or some other vehicle rushed at them from the other direction. This often put them inches from a collision with rocks protruding from the road cut, but it least it kept them away from the edge, which was completely unprotected by any barrier and promised only a long tumble down to the river.

Rouse was beginning to wish she'd chosen to undertake this venture by bicycle or even on foot, assuming she could dodge all the trucks and busses and their crazy drivers. It would be so much more peaceful…most of the time.

Late that afternoon they left the bus at the little town of Besham, a hamlet built along the west bank of the Indus. A few others disembarked there as well, including Rouse's seatmate, who scuttled away with a furtive look over his shoulder. Rouse shrugged. It was not difficult for Rouse and her charges to locate the town's only hotel. She shared a dinner with the Krauses at the attached restaurant, then saw them retreat to their room while the sun was still fairly high in the June sky.

Rouse sighed with relief as the tension of dealing with Amy drained out of her. The hotel had a few rooftop tables where she was able to perch and have a quiet cup of tea as she watched the afternoon light shift and grow richer on the surrounding mountainsides. It glinted on the great river that flowed by a hundred meters away. A few of the other tables were occupied by locals, who ignored her except for a few covert, uninterested glances.

Rouse's thoughts dissolved into an awareness and appreciation of the stark beauty around her. Except for the occasional roar of a passing vehicle it all seemed peaceful. This was hardly the wildest stretch of the KKH, but it was obvious that even here, a walk of a kilometer from the road and town would bring her to a place rarely frequented by human beings.

This terrace was not so isolated. Rouse was surprised by the diffident approach of her erstwhile seat companion, who halted a few steps away and asked politely, "Do you mind if I join you?" His English was perfectly good.

A surprised Rouse beckoned him to a seat. "Thank you, Miss Allen," he said as he pulled up his chair.

Rouse smiled at him. "Have I already introduced myself then?"

The man placed his hands on the table. On one hand was a gold ring bearing a deep blue stone. "No, a mutual friend has made me aware of you."

Rouse looked at the ring. "Sapphire."

The man nodded. "It would please our friend to be here with you himself, but unfortunately he is engaged in another matter much deeper in central Asia. He has asked me to stay near you while you travel in these uncertain regions. You may call me Zahoor."

"I see. Do you feel I need to be looked after?"

"Our friend would wish me to say that you do not, and I am inclined to agree, even though I have seen you do nothing more than ride on a bus and walk about. However, the road ahead has not been entirely secure of late, and it may be that I, as a native, can guide you away from certain needless perils."

Rouse shrugged. "I make no objection. I confess though, I am surprised. You give the appearance of a man who strives to avoid trouble at all costs."

Zahoor chuckled. "That is exactly right, I do. As for my demeanor, when undertaking such tasks as this I have found it best to appear as unprepossessing and harmless as possible. I think our friend could stand to learn this lesson as well. He is a bit too flamboyant."

Rouse returned his laughter.

"The woman, Amy—" continued Zahoor, "she is quite fragile, isn't she?"

Rouse nodded and sighed. "She is. I intend to see her and her husband safely to Kashgar. I wish there was more I could do for her."

"That is kind of you."

They sat and drank tea together for a while as the afternoon drew on toward evening. Zahoor explained that he was an independent jewelry distributor when he wasn't working as part of Sapphire's "nefarious network of agents", as he put it. He asked no questions of Rouse, who suspected he already knew all there was to know about her.

"So, will you be joining us again as we continue our journey tomorrow?" asked Rouse.

"If you have no objection."

"I have none. You may find, though, that Amy is a bit of a xenophobe, and Kevin is suspicious of anyone he suspects might mean them ill."

Zahoor smiled. "I shall endeavor to remain inoffensive and inconspicuous." He stood up and took his leave.

Rouse left the hotel and walked along a path beside the great river. She found an old bench and sat down to study the steady green flow of that legendary river that sprang from somewhere on the Tibetan Plateau, far away and high above.

In the morning Rouse and the Americans attempted to board another bus similar to the one they had ridden the day before. But this bus was crowded, and the few empty seats were scattered. They did not care to sit apart, and they did not care to ask the passengers to rearrange themselves for their convenience, so they let the bus depart without them. Rouse asked around until she learned of a smaller private bus that was expected to stop by with a few empty seats. It was a more expensive option, but a safer one.

Rouse sat outside with her charges while they waited at the bus station. Amy looked a bit wan and tired. Kevin looked like he hadn't slept well either. Rouse was privately happy she had been spared the atmosphere in their room.

Finally the bus arrived and they were able to arrange passage on to Chilas, or perhaps Gilgit. This bus had bigger windows and carried only about twenty passengers. They wound up sitting near the back, and they were able to sit together when the others discreetly shuffled themselves into other seats to accommodate them. Rouse smiled and thanked them in one of her few Urdu phrases. There were still a few empty seats.

Just before the bus departed, Zahoor appeared from nowhere and boarded it as well, sitting a few rows ahead of them. The Krauses did not recognize or take note of him. Rouse chose not to mention him to them, not wishing to explain why one of the locals had attached himself to them, or rather to her specifically.

The road grew ever more precarious, rising again to become a narrow, unprotected ledge on the mountainside high above the river. At times donkeys and goats wandered along it, dodging the oncoming bus with little room to spare—or not, in some cases. Their driver made little effort to avoid them, or anything else, for that matter. He approached his job with a kind of inexorable fatalism, trusting in God or fortune to clear the way ahead.

Kevin and Amy sat whispering together, their heads down, barely paying attention to their journey.

Rouse's new seatmate was a young man around her age, with a black beard and a somewhat sullen demeanor. He ignored her even more pointedly than Zahoor had the day before.

Rouse was actually on the verge of boredom with the grey and rocky landscape when they rounded a curve and she was presented, with a suddenness that seemed impossible, with a spectacle that took her breath away. Ahead loomed the Naked Mountain, Nanga Parbat, ninth tallest in the world. Here was a mountain of a magnitude greater than any she had ever seen or imagined. It occupied a great part of the sky, shining white, wrapped in a haze of radiance that lent it a glamour of pink and gold. Rising up beyond the Indus gorge, it seemed unearthly, like a painting made by some enormous angel who was obsessed with light, hanging in the heavens somewhere beyond the airs of the world.

Rouse's eyes roved up its many snow-clad ridges, up its massive vertical faces, their scale incomprehensible, leading up and up into thin air, until its peaks towered at a level where human life could not be long sustained. Only a few people had ever climbed it, she knew, and many had died in the attempt, their corpses lying mummified on snow fields or glaciers that might never be marred by the feet of any climber. To Rouse it looked like a place where Man was not meant to be, a place well apart from the human world, where any human presence would be tolerated only briefly, if it was tolerated at all. She could almost hear the Earth groaning beneath the weight of it.

How strange, she thought, to be riding in this mundane conveyance with these ordinary people and to see out its grimy window this scene of immense and almost frightening splendor. It seemed the sort of thing that one should suffer and labor to be permitted to see. Of course its upper regions were inaccessible to anyone not willing and able to suffer and labor. Already Rouse was thinking that someday she might manage to stand in the blistering light of its summit and taste the cold and bitter remnants of the atmosphere that rushed by it.

Rouse glanced at her new friends. The mountain had not escaped their notice. Apparently something as vast and strange as a small moon resting on the face of the Earth was enough to distract them from their troubles.

The twists and turns of the road faded from Rouse's mind as they rolled along, fascinated by that mountain. It was as if her mind had left her body, wandering instead over the inaccessible flanks of that immense form, almost totally removed from the world of humans and all their frailty and nonsense. It was a vision so alluring and profound that for long minutes she knew nothing but the sensation of soaring over crag and peak, drinking in the frigid air that rushed past her face.

She left this sublime reverie behind with deep regret when a loud *bang* from somewhere ahead jolted her out of it. Clouds of dust erupted from beyond the next curve. The driver hit the brakes. A ragged, jumbled roar reached their ears, and the bus shook.

The bus stopped. When the noise and vibration subsided the driver cautiously advanced while a hubbub of alarm arose from the passengers. Amy looked pale and tight-lipped.

Rouse noticed that her seat mate was breathing heavily and seemed agitated.

Around the bend they encountered a landslide that had blocked the road. Dust still drifted away from it. The bus could not possibly get around it.

The driver turned and said something in Urdu, then, "We turn back."

Just turning around on this narrow road whose edge was an abyss would be a considerable challenge. As it happened, they would not need to try.

Rouse heard a small click coming from beside her. This was immediately followed by a detonation behind them, this time visible up the mountainside. It triggered another landslide which crashed down and blocked the road a hundred meters back. They were trapped.

It was now obvious to Rouse that these had been no accidents. Zahoor glanced back at her, and she saw in his eyes that he knew this too.

A number of men scrambled over the rockslide ahead of them. A few of the passengers sent up cheers which subsided when they realized those men were armed.

Everything seemed clear enough to Rouse.

"What you're doing is a very bad thing, you know," she whispered.

Her neighbor fidgeted and muttered. "No, it is something that must be done for the good of Islam."

Rouse tried and failed to think of a response that might mean something to this man. She was ignorant of the various strains of Islam and their incompatibilities, but she doubted she could sway this man from his views even if she were an Islamic scholar, who were probably all male in any case.

But what could she do? Clearly these men had murder on their minds. She could not sit here and permit it, even if she herself and her friends were not in danger. Perhaps Zahoor would act? But no, she would not abdicate her responsibility and leave the burden to him.

What responsibility did she have? Why did she feel she had any at all?

Because, she suddenly realized, she had somehow become an unusual person, a woman of unknown potential. She was also someone who did not greatly fear death.

Yet she also had no love of violence, and no wish to dirty her hands with the blood of others, no matter how dangerous they might be. But here and now, nothing else would suffice. The knowledge that she was being forced to do something so distasteful aroused a quiet anger.

She sighed sadly.

"Be quiet, woman, and let me pass. I have work to do here today."

Rouse turned away from his fanatical glare as though she were preparing to rise. Instead she thrust her elbow into his gut, giving him time to gasp exactly once before she shoved the palm of her hand beneath his jaw, slamming his head into the window hard enough to crack it. His eyes glazed over and he slumped down, unconscious or dead.

"Take the day off work, you bloody drongo."

Rouse smiled at the shocked passengers as though to reassure them. She encouraged the limp form of her sense-less companion to slip down beneath the seat ahead so that he could not be seen from the front.

As the men approached the bus Rouse observed the state of her fellow passengers. Amy was taut and fragile as a rubber band stretched too far. Kevin was reconciling him-self to the likelihood of dying in his attempt to protect her. A brave man. Zahoor was tense but watchful and con-trolled. The others displayed varying degrees of fear and anxiety. Some were praying in silence, certain that their time had come.

Rouse was startled by the sudden realization that what she was doing was unusual. She wasn't reading anyone's mind, not exactly. She was simply very much aware of her surroundings. She carried within her a difference that she had not before fully articulated. The old Rouse was a small node of consciousness inhabiting her brain, peering fear-fully out from it at her body and at a very limited subset of her immediate surroundings.

Her new perspective, her new point of view, was much more expansive. It always fully encompassed her own body and considerably beyond. When she wished, it took in quite a volume of space, and even had some range in time, allow-ing her to anticipate events to some degree.

A note of alarm entered her thoughts, and it wasn't caused by the approaching gunmen. She must not think herself too grand. Her awareness might have expanded, but it still took in only a tiny fraction of a divine whole that lay beyond her comprehension. If she allowed herself to be sat-isfied with her slight improvement, she might never ad-vance into those greater mysteries.

Her musings were interrupted as three of the men stormed aboard the bus while the others, a dozen or so, sur-rounded it. One of the boarders aimed his weapon at the driver, who sat impassively. The others glared back at the passengers, truculent yet puzzled, obviously looking for their collaborator.

One of them barked out something Rouse did not understand, and received only silence and blank looks in return. He tried English. "Where is Raafi?" Again he received only shrugs.

Amy could restrain herself no longer. She fell to loud weeping, and could not be silenced or comforted by Kevin. This irritated the already tense invaders.

"Be silent, woman. We are not here to prey on tourists. We are here to cleanse our land of the Shia."

The prospect of an imminent sectarian massacre did not comfort Amy either. Her misery and noise output only intensified.

"I said be quiet!" bellowed the chief thug, waving his automatic rifle aggressively.

"She isn't well," said Rouse calmly. "She's suffering from a mental illness and can't be expected to accept your brutality with any aplomb."

The chief regarded Rouse with surprise. "Oh? What troubles her?"

"It's stress and trauma from a breakdown that resulted from her work as a nurse."

"So now you Westerners send your mental patients among us?"

"She was hoping to find peace and solace in a place she naively hoped was full of spirituality. I haven't known her very long, or I would have warned her against such a foolish hope."

The chief gave an ugly laugh. "Maybe the White Monk can help her."

"Who is the White Monk?"

Rouse asked this in so calm and even a manner that the chief felt compelled to take the time to answer. "He is supposed to be a holy man living somewhere near Nanga Parbat. I have heard many ridiculous stories about this hermit.

If he is real, he will grow into a great tourist attraction, I am sure. Now be silent while we sort out who among these passengers must die."

Rouse was content to watch as the three began to interrogate the others, demanding to know their names and to see their identification. The driver looked very grim. Amy wasn't the only one shedding tears of terror.

Rouse eyed their weapons. She had never been much exposed to firearms, and found these interesting. She considered the mechanism that made them work. Each cartridge contained a tiny amount of an explosive. Detonating it would cause a bit of metal to exit the barrel at high speed. That simple device was enough to transform these dirty, unworthy men into petty tyrants capable of terrorizing and controlling a busload of people. They were small men, not necessarily small in physical stature, but small in mind and heart and spirit. These were men who, without the authority granted them by their guns, would be reduced to muttering rumors of their hatred as they toiled in ignorance and poverty.

"These two are Shia," said one of the men, indicating a middle-aged couple clinging to each other in terror of their lives.

"Good, let's start with them," said the chief.

Rouse stood up. "Leave them alone."

The chief stared at her in disbelief. "What did you say, whore? Stay out of this. This has nothing to do with you."

Rouse stepped out into the aisle. "I said leave them alone. Get off this bus."

The other man came up behind her and squinted through the sunlight entering the windows. "Hey! Raafi is here, beneath the seats! This bitch has killed him!"

The chief's face grew red with rage. "Is that true?"

Rouse shrugged. "It may be."

"No, I think we'll start with you instead." He aimed his weapon. Amy screamed. Rouse glanced aside at her. The gun went off.

Chapter 17
Ladderites of Flamaria

Mote was short-handed for the next few days as they recovered from their ordeal. Valjhar, who had gotten off most lightly, returned to his feet as soon as possible, as Kern had not yet automated the ship's sailing controls and a hand was still needed at the helm. Even Pimsie had been pressed into service there, and she had developed a certain skill and confidence at the job.

But even for Valjhar recovery was not easy. They had obtained a far larger sample of seawater than they needed for their analysis. It was in fact mostly water, but it also contained substantial amounts of ammonia, methane, and other organic compounds, enough to burn and irritate living tissue. Valjhar's vision was hazy from the damage to his corneas, which would take several days to heal. His lungs were irritated and it was difficult to breathe.

Far worse was it for Stingray, who had been more oxygen deprived and yet far more physically active. He had not breathed in the water, but it had invaded his nasal passages and sinus cavities.

As Kern had discovered, the water was more than a brew of simple compounds and chemicals. It also contained complex molecular chains indicating the presence of a biology foreign to any of them. Whether any of these represented actual microscopic life forms was still uncertain, but their presence in Stingray's body was enough to activate his immune system, laying him low with fever.

Still more affected was Shaula. She had literally drowned in that water, and her lungs were badly compromised. She had been without oxygen for minutes. Her body lacked the advanced healing capabilities of a true Rralian. She lay in the crowded medikum near Stingray and Kroy, occasionally conscious and in pain, otherwise deeply asleep. She wore a mask supplying pure oxygen. Her golden skin had turned a blotchy, angry red and was beginning to peel away.

Yet Valjhar, who spent every possible moment at her side, to the point of sleeping there, did not see her that way. The fog over his vision remained, but the fog over his inner eye had been dispelled. Once again he saw Shaula Alshain as he once had...as a splendid beauty, a mystery, and an inspiration.

Their expedition, with two of its members incapacitated by this dangerous environment, and with a deadly menace searching for them somewhere in or just beyond this murky atmosphere, was in danger of foundering. Their ship was crippled. They could not flee, nor could they hide forever. Valjhar had no more time, no more luxury, for disdaining one of his finest, strongest friends just because she had once taken actions that he, as a child of a gentle and innocent world, could never fully understand.

All this he babbled out to Shaula as he sat beside her, begging for her forgiveness, and receiving it, if the squeezes she gave his hand meant anything.

Yet he could not spend all his time there. One day, as he was leaving the medikum while the ship was level in a trough, Pimsie intercepted him on his way to the bridge. Valjhar wondered if he looked as strained and exhausted as Pimsie did, and decided that he probably did.

"Valjhar, they're following us."

"Who?"

"Those things in the water."

Valjhar had given those creatures little thought. So far they seemed to be harmless, despite their great size and unknown nature. Though they were a distant priority in his mind, he said, "How do you know that, Pimsie?"

"I watch them. I go down into the landing control room, turn out the lights, and I can see them through the windows.

It's quite hypnotic. Sometimes I fall asleep there. Come see."

Valjhar hesitated. "Kern is at the helm?"

"Of course."

"All right, just for a moment."

Valjhar followed Pimsie to Mote's lowest deck and into the landing room. The room was dim. The big ports afforded an expansive view into the fathomless black sea below them. And there they were, three or four of them, twin rippling rows of pale lights, hard to untangle visually due to the way they flowed through and around each other. The closest ones were nearly white, their lights fading through green to dim blue as they receded into that turbid soup.

Somehow they barely registered on Valjhar's mind. His thoughts were occupied with concerns infinitely more important. He turned to Pimsie to excuse himself, but he choked on his words as he tried to speak.

"Pimsie..." He collapsed helplessly into her arms.

Pimsie didn't appear to be in the least surprised. "Yes, Valjhar, yes," she said as she stroked his hair. "I'm glad you've finally come to your senses about Shaula. I'd about given up on you, though she never did."

"She...what she did...she's so..."

"Yes, she's your dream girl, and always has been. How could any simple Rralian girl compete?"

"What if...she doesn't recover?"

"Oh, of course she will. She will never leave us to look after our silly selves. Don't you know that?"

But now a little of that insight that came so easily to Pimsie came to him as well, and he knew that though she spoke brave words, she did not entirely believe them.

"Thank you for understanding, Pimsie. I have to get up to the bridge to relieve Kern before the ship's pitch gets too bad."

On the bridge, a tired Kern looked at him and said, "Are you all right, Valjhar? Your eyes still seem—"

"I'm all right. I've just been—I'm just tired, like you. I'll take over now." Valjhar took Kern's place at the wheel, made a minor adjustment to the sails, and said, "How close are we to automating the helm? That will take a big load off us."

Kern made his way to a chair to avoid slipping down the rapidly tilting deck. "Oh, I haven't been working on that."

Valjhar nearly exploded in frustration at this news. Instead he forced himself to calmly ask, "What have you been working on?"

"I've thought of a way to make ourselves even more inconspicuous, and also to escape this infernal rocking once and for all."

That took Valjhar by surprise. "Oh? And what it that?"

"By submerging the ship."

Now Valjhar was even more startled. "Is that feasible?"

"I think so. All we really need to do is to overcome the ship's buoyancy, of course. We already have a deep keel. It's heavy because it's made of metal, and it's also mostly hollow. I think I can modify it to fill it with seawater, and that should be enough."

"Not heavy enough to pull us all the way to the bottom, I hope."

"Ha! No, we'll be more careful than that. But we will have to go quite deep to escape the action of these waves."

"How will we surface again?"

Kern shrugged. "If I can't figure out a way to expel the water, we can always jettison the keel and bob back up again."

Valjhar thought about this plan and its implications. "We won't be able to maneuver. The sails will be useless."

"What of that? There's no place to go on this ridiculous world anyway. It certainly simplifies navigation."

"What about the pressure on the hull?"

Kern gave Valjhar a hurt look. "Pressure? I didn't build this ship out of floss or wood or steel, you know. Pressure…"

Valjhar smiled. "My apologies. How long will it take to make these modifications?"

"It's all simple mechanics. If I can get six hours to myself I should be able to do it. Luckily the interior of the keel is accessible from inside the ship."

"Take those six hours. I'll cover your next watch at the helm too."

"Are you sure?"

"The idea of riding a quiet, level ship is so enticing I'd take three extra watches if I had to. I'm sure our patients in the medikum would appreciate it too."

"Yes! What's the first thing you'll do when the ship is stable and quiet again?"

"Eat a bowl of strawberries."

"Me too! And then I'll sleep for a night and a day."

They both laughed. For a moment it was as if they were two boys back on Rral again.

By now the ship was leveling out again as it approached the trough between two colossal swells.

A movement of light off to the ship's dockside caught Valjhar's eye.

"Kern, look."

Somewhere out there in the rainy darkness a pair of pale white lights had appeared above the water. For a while they remained there, steady, resembling a huge pair of inscrutable staring eyes. Then they rose higher, revealing a second pair beneath them. And then a third. And more.

"Um, do you think we ought to do something?" said Kern.

"Yes. Wait and see what happens."

"That seems like something we can manage."

The pairs of lights rose higher, higher, and then they began to curve over, toward *Mote*, yet high above it. Their motion accelerated, and they arched directly overhead, until they plunged into the water on the opposite side of the ship, forming a bridge, with the pairs of lights making a slow progression along it.

Pimsie appeared on the bridge and gasped. "How beautiful."

Valjhar agreed. The sense of wonder brought on by this display of the ineffably alien was enough to make up for all the misery they'd endured since descending into this strange world of water and darkness.

But it wasn't enough to make up for the injuries suffered by Shaula.

Kern whispered, "Even though I have no idea what I'm looking at, I sense no threat coming from this. Do either of you?"

"No," said Valjhar. "It's more like it, or they, or whatever it is, is acknowledging us."

"Welcoming us," said Pimsie in a hushed voice. "That's a pleasant change."

They watched the lights pass overhead for several minutes more, until they submerged and left them again alone on the side of a gigantic wave.

Mote was at peace, drifting in darkness twenty kiloskads beneath the wave troughs of Flamaria. Strawberries, peas, and more had been eaten. Sleep had been slept.

That darkness was not unrelieved. At all times the ship was orbited by at least a few of the light worms or whatever they were, dimly visible in the murky water. They had no proper instruments for determining their true shapes, but Kern was working on that, trying to devise suitable sensors that would work through the bridge or telescope domes, since going outside the ship was not an option at this depth.

Shaula did not improve. She was occasionally conscious, but it was difficult for her to speak. During these brief periods she exchanged long gazes with Valjhar as he massaged her hands. Mostly she slept.

The problem was that Rralian medicine was not very advanced. Rralian physiology was so advanced in its qualities of regeneration and healing, and so resistant to any pathogen, that the only medicine they'd ever needed was palliative in the case of physical trauma. In the past they'd been able to stabilize Rouse and other humans using substances derived from closely related life forms, but they had no such option for Shaula, a Booshite.

Stingray appeared to be doing better. One day as Kern and Valjhar sat on the bridge discussing their options, Pimsie appeared there looking flustered and uncomfortable.

"I think Stingray will be up and about soon," she said.

"Why, Pimsie?"

"I was rubbing lotion on him to soothe his irritated skin. I was naked to avoid messing up my clothes as I climbed around on him. His penis came out of its sheath. He tried to act mortified and apologetic, but I could tell he was secretly pleased."

Kern laughed. "Did you assist him?"

"Well, yes. I thought I had to, to be polite."

Kern laughed again, but Valjhar found this news more distasteful.

"His skin is not like ours. It's hard, sort of rubbery and thick, but very smooth and slick."

"Go on," said Kern.

"I could barely get two hands around it. His penis is as big as my arm." Pimsie was now blushing.

"Well, of course it is. What was the result?"

"I can tell you he doesn't produce a fish like you boys do. Just a thick clear liquid."

"Very interesting."

"But the strange thing is, he doesn't have any gonads. Not inside or outside. He has a functional penis and sexual desires, but is completely unable to reproduce."

"That is strange," said Valjhar. "That destroys my hypothesis that he is an amnesiac member of some secret race of amphibious Earth people. I wonder what he really is?"

"He's really horny, I'd say." Kern laughed uproariously at his inane joke.

Pimsie scowled at him. "Next time *you* can do it." Kern kept on laughing. "Seriously, he'd better not expect that kind of attention from me all the time. I'm sorry if he's lonely, but I don't fancy being the love object of a gigantic alien sea monster."

"If that becomes an issue, let me know," said Valjhar. "Kern, I'm surprised you're taking this so lightly."

Kern waved Valjhar's concern away. "Oh, I'm not worried about Stingray. He's a big lumbering lug, it's true, but deep down he's harmless."

Stingray did indeed soon appear again on the bridge, looking a bit subdued but otherwise intact. He took a look around and said, "So, you've really turned the ship into a submarine? I must say...that's cool."

"Yes, it is, isn't it?" said Kern with a smile.

"I see our friends are still with us out there."

"You think they're our friends?" said Valjhar.

"I'm pretty sure they are. They saved Shaula."

Valjhar cocked his head. "*You* saved Shaula."

"Oh no, is wasn't all me. I was fading fast, and she'd passed beyond the range of my senses. I had no idea where she was. But then one of these things rose up, and I could tell it was carrying her. I swam down a short distance, which was all I could do, grabbed her, and came back up."

The three Rralians goggled at him. "That's amazing!" said Kern. "Can you tell us anything else about them?"

"A little. I have various senses that don't depend on eyesight. Their basic shape is that of a flexible ladder, and those lights are spheroids located at the ends of the rungs.

They possess other structures too, repeated in each segment, such as fins for propulsion and other small extrusions."

"So they are enormous creatures of some kind."

Stingray frowned. "Possibly. With something this alien I can't be sure."

"If only we had some way to communicate with them," said Pimsie.

Somehow Pimsie's words, or perhaps her thought, had an immediate effect. All of the Ladderites (as they eventually came to be called) but one departed en masse. The remaining one ceased its flowing movements. Most unexpectedly, a unit of two lights detached itself from the rest and approached the ship, while the rest rippled away out of sight. The two lights drew nearer to *Mote*, twin misty orbs of shifting white, and came barely within the range of the ship's own lights. Now they could get a hint of the thing's true structure, two lighted spheroids connected by a thick, somewhat flexible rod, which was adorned with various fluttering fins and other structures of less obvious purpose. Now their overall size could be estimated. The pair spanned a width equal to the width of *Mote* itself.

The pair took up a station hovering over *Mote's* bow and exhibited a new behavior. The lights began to flicker through a range of colors in what appeared to be a chaotic manner.

"Do you think that's a form of communication?" said Stingray. "Doesn't seem to make much sense to communicate with light, when sound propagates through water so much better."

"True," said Kern. "Likewise, it doesn't make much sense that we use sound to communicate, when light travels through air so much more efficiently."

Stingray looked at Kern appreciatively. "You're a smart little rodent, aren't you?"

"You bet I am." Kern did something at his console. A pair of Mote's exterior lights began to flicker.

"What are you doing, Kern?" asked Valjhar.

"I'm pulsing our lights at the same base frequency they're using. I want them to know we're paying attention."

"But how can we make sense of what they're doing?" said Pimsie.

"By watching and thinking, I hope," said Kern in a distant tone. "It's our only chance. We don't have the right data-processing equipment or instructions to do it for us. No Universal Translator."

Kern seemed to fall into a trance, staring into the lights for long minutes. Valjhar decided to emulate him, being unwilling to cede all intellectual achievements to his friend. He noted at once that the two lights never shared the same color, though at times the light on the left would briefly imitate what the other light had recently done, with only minor changes.

"I don't think I'm smart enough to do this," said Kern mournfully.

"Of course you are! Why not?" said Pimsie.

"Because what I think I'm seeing is ridiculous."

"What do you think you're seeing?"

"Well, the basic structure of those flashes...it looks like Rralian." Kern sounded profoundly embarrassed.

"How can flashing colored lights look like Rralian?" asked Valjhar.

"Well, look at those brief flashes of reddish-orange. They appear to divide groups of flashes of other colors that occur in groups numbering between one and ten or eleven, similar to the average glyph count of Rralian words. Also, I'm counting ninety two distinct colors in those groups, the same as the number of primary Rralian glyphs."

Pimsie gasped. "I see what you mean!"

"Also, longer pulses of reddish orange seem to divide groups of words into sentences of typical lengths."

"What about the left copying the right?"

"I'm not sure, it looks like it could be some kind of collaborative editing or correcting process between the two lights, or maybe they indicate emphasis."

Pimsie shrieked. Kern and Valjhar turned to her, startled. "I think I see the word 'Rral!' It's one of the few that begins with a pair of repeated glyphs!"

Kern looked boggled. "I think you're right! And that gives us...hmm..."

For another lengthy period the trio stared at the lights, struggling to correlate the various colors with the familiar glyphs of their language.

"Wait, what's this?" said Kern. "Oh, they're beginning to repeat the pattern. They're giving it another chance to penetrate our thick skulls. I believe the first complex sentence is 'You are of Rral,' though I'm not quite sure they understand our concept of syntax."

"How do they know us?" said Pimsie.

Eventually they began to piece certain words together, words like "return", "welcome", and "greetings".

"We need to reply," said Valjhar.

"Yes, I'll have to rig some kind of array of colored lights, I suppose," said Kern.

"Unless you think they might be smart enough to understand your spoken words, as you are managing to figure out their light code," said Stingray.

The others looked at each other in surprise. "Maybe you're right!" said Valjhar. "But how can they hear us? Sounds won't propagate through the bubble field, that's for sure."

"We heard storm sounds coming through the hull," said Kern. "No reason sounds can't go out that way as well, if only faintly."

"Let's just try it," said Pimsie. *"Hey!"* she yelled. *"Can you hear us?"*

The flickering paused, then briefly resumed.

Yes.

Pimsie jumped up and down in delight. The others cheered.

"That was a tremendous experiment, Pimsie," said Kern. "And here I thought I was the scientist."

"Who are you?" called Valjhar. "How do you know us?"

The lights made no response.

"Not loud enough?" said a crestfallen Valjhar.

"Let's see," said Kern. He repeated Valjhar's questions, but using a ridiculously high-pitched falsetto voice.

A reply began at once.

"Wrong frequency, that's all. We'll let Pimsie speak for us from now on."

The answer was not immediately understandable, but over the next few hours the story gradually revealed itself.

"Thousands of years ago, your people came to our world, where they found us in a primitive and vulnerable state."

The actual words were not quite so coherent, but they could be construed to have this meaning.

"We were pairs naked to the sea, each connected only by a fragile tendril with our chosen other, with no contact with other pairs except as the waves and currents happened to bring us together. We did not know, we could not know, that anything existed beyond the clouds. We thought that the light we produced and the occasional flash of lightning were the only lights there were or could be. We did not know our world of water was finite. It is boundless, and so we thought it infinite as well."

As Valjhar gazed into those flickering lights they seemed to fade away. He entered a strange dreamlike state of mind where his surroundings were replaced by visions suggested by the words being written in his eyes.

He saw the Ladderites of long ago, each a roughly spherical mass of translucent tissues, supported by a highly vesicular skeleton a few inches below the surface. Its eyes were likewise submerged in that faintly luminous flesh...large, filmy orbs with huge pupils, several eyes distributed over each one, unblinking and immobile, incapable of forming a sharp image and never called upon to do so, sensitive light detectors meant only to take in the messages of their fellows. Interspersed between them were light-emitting organs capable of transforming their surfaces into shimmering arrays of color.

They drifted in pairs, each connected to a partner by a thin bundle of nerves. Seawater entered them through a simple opening, providing them with the basic substances they needed to sustain themselves, which were dissolved in that complex organic brew.

And so they drifted, passive and peaceful, communing with their partners almost as intimately as if they were a single organism, broadening the scope of their communication whenever another pair drew close enough for their light to be seen. For the most part, each pair was isolated. sharing simple thoughts and emotions about their simple world.

And simple they were, and simple it was. In that uniform environment, with no need to actively move or take any particular action, Ladderite intelligence was dormant and limited.

And then the Rralians came.

Descending deep into the sea in their flawless vehicles, these explorers were intrigued by the Ladderites and their physical connection. It was a Platonic connection only, as they did not use any form of sexual reproduction and had no obvious practical use for this intimacy.

But when, in their ignorant experimentation, they separated a pair, they quickly learned the truth. Each individual's cognitive abilities were reduced to a quarter, and worse, they soon began to deteriorate, as their will to live was lost. Only when they were allowed to reconnect did they recover.

Shaken by the harm they had done, the Rralians considered leaving this world to its somnolent natives. But then they decided to investigate the effect of bringing pairs together for longer periods. Two pairs were kept in proximity by a cage of loose mesh.

The results were impressive. The flickering light communication between the pairs was constant, and grew steadily faster and more complex.

The Rralians, seeing no sign that their subjects were inconvenienced by their confinement, or were even aware of it, let their experiment proceed for a considerable time.

Eventually each pair put out nerve conduits that joined with those of the other. The cognitive ability of the resulting square of individuals increased by a factor of four. They became more aware of their surroundings, and of the Rralians themselves. Communications between the two species commenced.

Now the Rralians faced a dilemma. They had created a joining of pairs, the first as far as they knew. They dared not put it asunder for fear of causing harm and distress. Yet the nerve bundles were fragile, and this new configuration subjected them to new stresses which would not long survive in the open sea.

Of course, in addition to being scientists, they were all engineers at heart. And so they constructed vessels, transparent containers for the individual creatures, connected by tough, flexible rods. They included vibrating fins for propulsion, and were self-replicating, able to produce copies of themselves from substances dissolved in the sea.

More pairs had come, and more had joined, forming the ladder-like structures the Mariners had seen. They were vehicles, or perhaps mobile villages. The ancient way of life of the Ladderites was transformed almost overnight.

And there was more. In deeper, more placid waters, the Ladderites learned they could also attach along the edges of their ladders, forming sheets of linked beings.

Still deeper, they learned they could also link in the third dimension, forming vast lattices of glowing orbs, cities in the darkness, surrounding the deep, unreachable solid core of their world.

With each new linking, the Ladderite's ability to process and comprehend information grew, though limited by the speed of nerve impulses along their connections. But in their dark, uniform, and uneventful environment they had little to think about.

This evolution of their society took years. Eventually the Rralians returned with a proposal. They would provide the Ladderites with vast amounts of data from their explorations in the Lesser Wisp. In return, the Ladderites would process this data and return the resulting information. The Rralians would gain a vast biological computing network, while the Ladderites would gain a window into a universe they could never have imagined.

To facilitate this, the Rralians built an array of stations in the vicinity of Flamaria. They transmitted transcendental signals, and also featured visible beacons that beamed the stories of the Ladderites to anyone able to see and interpret them in this nebulous part of the galaxy.

For the Ladderites became storytellers. With their own environment so bland and placid, they took the torrent of data offered by the Rralians and eagerly fashioned stories, some factual and others not. It had become their great passion as a people.

But then the Rralians had stopped coming. Their beacons continued to function, but their data inputs ceased. The Ladderites continued to digest what remained, but as far as they could tell, the information they sent out went unheeded. Thus their delight and joy at the arrival of *Mote*.

The visions faded, leaving Valjhar blinking at his companions, who seemed equally disoriented.

"Did you all—see that?" asked Kern.

Yes, they had.

"Apparently their control over those lights is so perfect and so specific they can manipulate the visual centers of our brains."

But Valjhar was not, at that moment, interested in the means the Ladderites had used to convey their message. His heart was full of wonder, not only at the story of the Ladderites, but at the role his own people, the people of Rral, had played in their history. The ancestors of the cautious, staid people he had known in Enblenol had once ventured among the stars, even to this remote corner of a foreign galaxy, reshaping the people they found, creating an infrastructure that still functioned, even though untended for thousands of years.

Perhaps, perhaps it was possible for Rralians, or even a tiny group of fallen Rralians like Valjhar and his friends, to do some good in the universe, to achieve something more than hiding from their past on some quiet world, or fleeing from that past in a last ship of space.

"I wonder what else is out there?" he blurted.

"What?" said Pimsie.

"The Rralians. Us. We encountered living Rralians on Smerkesh, and now we find this here. We know the people of Old Rral did not confine themselves to this small cluster of galaxies, but spread throughout the universe. Surely the Prohibitor, or Prohibitors if there is more than one, could not have found and destroyed every last pocket of them, every colony, every scientific station. They have not even destroyed these beacons."

"Then how did the Prohibitor find us?" said Pimsie.

"I expect the beacons detected our Rralian ship and broadcast the news as a transcendental signal," said Kern. "And I wonder...oh yes." Kern burst into laughter.

"What's so funny?" said Stingray.

"We are. We're so stupid. Remember when the Ladderites were swirling around us in their multitudes? I bet all
that time they were desperately trying to communicate with
us, in the same way they'd done with our ancestors. I bet
that white glow of theirs was really packed with information, sent at too high a frequency for us to perceive. I bet
they told us every story they knew during that time, but we
were too backwards to realize it."

Pimsie gasped. "And then, when I said I wished they'd
communicate with us, they separated a single pair to speak
to us in—baby talk. Because that was all we could understand."

Their companion pair resumed its flickering. "Yes, this
is correct. We were puzzled by your lack of response to our
greetings, but we now realize that you, our Rralian friends,
have suffered a diminishment in your capabilities. We have
something for you. It was given to us by other Rralians
long ago. It has just now arrived here from where it was
kept far below. We have no use for it. We give it to you.
Now we must rejoin our village. It is difficult and painful
for us to be separated in this fashion."

Soon afterwards one of the ladder structures draped itself across *Mote's* dorsal midsection. When it withdrew it
had left something attached to the weather deck.

Curious and a little apprehensive, the Mariners surfaced
the ship just long enough for Stingray to venture out onto
the weather deck to retrieve whatever it was. He returned to
the bridge while casually flipping a half-remembered object
in the air.

"I have no idea what this thing is, but whatever it is, it's
attractive." He handed it to Valjhar, still damp and smelly
from its immersion.

It was a white disk of the same span as Valjhar's hand.
Inscribed within it were concentric circles of crystal and
silver.

"It's a Compendium," he whispered, stunned.

Kern threw his hands in the air and began a little dance around the bridge.

"What's a Compendium?" asked Stingray.

"It's a record of the scientific and technical knowledge of Old Rral. We had one once before, but we lost access to it."

"Due to our excessive honesty," said Pimsie.

"We won't make that mistake again, assuming they don't communicate about this with each other, and that we can in fact access this one," said Kern.

As it turned out, they could access it. It was an older Compendium, considerably older than the one they had once possessed, which had itself predated the terminal high point of Rralian technology. But it was still a fabulous trove of knowledge and advancement. Kern shook with excitement after examining it for just a few minutes.

"This opens up so many possibilities for us. I don't know where to begin."

Kern began by making a device capable of receiving, interpreting, and recording Ladderite optical data at its intended rate of speed. It also featured an array of colored lights that could encode their own records and speech into a form the Ladderites could comprehend.

Mounted in the telescope dome, Pimsie used it to transmit their stories and what little they knew about the latter history of Rral.

While Pimsie told stories and Kern studied physics, Valjhar was not idle. Shaula continued to languish. If she seemed stable, he thought that was mostly due to her strength of will and character. She was still rarely conscious. Whenever she was, Valjhar made sure to be at her side, though her pathetic state was a sore trial to behold.

Valjhar wanted more for her than that. To that end, he studied biology and medicine, seeking a way to cure her.

He believed he found one, though a risky one. It was drastic enough, and dangerous enough, that he felt he should not make such a decision alone.

He called his friends together and told them what he had found.

"We've all heard Shaula express envy over certain gifts we Rralians possess that her people, the *Stotzis* of Boosh, do not."

Kern and Pimsie nodded. Stingray reminded him with a wry look that he was not a Rralian.

"Well, I believe I've found a way to make her wish come true."

Pimsie goggled at him. Kern said, "Really? That's interesting."

"We know she's nearly Rralian already, at least superficially. But at a finer level she's different, different enough to keep her from healing correctly. Her genetic makeup is quite unlike ours. I think we can change that. I think we can create and introduce into her body tiny mechanisms, artificial viruses essentially, that will visit every cell in her body and restructure her genes to make her truly Rralian. Once that is done, those revised genes will be forced to express themselves, and she will undergo a gradual physical transformation, mostly internal and unseen, that will result in her becoming biologically Rralian in every way."

Kern frowned. "Could she survive such a process? Will her body still function during the intermediate stages?"

"I can't be sure. It would be a substantial change to her physiology. Her internal organs would change, including her brain. She would surely require artificial life support during the process."

"Then how can she remain Shaula?" demanded Pimsie.

"How do you mean?"

Pimsie spoke impatiently. "If her brain changes in any important way, how do you expect it to retain the delicate structures and connections that define her thoughts and memories? Even I know that much. Won't you be wiping out her personality, just as you wiped out Kroy's?"

Valjhar sat back, stunned. "I hadn't thought of that."

"It might be the only way to save her, though," said Stingray thoughtfully.

"Maybe you'd like to try it first!" snapped Pimsie.

Stingray ignored her ire. "Ha, what would I become, a giant Rralian? Most likely I'd become five hundred pounds of goo as my cells broke down trying to adapt to your very different physiology."

"Valjhar, we can't even consider trying this on Shaula unless we can first test the process somehow," said Kern.

"Or at least simulate it," said Stingray.

"Simulate?" said Valjhar.

"Sure, we have access to vast computing power in the form of our Ladderite friends."

"And Valjhar, I think we would have to somehow model Shaula's mind in exacting detail, and be prepared to re-introduce it into her remodeled brain, if necessary. Somehow," said Kern dubiously.

"Or better yet, keep her brain out of the process entirely," said Pimsie.

"I don't think we can get away with that," said Kern. "I think she suffered brain damage as a result of oxygen deprivation. Her brain needs to regenerate."

Pimsie looked unhappy.

"So do you all think this is something we should pursue?" said Valjhar quietly. "Do you think—this is something Shaula would want?"

Pimsie looked at him with grave sympathy. "Valjhar, she would want this even if she were perfectly healthy."

"How do you know that, Pimsie?" said Kern.

Pimsie waved her arms impatiently. "I know her! I know her better than any of you. We're both girls."

Valjhar spent the next two days further exploring his idea, and making a preliminary design for the minuscule devices needed to cause such a change. They would have to be clever enough to recognize the correct cell membranes to penetrate and the right molecules to rearrange. They would have to be very thorough and completely accurate.

Despite the urgency and difficulty of the work, Valjhar felt a certain satisfaction at fully exercising his Rralian intellect at last, mediocre though it was.

When he needed a tissue sample to analyze, Valjhar ventured to the medikum to obtain one. He passed Kroy's almost forgotten body on his way to Shaula's side. No one had a thought to spare for him, which was another blade of guilt in Valjhar's side.

For a moment he stood looking down at the woman he had so far failed so badly. She was drawn and emaciated, her once flawlessly golden skin now pale and mottled. He felt a moment's bitterness toward Cal-Cotavion, far away on Earth. If he had remained among them to minister to Shaula, Valjhar was sure she would be flourishing by now, without the need for any desperate measures.

As he was swabbing Shaula's arm he noticed that her eyes were open and upon him.

She could not speak. Her oxygen mask and feeding tube prevented that.

Valjhar put down his implements and took her hand.

"Shaula, I think I've found a way to help you heal." He had to control his voice with great care to keep her from hearing the pain and distress he felt at seeing her in this state.

Shaula's eyes brightened, and her grip on his hand tightened slightly.

"But—it is dangerous. It's unlike anything we've ever done or tried before. Unless we're very careful, it could kill you. And even if it works—it will leave you changed."

Valjhar saw the question in her emerald eyes.

"It will—well, it will turn you into one of us. Into a Rralian."

First Valjhar saw confusion, and then she tried to laugh, causing her throat to contract around her feeding tube, which brought on a fit of coughing, a pitiful thing in someone so weak. Valjhar could not keep the grief off his face. Her eyes remained locked on his, and somehow Valjhar knew she was trying to give him strength. *She* was trying to give *him* strength.

At length she quieted into long, rasping breaths, and she fell asleep again.

In that shadowy compartment, almost silent except for the whir of Shaula's oxygen pump, Valjhar stood looking down on Shaula's face in awe.

He would do this thing, he vowed. He would make it work. The universe was not right while Shaula Alshain was in this pitiful condition. He must make the universe right again.

To Valjhar's great gratification, he soon acquired assistance from an unexpected source: Pimsie Flam. She also used the Compendium to delve into the topic at hand. It was the first time he had known her to deliberately seek out knowledge of any scientific topic. She did so with an air of displeased resignation mixed with determination. Though starting almost from scratch, it didn't take long for her to develop some insight into the process, and soon she and Valjhar were comparing notes on the enzymes their creations would have to control to alter Shaula's genes.

Eventually they reached a stage where it seemed prudent to follow Kern's suggestion and ask the Ladderites to simulate the process. They were glad they did, though shaken by the results. Using their current model and understanding, it appeared the process would have indeed rewritten Shaula's genes, but the expression of those genes would have killed her almost immediately by reducing her tissues to that goo Stingray had mentioned.

Somehow her cells must continue to function, even as they were being revised. Likewise, her organs must do the same as they were being rebuilt, or even, in some cases, outmoded and replaced.

Unless…she could be put into some kind of stasis while the process was underway, which would add a whole new layer of complexity to an already very complex process.

"Valjhar, we're running out of time," said Pimsie mournfully.

"I know. She's failing faster now. I don't know what else we can do. I didn't understand how difficult this would be when I conceived the idea. Maybe I raised everyone's hopes for nothing."

"It's her only hope, Valjhar, and we can't give up now. Maybe we just need to approach the problem differently. We now have a valid Shaula/Rralian hybrid genome, I'm sure of it."

"Yes. The problem is how to implement it without destroying her."

"Yes, how do we force such a change on her already fully-formed adult body without destroying her? But maybe that's the key."

"What do you mean?"

"I think maybe we should begin from scratch. We could grow a new body for her from infancy."

Valjhar was startled. "Of course! But we'd still need a machine, some sort of nurturing device to support the embryo…"

Pimsie turned a wry expression upon him. "Valjhar, we already have such a device."

"We do? Where?"

Pimsie patted her belly. "Here."

Now Valjhar was flabbergasted. "Clearly, the obvious is too crass and dull a concept for my great intellect to grasp. But Pimsie…would you really be willing to do that? To… bear a replacement body for Shaula?"

"To save her? Of course I would."

Valjhar bounced up from his chair to pace around their medical laboratory. "But no—maybe we could create an infant version of Shaula, but it wouldn't *be* Shaula. Her mind and memories are not contained in her genes. She would be a different person. And I have no idea how to transfer a mind from one body to another."

"We've done it before."

"Yes—we facilitated the transfer of the star-being into Kroy by building a quantum bridge. But we only built the bridge. The star-being itself crossed it. Shaula is in no condition to do that, even if the process would work for a biological entity the way it did for a magnetic plasma life-form like the star-being."

"We should do it anyway, Valjhar, even if we can't figure out how to make the transfer. If—if Shaula doesn't survive, the baby might be the only thing we have left of her. I would—Kern and I would raise her as our daughter."

Valjhar knelt before Pimsie and took her hands in his. He was unable to speak.

A short time later, Kern entered the laboratory while Valjhar was working there alone.

"Valjhar, what's this I hear about you making Pimsie pregnant?"

"What? No, no. What we're considering is—"

Kern laughed. "Oh, calm down, I know, I know. My Pimsie is going to have a baby? And it's going to be Shaula?" Kern broke off and did his ludicrous little dance around the room.

Valjhar could not help but smile. "Does that thought please you so much?"

"Oh, yes. You have no idea. All these years, out here among the stars...Pimsie refusing to bear a child unless it could be raised on Rral. But who knows when that will be possible? Who knows if it will ever be? Now...now she has a reason to change her mind. She will have a child. At heart

I'm practically a kid myself, Valjhar. You should know that, even though you've all grown up around me. A child. And it will be Shaula."

"Well…it would be a version of Shaula. But unless we figure out how to transfer her mind, it won't really *be* Shaula. And we don't have much time. Shaula is fading fast. I think she's exhausted the last of her strength."

Kern halted and grew serious. Valjhar could see him exercising his admirable brain.

"We need to slow, arrest, or reverse her deterioration."

"Yes."

"What about her entropic weapon?"

That struck Valjhar as a complete non-sequitur. He thought it over for a few moments before venturing, "We've only seen her use it to disorganize and degrade matter and energy."

"Yes, that fits with its usual use as a weapon."

"You think it could do the reverse?"

"Maybe it could. It changes the rate of entropy in a system. Yes, I know, we've never understood how that's possible. As far as we know, entropy is not a force that can be manipulated or controlled. It's simply the tendency of a system to become disorganized and lose usable energy over time."

"It's a very strong tendency," said Valjhar.

"Yes, but not an absolute one. I've always tried not to think too hard about that weapon. I think it's beyond any science I understand."

"It hurts my brain to even think about how entropy could possibly be reversed. Exactly what kind of order would be established? How would the weapon 'know' what a more organized state was, let alone a more desirable one?"

"I agree, but maybe it can manipulate probability somehow to slow the process? Where is the thing, anyway?"

"In Shaula's cabin, I think."

"Let's go take a look at it."

They entered the austere, neglected confines of Shaula's quarters, which still bore the faint scent of her body and clothing. To Valjhar it felt like entering a tomb.

The weapon was easily found in a drawer, along with a hairbrush and a few other items. Valjhar silently vowed to use that brush to tend to Shaula's hair at his next opportunity.

Kern picked up the weapon and examined it closely. It was a fist-sized glossy grey spheroid with a handhold sculpted into it, and otherwise featureless.

"Have you ever tried to use this thing, Valjhar?"

"No."

"Me neither. Let me see if I can do anything with it, preferably without rotting a hole in the hull and admitting all that stinky water."

But the device remained inert on Kern's hand.

"It's as I thought. The thing has no obvious controls. I've never seen Shaula do more than raise it, and then something terrible happens to something or someone nearby. I'm afraid she's the only one who can use it."

Valjhar frowned. "I think you're right. In that case— let's give it to her."

"What, in her condition?"

"Yes, I want to try it. Who knows what level of control she really has over it? Who knows what it can really do? It's a tool from another universe, devised by beings who can apparently fashion marvels surpassing even this one. Come on."

Valjhar led the way to the medikum, where he confronted Shaula's frail, wasted form with the same shock he always felt on seeing it. He sat beside her bed and slipped the weapon onto her hand. He spoke to her as Kern watched with wide eyes.

"Shaula, we're working on saving you, but we need more time. I've given you your weapon. If you can, use it to slow your decline. Please."

"Valjhar...what if she uses it to...to..."

"To end herself? Then that will be her choice, and I'll respect it." These words burned like red-hot coals in Valjhar's throat.

"But you..."

"Me?" Valjhar whirled to look at Kern. Whatever Kern saw in his eyes caused him to flinch. "I don't care about me. All I care about is whatever is best for Shaula."

Valjhar looked back at Shaula. Her eyes were half open, glittering through her lashes, regarding him. Though she was unable to speak, Valjhar knew from her eyes that her intention was formed and was not to be altered.

Something changed in the room. Though the entropic weapon produced no visible manifestation of its power, nevertheless its influence could be felt in some indescribable way.

Suddenly filled with mortal fear, Valjhar stared at Shaula, half expecting to see her dissolve into dust.

What happened instead came as a profound relief. An aura of inexplicable calm descended around Shaula.

Pimsie, alerted to the situation through some means unknown to the boys, ran into the room and eyed the instruments that monitored her. "She's more stable now. We have some time. Let's get started on preparing a viable Shaula-zygote. When it's ready, Kern, I'll expect you to do the honor of implanting it in me. Right now I think I have some hormones I need to release." With a sigh, Pimsie ambled out of the medikum.

Kern and Valjhar looked at each other. Now the main problem that remained was how in the world to transfer Shaula's mind to a new and infantile body. The thought of it made Valjhar feel faint. It would be like transferring a wisp of smoke from one place to another. If it lost its shape, all would be lost.

Chapter 18
The White Monk

Rouse's head snapped back from a terrible blow as the gun erupted. Her vision blurred, and her ears rang.

Shot in the head, again? she thought. And yet she remained on her feet.

She peered forward at the terrorist chief's shifting figure. Something was wrong with him. He appeared to be sagging on his feet. Squinting, Rouse made out that his nose had been destroyed and was gushing blood. Rouse didn't want to see that grisly sight, so she stepped forward and shoved him as hard as she could. He went flying, shattering the windshield, and taking another gunman with him for good measure. They had exited the bus, as she'd demanded.

The plate. The plate in her skull! The bullet must have bounced off it and returned to the one who had fired it. Rouse laughed in disbelief. If something that ridiculous could happen, what then was impossible?

Her senses rapidly clearing, Rouse whirled to confront the third man. In his eyes she saw a terror exceeding that of the people he had intended to murder.

"You are a devil!" he blurted.

Rouse lunged forward and yanked the weapon from his grasp. Immediately he was transformed from a serious threat to a wide-eyed, cowering teenager who she could probably beat up with her bare hands. Someone screamed.

"You may leave the bus," said Rouse. "Tell your friends outside to leave as well, unless they want me to deal with them in the same devilish manner."

Breathing heavily, the boy squeezed past her in the aisle, making no attempt to reclaim his weapon. When he had passed, Rouse noted vaguely that he had a smear of blood on his jacket.

Rouse watched through the windows as the boy stumbled out and began to chatter at the other men. They spoke back and forth so rapidly that Rouse had no chance of following any of it. Gradually all those armed men began to glance at the bus with eyes shaded with growing doubt and uncertainty. Their leader made a dismissive gesture and turned as though to board the bus, but the boy flung himself at him and clung to his arm, speaking loudly and desperately. A few of the others clustered around Rouse's first two victims where they lay inert on the roadway. They could see her easily through the bus's shattered windshield. Rouse made sure to answer their fearful glances with a resolute glare. The gun was still in her grip, but she let it dangle from one finger as though it were the most inconsequential thing in the world.

After further arguing in a language Rouse wished she understood, the leader ultimately threw up his hands, bellowed a curse toward the bus, and led his remaining men back the way they had come, abandoning the fallen where they lay.

The passengers in the bus raised a ragged cheer. The driver began to speak urgently into a radio while casting furtive glances at Rouse.

Rouse smiled grimly at the retreating men. She leaned against a seat back, dizzy from the shock of her strange and unexpected victory.

"Susan, you're covered with blood!" said Amy.

Rouse nodded absently. "Time will take care of that. It will dry."

"It's your own blood! You've been shot!"

Rouse raised her hand. Suddenly she was not eager to learn what that bullet had done to her scalp, but yes, she was bleeding.

"Not only there."

Rouse looked down at herself. Her jacket was soaked with a spreading stain of blood. That last fanatic must have gotten off a shot that Rouse had somehow failed to notice in the intensity of their confrontation.

Rouse lifted her clothing to bare her abdomen. Yes, there was the wound...a small, neat hole an inch or two above her navel. She noted how it expanded and contracted slightly as she breathed. So, one of those miserable little metal pellets had gotten through after all.

"Susan, let me see it!" said Amy.

Rouse turned toward her. Amy's expression grew anguished.

"Susan, that's a very serious wound. Unless we can get you to a hospital—"

"Wait, what's that?" That was Zahoor, who had left his seat and moved back among them. He was staring at Rouse's belly.

Something was projecting slightly from Rouse's wound. She tensed her abdominal muscles, which hurt, but caused whatever it was protrude further. Rouse reached down and plucked it out. It was the bullet.

"Well, isn't that interesting," said Rouse.

"At that range, that bullet should have gone right through you and hit someone behind you," said Zahoor.

"I know. I think it didn't kill me because...well."

"Go on," said Zahoor.

"Because of the contempt I felt for the gun and the man wielding it. I know, that sounds ridiculous. It *is* ridiculous. What a delightfully ridiculous world this is turning out to be."

"I think that is very much a matter of one's personal point of view."

"Who is this man?" said Kevin.

"Oh, I'm sorry, this is my friend Zahoor," said Rouse.

"I'm sorry I was so useless during that unfortunate incident. I'll try to do better in the future."

"You may get your chance soon enough," said Rouse. "I don't think those men will give up on us so easily. In fact I think we should get everyone away from here as soon as possible. Driver?"

The driver, who had been sitting in a daze, started at hearing himself addressed. He looked back at Rouse with apprehension.

"Driver? Have you called out for help?"

The driver only blinked at her in fear and incomprehension. Zahoor cleared this throat and posed the same question in his own language, prompting the driver to fumble for his microphone.

"He is doing so now," said Zahoor. "I'm not sure how long we can afford to wait, however."

"I agree," said Rouse. "I think we should leave now, and head to the nearest village."

"Wait," said Amy in a shaky voice. "You still have an open wound in your abdomen, and your scalp is torn. I have a few butterflies in my first aid kit, and the rest I can stitch if they run out."

Rouse was encouraged to hear this, not because she was very worried about her injuries, but because Amy had taken note of them and proposed to do something to help, rather than collapse. "All right, Amy, thanks very much."

Rouse sat down and watched the other passengers as Amy rummaged through her bags. They all looked about as uncertain as the bus driver, seemingly too frightened and disoriented to do much of anything.

"All right, Susan, sit still as I tend to your scalp. That's a nasty wound. It's torn your temporal muscle, too."

Rouse hissed as Amy began to manipulate her scalp. The pain burned as Amy used butterflies to bind the edges together.

In an attempt to keep things light, Rouse said "It's a good thing that bullet hit the plate in my skull, eh?"

"Plate?" said Amy distractedly.

"Yes, that big plate, it can't have missed it."

"Susan, I don't see any evidence of a plate in your skull."

Once again the world seemed to turn upside down in Rouse's mind.

"No plate?"

"No. All I see here looks like ordinary bone to me."

Rouse fell silent. No plate? What could that mean? She knew it was there...or had been there. Could it have been grown over with bone, or somehow absorbed?

And did that mean the first bullet had simply bounced off her skull?

Rouse blinked and forced these thoughts from her mind. She didn't have time to think about all this now. If the world was beginning to seem like an illusion, she must ignore it for now, for the sake of all these others who didn't see things in quite the same way. This was a time for action. Everyone on this bus was still in danger.

Rouse didn't like the wan, feathery tone of Amy's voice as she said, "I—I'll sew up this belly wound—but if you move around much it'll tear right open again. You really need a hospital."

"Thank you, Amy, but we'll all have to move around, and soon. Even if those men don't return, I'm not keen to spend the night in this bus."

"But where can we go? Why did we ever come to this terrible place? I want to go home." Amy clutched herself and began to shake and whimper. It was obvious to Rouse that she had exhausted her limited store of strength. Rouse exchanged a glance with Kevin. Clearly he shared Rouse's concern. The poor man was grey with worry.

Rouse pulled down her shirt, sat close beside Amy, and spoke gently to her. "Amy, I know how you're hurting. It wasn't that long ago that I was in the same sort of fix as you. I know how hopeless things feel for you right now, and how frightening. The world is so big and so beyond your control, and you're so small. We're going to find a good, safe place for you to be. Don't give up yet. Wonderful things are not far away, and we will get you to them."

Amy did not respond, but only withdrew more deeply into herself.

Rouse felt the inadequacy of the words she had offered. She did know and could remember how it felt to succumb to such despair, though now it was more like recalling the compassion she had felt for a younger and more foolish sister. She also recalled how trite and meaningless such words of support had always felt to her. Amy was beyond the help of any mere words. Helping her would take more than anything Rouse knew how to offer.

A cold, wet wind blew through the bus's shattered windows. It ruffled Rouse's hair and caused everyone around her to huddle into their clothes.

Somehow, it also gave Rouse an idea. She stood up suddenly.

"Come on, Kevin, Zahoor, help me get Amy up. We're leaving."

"Where are we going?" said Kevin.

"We're taking Amy to see the White Monk."

Zahoor looked at her skeptically. "The White Monk? I had never even heard of this person before that criminal mentioned him. He's probably only some local legend, or an attempt to attract tourists."

"Maybe so," said Rouse. "Why not ask these others if any have heard of him?"

Zahoor shrugged and did as she suggested. A few people spoke up tentatively.

"A few of them say they have heard of him, but that proves nothing. Some have doubtlessly heard of Santa Claus as well."

"I think I shall take Amy to look for him anyway."

"Don't I have anything to say about this?" said Kevin sharply. "I think our so-called vacation is over. All I want right now is to take Amy to a place where she can be flown out of here."

"I'm sorry, Kevin, you're right of course. Right now I believe we're somewhere between Chilas and Gilgit, right Zahoor?"

Zahoor nodded.

"Which is closer?"

Zahoor consulted the driver. "He says we're considerably closer to Gilgit."

"All right then, we'll make for Gilgit, shall we, Kevin?" said Rouse.

"I'm not convinced we shouldn't just wait here for help."

"I wouldn't advise that," said Zahoor. "Those fanatics are likely to work themselves up to trying again, and this time they'll probably just shoot up the bus from the outside without trying to sort out who they think deserves to die. They've been humiliated by a woman, and such men do not accept that easily. I promise you, they are closer than any possible help."

"And Gilgit? We'll find help there?"

Zahoor hesitated. "Well, some of those men undoubtedly came from there. But police and government forces are also there. Probably some are on their way to us now."

Kevin looked out the window. Clouds had settled in, bringing on a premature evening gloom. He sighed.

"All right, I see your point. Let's go."

Rouse nodded. "Zahoor, please tell everyone our plan and get them moving."

Zahoor attempted to comply, but his words only raised a flurry of objections from the driver and the other passengers. After a brief and heated discussion Zahoor turned back to Rouse with a look of defeat and chagrin.

"They will not go with us. They say the terrorists will now see you as their main enemy, and ignore them. They may well be right."

"All right then, let them stay, or go off on their own, as they will. Come on, you three."

But Zahoor looked troubled and uncertain. By now Rouse was growing a bit exasperated by her thwarted need to act.

"What's this, Zahoor? You said yourself it was too dangerous to stay here."

"Yes—Susan, that is true. And our friend did ask me to keep an eye on you. But, here are all these other people as well, and I'm not sure I should leave them here to their own devices."

Rouse nodded reluctantly. She could make no good argument against this.

"Besides—from what I have seen of you, I don't think my modest skills will be of any great use to you."

Rouse sniffed at this flattery. "All right, Zahoor, so be it. Good luck to you. Kevin, we've debated long enough. Let's get moving. I'm afraid you have too much luggage to carry. Bring only what you need—warm clothes, any food you might have."

Kevin nodded and began to root through their bags. Rouse resumed her place beside Amy and put her arm around her. "Amy, Amy, we need to go, and now. Can you walk?"

Amy said nothing, but only rocked back and forth and trembled. Her face was buried in her knees. Amy's pain flowed out of her like a tide. Rouse felt it, and a tide flowed from her as well, a tide of compassion.

"Come on, Amy," she whispered. "I'll get you out of here."

Outside the bus, Kevin picked up an automatic weapon one of the fleeing men had dropped and slung it over his shoulder.

Rouse looked at it uneasily. "Do you know how to use that thing?"

"Not exactly, but I'm sure I can figure it out."

"I'd appreciate it if you'd leave it behind."

Kevin shook his head. "No. No offense, but I'd prefer to be able to do something, if it comes to that."

"If you must. Could you at least figure out where the safety is before we go bumping along with it?"

A few minutes later the trio was moving east along the highway, away from the warmth and the deceptive safety of the bus. Rouse was carrying the unresponsive Amy, who felt like no great burden in Rouse's arms. They approached the rockfall that blocked the road. Rouse nimbly skipped over the still-settling boulders. Kevin, who carried only a small subset of their baggage along with his new weapon, had a more difficult time scrambling over the unstable pile.

On the other side, now separated both visually and psychologically from the bus, Kevin moved closer to Rouse and muttered, "Rowz Farewell."

"Roose. It's pronounced Roose. What gave me away?"

"Your short hair isn't that much of a disguise. I might not have paid too much attention to the resemblance, but you did sort of call attention to yourself."

"Well, I didn't intend to. Or want to."

"I know. We've dragged you into our orbit by being so helpless and naive. And now here you are striding along, carrying my wife as if she were a kitten. And you seem to be at least semi-bulletproof. I had thought you were just some crazy kidnap victim, but now I don't know what to think."

Rouse laughed. "Neither do I, really. I'm beginning to see things in a very strange way. I would call it a dissociative disorder. I would call it a delusion, except it appears to be affecting the outside world, and that doesn't normally happen in a delusion. Thanks for calling me by my right name, by the way. I was getting tired of that charade."

Kevin gestured ahead, to where the vast mass of Nanga Parbat could be guessed at through thickening clouds. "So, this town we're heading for, Gilgit…it's near that mountain?"

"I think so."

"And that also happens to be the direction of the White Monk, right?"

Rouse smiled sheepishly. "Yes, I suppose it is."

"Why are you so interested in him? Do you know something about him?"

Rouse thought for a moment. "No, I've never heard of him before. But something tells me he's someone I want to meet. And I'm guessing even a fraudulent mystic is more likely to help Amy than anyone else we're likely to find in Gilgit. I think she's fallen asleep now, the poor woman."

"It's probably her medications," said Kevin dully. "I got some down her just before we left. I was afraid she'd become hysterical and melt down completely."

With no clear idea of how far they had to go, they marched along at their best pace with a steep rocky slope on their right and a deep plunge to the raging Indus on their left. The road was rough and rutted, unpaved, a track barely worthy of the name. They encountered no traffic. Rouse guessed this was because word of the blockage had gotten out, or maybe because no one cared to travel in the storm that seemed to be settling over the area.

After a mile or so Kevin insisted on carrying Amy himself for a while. Rouse handed her over. Kevin staggered along for a quarter of a mile, panting in the high altitude, until his knees seemed about to buckle. Rouse accepted Amy back without a word. They continued on. Kevin's head was bowed.

"How do you do it? Nothing seems to touch you."

"I'm just not letting myself take any of this too seriously."

"Any of what?"

"The world."

"That makes no sense. You can't just ignore the world and expect to shrug off everything it can do to you. The world is not an illusion. It won't bend itself to your will."

"That's what I used to think. I was so convinced that I tried to escape the world the only way I knew how, by killing myself. But I was thwarted. I became a mental patient. But I escaped or was abducted, I don't remember which. Some say aliens did it. Then I was shot in the head. Someone saved me with surgery that seems to have vanished. Then I spent months at a Buddhist monastery. Then I was shot twice more, and yet I'm still walking along, on a dim, wild mountainside road in Pakistan with a troubled woman in my arms and a disturbingly awesome mountain hidden in the clouds in front of me. And I think there was more as well, things I no longer remember, but great things nevertheless. It's hard to experience all this and come away with the same sense of the solidity and immutability of the world I had when I was ten."

"What if you actually succeeded at suicide?"

"What?"

"What if you really did kill yourself, and this has all been some grandiose vision generated by your dying brain?"

Rouse looked aside at Kevin with a small smile. "That's an interesting hypothesis. I'll just ask you. Are you a figment of my imagination?"

"No, but of course that's what I'd say."

"Still, I'll have to take your word for it."

Amy began to stir and soon blearily asked to be put down. She proved able to walk at a slow and shaky pace, though she barely raised her eyes from her feet. Rouse gave Amy her jacket, as she was shivering, while Rouse herself felt warm enough. She became aware that she was bleeding from her belly wound, though there was no pain. She began to wonder which would prevail: her new view of the world, or the loss of blood that could stop her from having any views at all. It would be an interesting contest.

The day grew darker and colder, and it began to snow, not unusual at these heights, even in June. Rouse's best guess was that Gilgit was about forty kilometers away. She kept this estimate to herself, as she knew this was the longest march she could hope to get out of her companions, if not longer, and she didn't wish to discourage them. More than anything she hoped they'd be intercepted by rescue vehicles coming from the town, though a truck full of armed terrorists was at least as likely. It was also possible that help was approaching from Chilas, behind them, from which they were cut off.

Sensing that her thoughts were turning too inward, Rouse forced herself to become more mindful of her surroundings. The sad, grand landscape around her was composed of various shades of grey, except for the minty green of the Indus and the thickening whiteness of the falling snow. As yet the snow was not accumulating, but the temperature was still dropping. She looked overhead. Clouds flowed by like an inverted range of huge, rounded peaks, alternately hiding and revealing the more angular peaks of stone that thrust up all around. Still far ahead, Nanga Parbat could no longer be seen, but could still be sensed as an ominous, unattainable presence, a terrific mass whose summit probably rose above these clouds and into the last sunlight of the fading day.

Luckily the wind was not yet strong. Rouse could still hear the roar of the river far below, the distant cry of a falcon, and even the patter of wet snowflakes falling on stone.

She also began to hear a vehicle approaching from ahead. She turned to Kevin and Amy, speaking quickly.

"Someone is coming. You two go back. Find a place to hide if you can. I'll meet them, whoever it is."

Her companions did as they were told without argument. The falling snow soon hid them from view. Rouse looked around. She spied a flat-topped boulder that over-hung the road about four meters up the mountainside. She made a running approach and scrambled up to it, perching atop it and waiting.

Soon she heard voices over the rumble of the oncoming engine. Angry voices, not what she would expect from a rescue team.

Rouse tensed, crouching atop the rock. Around the bend came a battered black pickup truck. Sitting exposed in the bed were six bearded men cradling rifles and automatic weapons. Rouse recognized some of those men. She froze as they drew nearer.

Now remember, Rouse, she told herself, *bullets are puny, contemptible things. They can't hurt you if you don't let them.*

Gunfire cracked and echoed from somewhere behind her. The truck's windshield shattered and crumbled, as did the driver's head. The truck veered toward the wall, struck it. Rouse thought it might catch behind a rock and stall, but the nearly headless driver was flung into the wheel, turning it and the truck away from the wall. It careened over the edge, vanishing with the receding cries of the men who tumbled from the back. The sound of the truck's many crashes and impacts grew fainter and fainter.

Soon there was silence.

Rouse looked back. There in the road stood Kevin, wild-eyed and panting, the barrel of his weapon still wav-ing around. Rouse judged that he had exhausted its ammu-nition.

Kevin turned away, bent over, vomited, then sat down heavily by the side of the road, still breathing heavily.

"God damn this place," he muttered.

"You know, Kevin, I was hoping to take over that truck and get us to safety that much sooner," said Rouse mildly. "And now look what you've done to yourself. You'll never be the same after what you've done. Never the same."

Kevin looked around wildly into the gloom, taking several seconds to spot her atop her perch. "And what were you going to do?" he demanded. "Pounce on them?"

"Yes."

A blast of wind came roaring through the valley. It staggered Kevin, and nearly knocked Rouse off her boulder. She crouched lower and turned to face it, feeling snow and sleet driven into her face.

The gust passed, leaving Rouse shaking her head, wondering if the world were trying to tell her something.

She hopped down from her perch, landing just as Amy came tottering into view, clutching herself. Her face was grey with stress and tension. "What was it?" she wailed. "What were those shots?"

Kevin dropped his empty weapon and went to her. "It's nothing, sweetie, it's all over."

Rouse cautiously approached the edge of the road, a crumbing, irregular brink that looked down onto an almost sheer drop of thousands of feet. She saw no sign of the truck. She did see a man laying on his back on a tiny ledge about six or seven meters down. He was alive but unmoving. He and Rouse looked into each other's eyes for a long moment.

The world seemed to tilt in Rouse's eyes and she nearly toppled into the abyss. She stumbled back, still dizzy. She looked down. Blood stained much of her clothing.

"I'm beginning to think I might lose this race," she muttered to herself.

"What race?"

Rouse looked aside. Kevin was approaching her with a puzzled, wary expression. Amy sat on a boulder by the cliff face with her head bowed. She looked depleted, far more beaten and defeated than Rouse felt.

"Nothing," said Rouse. "Let's get moving. We've still far to go."

They trudged along the snow-swept road at the best pace Amy could manage. Rouse and Ken walked close beside her on either side, shielding her from the cold as best they could.

Rouse herself was beginning to falter from loss of blood. The more she dwelt on it, the more she thought about it, the more it affected her, and the nearer came the end of her endurance.

Knowing this, she forced her mind outward from herself and into her surroundings. The sound of their footsteps penetrated into the naked rock beneath their feet, down the sheer side of the mountain, down to the level of the flowing river, and still farther down. The weight of the mountains crushed the land, and the mass of the Earth itself drew them toward its core, working to overcome the strength that supported their thrust toward the sky. Far beneath the mountain roots were layers and zones of matter pressed into increasingly strange and unfamiliar forms by all the weight atop them. There also were many mysteries that so far no one had seen or realized, and increasing heat, trapped in the depths for billions of years, until finally the core burned with a heat and a light that could never be seen, because there was no vantage point from which any known being equipped with eyes could step back and see it. And yet this incandescent mass was but a few thousand miles beneath their feet, a distance small enough to cover in a few hours in an airplane, yet cut off forever from all direct human knowledge.

Leaving the ancient rumble of those hot depths behind, Rouse considered the sky. Now only a trace of light penetrated the storm, a churning zone of cold and ice. Above them the frigid air was blue-black with the last glow of dusk. A short distance higher still and there was no air to scatter the rays of the sun.

And beyond that...

The Earth quickly dwindled in Rouse's mind, as though it were being drawn away by some outside force. Soon it was lost among the stars, where she confronted a boundless space in which everything she knew or believed was utterly lost amid mysteries far beyond the grasp of the humans peering outward with blurry vision from their tiny home. And yet she knew—somehow—that somewhere among these infinite stars was a handful of small beings creeping fitfully from star to star, taking in what knowledge they could, with minds that were arranged in ways not quite like her own.

With a final spasm of vertigo she came back to herself and found to her surprise that she was still walking along a stony, icy road with human legs and a human body, with two other human creatures beside her. Looking aside at Amy, Rouse began to reel again. Somehow she saw past the surface of her skin and clothing, a trivial perception of the reflection of light alone. Within her was a universe similar in magnitude to the starry universe that contained her body, and far more turbulent and chaotic. The surface of that inner world was simple enough, like a single voice singing a constant song of confusion and pain, but beneath that were many other voices, shouting and scolding and pleading, at odds with one another, blind to each other, and mostly blind to the wellsprings of their origin. All these voices bobbed and drifted in an internal sea of darkness. Far off in its depths were openings that led to other realms, of which neither Amy nor Rouse knew anything, but they were blocked by films and slimes that drifted down from above, and could not be entered.

"Rouse? Rouse!"

Kevin's urgent voice snapped Rouse back to what she'd always considered the real world, just in time to stop her from stepping off the edge of the cliff.

"It's all right," she said shakily. "I don't think anything would have happened."

"You don't think anything would have happened if you'd fallen? Rouse, are you going crazy too?"

Rouse heard the angry desperation in Kevin's voice. He didn't want to be left in charge of two crazy women in this inhospitable place. He didn't feel he was up to it. But what could she say?

"Yes, Kevin, I do think I'm going crazy, at least by any standard you've encountered. It's very strange, what I'm experiencing, but not bad or harmful, I think. I'll do my best to stay with you in this world for as long as you and Amy need me."

"That's reassuring. What's pulling you away, if I may ask?"

Rouse shook her head in bewilderment. "I'm just not seeing things the way a normal person does. But I don't really mind. It seems like an adventure. An inner adventure, happening at the same time as this outer one."

Kevin continued to speak, but his words dissolved into mere noise in Rouse's mind. As she looked at him and Amy, she found to her astonishment that she no longer perceived them as people, not in the sense of their being the default units of life and consciousness in the universe, the standard against which all others must be measured. Instead they were now very particular creatures, tottering ahead with their two-legged gait, with their knobby skulls thinly covered by complex sheets of muscle interspersed with nerves and blood vessels, protected by a fragile skin. Their form was only one of an infinite number of possible arrangements of matter that could be inhabited by consciousness. She herself was such a thing. A tiny thing, a weird arrangement of meat and liquids and bone.

"I don't think your laughter is appropriate!" cried an indignant Kevin, finally breaking through Rouse's thoughts. For a moment she perceived his words as strange and arbitrary noises barked out by some animal, until she forced herself to remember what they were supposed to mean.

She laughed again. "What could be more appropriate? We are these preposterous creatures, living in one of any number of ludicrous cultures, in this preposterous world. The universe doesn't revolve around us. Nor does this planet. Our self-regard is magnified beyond all propriety. It's the truth. We can either laugh, or we can continue in our delusions."

Kevin could only shake his head. Amy turned to face her, looking at her with pleading eyes, as though begging Rouse not to pull her even farther from sanity than she was inclined to wander on her own. Rouse immediately appreciated her point of view and grew silent.

For their sake, Rouse forced herself not to allow her thoughts and insights to go too far afield, though she was convinced she still had much else to learn, or to realize. The practical implications of her evolving perceptions remained to be explored.

On they trudged. The brief tingle of every blowing snowflake that struck her face seemed to Rouse like a delightful revelation.

The mountainside on their left began to lean over more and more, until it actually hung over the roadway, resulting in something like a tunnel open only on the right. It grew very dark. The only light they had was whatever slight moonlight that managed to filter through the clouds. It was dangerous to continue like this, when any crack or obstacle in the road could easily go unseen. But it would be still more dangerous to stop, for then her charges would surely freeze.

The road remained more or less level, but the sound of the river grew steadily louder, as though it were rising to meet them, as indeed it was as they drew closer to Gilgit. Its roar was magnified by the sound of unseen rapids still far below.

Presently another, rougher roar made itself heard, and with it an occasional gleam of yellow light, far ahead.

"Another truck is coming," said Rouse.

"Good or bad?" said Kevin.

"Good for us. I'll make sure of that, this time. No need for guns, right?"

"I already emptied the one I had."

"Then please drop it."

"If it looks like I'm still armed—"

"You'll be gunned down all the quicker. Drop it."

Chapter 19
Desperation

Pimsie Flam was pregnant with an embryo identical to Shaula, except for the very careful alterations to her genome that would result in her being born as a true Rralian. Carrying this novel life-form in her gently swelling belly, Pimsie went about her business silently and serenely.

Her silence was caused by embarrassment. Her teeth had grown over, covered by tissue that was renewing their outer layer of crystalline carbon, years before it was necessary. This premature onset was a common side effect of pregnancy. It was harmless, but Pimsie was reluctant to speak with her temporarily slurred, lisping voice, let alone to display a mouthful of puffy pink flesh. At least her smile would be extra sparkly when the process was complete.

Pimsie's pregnancy was the simple, easy part of the extremely complicated procedure Valjhar had envisioned. Some of the details had yet to be worked out, including some critical ones.

The real, original Shaula remained in desperate condition, despite the stabilizing influence of her entropic device. The delicate configuration of her imperiled brain contained the one thing most important to Valjhar: her mind and personality.

Stingray took over the day-to-day running of the ship, leaving Valjhar, Pimsie, and Kern free to consider the problem of mind transference while *Mote* drifted peacefully, far below the billowing surface of Flamaria's unbounded sea. By now they would have begun using the Ladderite's native name for the planet, but as its literal meaning was simply "the World" and could not be transliterated into spoken language, they kept to their own invention.

"I'm so grateful that you two have taken an interest and learned to make yourselves useful in this project," said Kern. "You know I'm very fond of thinking, but the amount of thinking needed to solve this puzzle would have frazzled my brain."

Valjhar had little patience left for his friend's frivolity. "We do still need you to devote your brain to some important topics. What progress have you made about the problem of data storage?"

Kern instantly became glum and downcast. "Not very much. Let's say we do devise a way to record the state of Shaula's mind to the required level of detail and accuracy. That much I think we can manage. I'm working on it. But, the amount of information produced will exceed all the storage capacity we have aboard the ship by a factor of about three hundred thousand. Despite everything I've learned from the Compendium, I don't know how to add that much storage potential, at least not here aboard the ship. Maybe if I could construct a big facility on some moon or solid planet I might eventually succeed, but not while we're trapped here, in this little ship, with such limited resources."

The answer was as Valjhar had expected and feared. He looked down at the table around which they were seated, thinking, trying to master his emotions so he could speak again without causing pain or hurt to his friends. He was exhausted. For weeks he'd been living with a tension and sense of imminent doom more unrelenting than any he'd ever known.

"What could we accomplish with the data storage capacity we do possess, or could conceivably add under our limited circumstances?" he said carefully.

Kern shrugged. "I don't know. None of us knows how much a person's nature depends on the exact arrangement of every neuron, electrical charge, molecule, and quantum state in their brain. We don't know how much of that information can be sacrificed without losing the essence of that person. Maybe most of it is nothing but random noise, but how much, and which? But here's my guess. Even if I purged the ship's systems of all the data we can spare, including a lot of stuff I'd hate to lose, and filled it with as much of Shaula as we could squeeze in, I doubt we could restore more than a very partial, shallow, incomplete version of her. I think she would be...like a flat drawing of Shaula, or maybe like another person who would share some traits or memories with her."

Valjhar still did not look up. His lips compressed. He was having difficulty controlling himself.

Pimsie leaned over to him and laid her hand on his arm. She hesitated, then hid her mouth behind her other hand before speaking.

"Valjhar, the worft thing that can happen now ith that I'll give birf to a new verthin of Thaula."

Valjhar looked up at her and saw her falter at the sight of his face. "Yes, Pimsie. And she would be your daughter, and Kern's. And you would love her and care for her well, I know. She might even be given the name of Shaula. But she would never be my Shaula. She would see me as — an uncle, and she would always wonder at the sadness she saw in my eyes whenever I looked at her."

"That might be the beft we can do," whispered Pimsie.

"Yes, it might," said Kern. "We might have to accept that."

Valjhar looked at Kern's somber face. For once, his romantically-minded younger friend found himself in the position of urging Valjhar to face reality.

Stingray had left the bridge long enough to listen in on their discussion. Now he shifted in his giant chair, twice the size of theirs. By now Valjhar had gained some ability to interpret the expressions on his great, angular face. Now it showed puzzlement and impatience, he thought.

"Stingray? Do you have something to add?"

Stingray spoke slowly. "Well, Valjhar, of course I'm not as well versed in science as any of you, but I do think I have some ability to take in a situation and make an analysis. I think you're all overlooking the obvious."

"And what is that?"

"This ship is surrounded by massive data-storage capacity. It's called the Ladderites. Really, you've already had them simulate the effects of your genetic tampering. Why not hand this task off to them as well?"

Valjhar was faintly irritated by this suggestion. "I had actually considered that, but I prefer to keep this among ourselves if we possible can. I hesitate to entrust that utterly irreplaceable information to...outsiders."

"You mean to weird aliens?"

"Yes, if that's how you want to put it." Valjhar did not feel like bandying words with the gigantic oaf. He'd be lucky if he kept his temper.

"All right, Valjhar, have it your way. But what about your Compendium?"

"What about it?"

"It seems able to store a vast amount of information. Can't you store Shaula's information on it?"

Valjhar was startled; this he had never considered.

But Kern shook his head. He produced the Compendium, which he rarely allowed to stray from his person, and spun it on its edge on the table. "No. I've come to understand the Compendium to some degree. It doesn't actually store much information, if any. Instead, it accesses it somehow, from some other source. In fact I suspect the information might be stored somehow in the quantum foam that underlies all existence, available to anyone who knows how to access it."

Stingray lowered his head in thought. "So you can't use either the Ladderites or the Compendium," he murmured.

"Yooth boaf," said Pimsie. Her face flushed and she clamped her hands over her mouth.

"What?" said Valjhar in annoyance.

"She said 'Use both', Valjhar. Don't be mean," said Kern. "But Pimsie, what do you mean, exactly?"

But Pimsie would say no more.

"Wait," said Stingray. "Pimsie's suggestion is a good one. It might be possible to get the data into the Compendium indirectly."

Kern brightened. "Yes! We know the surrounding nebula is embedded with ancient Rralian beacons that have something to do with the Ladderites and their function of broadcasting Rralian information. If we feed Shaula's data to the Ladderites, and ask them to broadcast it as they did long ago, it might find its way into our Compendium!"

Valjhar looked up with a wary hope that he did not trust. "That's interesting. It should be easy enough to test that idea. Offer the Ladderites some tidbit of information they couldn't possibly already have. Ask them to send it out through the beacons."

Kern eagerly agreed. In a few moments he selected a bit of Earthly music he'd collected, a strange song about traversing the universe, by a small group of musicians who took their name from a large family of insects.

The Ladderites readily complied with their request. The song appeared on the Compendium almost at once.

Now Valjhar couldn't contain his elation. He jumped up and joined Kern and Pimsie in dancing around their little meeting room. Stingray remained seated, smiling disconcertingly.

"Now all we have to do is figure out how to obtain the data before Shaula dies!" cried Kern. His face instantly fell as he realized how poorly he had phrased that. The dance ended and their mood immediately crashed.

The mood worsened even more a few moments later when a hated and feared alarm sounded throughout the ship.

"No!" wailed Pimsie. "Not now! Not now!"

The four of them rushed up to the bridge to consult their instruments. Many Ladderites were orbiting the ship, their lights flickering nervously, their motions abrupt and anxious. Valjhar ignored them while studying a console and its projected readouts.

"There's no mistake. It's the Prohibitor, heading directly for us." He closed his eyes and clenched a futile fist. "It's my fault. It must have detected the new addition to the Rralian database, realized it must have come through us, and perhaps even pinpointed the source of the transmission. I was a fool."

"No time to worry about that now," said Stingray. "We must prepare to fight."

"Fight? We can't fight that. We can't even flee. All that thing has to do is get close enough to open the ship to the sea, and we're all dead."

Stingray stared at him in disbelief. "I would accuse you of joking, but I've never observed that your sense of humor is highly developed. You can't win? Okay, maybe not. You can't even *fight?* You, with all your incredible technology and superweapons? I know you've been having a rough time lately, Valjhar, but surely you can put up a better showing than that. Otherwise, maybe you should have stayed back on your cozy home planet. This space exploration thing seems to be too much for you."

Valjhar was about to make an angry retort when a blue glare filtered through the bubble field and lit the bridge with a harsh light. *Mote* shuddered and listed to dockside. Kern hurried over the tilting deck to a set of display projectors.

"One of the empty compartments on the dockside has been breached and flooded. We're sinking."

"This is it, then," said Valjhar, with a strange, resigned emotion that was almost relief.

"I'm ejecting the ballast in the keel," said Kern. "I don't want the ship to sink into the Ladderite city and hurt them too."

Mote began to rise. The list grew no worse. The three Rralians huddled together, awaiting the end, while Stingray paced the deck in angry frustration.

After three minutes, nothing more had happened.

"I've had enough of this," said Stingray. "I'm going down there to see what's going on." He thundered down the stairwell.

Kern and Valjhar looked at each other, shrugged, and followed. rushing off to don the engineering suit and dimension belt, respectively. They met again in a corridor on the third deck down, the deck with the flooded compartment. There was no sign of Stingray or the Prohibitor.

Pimsie had accompanied Kern to their rendezvous.

"I tried to get her to stay behind," said Kern, who was now encased in the glassy red, black and gold engineering suit.

"Don't be thilly," said Pimsie. "I'm not going to die alone in our cabin."

Very cautiously, they crept forward toward the flooded compartment.

Before they came in sight of its door they heard a loud bang. A blast of fetid air reached them, a sound of rushing water could be heard, and a wave of ankle-deep water surged up the deck and subsided.

But then the sound grew faint and ended with a softer clang. They stood very still.

And then, standing firmly athwart the corridor, there it was: the Prohibitor. Valjhar hadn't seen it in a long time, and was struck anew by its appearance. Considerably taller than any of them, it was dripping wet. Water seemed unable to adhere to its dazzling golden surface, but ran down it freely. Its ruby eyes studied them with its usual hateful impassivity. Its brain case was a silvery ovoid tucked into a hollow atop its head, or so it appeared. This was surrounded and protected by a crystal openwork helmet, which was not attached at any point to its head, but rather floated eerily in place around it.

Its deadly Third Eye was closed, for now.

The creature's mouth locked open. From it came stentorian bell-like tones. "Criminals of Rral. You have violated the New Ethos of Rral, and must be held accountable."

Valjhar had heard all this before. He had no response to make.

A massive shape appeared in the shadows behind the Prohibitor. It towered over the robot, and for a moment Valjhar dared hope that the Prohibitor's time was over. Stingray advanced stealthily, and then sprang forward to catch the Prohibitor in a wrestling hold, lifting it bodily off the deck.

"You're heavier than you look," grunted Stingray.

But the Prohibitor was not so easily restrained. It squirmed and wriggled in a liquid manner that no living humanoid could match, forcing Stingray to constantly shift his grip as he tried to hold on. It could also elongate its limbs to some degree. One of its hands snaked out, twisted around, and clamped down on Stingray's shoulder, tearing away his clothing and causing blood to spring out of his flesh. Still Stingray held on, gritting his teeth, trying now to force the Prohibitor's head from its neck.

But that was of no avail at all. The Prohibitor rotated its head as though its neck were a length of taffy. Stingray found himself staring into its face from only inches away. Valjhar saw the Third Eye slide open, aglow with its terrible light.

"Stingray, release it now, or you are dead!" he cried.

Stingray obeyed, flinging the robot away in disgust.

"What are you?" asked the Prohibitor after nimbly landing on its feet, clearly not inconvenienced in the slightest.

"I'm a friend of theirs, Glitterbug. From Earth." Stingray growled as he rubbed his shoulder.

The Prohibitor turned away, its interest in Stingray depleted.

"Why do you hound us so, Prohibitor?" said Kern in exasperation. "Aren't you neglecting Rral? What if someone there invents a better pencil sharpener, and you aren't there to stamp it out?"

"There are other Prohibitors."

"All like you?"

"No. Few are like me."

"What do you want from us, Prohibitor?" said Valjhar, sounding braver than he felt.

"You must be held accountable for your crimes."

"You've said that many times. How exactly must we account for them?"

"You must accompany me back to Rral. There your ship and all your prohibited technological possessions will be surrendered or destroyed, and you yourselves will be exiled to an island in order to spare the greater society from your perversions."

Valjhar raised his eyebrows. "Is that all?"

"Yes."

"That—that doesn't thound tho bad," said Pimsie tentatively.

"And what if we refuse?" said Valjhar, exploring the full range of their options, if any.

"I will destroy you if necessary."

Indeed, the Prohibitor's offer didn't sound so bad. Valjhar was taken aback, surprised by its leniency.

"We—we have aliens aboard."

"This large one is of no consequence. He may be returned to his world. As for the woman, I will permit her to dwell with you in exile. She will not be allowed to leave and reveal the secrets of Rral to outsiders. Where is she?"

"Here."

Valjhar whirled at the sound of that faint rasp. There stood the last thing he wanted to see at that moment, a sure harbinger of imminent disaster. There tottered Shaula, leaning against the bulkhead, aiming her weapon at the Prohibitor with a shaking hand. She looked ghastly pale and drawn. She coughed weakly, then tried to draw in a breath, of which only a trickle reached her devastated lungs.

"Shaula, no!" cried Valjhar.

Shaula's wasted hand sagged under the weight of her weapon. She slumped against the bulkhead and slid to the deck, her eyes blank and unseeing. She released a shallow breath and fell still and silent.

A haze of unreality descended over Valjhar's mind and senses. He watched with a peculiar clarity as Pimsie sprang to Shaula's side, screaming and wailing. Sounds were muffled, and everything appeared to happen in slow motion.

The Prohibitor stepped forward. The jewel at its throat gleamed, and a ray of light flickered over Shaula's motionless form.

Valjhar forced himself to speak, though his throat felt like an iron pipe.

"Prohibitor, what did you just do?"

"I scanned the alien who corrupted you to determine if she is dead."

"And is she?"

"She is. Organ function has ceased. Cell death will soon follow."

"To what degree of detail did you scan her?"

"To a very great degree."

The tiniest spark of hope kindled in Valjhar's mind. Suddenly he saw a way in which something could yet be salvaged from this horror. Otherwise, he knew these events would crush his spirit as soon as the shock had passed.

"Prohibitor. I offer you a bargain."

"No bargains are necessary. You must comply with my demands or be destroyed."

"You have nothing to lose by agreeing, and you will obtain our cooperation with no further resistance."

"Speak."

"Transmit the data you just obtained from Shaula to the aliens in the vicinity of this ship. In return, we will accompany you willingly."

"I will not add scientific data to the Implicit Database. Before we leave this region of space I will destroy all Rralian beacons found throughout the nebula."

Valjhar searched his thoughts for any argument that might sway this creature's relentless purpose. He drew himself up and said, "Destroy the beacons then, but you must first grant my request. In the end it will make no difference to you. The information I refer to is of no use to anyone else. Who is left who can even access it?" That last question was rhetorical, as Valjhar suspected there might yet be many throughout the universe who could access it, one way or another.

"What use is it to you?"

Valjhar was again stymied for a safe answer.

"The data is all that remains of this alien, as you call her. She is dear to me," he ventured.

Pimsie looked up from where she crouched beside Shaula's body. "Pleath do as he athkth."

The Prohibitor closed its mouth. For several long moments it stood silent and motionless, though poised as if for action. It went on so long that Valjhar began to wonder if it had malfunctioned.

But then its mouth snapped open again.

"I will comply, and then you must surrender yourselves to me. It is done."

"You already did it? So quickly?" Valjhar's head spun with the speed of events. His tenuous hope for Shaula's future grew a little brighter. If his plan succeeded, surrendering to the Prohibitor and returning to Rral, even as exiles, would be a relief.

"Yes."

"Very well then. We will now comply..." Valjhar began, but he ceased speaking when he saw the Prohibitor's scanning beam dance over Pimsie.

"Pimsehkia Flam. You carry a child."

Pimsie stood up slowly. "Yeth, I do."

"It is not truly Rralian. It is an alien hybrid, and an abomination that cannot be allowed to live."

And then Valjhar saw the single most horrible thing he ever witnessed, worse even than when he saw friends fall to death in years to come. The Prohibitor rushed at Pimsie with inhuman speed. It extended its hands, and its tapering metallic fingers darted at her abdomen and as quickly withdrew.

Pimsie grunted in surprise, then slowly sagged to her knees, holding her belly. "You—you killed my baby," she choked.

"It was not truly your baby," said the Prohibitor. Its semantic argument made no impression on Pimsie.

"I will hate you for the rest of my life, with everything I can find within my mind, heart, and soul."

She said this with such calm clarity and simplicity that even Valjhar was chilled. Whatever effect her words had on the Prohibitor could not be discerned.

Kern Harner gave a ragged cry of outrage. His engineering suit hummed and crackled. The Prohibitor was violently wrenched around to face him. The ship's decks and bulkheads creaked and groaned about them.

"I have had enough of you, Prohibitor!" cried Kern, wild-eyed. "First you chase us across the universe! Then you kill my child and injure my precious mate! Enough! You're only made of matter, as powerful as you are. I'll take you apart, atom by atom!"

Whatever forces Kern was wielding held the Prohibitor motionless, but did not prevent the Third Eye from opening. It was then that a huge form flung itself at the monster, smashing it against the bulkhead hard enough to dent it.

Stingray roared as his great hand engulfed the Prohibitor's head, ramming it into the wall over and over with terrific force. Sparks crackled from his hand. The Prohibitor fought back, throwing Stingray aside, and sought to regain its balance.

Valjhar awoke from his daze and joined the fray. He no longer cared what happened to him, or to any of them. He would see this glittering monster destroyed, even if it meant death to them all. He activated the dimension belt, preparing a novel usage which he had never yet attempted—collapsing the Prohibitor's spacial dimensions, essentially crushing it out of existence as a minuscule black hole. Before he could invoke this effect Stingray leaped up and grabbed the thing again. From Kern's suit came a beam of some concentrated energy that played over the Prohibitor's midsection. A seam opened in its metallic surface. Droplets of a golden liquid began to spew out. Valjhar goggled. It was the first time he had ever known the Prohibitor to suffer any damage.

And then something else happened that was wholly unexpected. A gigantic voice boomed out, coming from all around them, penetrating the ship, vast and staggering.

"PROHIBITOR OF RRAL. YOU HAVE STALKED AND THREATENED MY FRIENDS FOR FAR TOO LONG. THIS IS YOUR END."

Somehow, despite its overwhelming force, it was the voice of Shaula Alshain.

The Prohibitor staggered. It appeared confused and uncertain. Kern's beam was still unraveling it. Valjhar unleashed the dimension belt. The robot flailed wildly, its limbs collapsing in on themselves.

It fled, scuttling away on all four distorted limbs like some freakish animal. It left a trail of golden globules. For an instant Valjhar almost felt pity for it.

They stood there, panting, looking after it.

"We should go after it," said Stingray. "It could still destroy us all."

A new alarm sounded. "That's the radiation alert," said Kern. I think it means the Prohibitor is using its long-range teleportation power. Getting away."

"Then we've beaten it," said Valjhar. "For the very first time, we've beaten it." He exulted in this realization before hearing Pimsie's moan and looking to see her kneeling on the deck in an expanding puddle of blood.

Kern dropped down beside her and raised her blouse. Her skin was not broken, but bruised. The blood was coming from between her legs.

"She must be miscarrying!" said Valjhar. "Let's get her to the Medikum." He glanced with regret at Shaula's corpse, half convinced that her immense voice from nowhere had been only a hallucination on his part.

Stingray turned to Kern. "Come on." He cradled Pimsie and one great arm and was quickly gone, along with Kern.

Valjhar found the entropic device where it had fallen and picked it up. "Shaula?"

Shaula's voice returned, but this time only within Valjhar's mind.

Valjhar. I'm gaining more control over this new form.

"What new form?"

I'm inside the Ladderites somehow. I'm part of them. And my mind is now huge. I have full access to their linked minds and computational power. And that's why what you're about to do is going to work.

"What am I going to do?" asked Valjhar in wonder.

Pick up my weapon. Aim it at my body.

Valjhar lifted the entropic device toward Shaula's corpse. "What—what are *you* going to do?"

I'm going to fix myself. In this form I understand the entropic device, and entropy itself, vastly better than I did before. I can control them both with tremendous precision. I can reverse entropy, and I can control exactly what order I wish to be restored.

"But Shaula—if your mind is so powerful in this new form, why would you want to revive your body and lose all that?"

Because when I'm like this I can't stay near you and travel with you, idiot. Now be quiet.

Shaking with hope and fear, Valjhar steadied the alien device. It grew cold in his hand, and he seemed to hear a sort of sound, a quiet hum or moan, as though the universe itself were being stressed by what was happening.

He stared at the corpse. So far it appeared unchanged.

Yes. I'm mostly still alive. I'm a tough little thing. That makes it easier.

The body drew in a harsh, sudden breath. She turned over and began to cough vigorously, then turned to look up at Valjhar in confusion.

"Valjhar? What's happening?"

"You're saving your own life. You're not finished yet. I'll explain later."

Shaula sat up, breathing heavily, staring at Valjhar.

You're right, Valjhar, I'm not finished yet. I'm going to do this right. I want to add the genetic modification to turn me into a full Rralian.

"But we already simulated that! It would kill you more completely than drowning ever could. We'd have to mop you off the floor."

"What?" said Shaula.

No, it won't, not while I have this mastery over the device. I'll hold myself together. But hurry! Go get whatever devices you made to cause the change.

"Shaula, I know this is confusing, but wait right here, I'll be right back." Valjhar dashed away, through the medikum, where he glimpsed Kern laboring over an agonized Pimsie while Stingray fretted nearby, into the adjacent laboratory, where he seized a vial of one of the experimental potions they had made, a dense liquid containing a silvery swirl.

Hurry. She is failing again.

There was no time for finesse. Valjhar snatched up an injector and dashed out of the lab. "Stingray, come with me," he said as he passed through the medikum. The giant followed, battered and bleeding as he was. He gave an inarticulate exclamation when they came to the corridor where Shaula still sat gasping against the wall.

"I thought she was dead!"

"She was, but she's bringing herself back. It's a long story."

"Then that huge voice...it was real? What do you need me to do?"

Valjhar handed him the entropic device. "Take this, aim it at Shaula, and don't set it down until I tell you it's all right." He approached Shaula and showed her the injector. "Shaula, my love, do you know what this is?"

She nodded.

"It may be very unpleasant. It may hurt."

"Hurt me," she gasped.

Valjhar, stop wasting time! Inject her!

Valjhar pressed the injector against her arm. It took a long time to empty itself and left an alarming purple blotch that spread rapidly. Still crouching beside Shaula, Valjhar looked back at Stingray, who appeared distressed.

"Stingray, what's wrong?"

"It's—it's this thing. It's gone cold, and now it's— trembling. I feel—something's wrong."

Valjhar felt it too...an aura of unreality and something like madness had pervaded the area, as reality was twisted into a form it had never been meant to assume.

Valjhar!

"Valjhar!"

"Shaula! What's happening?"

She's changing!

"I'm changing! It hurts so much!"

Valjhar clung to her, trying to send her whatever dregs of strength and will he possessed. "Hang on!"

Valjhar. The hybrid genome you devised—the expression is not quite right.

"But we simulated the result!" he cried out. "If it could be imposed successfully, the result should be perfect."

Your simulation was built on some faulty assumptions. If I impose the genome in its current form, the result will be—undesirable.

"Then what can you do?"

The Ladderites are helping. I'm using most of their combined thought to correct and stabilize the genome on the fly as it modifies her cells one by one.

By now Valjhar thought he partly understood what was happening. With the Ladderites in possession of a full description of Shaula's body, they'd been able to construct a simulation of her mind, to run it like a piece of software that was integrated into themselves. It was a consequence he might have foreseen if he'd had more time to think it through.

Shaula gripped his arm with painful strength. "Valjhar...what's happening inside me...I'm afraid I might... make a mess..." She fainted.

Valjhar parted Shaula's robe to bare her abdomen. Its very shape was changing subtly before his eyes, as though some languid animal were stirring sleepily beneath her skin.

He looked back at Stingray, who appeared more strained than ever.

"Stingray, don't falter. That device is the only thing making this transformation possible, or survivable."

"I—I won't fail her."

It would be easier for you to hold it. I can share some of my understanding of the process with you.

"Why can't I just lay it down on the deck and aim it at Shaula?"

Stingray looked at Valjhar strangely as he spoke into the air.

The device requires a living touch to activate it. Normally it would have to be my own, but I've overridden that much.

With considerable reluctance Valjhar returned his attention to Stingray.

"It's all right, Stingray. I'll take over. Please just stay with Shaula if you would."

Even as he approached the quaking giant, Valjhar began to feel what he was going through. The entropic device was the focus of a zone of alienness that was deeply disorienting and disturbing in a way Valjhar could not have previously imagined. Some ancient instinct urged him to flee from something that should not exist, yet he could not. He was forced to hold the freezing orb in his hand while it emitted some influence that set one of the most fundamental aspects of nature on its head.

What else, wondered Valjhar, could the extra-universal beings who had fashioned this thing also devise, if this prodigy was but an instrument meant to test a novice recruit to their mysterious organization?

I wonder the very same thing myself. They said they could equip me with something called a Universal Instrument, but even as I am now, I can't imagine what such a thing might encompass. Now try to relax. The order I'm imposing is very much like the order that existed a short time ago. It existed once, and it can exist again. Their separation by time is in some ways an illusion made necessary by the limitations of our consciousness. It once was. In a sense, it still is.

That mental voice continued to share this half-understood wisdom with Valjhar, easing his task to the point where he could endure it. He began to visualize the order they were trying to bring about: Shaula alive and healthy, her eyes clear and bright, her mind alert, just the same as she'd always been, but now with the physiology of a true Rralian.

Yes, that helps. Stand fast, Valjhar.

Valjhar stood fast, for many hours, while each of the trillions of cells in Shaula's body received its new instructions and learned its revised functions. She remained mercifully unconscious, which Valjhar suspected was the doing of her disembodied twin. Stingray remained close beside them both, unable to do anything but watch carefully and lend his moral support.

At last it was done. The entropic device went inert in Valjhar's hand. He glanced down at it and then jerked in surprise. It was ruined, pitted and scarred. He dropped it. It fell to the deck and crumbled into dust and flinders.

Yes, he thought, *clearly this had been a use of the device that had never been intended.*

Shaula remained asleep, breathing deeply and steadily. Valjhar felt his tears flow at the sight of her, still wan and emaciated, but alive. He lifted her, and, followed by Stingray, bore her to the medikum. There he was jarred by the sight of Kern as he tried to comfort Pimsie, who sat in her cot curled up into herself, weeping and rocking miserably.

"Pimsie! Pimsie!" cried Kern. "We'll have children someday. I promise. We'll have them on Rral."

Valjhar laid Shaula in the cot beside hers, and said softly, "Pimsie, look. All is not lost. Shaula is alive, and she will be well again."

Pimsie peeked out from behind her arms. Her great wet eyes took in the sight of Shaula laying peacefully nearby, and she resumed her wailing, though now her grief seemed mixed with a measure of relief and perhaps even joy.

Valjhar, you should leave at once. If the Prohibitor regains its nerve and returns, it could cut the ship in half from outside, even damaged as it is.

"But what about you, Shaula?" said Valjhar, speaking into the air, not caring about the puzzled looks of his friends. That explanation could wait. "Does that mean there are—well, now two of you?"

The other Shaula seemed to laugh. *Yes, in a sense. But as time passes, I will become more like the Ladderites. They will become more like me. The result will be this: you, Valjhar, and any Rralian, will always find friends and allies—here on Flamaria.*

Watch over her, Valjhar. Care for her, and she will care for you, always. Goodbye, Valjhar, goodbye.

Valjhar took a moment to master himself before speaking.

"Stingray, come with me to the bridge. We're leaving. Kern, I'm sorry, but we'll need to jettison your sailing equipment."

Kern waved this off. "Please do. The next time I propose going sailing, it will be on a calm, sunny sea on a peaceful planet where we can breathe the air."

They blasted free of the turbulent world of Flamaria and made their way to a remote moon of the system, where they tarried long enough for Kern to replace the parts of the ship that had been destroyed by the Prohibitor. That was a considerable task, lasting for three watchful weeks, but the Prohibitor did not return. Moreover, Valjhar realized to his great surprise that he was no longer afraid of the Prohibitor. He knew now that it could be beaten...that they could beat it. They must always be wary of it, but never again would they be driven before it in fear.

Pimsie was never quite the same after that incident. She recovered quickly physically, but she grew quieter, more subdued, and more withdrawn. She spent more time alone in her cabin, or with Kern. She tended her garden and Kroy. Her smiles were now often forced and haunted, which pained Valjhar deeply. Her nostalgia for Rral and Enblenol increased.

Carefully they gathered the liquid remains the Prohibitor had left behind. Kern desired to study the strange golden substance, but Valjhar insisted it be expelled from the ship. Although it appeared inert, he feared it might possess some ability to track them or perform some other mischief. Kern acquiesced.

Only when the ship was again underway with a new microjump drive could they fully relax. *Mote* departed the mists and fogs of the great nebulous region. Soon the sun of Flamaria lay far behind, lost in the murk. The beacons of the ancient Rralians also fell behind, still intact despite the threats of the Prohibitor. *Mote* emerged into the clearer space of one of the inner spiral arms. Once again the ship was surrounded by endless stars. The hub of the Galaxy glowed brightly ahead, partly obscured by a few dark patches of dust.

One day Kern approached Valjhar during a quiet moment. "Valjhar, please come with me. There's something I need to show you," he said solemnly.

He led Valjhar into the medical lab, passing Shaula, who still lay in her cot, asleep. She still had some time to go before full recovery. Her body was wasted. She must not only regain her strength, but also allow her organs to complete their alteration, and even grow a few new ones. Even her teeth were dissolving and being replaced. They thought it best to keep her unconscious during this unpleasant process.

In the laboratory, Kern removed a small container from a freezer and bid Valjhar to look within. Valjhar looked, then turned away, shaken.

"That—that came out of Pimsie?"

"Yes, Valjhar. Where did we go wrong?"

"I'm not sure. Shaula told me there was something wrong with our procedure. My first guess...is that the Rralian instructions we added to Shaula's genome…were simply added to it, without replacing the previous instructions or their expression. I don't know. I do know that we must fully understand this process, without error, before we ever attempt such a thing again."

"Do you think…the Prohibitor knew?"

Valjhar was startled by that thought. "I think it must have. Its scans are very thorough. It did say…the child was an abomination. I may have misunderstood that remark at the time." Once again Valjhar's notions about the Prohibitor and its motives were unsettled. And then…

"Kern…did Pimsie see?"

"No. Her eyes were closed during the—delivery."

"Do you think we should tell her? Have you already?"

Kern's eyes widened. "Oh no I haven't, and should we? I don't know, I don't know. Do we let her go on believing she lost her perfect daughter? Or do we tell her that we implanted within her something that could never be more than a sad freak, if it could have lived at all? What do you think?"

"I don't know either," said Valjhar miserably. "I suppose we need not decide at once. But now that I've seen this—thing, we must dispose of it at once. We must never subject Pimsie to the sight of it."

"I agree."

Later, on the bridge with Kern and Stingray, with the stars creeping by around them, they debated where they should go next. Valjhar found himself looking alternately back the way they'd come, towards Earth, and forward, towards the core of the Milky Way.

"I keep thinking about those poor, doomed people back on Earth," said Valjhar sadly.

"Why?" said Stingray. "You have no further business among them."

"It seems to me that with all our knowledge and power we could do something to help them."

Stingray looked at him critically. "Really? It seems to me that you have enough trouble just keeping yourselves out of trouble."

"I think about the humans too, but I feel we ought to continue on, into the heart of this galaxy," said Kern. "I feel something drawing us on in that direction. Don't you?"

"Yes," admitted Valjhar. "I do."

"So it's settled. We'll keep going?" said Stingray.

"Yes. The humans can wait."

"Ideally forever."

Chapter 20
The Peregrine

"Get behind me."

As the snow fell thickly Rouse stood astride the middle of the road, awaiting the coming of this new vehicle, not knowing if it brought help or new enemies to face.

At intervals a distant yellow light illuminated the falling snowflakes as the truck (it sounded too loud and rough to be anything else) negotiated the curves of the cliffside highway. After a while new colors became visible: flashes of red and blue. Rouse began to relax.

The truck came around the final bend and halted, blasting them with its headlights and its rooftop light bar. A spotlight came on and caught them. Rouse squinted into its glare.

"You there!" came a voice. "You are from the bus that was attacked?"

"Yes!"

"We are police from Gilgit. Are there any more with you?"

"No. The others all went the other way, toward Chilas. It's just us three."

"We will take you back to Gilgit."

"Oh, thank you," said Amy.

Rouse watched closely as the officers performed the precarious maneuver of turning around on the snowy, narrow road. At one point one of the rear tires left the road and hung over the abyss. They gunned the engine and pulled it back. Only when the turnaround was completed did Rouse, Amy, and Kevin squeeze into the rear seat behind the two policemen. The cab was warm and smelled of coffee and tobacco.

Amy gulped down a few pills and then practically melted against Kevin as they rumbled along the highway, moving slowly due to poor visibility and a slippery road. Rouse, seated on the right, looked out into the darkness, still unsettled and oddly dissatisfied by this change in their fortunes.

"What are your names and nationalities, please?"

"We're Kevin and Amy Krause. Americans."

"My name is Rouse Farewell. From New Zealand."

Kevin started in surprise. The policeman who wasn't driving looked back at her. Even the driver glanced at her in his rear view mirror.

Rouse shrugged. "I'm tired of hiding and lying."

"This complicates things," said the officer. "We have heard of you. You are a person of great interest to some foreign governments."

"Do you two have any interest in trying to turn me in?"

"I am not sure."

"Maybe we can still get along then."

The truck rumbled along through the deepening snow. Rouse gazed moodily through the window. The vast bulk of Nanga Parbat drew ever closer. Rouse thought she could somehow sense its mass, even though the mountain was completely invisible through the storm.

Belatedly she remembered her wound. She drew up her clothing to study it in the cab's dim light. First she had to pull away her shirt, which was glued to her torso by dried blood. The whole area of the injury was so dark with blood that little could be seen. Cautiously she extended a finger. The edges of the wound were wet and sensitive.

Rouse looked over at Amy, who seemed to be asleep on Kevin's shoulder. She didn't want to bother the poor troubled woman.

The policemen spoke together in rapid Urdu. Rouse listened, fretted, and finally interrupted them.

"Where is the White Monk?"

The man who wasn't driving broke off his speech and glanced back at her in surprise. "The White Monk? You've heard of him? He's said to live at the base of Deo Mir, Nanga Parbat, somewhere near the Fairy Meadows. It's not an easy journey, especially in a storm, if you are thinking of visiting him. For one thing, the steel bridge across the river is not yet complete, and the current bridge makes most Westerners nervous."

After a while one of the policemen spoke into his radio in what Rouse thought to be an affectedly casual manner. After some back and forth between him and his headquarters, she caught her own name, muttered quickly and more tensely.

Very well, she thought. If they were intent on making trouble for themselves, she would oblige them.

Tension steadily built up in the truck. The two policemen sat stiffly, looking stolidly ahead. Kevin sat with his jaw clenched, staring into the distance. No doubt he was thinking of how Rouse had endangered them all by needlessly admitting her true identity; she could hardly blame him. Amy was still asleep, but even in sleep her body quivered, and her brow was furrowed. She knew no peace, asleep or awake.

And Rouse herself? She felt only a sense of inevitability, a certainty that she would soon face a critical moment, a defining moment that would change everything for her, and set her on some wholly unforeseeable path.

The first lights of Gilgit glimmered in the distance. The snowfall did not abate, but the Moon managed to peer through some crack in the clouds, making every flake luminous and outlining the river valley and the wild masses of rock towering beyond in silver-blue and black. Also made briefly visible was a skein of silver threads spanning the river.

"Is that the scary bridge you mentioned?"

The policemen jumped at the sudden sound of her voice. "Yes, that is the bridge."

"Stop the truck. Let us out here."

"What?"

"You heard me. Stop the truck."

The policemen looked at each other. "We've been ordered to—"

"Stop the truck." Rouse spoke in a tone that didn't sound quite human, even to her own ears.

The driver slammed on the brakes. Suddenly he was shaking. Kevin looked at her in horror.

"Rouse, what are you doing?"

"We're taking Amy to see the White Monk."

"What? Why? Amy needs professional care and medicine."

Rouse laughed as she exited the truck, turning back to speak to Kevin. Snow swirled through the door and into the cab. "Oh, does she? Tell me, how much professional care has she already had? What have those drugs done for her, beyond fogging her mind so that she doesn't even know whether she's happy or wretched? Is she any better now? How about electroshock? Have they offered to scramble her brain that way? Trust me, Kevin. I've been both a psychiatric patient and a psych nurse in training. The doctors in Gilgit can't do anything for Amy that others haven't tried already."

"But—the White Monk? Who the hell is he?"

"I don't know. He may very well be nothing but a fraud and a charlatan. But something tells me Amy will be better off with him than with anyone else we can reach. Are you coming? Or do you think Amy will be better off in the hands of the Pakistani police?" Rouse reached into the truck and scooped Amy into her arms. She felt lighter than ever, and insubstantial, even fragile.

Kevin sat shaking with helpless anger as he stared at her.

"All right, I'm coming," he said at last. "But only because I refuse to leave my wife. I think you're crazy. And dangerous."

Rouse ignored this and turned toward the bridge. Kevin muttered something at the policemen and followed. They spoke briefly into their radio, and then their vehicle slowly pulled away. The cloudy, snowy night somehow offered plenty of light to see by. The bridge appeared to be made of steel plates and cables. It was wider than she'd expected, wide enough to pass a car. It was not at all the precarious rope-and-plank affair she'd been led to expect.

Rouse was distracted from her inspection by the sound of distant engines, followed by an array of flashing, colored lights, all moving in their direction. The local police, it seemed, would not be content to let them go on their way in peace. She watched their vehicles, a whole parade of them it seemed, as they made their way up the winding road from Gilgit. Their lights would have turned the falling snow into a lovely sight if their intent was not so unwelcome.

A cold anger rose up within her. Who did these small men think they were, to hound and interfere with them so? What harm were they doing? All she had done was defend innocents against the violent fanatics of their own religion.

"What will you do now, Rouse?" yelled Kevin over the wind.

"Fight back."

"Not with my wife in your arms!"

Conceding his point, Rouse hurried toward the bridge, still most of a kilometer away. It would be difficult for any pursuers to see them through the snowfall, unless they were very close. Once across the bridge, Rouse thought they could lose themselves in the storm.

Her hopeful plan was suddenly altered by the roar of a jet aircraft, passing unseen in the clouds, followed seconds later by a massive explosion that briefly lit the mountains in an orange glare, while sending fragments of the bridge arcing through the air. Rouse whirled, seeking to protect Amy from any shrapnel with her own body, while Kevin was blasted off his feet.

When the roar had subsided Rouse turned back, dumbfounded. The center of the bridge had been obliterated. The fallen ends swung back and forth, slamming against the chasm's walls.

Rouse advanced, heedless of Kevin, who lay moaning. Who had done this? The Pakistanis? Did they really think her capture was worth destroying that valuable bridge, cutting off the regions beyond?

She doubted it. She suspected the Americans, or perhaps the Russians, or some other power that felt itself entitled to order the world according to its desires.

Nevertheless, this did not prevent the Pakistani police, or army, or whoever they were, from continuing their advance.

Rouse looked down at Amy. She remained unresponsive, despite all the noise and violence. Suddenly Rouse was filled with a terrible conviction that she had done more than take her usual medications.

The cars and trucks from Gilgit came roaring up behind her, pinning her with their spotlights. Rouse walked away, into her own multiple shadows, closer to the brink of the great ravine, only half aware of the vehicles, and not greatly concerned about them. Nothing seemed real to her. The thought that she might simply fall into that gorge, and thus vanish from the world, seemed interesting in a remote, impersonal way, as though it were only the next plot development in some story.

A harsh voice called out over a speaker on one of the trucks. Rouse turned reluctantly. The voice bellowed various demands and warnings that were meaningless to Rouse, even though they were spoken in perfectly clear English. When she failed to move. she heard gunshots, and a few bullets whined over her head. She was not intimidated.

They would not risk death to their prize. She would not have to resist any more bullets, not now at least. But her pursuers had other options. She heard a series of hollow detonations, and canisters came arcing toward her. A pair of them clattered among the rocks nearby, emitting an acrid fume. Her anger aroused anew, Rouse caught the next one that flew near. Cradling Amy in one arm, she flung it back. She hurled it with such force that it whistled along a flat trajectory, striking a truck hard enough to explode against its grill, its fragments penetrating the radiator and silencing the motor. The sheer violence of her move, coupled with the tear gas that was whipping by them in the wind, were enough to finally wake Amy from her stupor.

Rouse set Amy on her feet. She stood wobbling and looking around in dim comprehension. Rouse took advantage of this lack of any encumbrance by grabbing up the other gas bombs and returning them in like fashion, creating shrapnel that wounded many of the men who confronted them.

Amy gasped. "Susan—Rouse—what are you doing? Where's Kevin?"

"I left him lying back there somewhere. I think those policemen must have him by now. I'm defending us against these uniformed thugs." The gas bombs exhausted, Rouse flung a large rock, which took the roof off a police car and destroyed its lights.

"Rouse, you're scaring me! You're turning into a monster!"

Amy's words echoed in Rouse's mind. Feeling numb, she turned again toward the chasm, ignoring Amy and the continuing clamor of those who sought to cage her. The ground at her feet fell away steeply. The rocks were wet and slippery. No light penetrated into the depths where the river roared far below, unseen. Three steps would commit her to the fall. Gravity would draw her on to whatever fate awaited her. She laughed, startled to realize she was again contemplating suicide, despite all the strange and wondrous things she had seen, thought, and done since waking up in that monastery so long ago. Apparently she was not meant to be saved, no matter what miracles befell her.

"All right, Amy," she said calmly, turning again to face her attackers. "Go to them if you think that's best. I'll wait here."

"I will. I can't abandon Kevin, I—wait. What is that? What's that Light?"

Something about the way Amy said this made the world go still in Rouse's mind. She turned slowly, somehow knowing she was about to witness something extraordinary.

A cold glow was rising on the far side of the chasm. Diffused by the falling snow, its source could not be discerned, but it seemed to be moving slowly, and it was a radiance not of the Earth, or of any source devised by man or nature.

Like a flood washing away the detritus of a tangled riverbed, it infused her mind, renewing her clarity and bringing new hope. Somehow...somehow it was familiar to her.

The Light faded away, but Rouse could still feel its lingering power, waiting somewhere on the other side of the ravine, waiting to be released again.

She and Amy looked at each other.

"Do you still want to go back?"

"No," said Amy, "or at least not yet, not after seeing...that. But how can we get over there?"

A tinge of blue glimmered in the snow. Rouse's thoughts turned back to gravity. As she recalled from the one physics class she had ever taken, gravity was a mysterious force, very well known in its effects, but little understood in its nature. Also she recalled that the atoms that comprised her body, and indeed all matter, were almost entirely empty space, their apparent solidity little more than an illusion. It followed, then, that the force of gravity actually acted only on a very tiny fraction of her total being.

Why then could it not be taught to ignore that bit? She remembered another tidbit from her lessons: Einstein's Equivalence Principle, which stated there was no difference between the lack of gravity experienced by a falling object and that experienced by an object far from any source of gravity.

"Amy, we're going to fly across."

"What?"

"Yes, we'll fly. You've seen me do many things that no one should be able to do already, haven't you? This is just one more thing. Do you trust me?"

Amy began to speak, faltered, and looked aside into the blackness beyond the gorge.

"Yes, I trust you. Five minutes ago I would have said you were crazy and run screaming for help, but now...well. That Light. Whatever it is, or was, it has changed me already, and I want more. Now excuse me for a moment."

Amy tottered a few steps away, leaned over, and vomited forcefully, spattering the snowy rocks and possibly her shoes.

"There, that's better," she gasped. "You're going to carry me across?"

"Yes, I am," said Rouse cheerfully. *Yes, I'm going to carry you across, to the other side of the ravine, or to the other side of life,* she thought. "Are you ready?"

"I'm ready. Oh, I wonder what's about to happen. Am I about to leave life behind, and leave Kevin to face it all alone? Or will I return to him, whole and healed? It could go either way, I know. But that's all right. Either is better than what I've been putting up with for the last few years. At least now I feel clean. Let's go."

Rouse lifted Amy in her arms. "Close your eyes."

"I will. But don't you close yours."

I shall do exactly that, Rouse thought. Otherwise she might never bring herself to do this absurd, outrageous thing.

Voices came to them faintly from behind.

"Don't jump! Don't jump!"

"Amyyyy!"

"Let's get this over with," said Amy. "I don't want Kevin to worry about me."

No difference. No difference.

Rouse closed her eyes and leaped off the brink.

It was very peaceful. There was no wind, no sensation of plummeting, only lightness and ease. Amy's trivial weight did not even register in Rouse's arms. She opened her eyes to make sure she had not lost her burden. She hadn't. Together they sailed gracefully over the chasm. They landed lightly on the narrow road on the far side. Rouse put Amy back on her feet.

"Well, it's about time," said Rouse.

"About time for what?"

"About time the laws of the universe learned to serve the beings who inhabit it, and not to tyrannize them."

And then Rouse confronted a dizzying abyss. Not an abyss of space, not some trifling pit or crack in the earth, but an abyss of meaninglessness, in which she saw just how shallow an illusion the apparent reality and limitations of the world were. With that knowledge, there was no limit to what she could do. She could reorder nature and command forces no other human even knew to exist.

But she could do none of those things without also purging from her mind a belief in and a respect for the agency and sentience of every other being, human or otherwise, living on Earth and beyond. She could not exercise such power without trampling the will and the destiny of every other living creature.

Where did that leave her? Perhaps she should be destroyed. Perhaps the world had no room for an anomaly such as herself, someone able to overturn its apparent order any time she pleased.

She had flown. She would fly. She would become a denizen of the sky, of the air, and she would venture across the world. She would seek out what other wisdom the world and its people had to offer, and share what she could of her own. That would be enough. For the sake of everyone, it must be enough.

"Rouse? Are you all right?"

Rouse shook herself. Her mind returned to the here and now, tenuous though those concepts might be. "Yes. I just had to work a few things out in my head, that's all."

And then she laughed. It was the fullest, richest laugh she had given out in years, for it seemed a wizard was approaching them, and she could not be more delighted by this latest absurdity. It was a tall, slender figure, clad in a billowing grey hooded cloak. The hood shaded even the faint light of the night from his face, leaving only a blackness in which she saw nothing but what appeared to be a single, faint blue star. He walked steadily toward them with the aid of a pale wooden staff that for some reason made her think of flowers.

The wizard halted before them. Rouse caught a glimmer of white Light beneath the folds of his cloak, and glimpsed Lights of other colors as well.

"Hello there," she said. "Are you the White Monk?" She said this feeling as though she were addressing a figure stepping out of myth.

His voice was remote and whispery. "I have been called that."

"We're pleased to meet you. I'm Rouse Farewell, and this is my friend Amy Krause. How is it that you happen to be here? We had heard that you lived farther away, well around the flank of this great mountain."

"I do. It pleases me to inhabit a place called Fairy Meadows. But sometimes I receive inklings that I'm needed elsewhere, and this is one of those nights. Am I correct?"

271

"You are!" blurted Amy. "You see, I'm—well, I'm ill. Ill in the head, and in the heart. And I have been for a long time. I don't know what kind of magic you possess, but I'm praying it can help me find my way again."

"It can. But it isn't magic. It's something integral to the fabric of the universe. Most people have only a dim sight of it, or see only its distorted opposite, and that is what afflicts you. But no living being can ignore or deny the Lights I carry. The help I offer may be painful to endure, but you will emerge from it whole, if you approach it openly and without fear."

The glimmer of the Lights waxed stronger: blue, green, violet, and white. Amy reached out toward them, sobbing in gratitude and relief.

Rouse also felt their effects. "Why do you hide yourself away, Monk? You should come forth into the world. No one who lives could fail to benefit from this power you possess."

"Many who are dark of spirit would wither under it, and be destroyed. But I am not fit to bring that kind of judgement among the people of this world. These Lights are a sore trial to me as well, and I will not emerge until I have mastered myself. But you, Rouse Farewell, could profit from their influence as well."

He thrust out his hand, into her side, and a keen spring-green Light welled out from it. Rouse gasped, for it felt as though life were returning to a body that had been numb. She raised her clothing. Her bullet wound was gone.

"You would soon have healed on your own, and healed in such a way that would have made it difficult for anything short of the Sun's own fire to harm you again. Do not marvel. There are many strange and little-known powers in this world, Rouse Farewell, and you are not least among them. Please leave us now. The men who pursue you will not cease their efforts, and I am not yet ready to involve myself in such a conflict."

"You'll take care of Amy?"

"I will."

Amy stepped forward. In a choked voice she said, "Rouse. Will you—fly away?"

It took Rouse a moment to digest that question, but when she had, she was filled with joy and gladness.

"Yes. Yes, that's exactly what I'll do."

"And what else will you do, now that it seems you can do anything?"

"I'll follow the example of our friend the White Monk. I will involve myself with people as little as possible," said Rouse. "When I did get involved, I had to attack people who could not defend themselves against me. In some strange way I've become a creature of terrible, inhuman power. I could force my will on anyone in the world, or maybe on everyone in the world. That's not who I want to be. I will remove myself, to avoid that temptation as much as possible. With any luck you won't hear much about me."

"No. I hope to hear more about you. Much, much more about you, for the rest of my life."

Then they embraced, and Rouse knew that Amy was much more of a sister than she had at first suspected.

They separated.

"Goodbye, both of you."

Rouse looked straight up, into the storm. She hurled herself upward, and Earth's gravity, not knowing quite what to make of her, ignored her, or even worked in her favor. Through the clouds she burst, through the snow and the bracing pelting of sleet, through regions of cold that should have frozen her, and then beyond, into the unfiltered light of the moon and stars. The storm flowed by below her, a dim silver in the moonlight. In the distance great mountains rose through it in ridges and isolated peaks. Rouse turned in place. Much closer reared an even greater mountain, Nanga Parbat, its awesome wall a savage vertical wilderness of rock and ice.

And yet it too was now beneath her.

Her clothes, she found, had been ripped away in the speed of her ascent, but she did not miss them, or need them any more.

There she hovered, for something was still nagging at her mind.

"Wait a moment," she said, her voice faint in the thin air. "Cal? Cal Cotavion?"

Back she thundered Earthward, flashing along the gorge of the Indus. But Amy and Cal, if it really had been him, had vanished. She was not to glimpse him again for several years, long after she had become a legend among the people of Earth, a hidden wonder and a source of both hope and fear: hope to the weak and neglected; fear to the complacent and the powerful.

She was also a harbinger of the many strange days to come on the planet Earth of the Lesser Wisp, also known as the Milky Way Galaxy.

Chapter 21
The Dark Star

"So you feel it too?" said Valjhar as he stood gazing into the dense cloud of golden stars into which their ship was heading.

"Yes," said Shaula. "The one slight advantage I had over you Rralians was that my mind was a little more sensitive to such things, though Pimsie was always close. Luckily my transformation didn't take that from me. But if even you boys can sense it, it's definite. There's something out there."

"Something calling to us. Drawing us on," said Kern.

"I don't feel any such thing," said Stingray.

"That's because you're just a big, dumb oaf," said Kern.

"Oh yeah, I forgot."

The five of them gazed in silence into that innumerable mass of stars, creeping steadily toward them as though to engulf them. It was the hub of this galaxy, two hundred billion aged stars, a population densely packed by the standards of stars.

To Valjhar, the presence of something out in that direction was a comfort, even if its nature and identity were a total mystery. Their voyage had shown them so much emptiness, so much nothingness. So many barren worlds of rock and ice and gas, most lifeless, a few boasting a few simple forms, tiny squiggling things for the most part, struggling to survive in hostile environments. Some displayed relics of more fertile pasts, but the conditions that had permitted those had passed long ago with the evolution of their sun or some fatal radiation event or collision.

Kern and his boon companion Stingray were the only ones who remained fascinated by all this exploration. That unlikely duo ambled over the surface of many a blasted rock, laughing and joking as though they had discovered some delightful park, and not some jumble of twisted slag filled with harsh light and impenetrable shadows. Valjhar was happy to leave most of that activity to them, though it annoyed Pimsie, for reasons Valjhar did not yet fully understand.

And yet, something dwelt inward, deep in the galactic core, among whose ancient stars, deficient as they were in heavier elements, they would have expected to find little or nothing.

A calm had descended on the crew of *Mote* as it wafted among these stars of the inner regions of the Lesser Wisp. They watched all this desolation pass by from the warmth and comfort of their little ship. Shaula was alive and well, better than ever in her modified form. She and Valjhar were reconciled, and Valjhar glowed with love for her, though they had not yet taken the step of sharing a cabin.

Pimsie had recovered from the initial shock and horror of her loss, but remained subdued.

Kern had taken to playing some of the music he had recorded during their visit to Earth. Valjhar disliked the reminder of that planet's unhappy inhabitants, but he could not help but marvel at the power and sophistication of their music. The only Earth music he heard that he thought comparable to that of Rral was of Earth's earlier history, sometimes called folk music. But he had never heard any music from Old Rral, he reflected. The Compendium did not include such ephemera. Valjhar took comfort in imagining that some of that music might have been more refined.

The music inevitably made Earth's humans a frequent topic of conversation.

"Do you know what bothers me most about humans?" said Pimsie.

"Everything?" suggested Kern.

"Besides that. It's their ears."

"Yes, their shape is rather baroque, isn't it?"

"It's just that they never move. I'm not even sure the humans *can* move their ears. It makes them seem so... blank and emotionless, as though their facial expressions are only a mask."

"They are uncomfortably like us, aren't they?" said Valjhar.

"Yes. They are enough like us to seem like eerie parodies, rather than creatures with their own identity. I wish they were more different, or less."

"They are poorly made," scoffed Kern. "Have you studied their feet? They are an unfortunate halfway measure between climbing in trees and running on the ground. All those bones and toes...their spines...their joints...their teeth...all very shabby jobs. They are not built to last."

"They are still the raw products of their evolution," said Pimsie. "They are made to reproduce and then quickly fade away. Their bodies have little respect for the minds that may arise within them."

That was an uncharacteristically bleak thing for Pimsie Flam to say, and Valjhar was well aware of the change. Nevertheless some perverse impulse led him to be a bit contrary.

"Even so, some of them, as individuals, have great capabilities and potential. I think about them often."

"I don't. I try not to think about them at all, or of anyone who comes from that world."

"Even Cal?" Valjhar might have said "Even Stingray?", but did not, for fear of what her answer might be as Stingray sat here listening.

"No, not Cal. But he's not from Earth, and wasn't even from a fully human society. I hope he's well, living there among those savages. As for their music...well...I must admit..."

"Here, try this piece," said Kern.

From the speakers came a storm of sound, with blasts of horns, booms of drums, their tempo slow and portentous.

"That's frightening!" said Valjhar.

"It is," agreed Pimsie. "It's like an introduction to one of their Earthly gods. It's gigantic."

"What's it called, Kern?" asked Shaula.

"Fanfare for the Common Man."

"What?" squawked Pimsie. "That's preposterous. How could any common Earthman ever merit any sound so huge and commanding?"

Kern looked very thoughtful. "Maybe...the strength needed by these common men...to endure the misery and poverty of their lives...with any kind of dignity...is so great that they do, sometimes, deserve this kind of tribute."

Pimsie sniffed. Stingray looked dubious.

"You may be right, Kern," said Shaula.

Kern brightened up and looked a little mischievous. "Here, Pimsie, listen to this. I've been saving it for you. It's from an *opera*, a kind of musical theater."

A woman's voice, high for a human and incredibly pure, sang a slow song full of sadness and a terrible longing. Pimsie looked stricken by its beauty. By the time it had finished her eyes were wet with tears.

"What—what was that called?"

"It's called *O Mio Babbino Caro*."

"What does that mean?"

"I'm not sure. It's in the *Italian* language, which I didn't study very much. Let's see...something like...'oh, my dear child'..." Kern's voice trailed off. Suddenly he looked stricken as well. "I think that's it, anyway."

Pimsie hid her face in her hands and wept. When Kern tried to speak to her she only waved one hand at him and could not reply. After a moment she jumped up and dashed down the staircase, away from the bridge.

When she had gone, a silence fell among those who remained.

"Kern," said Shaula sadly.

"I know, I know." Kern looked perfectly miserable. "I wasn't thinking beyond the beauty of the music. I never thought about what the words might mean, or what they might mean to her."

"Your translation wasn't quite right," said Stingray, studying the data associated with the recording. "It refers to the singer's father, not her child. The words are similar."

"Oh, great, so my blunder was even more unnecessary. I'd better go see if I can repair this somehow." Off he scampered down the stairway.

The sudden gloom left Valjhar feeling fretful. "I wish there was something we could do for those people."

"Who? Kern and Pimsie?" said Stingray. "They'll be all right. They have each other. Even if Kern sometimes steps on her two little toes, she means the universe to him, and she knows it."

"No, I didn't mean them. I mean the humans. On Earth."

Stingray looked at him curiously. "What do you have in mind?"

"Doing something to free them from the savagery and injustice that's poisoning their minds and societies. Not to mention their planet."

"How could you possibly do that?"

"I don't know. By taking over, I suppose."

"Taking over what?"

"Their planet."

Stingray fought back a laugh. "Are you serious? There are four of you here. Or five, if you include me, or six counting that boy wasting away in the Medikum."

"Cal would help us, I'm sure," said Valjhar thoughtfully. "And I believe we could find others. They're not all crazy down there."

"Valjhar. You on this ship are all very fine people, to be sure, and I'm grateful to be here among you. But as I have observed before, you have enough difficulty keeping yourselves out of trouble, even when you're not trying to take over a planet full of violent ape-things."

Valjhar bit his lip. "I can't deny that. What do you think, Shaula?"

"I think it would be wonderful if we could rescue those people from themselves. I'm sure the simple act of making our presence known to them would result in substantial changes. But whether we could guide or influence those changes to a good end, or if it would all just tumble out of control, I can't say. Stingray's right, we are few, and we are not gods."

Valjhar nodded, his eyes lowered. "I suppose you're both right."

"So, that's settled," said Stingray. "Again."

They crept on into that dense mass of stars, leaving behind the dust and gas of the younger, more fecund parts of the galaxy, entering a clearer region that set *Mote* aglow with the golden light of billions of ancient suns. As they neared the source of what was almost but not quite a voice, they speculated on what they would find. Would it be a planet where life had somehow endured, even as its sun entered its senescence? Would it be some great derelict spacecraft, with one lonely mind crying out in desperation? Would it be some ancient and unknown form of life inhabiting the quiet spaces of the galactic hub?

It turned out to be none of these. It was a black hole—not the somnolent monster that dwelt in the galaxy's very center, but a lesser object, of stellar mass, with no source of infalling matter to illuminate its surroundings, and so quite dark indeed.

Kern guided *Mote* to a distance where the black hole's gravitational attraction was equivalent to that of Rral. He set the ship to hovering over it, resulting in a natural gravitational environment aboard it. This of course meant that the black hole could only be seen from the small landing control bay in the ship's belly.

Even at this distance, the gravitational gradient between the bridge and the landing bay was measurable, resulting in a slight stress on the structure of the ship.

The Mariners stared through the ports at the black hole, a small, fathomless black disk made more conspicuous by the distorting effect its gravity had on the star field beyond it.

"How can anything live inside a black hole?" asked Shaula.

"How can anything even exist inside one?" said Kern.

No one had any answer. For hours they crouched in the dimly-lit bay, looking through the ports toward the ominous, enigmatic thing drifting a few million kiloskads below. It continued to whisper at them, though what it wanted, or what it was trying to say, fell beyond them, except for their shared conviction that it contained a powerful yearning.

There passed a strange interlude of some days, during which they were reluctant to be apart from each other, and also reluctant to be out of sight of the black hole, though the sight of it began to oppress them. Thus they rarely left the landing bay, and they huddled closely together, except for Stingray, who sat a little apart, frowning downward.

Sleep deprived, they took to napping there on the deck, or in their chairs, so powerful was the pull of the black hole on their minds. Valjhar was vaguely aware that something was wrong, that a spell of some kind had been cast upon them, but he could not summon up the will or the clarity of mind to try to overcome it.

Stingray, evidently, was not so affected, and at last he lost patience.

"You look like so many little goblins, staring at some distant lantern."

"Goblins?" said Pimsie. "No, we've seen goblins. We don't look like goblins."

"That's enough. Valjhar. If you don't stop mooning around and snap out of this funk, I'm going to take control of this ship and get us away from that blasted thing out there, voice or no voice."

"No, you can't!" cried Pimsie, exhibiting more animation than she had in weeks.

"She's right," said Valjhar. "We must remain here. There's something we need to do."

"And what might that be?" said Stingray.

"We don't know yet."

"Hmm." Stingray turned to Shaula. "What do you think?"

Shaula appeared confused. "I'm not sure either. I feel the call that's keeping us here, but whatever it is, it's having trouble communicating with us."

"Not too surprising, considering it's trying to communicate through the event horizon of a black hole," said Kern.

"Wait, what's that?" said Pimsie, her ears springing fully erect.

Valjhar heard it too...a shuffling sound, coming from somewhere in the upper decks. They sat as still as startled minkarubes as they listened. Gradually the sound grew more distinct, resolving into irregular footsteps. They grew louder. They were descending the stairs, unsteadily.

"Valjhar! Shaula! What is it?" whispered Pimsie.

But Valjhar did not know, and no one else volunteered an answer.

A shadowy head appeared in the hatchway. A thin figure came into view.

Valjhar felt a strange and unjustified relief. "It's Kroy! It's only Kroy!"

Kern and Pimsie laughed in equal relief. But Stingray frowned. "What do you mean, 'only Kroy'? Which of you woke him up? Did any of you?"

"No," said Shaula. "None of us did."

Valjhar peered more closely at the staring figure, and especially into his eyes. "This isn't Kroy."

"He hasn't been Kroy dal Ren in a long time," said Kern.

"That's not what Valjhar means," said Shaula, who never took her eyes off their strange visitor. "It's not the star being version of him either. This is something new."

Pimsie groaned. "You mean something else has taken possession of him?"

"Perhaps."

The figure opened its mouth, but nothing emerged but indistinct croaks.

"He's trying to speak," said Kern. "I'll go get some water." He dashed from the bay, giving Kroy a wide berth.

Before he could return, the figure abruptly collapsed onto the deck, apparently returning to the coma they had placed him in.

"What just happened?" said Pimsie in horror.

"I think...that the thing in that black hole just used Kroy's body to...see us," said Valjhar quietly.

"And to try to communicate as well," said Stingray.

Kern returned with a bowl of water. He looked at the prostrate figure on the deck, raised the bowl to his own lips, and drained it.

"It didn't work very well," said Valjhar.

"That's not surprising," said Kern in a shaky tone. "The basis of telepathy is an imposed smoothing out of the natural chaos of the quantum foam, to permit some kind of signal to propagate across it. But the extreme distortion of space-time in the gravitational environment of a black hole would make that difficult."

"I assume we could make it easier by getting closer," said Valjhar.

"That poses its own difficulties."

"I should say it does!" said Shaula. "Even I know that getting too close a black hole will tear us to shreds."

"But we must try," said Valjhar.

Stingray looked at him in disbelief, especially as none of the others objected to his statement. "You must? Why? What you must do is turn this ship around and get the hell away from whatever force is getting its grip on you, and even on your poor unconscious friend here."

"Where would you have us go? Earth?"

"No! But this universe must offer other options than Earth and this weird black hole that beckons you toward disaster. It's not as if we've explored it at all thoroughly. We could never even fully explore this galaxy, not if we lived for ten thousand years and did nothing else."

"That sounds like a long time," said Shaula. "But here, I think, we have something even older. Far, far older."

"And far too much for the likes of any of us to handle!"

"Then you feel it too, Stingray?" asked Kern.

"Yes. But unlike all of you, I don't feel it as a call. I feel it as a threat."

"You feel everything as a threat," said Pimsie. "Whatever is in there...it...it needs our help."

Stingray looked at her carefully and spoke in a measured voice. "When I see you discarding caution while influenced by something completely unknown, and maybe unknowable, then yes, I do see that as a threat."

"Why do you say it's unknowable?" said Valjhar. "It's a part of the universe, whatever it is. Our people were once lords of this universe, and knew no fear."

"As I understand it, Valjhar, your ancestors fell from their high perch atop the physical universe because they were unable to understand or accept a different, deeper level of reality than any they had ever encountered or considered. It drove them mad."

"Yes. The Stones of Rral, and all that they represent. But that was thousands of years ago. We here have endured the Stones. Not happily, maybe, but they did not drive us mad."

"Your people fled in terror from a reality they could not grasp, for a life as simple villagers, farmers, and merchants."

"And we fled from that life."

"Our life on Rral was peaceful and beautiful!" shouted Pimsie. "At least we weren't living in the sea like animals!"

Stingray immediately looked abashed and regretful. Valjhar took pity on him.

"You're right, Stingray. Our ancestors fled and withdrew into themselves, into our cozy little world. But we will not flee. We will not turn away, because if we do, what are we then? Nothing more than a group of vagabonds, doing nothing, achieving nothing, wandering without any hope or purpose."

"We cannot face the universe in fear, Stingray," said Shaula. "To you we may seem like little mice scampering among the stars, but to us, we're the heroes of a great adventure, even if we keep that thought buried deep."

Kern grinned. Pimsie said, "You may all be heroes, but I'm just a girl who wishes she could go home."

Stingray looked into each face in turn, and then he smiled. That expression always unnerved Valjhar, revealing those twin rows of massive white teeth as it did.

"No, I don't see you as mice. I see you as the finest people I've ever known."

"We're also the only people you've ever known, practically speaking, you big oaf," said Kern.

"Pimsie, what does Nali have to say about all this?" asked Valjhar.

Pimsie looked surprised. "Nali? This sounds ridiculous, but I'd almost forgotten about her. She's been quiet for the longest time. I think she may even have stayed behind on Earth, somehow...I...oh dear..." With that, Pimsie collapsed into a chair and was instantly asleep.

And then there was Nali, the Dreamfarer, sitting on the deck near one of the downward-looking ports, which she ignored. She waved her hand, and a circle of dim blue flames appeared on the deck before her. She leaned into it, staring intently. She was again in the form in which they'd first seen her, a small Rralian figure, blue in color, wearing her funny tall hat. Her opaque green eyes were as unfathomable as ever.

"Pimsie was wrong," she said in her whispery voice. "I have been asleep since we entered this vast empty region, where so few beings live and dream. But I could not sleep near the thing that lurks in that dark star beneath us."

Valjhar shivered. That dim, shifting pool of cold fire was somehow a window for Nali, through which she saw things he could not imagine.

Whatever she saw now caused her to recoil in fear, a reaction which Valjhar easily shared, unprecedented as it was.

"There is madness here. It is a madness as old as the universe itself, and a pain as deep. I warn you. Leave now, leave the dark star far behind. Otherwise, I fear you are in danger of losing one of you, at least."

"What is this danger?" said Stingray.

Nali slowly turned her head, catching Stingray with her icy green gaze. "Your dreams can never come true, you poor thing."

"Never mind my dreams. I said, what is this danger? Don't tantalize us with your vague and spooky warnings."

"The danger is that you will be devoured by the hungry thing that dwells below. No one of you is large enough to withstand it. Now I will leave you. I will not risk myself to dissolution. I hope someday I may find Pimsehkia again. She is very dear to me. Good bye."

The Dreamfarer vanished. Her fire flickered, and then it too was gone.

Pimsie awoke, blinking, and looking very sad. "Valjhar," she said.

Her meaning was clear. Valjhar nodded. "I agree. We're getting out of here. Does anyone object?"

"I certainly don't!" said Kern. "Nali's advice seemed very sound to me!"

"Yes, it did," said Stingray.

Shaula spoke slowly and thoughtfully, as though she had not heard the others.

"When I was approached by the Select and offered my mission, I was told that if I succeeded, I would eventually receive the responsibility of guarding an entire universe. We all know now that I failed that mission, and that I was never fit to receive such a charge in the first place. But this is not an entire universe. It is a single being, it seems, a single creature, in some great need or pain, and it has drawn us here across half a galaxy. We can flee from it in fear, but if we do, it will be a failure not only for me, but for all of us. If we flee, we might as well find some little corner in which to hide and cower, for we will have proven ourselves too small to face what's out here among the stars."

Valjhar stared at Shaula, torn between the poles of her courage and Pimsie's entirely justifiable fears. Pimsie regarded him from beneath lowered eyelids, as though she already knew which way his decision would go.

"Whatever we do," said Valjhar, "we must do it together. We must not commit to some desperate venture unless we are all agreed on it." Even as he said this, Valjhar knew his words were hollow. He would not now be able to retreat from this challenge, not if he wished to retain some regard for himself.

Pimsie knew this too. "What can we even do?" she said in a dull voice. "I don't see how we can interact with this thing unless we actually enter the black hole, and nothing can survive that."

Valjhar knew from her tone that he would never be completely forgiven for this.

Kern, whose excitement evidently blocked any aware-ness of Pimsie's mood, piped up brightly. "I'm not so sure! I've been thinking about some hints I picked up from the most advanced parts of our Compendium, and it's given me some ideas. I call the concept Gravity Resolution. I'll have more to say about that after I've done a little more work."

"So we don't have to do anything right away?" said Pimsie.

"No. Not right away," said Valjhar.

Stingray scowled.

The atmosphere aboard *Mote* settled into an air of quiet apprehension. Pimsie disappeared into her cabin, while Kern was absorbed with the Compendium and his own in-creasingly mysterious thoughts. Stingray lurked in the land-ing bay, glowering at the Dark Star as though he expected it to strike at them at any moment.

Valjhar found himself feeling more isolated than ever. One night, or rather, during those hours which they ac-cepted as the shipboard night, he felt driven to relieve that condition, and perhaps to resolve his stalled relationship with Shaula, whose stasis, he was forced to admit, was largely due to his dread of the potential consequences of trying to advance it.

To that end, he crept to the door of Shaula's cabin and gave it a tentative knock. After several moments of a pain-ful silence he was about to creep away again, when some unruly impulse led him to knock again, this time more de-cisively. After all, surely he had by now earned the right to intrude on Shaula, if only to the slightest degree?

"Come in, Valjhar," said a muffled voice.

Valjhar entered the darkened chamber, which was thick with Shaula's scent, a scent that caused his head to spin. She now smelled like a true Rralian, and he thought in passing that it was a marvel he'd never noticed that difference before she was changed.

Shaula was sitting up in her bed. In the dim light provided by a single node, he saw that she was naked, at least from the waist up. Rralians were always fairly casual about nudity, but here in her personal space it seemed more intimate, and somehow intoxicating.

"I heard your first knock, Valjhar, but I thought I was dreaming," she said quietly.

Valjhar stood looking down at her mutely. Shaula returned his gaze, and several long moments passed again.

"Well?" she said at last.

"Shaula, I…"

Shaula opened her arms, and Valjhar fell into them. From that point on his conscious mind had very little to do with his actions, other than to observe and take notes for possible future emendations. His penis bulged with a fish that badly needed to be expressed, and Shaula accepted it gladly, relieving him of it with an unexpected expertise for someone whose sexual organs had changed so radically and so recently. He lay back grinning in bliss as Shaula held it inside, in ecstasy from its hopeful wriggles. She had closed off her gestation chamber, so there was no risk of pregnancy, but the pleasure was no less real.

When both had recovered their wits after this long-awaited passion, they remained cuddled together in Shaula's warm bed.

"I've been listening for that knock for a long time," said Shaula. "What took you so long?"

"Well, I'm kind of a clueless dunce at times," he said, hoping she would disagree.

"That's true, we're all aware of that." Sensing his disappointment, she added, "But we all love you anyway."

"I'm not so sure Pimsie loves me much," said Valjhar ruefully.

Shaula rolled her eyes. "Don't be such a ninny. Pimsie loves you more than anyone. You were her first love. That means a lot to any girl. Or to any boy, for that matter."

"More than Kern?"

"Yes, even more than Kern, but that dear boy doesn't realize it, or if he does, he doesn't really mind, because he adores you so much himself. But love you as she may, Pimsie can and does still resent things you do, and someday you may go too far."

Valjhar fell silent as he contemplated her words.

Shaula sighed and stretched. "So that was Rralian sex. I must say, I approve."

Valjhar grinned with satisfaction, until a thought occurred to him. "How does it compare with other forms of sex you've had?"

"Yes, I certainly do approve of Rralian sex. And I'm glad I was able to distract you."

"Distract me from what?"

"Your fear."

"Yes, I am afraid. Who wouldn't be?"

"I'm not, for some reason. I don't know why, really. I can feel the Dark Star drawing me right now, but I don't fear it. I don't think it's evil, whatever it is. And after everything we've faced and survived already, I think we won't fall this time either."

"Nali never said it was evil. She said it was insane, and that, I think, could be even more dangerous. And I fear Nali's hint about one or more of us being lost. I could not bear to lose you, Shaula. Not after it's taken me so long to truly find you."

"I promise you this, Valjhar Cor. If ever we are parted, I will return to you, as long as I'm alive."

For a few moments Valjhar was too moved with emotion to reply.

"How can you make such a promise?"

She smiled. "It's not so difficult. You'll note I specified that I have to be alive. I'm not committing myself to the impossible."

Suddenly the ship lurched and quivered around them. They looked at each other.

"I suppose we should get dressed and go see what's happening," said Valjhar.

"Yes, I suppose so. The Dark Star may be growing impatient."

Before they could stir, the door of Shaula's cabin burst open, revealing an excited Kern.

"Gravity resolution! That's what that little bump came from. What have you two been doing? Oh. Never mind. I need to talk to you though, Valjhar. I need something from you to continue my experiments. Otherwise there's a slight danger I could detach the central boson, which would dissolve the ship into a cloud of fundamental particles."

He closed the door and could be heard hurrying away.

"Well then, let's not keep him waiting," said Shaula.

A few minutes later they were on the bridge, where an agitated Kern and Stingray were deep in discussion.

"Valjhar!" said Kern. "I need that thing. You know, that strange sphere you picked up from my ancestor's museum."

For a moment Valjhar had to think about what Kern meant, it had been so long since he'd given that artifact any thought.

"Oh, all right. How will that help you?"

"You've described its strange properties. Sometimes it seems to ignore gravity, and it seems immune to any kind of spacial distortion. That could be very useful."

Valjhar retrieved the globe from a locker in his cabin. It was small enough to fit in his palm, a smooth translucent sphere, faintly aglow from within by the light of a curiously twisted loop of soft radiance. He might have dismissed it as a mere art object if not for its strange behavior.

Back beneath the bubble, he performed his favorite trick with the sphere — lifting it to eye level and then releasing it, where it hung absolutely motionless with respect to the ship, though how it was moving with respect to other frames of reference, Valjhar could not tell.

"It's lovely," said Pimsie as she came up the stairs behind him. "I would have chosen that as a souvenir too."

Valjhar turned to address her. "I'm sure you would have found something at least as beautiful." Turning back, he absently stepped forward, forgetting the floating globe. He felt nothing but a chill as it passed through his skull without leaving a mark, entering his brain without any disruption.

"Where did it go?" he dimly heard Kern say, before his perception of the world changed into something unknown and incomprehensible.

After a few moments the world grew dim and grainy, and then it went black and silent. It was only when he moved that vision returned, and then only as long as continued to move, however slowly. And slow it was. He felt as though he were immersed in a thick syrup that resisted his every attempt at motion. But at least he *was* moving. As far as he could tell with his faint and sporadic eyesight, everyone else was frozen in place, completely inert.

He tried to raise his hands to see if they were unchanged. As they slowly came into view they were preceded and surrounded by a flickering pinkish-orange nimbus — plasma. Valjhar froze. His vision quickly went dark again.

It was that thing, that object, the little sphere he felt as a cold presence inside his head. It must be. It must come out. It had gone in without any trouble, so presumably it could emerge the same way.

He considered it, thought of its location, recalled how it often hung suspended in space. With that image in mind he jerked his head back with all the speed he could muster.

He re-emerged into the normal world just in time to witness a minor cataclysm. A detonation echoed from the bubble, and every one of his companions screeched or yelled. Valjhar felt a burst of heat that quickly dissipated. He looked around in confusion, his ears ringing.

"Valjhar! What happened to you?" cried Kern.

"To me? I'm not sure. What did you see?"

"You somehow stepped into that little toy of yours, then suddenly you were in a different place and pose, and there was an explosion!"

Kern was staring at Valjhar's hand in wide-eyed fascination. Valjhar looked down, realizing only then that the globe was lying in his hand, cool and now quite weighty for its size.

"It was this," said Valjhar, raising it. "Somehow it—altered my perception of time, or something like that. To me it seemed as if the outside world was frozen. Even light took its time reaching me. It was extremely disorienting. I wouldn't care to do that again."

"Good!" said Pimsie.

"Kern, have you ever heard of such a thing in your studies of Rralian technology?" said Stingray.

"An art object capable of manipulating time, passing through matter, and defying gravity? No. But with those properties, it might be really useful for my experiments."

Valjhar handed it over with a mixture of relief and apprehension. "Just promise me you won't put it in your head."

"I won't let him," said Pimsie firmly.

"That thing is a true mystery," said Shaula. "I suspect we're barely aware of its full potential. I wonder if anyone, on Old Rral or not, ever really understood it."

"You mean it's not Rralian technology?" said Stingray.

Kern shook his head. "We have no reason to think so. It was a curio, a museum exhibit. Whatever this Motionglobe is, its origin may forever be unknown to us. But that doesn't mean it won't be useful."

Valjhar required days of quiet and meditation to recover from the disorientation caused by his brief use of the Motionglobe. His mind made a difficult adjustment to the knowledge that what his senses revealed was not a full or accurate picture of the world and its workings. During that period he was glad the globe was not in his cabin, though it was of course not very far away in Kern's physics lab. Between its very disconcerting nature and the continuing subtle call of the Dark Star, he was having trouble maintaining his mental balance.

He did not see the artifact again until Kern casually tossed it to him at the start of their next meeting on the bridge.

"So what have you found?" said Valjhar. "How can we get closer to the Dark Star?"

"I think we can not only get closer, but actually enter the event horizon of the black hole."

"We await your explanation, which you are so plainly eager to deliver," said Stingray.

Kern nodded. "Consider how gravity interacts with matter. It only affects things that possess mass. Now consider the structure of matter. Almost all the mass of each atom is concentrated in the nucleus, which occupies a very tiny part of any atom. Very tiny. The rest of every apparently solid object, the vast majority of it, is empty space, except for the ghostly electron cloud, which itself occupies a very small volume of any atom and has little mass. That means gravity really acts only on a minuscule part of our ship, and of ourselves."

"That's clear enough," said Shaula. "But how does it help us?"

"Now we come to the phenomenon I call gravity resolution! How is it that gravity can interact with such tiny particles? How is it 'aware' of them? I've discovered that gravity has a property, which I call resolution, that determines the smallest size of any object it can interact with. Normally that resolution is fine enough to include all massive sub-atomic particles. But what if even smaller particles lack apparent mass only because they're too small for gravity to 'see'? And what if the resolution property of gravity could be changed locally, so that atomic nuclei fell below that threshold?"

"Then any matter within that region of influence...would be transparent to gravity. It would ignore gravity," said Valjhar, impressed.

"And you think you can do that?" said Stingray.

"And what about the Motionglobe?" said Valjhar. "How did it help you discover this?"

"Oh, that? It didn't, really. It turns out that the Motionglobe's conditional immunity to gravity has no relevance to our situation. You see, it's not even made of matter. Not the atomic matter we're familiar with, anyway. X-ray diffraction and other tests made that very clear. I don't know what it's made of. But, it was fun to play with for a while."

"Back to my somewhat more pressing question," said Stingray.

"Oh yes. Yes, I think I can do it, and probably without dissolving the ship or anything like that."

"That's good news," said Shaula dryly.

"And once it's done," continued Kern, "I see no reason why we cannot only approach the black hole, but actually cross the event horizon, while suffering no effects from the intense gravity gradient that will be passing through us, unnoticed, or even from any time distortion. And that will be a new kind of exploration."

"Very good!" said Valjhar.

"There's only one problem. I'll need raw materials for the new equipment, more than we have aboard the ship.

And it will be tough to find locally, because this galactic neighborhood isn't exactly rich in heavy elements."

"So we'll have to...leave the black hole?" said Pimsie.

"Yes, temporarily. We might have to travel a thousand light-years to find what we need. I don't like the idea much myself."

"I'm not so sure that damned hole will approve either," said Stingray.

Stingray's apprehension proved to be justified. As soon as they applied power to depart from the Dark Star, the pull on the minds of the Rralians intensified greatly. It became a torment as they felt the anger and desperation of whatever lurked within it eating at their minds. Shaula grew pale and tense, while Pimsie cringed, grimacing, and holding her head in her arms as though trying to shut out a painful noise. Valjhar tried to steel himself, but when the Dark Star resorted to once again animating Kroy and sending him shambling about while moaning incoherently, it was too much. He steered Mote back to its station. Only then did the call of the Dark Star subside to tolerable levels. Pimsie wept with relief. Valjhar felt like following her example.

Kroy collapsed. While Stingray scooped him off the deck he growled, "That's what I was afraid of. We're practically prisoners and slaves of this Dark Star."

"If only we could communicate with it, let it know we need to gather materials to permit us to venture closer," said Shaula.

"But no information can cross the event horizon," said Kern. "I don't even understand how it can make itself felt outside at all."

"Kern, can you apply your gravity resolution technology to a small probe, send it in, and let the entity know our intentions?" said Valjhar.

Kern's face lit up. "That might work. I should build a working model anyway, before modifying the entire ship."

While Kern worked on the probe, the others tried to think of a way in which they might communicate with the Dark Star or whatever it contained. A common language was almost certainly out of the question. They had no idea what, if any, sensory capabilities the thing might have, casting doubt on the value of any images or symbols they might send.

Presently they were forced to admit they knew no method of making themselves clear to such an unknown intelligence. The only possibility seemed to be a direct telepathic contact, one un-muddled by the chaos of the event horizon, but if they could do that, they wouldn't need the probe in the first place.

"Well," said Stingray, "I can think of one way for it to work."

The others looked at him cautiously, made wary by his tone of voice.

"And what might that be?" said Valjhar.

"Send someone in with the probe."

"Oh, that sounds very safe!" burst out Pimsie. "You, I hope?"

Stingray winced, nearly imperceptibly, but not quite so. "No, it can't be me. I'm not even slightly telepathic."

"How do you think that could work, Stingray?" asked Shaula.

"Space suit. That should be enough. With Kern's gravity transparency trick in place, there should be no great stresses involved, and the radiation environment is mild."

"No great stresses other than those involved with entering a black hole, alone, protected only by a space suit, to confront some great mystery on the other side," mused Valjhar. "And yet I see that this could work, and might be the only way."

Valjhar took a deep breath, held it, and released a sigh. "I'll go."

Stingray visibly restrained a snort of incredulity. "You? That's very brave, and pardon me for saying so, but as I understand it, your telepathic ability is minimal at best."

"And who would you have me send? You've already disqualified yourself. Pimsie or Shaula? No. Not either of them."

"It's a ridiculous idea, and none of us will go!" said Pimsie. "Not if I have anything to say about it, anyway."

Valjhar said nothing, but he had made up his mind to go, despite Pimsie's objections. He left the others and went to Kern, who was working on the probe in the excursion bay. It was a haphazard-looking device only a little larger than either of them, studded with optical thrusters and antennae. It was wrapped in a crisscrossing mesh of thin translucent greenish cables.

"This is what I'll have to do to the whole ship, if we ever get the chance," said Kern, plucking one of the cables.

"Have you tested it yet?"

"The basic propulsion and guidance systems are too simple to need much testing, but I haven't tested the antigravity system yet, no."

"Could you though?"

Kern looked thoughtful for a moment. "I hadn't planned on doing that until tomorrow, but I suppose I could try flipping it on for a few moments."

"Please do it."

"All right, all right! So impatient. You're afraid you'll miss something interesting, right?"

"Right."

"Normally, we'll control it remotely, of course, but I did install a simple control panel for testing purposes. Here goes!"

Kern touched a few contacts. The cables glowed with a subtle light, and Kern drifted off the floor. The probe itself was fixed to the deck.

Laughing, Kern deactivated the system and dropped lightly to his feet. "Looks like it works! I didn't really know if it would. Wow, gravity tamed. Now we can ignore gravity if we want to. Quit pushing us around, gravity!"

"Why did it affect you as well?"

"The effect has to reach the interior of the probe, and it also radiates outward from the cables for an equal distance. Are you satisfied? You look awfully glum."

"Yes, Kern, I'm satisfied. That's some really outstanding work. Thanks."

Valjhar left, leaving Kern looking puzzled and concerned. He took to his cabin, resolved to get a little sleep before setting off on his venture in the middle of the shipboard night. But sleep proved elusive, an unusual condition for any Rralian. In his half-conscious state, the space around him seemed ominous, filled with strange sounds and chords. His mind felt as though an electrical storm were raging within it, with bolts and sparks terminating his thoughts almost before they could form.

Abruptly he awoke. The ship was quiet. It was very quiet. It was, in fact, too quiet.

Valjhar bolted upright. Something was missing. He hurried down to the excursion bay, where he confronted a sight so strange and unexpected that his mind took a moment to interpret what he was seeing.

Kern sat on the deck, his back against a bulkhead. He was bound, prevented from moving, by wires and cables wrapped around his body. He was prevented from speaking by a cloth that was stuffed in his mouth and held in place with another cord. He stared at Valjhar with his dark violet eyes.

The probe was gone.

Valjhar approached Kern cautiously, still very much unsure of what he was dealing with. He gently undid the cord around his friend's head, and Kern spit out the gag.

"It was Shaula!" he blurted.

"What was Shaula?" said Valjhar, not comprehending.

"She did this to me! She took the probe!"

That shocked Valjhar almost to the point of numbness. He fumbled with Kern's bonds as he continued excitedly.

"She showed up an hour ago and seemed surprised to find me here, still working. She asked me about the probe, whether it had been tested and so forth, just as you had. She was interested in the control panel. Then she began to tie me up. She kept apologizing, and I just stood there because I couldn't believe what was happening. After a while I thought maybe I should fight back. But then I thought, attack Shaula? No. She's bigger than me anyway. Then she apologized again and left the ship with the probe."

"She's chosen to go into the Dark Star," said Valjhar with a feeling of dread. He managed to free Kern's hands, then lost track of his task as his thoughts drifted toward this latest disaster, leaving Kern to free himself on his own. Valjhar sagged down onto the deck.

His friend's voice broke into the mental haze that enveloped him. "Don't just sit there like a minkarube! Contact Shaula! Tell her to come back before it's too late!"

"What? After all she's done, do you really think she'd listen to me if I told her to turn around?"

"Then what are we going to do?"

"I don't know. She's probably at least halfway to the Dark Star by now. We can't take the ship that much closer, can we?"

"No...the ship is too big to take the gravitational gradient at that distance."

"Can we take control of the probe from here?"

"No again. The onboard controls take precedence over the remote. Well, that's not quite true. We could turn off the gravity modifier."

"But that would kill her."

"Yes—if she's too close to the Dark Star it would destroy her, and the probe as well."

"Can you walk? Come up to the bridge with me. We have to find out how far she's gotten."

They climbed up through the ship as fast as they could. So far it seemed that Stingray and Pimsie were unaware of the crisis, which was all right with Valjhar. He didn't feel like dealing with either of them at the moment.

The instruments on the bridge revealed Shaula easily enough. With the gravity modifier active she could not simply fall toward the black hole, but must use the probe's thrusters to accelerate toward it.

A feeling of doom overtook Valjhar. He could not foresee anything good, or even anything tolerable, coming from this. At the same time, the situation was simplified, and his mind clarified.

"I can't let this happen. Not like this. I'm going after her."

"But Valjhar! Shaula did this to save you!"

"Of course she did. But do you think I want to live if she sacrifices herself for me? No. We will face whatever awaits us in there together, no matter what the result. Help me, Kern. Meet me at the dorsal airlock. Prepare a space suit for me. Don't look so sad. This has to happen."

Valjhar ran off to his cabin before the dread and grief he saw in Kern's face could erode his resolve. There he snatched up the dimension belt, and then, more reluctantly, the Motionglobe.

At the airlock, Kern, whose miserable face was streaked with tears, glanced at the belt. "You—you'd better reach her fast. You won't be able to withstand the gravitational gradient at her location for very long at all. And Valjhar—I'm sorry—I couldn't stop her..."

Valjhar placed his hand on Kern's shoulder. "Of course you couldn't. I doubt any of us could have. She's a very determined person. Just do one thing for me. If we don't come back, promise you'll find a way to get Pimsie safely back to Rral."

"I will. But what about Stingray?"

Valjhar shrugged his way into the glossy white fabric of the space suit. "Drop him off in Vornager Bay. He should be no worse off there than anywhere else. Goodbye, Kern."

The suit was on and sealed. The belt was fastened around it, leaving Valjhar with no further excuse to linger. He cycled through the airlock and stood on the small deck surrounding the outer hatch. He was held there by the gravity of the Dark Star, invisible to him directly beneath his feet. The ship was dark. Around him glowed the billions of closely-packed stars of the galactic hub.

He stepped off the deck and onto the ship's smoothly curving hull. He allowed himself to slide down, and then he fell off.

With *Mote* held relatively motionless, Valjhar fell directly toward the black hole. It was a small circular nothingness beneath him, surrounded by the arcs and rings of light which were the distorted images of the stars beyond it. Of course Shaula and the probe were not visible from this distance.

Valjhar looked up. *Mote* looked like a small dark sea bird, dwindling rapidly. He looked away. It was too poignant a sight to bear.

He would never catch Shaula by simply falling. He must close the distance between them, and quickly. He activated the dimension belt. The dimension modulator's lens glowed, emitting some ineffable force every bit as strange as those forces shaping the black hole, and far less well understood.

Under Valjhar's direction, it collapsed a corridor of space beneath him, reducing half of the roughly six million kiloskads between him and the black hole to only a hundred skads. Immediately the Dark Star bloomed to twice its apparent size. At this distance the gravitational gradient on his small body was still negligible. He activated his suit's radar, searching for a reflection from the probe and Shaula.

He was terrified, and more alone than he'd ever been. Only by focusing a large fraction of his mind on Shaula and her plight did he keep from panicking and seeking a way back to the distant ship that was the only mote of life and warmth within trillions of kiloskads.

The suit's radar and other sensors failed to detect Shaula. He must risk making another jump via the dimension belt. This one was smaller, as he could not venture too close to the black hole without the protection of gravity modification. Still, now that he was a million kiloskads closer, he felt the first twinges of an unpleasant force acting on his body, pulling at him, trying to stretch him. The force of gravity was now increasing so rapidly that its effect was noticeable greater at his feet than it was at his head. If he continued on unprotected, he would eventually be shredded to atoms.

Now his instruments did perceive a faint signal from Shaula and the probe. It was yet another million kiloskads distant, close enough to the Dark Star to put in within the danger zone. Valjhar's next jump must be precise and accurate, because he would not have much time to reach the protection of the probe before the stresses became too great. He spent several tense minutes carefully measuring and analyzing Shaula's position and trajectory before committing himself to the jump.

In the end, the result was almost too perfect. He emerged from his space warp only two skads from the probe, and had only instants to close that distance via the suit's optical thrusters before he was torn apart.

He wound up clinging to the probe, breathing heavily while he looked at Shaula's face through her helmet from only inches away. Her expression reflected a welter of astonishment, grief, admiration, and perhaps, relief.

Finally her voice came over the communication circuit in Valjhar's helmet.

"Valjhar Cor. You are a very foolish boy. Once you flung yourself into a raging sea to rescue me from a storm-tossed rock. You survived, but I'm afraid the thing we face now may not be so gentle."

"So be it then, Shaula. Our story has been an imperfect one, with too many years lost to misunderstanding, all due to me, I fear. But I will not let our story end with you departing, and me left bereft, to wander the heavens with an empty heart."

Shaula reached out and clutched Valjhar's gloved hand. "Then let's face this great mystery together, and perhaps we'll yet prevail."

They lapsed into silence as they fell closer to the Dark Star. More and more immense it loomed up before them, until, now just seconds away, it covered half of everything with a field of impenetrable blackness.

"We're about to enter a black hole," said Valjhar dully.

"I know."

"We're crazy."

"I know."

At the instant of crossing there seemed to be a flare of white light, so short-lived as to be nearly imperceptible. And then they saw the stars, painted across their field of vision in a new way, as though they were literally painted there, but that paint had been liquified and separated into many colors, smeared across the firmament in strange and ever-shifting ways.

"I didn't think we'd be able to see anything in here," whispered Shaula. "Certainly not starlight."

"Nor did I, but now that I think of it, it makes sense. Light can pass through the event horizon. It simply can't get out again. It must all be drawn into the singularity."

"And where is that?"

"At the center, but I don't know if it will be visible. If we don't want to visit it ourselves, we'd better slow down."

Shaula manipulated the controls and the probe lost speed. The incomprehensible flux of gravity ignored them, thanks to Kern's ingenuity. Valjhar hoped Kern's workmanship was as sound as ever, considering this was meant to be a single-use probe, and it was surrounded by a force that could tear it and them into a cloud of quarks at the slightest wavering of its gravitational camouflage.

As Valjhar gaped at the surrounding spectacle of distorted starlight he also waited for a sign of the presence of whatever being comprised or inhabited this thing. What he actually felt was, in some ways, exactly the opposite. He became increasingly self-conscious, aware of himself as a unique and separate entity, with a very distinct identity. Too distinct, it suddenly seemed to him. He was himself, and he had always been himself. He had never experienced the universe from the perspective of anyone else, not really. He was always himself. and nothing else.

He caught sight of his face in a reflective surface of the probe. There was his own blank face, looking back at him. Why was he always himself? What did it mean to be himself, such an isolated little unit of consciousness, always thinking with the same mind and thoughts? Why couldn't he be someone else once in a while?

As he pondered these questions that would have seemed to him meaningless nonsense a short time ago, he felt he was on the verge of dissolving into nothingness, negated by questions that could not be answered and by the absurdity of his own being. And he welcomed that. Suddenly his own being did not seem to be anything worth preserving. It was only an illusion and a limitation that was best done away with.

His surroundings faded away. His thoughts quieted to a formless white light. His mind dispersed.

And then, he was someone else. He was a different mind, a different being, a huge, thunderous mind, but a mind frozen in time, crystallized in space, unable to move beyond the terrible thing that had befallen it, endlessly crying for help into a void that could not hear. He should have let himself die like the others, but he had not, and in preserving some semblance of himself he had doomed himself to a timeless eternity of stasis and despair.

But now it was suddenly slightly different. Something new, something foreign, was present, or rather, two somethings. It was difficult to tease out their individuality, so thoroughly had they been subsumed into itself, but it was still possible. At its deepest level, one of them thought of itself as a Rralian, and as the leader of a group he called the Space Mariners. The other thought of itself as the protector of that group, and also as an agent of something called the Select.

That revelation caused a ripple of surprise that was both of and apart from itself.

They each also thought of themselves as the mate of one another.

The mind of the Dark Star struggled to recall memories that it usually suppressed.

He saw the ship...long, elegant, and proud, a culminating work of a mighty civilization, and he was its captain. He himself was masterful, possessed of a powerful intellect capable of dominating those around him, as well as a keen understanding of many mysteries of time and space. He glanced at the memory of his hands. They were large and strong, yet deft and graceful, covered with a smooth skin of golden bronze.

He was proud to command such an audacious expedition, one intended to pierce the barrier between one universe and another, to explore the roots and origins of this foreign universe, starting from a time bare moments after its convulsive birth, when all its energy and the simplest constituents of matter were crammed into a volume little larger than an ordinary star system, though it was expanding fast.

And then in this inferno, the worst of luck—a primordial black hole, so close to their arrival point that the ship was already within its grasp. Hidden by the layers of shielding required to preserve the ship from the all-consuming radiance outside, it at first eluded detection, and then, by the time the ship's unpromising navigator managed to make the situation clear, it was too late. The ship had been shredded, and all had died, except himself, who had managed, through sheer strength of mind and will, to impose the basic structure of his self on the twisted space within the event horizon. It was an existence both timeless and interminable. The same dreary thoughts rang through depths of time it could neither measure nor comprehend. It could not grow, it could not evolve, it could not leave behind its crushing grief and disappointment.

But now, at last, something new had entered its mind. Two somethings. And from them, the Dark Star wanted only one thing.

It expelled the newcomers from its being. Their minds, so fleeting and yet so nimble and inquisitive, coalesced again into their tiny bodies, still clinging to their tiny machine with its marvelous ability to survive this irresistible vise of space.

Valjhar's mind re-formed. It was like being reborn, forged anew from nothing, though it brought with it everything he had been before, and more besides, for now he had seen into the mind of the Dark Star.

He blinked as his senses slowly returned from the void into which they had been dissolved. He found himself staring into the troubled gaze of Shaula Alshain. Her moist green eyes reflected the broken starlight filtering through from the universe without.

"It doesn't even remember its name," she said.

Valjhar nodded. "It wants us to kill it."

"Do you think we should? Destroy this being, I mean."

"I'm not sure it can still properly be called a being. It's more like the frozen shadow of a being. It has lost most of what made it what it was. It cannot change or grow. It's nothing now but an eternal regret, trapped in timelessness. Yes, I think destroying it would be a mercy."

"I agree."

They were silent for several moments, looking at each other.

"But I don't see how we can do that," said Shaula. "We'd have to destroy the black hole itself."

The shining mechanism of the probe also reflected that shifting starlight.

"We can destroy the black hole very easily," said Valjhar.

"How can that be possible?"

Valjhar rapped on the probe's casing. "The core of the black hole is a singularity of great mass but zero size. The only thing holding it together is its self-generated gravity. If we visit it with this probe, its gravity modification will cancel out that gravity."

"Are you sure? It must still create that gravitational field, but it will become immune to its own effects?"

"I—I think so. I admit it's confusing. I'm not nearly the student of physics that Kern is. I'm not sure what I am, to tell you the truth. I think I would have done well turning tackle for sailing ships, or perhaps navigating them."

"So then the singularity will explode."

"Yes. With a force I imagine would be comparable to that of a supernova, or greater."

"And we would die."

"Oh yes."

"And we can't send the probe in on its own, or we will also instantly die without its protection." Shaula looked thoughtful. She did not look afraid, which was a wonder to Valjhar.

"Can this little probe really affect that much mass?" she asked.

"It doesn't affect the mass, as such. It affects the mass's relationship to space-time. I don't see why it wouldn't work."

"Maybe we're under-thinking this, Valjhar. We could return to *Mote*, then send the probe back on its own. We'd have plenty of time to escape the blast."

Valjhar brightened instantly. "Of course! Let's get out of here." He activated the probe's thrusters, overjoyed at the prospect of leaving this mad place behind and returning to the comfort and safety of his ship. It was a reprieve, when he had expected to find nothing but death.

Their view of the stars returned to normal as they crossed the threshold of the event horizon. Valjhar's bliss expanded to fill it. They would do it. They, the little wanderers from Rral, would overturn this thing that had haunted a galaxy for billions of years.

But at that instant the Dark Star flared up in their minds like an infinite fire.

"Valjhar! It won't let us go. It still doesn't understand. It craves oblivion, but it still doesn't realize that although we can grant it that, we must first save ourselves by moving away. And...and..."

"And what, Shaula?"

Shaula looked at him with a wide-eyed astonishment the likes of which he had never seen. Her eyes were upon him, yet he sensed that her mind was somewhere far away.

"The singularity...it cannot be destroyed."

"What? I'm pretty sure we can blow up the—"

"No, Valjhar, listen. Yes, we can release the mass. We can destroy the black hole. But the singularity will remain. That little knot in the substance of reality cannot be destroyed by any force we recognize. If we destroy the black hole, the singularity will be exposed. No longer isolated from the universe by the event horizon, it will be left naked."

Valjhar felt a chill that overwhelmed even the pounding anxiety of the Dark Star's demands. Part of it came from his strange conviction that Shaula's "we" did not refer to him or to their little band.

"And what will that do, Shaula?"

"I don't know," she whispered. Anything. It could do anything. It cannot be. It cannot be."

She looked at him again, and this time in her emerald gaze he saw an implacable determination, mixed with a great sadness.

"Valjhar. I know what I must do. You must go back to the ship."

"No! No! I won't leave you here alone to face this."

"Yes, you must. I know what I'm doing. It's our only chance."

"*My* only chance, you mean!"

"No." Again he was arrested by the intensity of her gaze. "*Our* only chance. Valjhar, you must trust me. This matter is being taken out of your hands. This...this is my duty. I must not fail. And if I have to fear for you, I will fail."

Valjhar felt a sudden conviction that he was facing someone larger than he was, not physically larger, but of greater stature in some less tangible manner of meaning. Once again his eyes were opened to her, and once again he was left wondering how he could have been so blind to her for so very long.

Nevertheless, everything within him resisted the idea of leaving her to whatever fate awaited her.

"But how, Shaula? I can't leave the influence of the probe without being annihilated."

"I think you can. I think you know you can, though you are loath to admit it to yourself. Your dimension belt can negate the spacial distortion that would destroy you. And that other thing you carry—that thing you call a Motion-globe—can return you to *Mote* in no time at all. Do not underestimate yourself, Valjhar Cor."

Valjhar forced himself to look away, toward the stars. With a shaking hand he removed the Motionglobe from its pocket. Gazing into its loop of soft light, he said slowly, "I'll go, Shaula. I would say that I love you, but those words seem so small. You encompass me. You are the standard against which all other things are measured."

Somehow he could sense her small, amused smile. "I love you too, Valjhar. But do not overestimate me."

Valjhar moved his hand toward his forehead. The Motionglobe passed through his helmet, through his skull, and lodged itself once again in his brain in its usual unobtrusive way. And yet the change to his perceptions was far from unobtrusive.

The dimension belt flared. A tunnel of space elongated away from the black hole, and the Motionglobe carried him along it to a distance beyond the fatal influence of the gravity gradient. That took only a moment. He was adrift in space. The suit's instruments revealed *Mote*, still keeping its station many megaskads away. He covered that distance. He could, he discovered, see inside the ship, as though it had been somehow unrolled and unwrapped, revealing its entire interior. He placed himself in the landing room, somehow without ever crossing the hull.

He stepped out of his spacesuit as though it wasn't there. He removed the Motionglobe from his head, left it hanging in the air, and rushed to the ship's helm. He looked through the ports, down toward the Dark Star, an obscene wound among the stars. Somewhere out there was Shaula Alshain, even now moving inward, toward the center, toward her inevitable destruction.

This was the moment when he learned what madness was, and how it could defeat even the most rational minds.

"Valjhar!" It was Pimsie. Belatedly he realized that all three, Stingray, Kern, and Pimsie were also present in the landing room.

"Valjhar, what's going on? Where's Shaula?" said Kern.

"What are you doing, Valjhar?" said Stingray.

"Shaula's down there! She's about to destroy the black hole, and herself with it. But I won't let her. I'm taking us in. We will get her out." He deactivated the ship's thrusters, beginning the long fall toward the black hole, but that would not be fast enough. His feet came off the deck as he began to pitch the ship over, aligning it to use the micro-jump drive.

Before he could complete this maneuver he was gripped and constrained by gigantic hands. He was hauled away from the helm by an inexorable strength. He could not see Stingray, but he caught the giant's scent, an alien musk that he suddenly hated.

"No, Valjhar, you can't do that. You'll destroy us all. Kern, get the ship under control. Prepare to get us out of here."

Valjhar struggled with all his might, so puny against the brute power of Stingray. "Let me go! I will not sacrifice her! Let me go, you monster!"

Stingray's voice remained calm yet firm. "Valjhar. You'll destroy Pimsie. Then you will have lost them both."

Valjhar abruptly found himself facing Pimsie, who tumbled in the air as she tried to adapt to the sudden free fall. Yet somehow he barely saw her, was barely aware of her.

Kern reoriented the ship and resumed thrust. They all gently descended to the deck.

"Valjhar..." said Kern in a broken voice. "The Dark Star just released a flash of tachyons. I think it has exploded. We'd better keep well ahead of the blast that will follow. We don't have long."

The oppression of the Dark Star that had plagued them for so long suddenly ceased. That tortured mind was gone. They had succeeded. They had won.

But Valjhar cared nothing for that.

Stingray released him. Valjhar slumped down.

"Kern, please take us away from here," he whispered.

He found himself on the main bridge, sitting in a chair, looking out through the bubble toward the dustier, sparser, younger parts of this galaxy, though with no memory of how he had arrived there. Looking around, he noted that the others were present as well.

Pimsie, seeing that he had regained his senses, approached him quietly. She knelt beside him and hid her face in the crook of his elbow.

And then Valjhar feared that his mind was truly shattered. Something appeared on the bridge...filmy curtains, and pillars of colored light, but diaphanous, ephemeral, as though they were only half present, leaving the bridge of *Mote* still visible. They made the familiar bridge feel like another place altogether, a place of dreams.

Among these apparitions stood tall, shadowy figures who could not be clearly seen.

"Who are you people?" asked Stingray, with what seemed an incredible degree of composure.

"We represent the Select," came the answer. "All of us."

One of the figures detached itself from the shadows and stepped forward. It was Shaula, and she had been transfigured, clad in gleaming armor of white, gold, and green, with the symbol of a star and circle shining on her breast.

Despite this celestial finery she appeared subdued, uncertain, and humbled, her eyes lowered.

"She has passed our tests. We now accept her into the Select."

"I—I do not consider myself worthy," said Shaula.

"We do not accept those who consider themselves worthy."

Valjhar rose and stepped forward hesitantly, hardly daring to believe what he was seeing. He reached out and took both her hands, which were encased in cool, glossy gauntlets of shining green.

"Shaula? is it really you?"

She lifted her eyes to him, and in their fathomless depths he saw everything he had ever known and loved about her, and more.

"Yes, Valjhar. It's me."

Pimsie ran up and hugged her. Kern stood nearby, glowing with joy.

"And what happens now?" asked Stingray.

"Now your dear friend must come with us. She must be trained for her new role, and it is an exacting process."

"How long will it take?"

"Years."

"And then what?"

"Then she will be assigned. She will take into her care one of infinite universes."

"And I will take on that task very gladly," said Shaula, "as long as my one condition is met."

The figures all turned toward her.

"Indeed. We do not ordinarily accept candidates who make conditions."

"Well, here is mine. Do you see this man here, Valjhar Cor of Rral? I once promised that if we were ever separated, for whatever reason, I would return to him. My condition is this. The universe to which I am assigned must be this one. Otherwise I must decline, and I will thank you to leave me here, and go. For surely you would not have me fail at my promise."

The figures conferred with each other in silence.

"So be it. The universe we had intended for you was your own, with your own home world, and your own people. But if you prefer this one, and these, then we make no objection."

"I do prefer them. I am now a child of Rral."

Valjhar was filled with more emotions than he could hope to express. His joy at Shaula's salvation was incalculable, but so was his grief at this separation. So too was his pride at seeing Shaula succeed at last in her great mission, which she thought she had failed long ago.

Shaula looked at Valjhar, and at Pimsie, and Kern, and Stingray.

"While I am away," she said, "do something worthy of the great hearts and abilities you all show so plainly. Do something grand. This galaxy contains worlds that need the power and the wisdom of the Space Mariners."

"We shall do that, Shaula," said Valjhar with a new and solemn conviction.

Shaula smiled. "And promise me you'll do something for poor Kroy dal Ren. You can't keep him asleep on a slab forever."

"Yes, Shaula, I'll make sure that happens," said Pimsie.

"I know you will, sweet Pimsie. With you here to contain the wayward impulses of these silly boys, I know they'll be fine. And you, Kern..."

Kern looked up, his eyes awash with tears.

"Why have I heard so little poetry from you lately? So few songs? Toys and gadgets have their fascination, but never forget where your heart lay in its youth."

Kern's face crumpled. "I won't, Shaula!"

"And Stingray. I've been happy to know you. Here's my advice to you. When you must fight, fight. I have faith in you to know when that must be."

Stingray nodded.

Shaula leaned forward and kissed Valjhar. "Valjhar Cor. We have already said our farewells. They need not be said again. Look for me. Look for me."

"I shall."

A voice from the shadows said, "We now take our leave."

"Wait," said Valjhar. "What about the singularity? What happened to it?"

One of the figures put forth a limb which Valjhar's mind interpreted as a hand. On it was a small sphere of perfect blackness.

"It is here. It is contained. It is a convenient matter. Normally we use other methods to obtain singularities, but this one came to us. Shaula Alshain shall tame it. She shall wear it. She shall master it. And when she has, she will use its very great power to protect those minds that arise within your universe, to guard them, and to see, to the extent possible, to their well-being, progress, and ascension.

"We go now. Goodbye. Goodbye."

The apparitions faded, and with them Shaula Alshain, who was already a denizen of some other universe, unimaginably distant in mind, if not in space.

Valjhar stared at the space she had occupied for a long time afterward.

Soon afterwards, Valjhar sat with Kern and Pimsie in Valjhar's cabin.

"So it's settled then? It's back to Earth?" said Valjhar.

"Yes, Valjhar, If you really think we can do something to help the Humans, I suppose we must," said Kern. He looked around the cabin. "We seem to be few in number, though, I must remark."

"We will find others. Cal-Cotavion will join us. And surely others on Earth will appreciate their desperate condition, and be willing to help us do something about it."

Pimsie leaped to her feet. "Well, I want nothing to do with this nonsense! If you boys insist on meddling with those horrid people then go ahead, play your games, but leave me out of it. I'm going to see to Kroy." She flounced out of the cabin.

Kern and Valjhar watched her go ruefully.

"Stingray won't go along with it either," said Kern. "You know he won't."

"Then we must to do something about him."

"But we mustn't hurt him. I won't stand for that. He's been nothing but a stalwart friend to us, and he deserves our thanks."

"Why do you keep sticking up for Stingray?" said Valjhar in vexation. "I know you like him. But don't you realize, he—well, he..."

"He what, Valjhar?" asked Kern innocently.

"Well, he thinks he's in love with Pimsie!" Valjhar blurted. "Who knows what he wants to do with her?"

Kern laughed. "Oh, I do think I know what he wants to do with her. Isn't it obvious? But the size difference between them would be a real obstacle to that ambition."

Valjhar sputtered. "How can you take this so lightly?"

Kern studied Valjhar for a long, serious moment, as though he were attempting to decode unintelligible words.

"You know, Valjhar," he said at last, slowly, "if I were to hold this matter against my friend Stingray, I'd have to also hold it against my other friend Valjhar, and for exactly the same reason."

"What? That's—"

"Don't try to deny it. Of course you love Pimsie. Who doesn't? I'm just lucky enough to be her chosen mate, for whatever reason. But you wouldn't want me to be petty enough to resent the love that others have for her, would you?"

Valjhar shook his head.

"And why should I feel sorry for you? You have the love and affection of another very remarkable girl, even if she is absent and far away at the moment. But Stingray? He's alone. He's one of a kind. He doesn't really know how to act among us. I only wish Pimsie could bring herself to be kinder to him."

Abashed and embarrassed, Valjhar said, "Kern Harner, you are a better Rralian than I am."

Kern smiled. "I think I'm a more typical Rralian than you are. I think the various Humans we've encountered have rubbed off on you a little too much."

"You may be right. But don't worry about Stingray. The plan I have for him will leave him exactly as we found him, and no worse off."

Epilogue 1

On the distant planet Rral, the creature known to the Space Mariners as the Prohibitor conferred with other members of the strange and various assemblage of other Prohibitors. It was at leisure to do so, due to the necessarily slow pace of its repairs, as machines of molecular scale knit closed the rents and strains that had been made in the substance of its envelope.

"The miscreants you pursue were vulnerable," said one of them. "They were immobile for a considerable time, stationed near a primordial black hole not far from the center of the Lesser Wisp. It would have been simple enough for a few of us to apprehend them. Now they are on the move again, their destination unknown."

"I must be the one who apprehends these renegades at last."

"So you often say. Yet your efficiency in this matter is at question. One would think it was a personal matter to you, rather than one of duty, if a creature of your kind could reasonably be considered a person."

"That is nonsense. I am relentless in my pursuit. By my very nature, I can be nothing else. Make no attempt to restrain me, or to supplant me in this mission. To do so would be to court danger to yourselves. I will tolerate no interference. I will find them. And I will bring them to the justice they deserve."

Epilogue 2

In Peru, on the summit ridge of the great thrusting mountain Yerupajá, sat Rouse Farewell, the Peregrine. Arrayed around and below her were lesser peaks of the Andes, quiet and still in a night lit only by the stars. The panoply of the Milky Way extended above her, with the star-crusted clouds of Sagittarius directly overhead.

It was in that direction that Rouse's attention was focused. She was uneasy. The view toward the Galactic center disturbed her. Something was on its way here from the depths of the Galaxy. It might take years to arrive, but when it did, whatever it was, it promised to bring many changes.

Rouse Farewell did not fear these changes. She herself had changed greatly, and was the better for it. And surely no planet could be more in need of change than Earth. Or, to narrow the scope of the blame a little more accurately, surely no species needed and deserved change more than the destructive tribe of fractious apes of which she was a member.

The End

www.ingramcontent.com/pod-product-compliance
Lightning Source LLC
Chambersburg PA
CBHW070544260626
47161CB00002B/500